# FOXGLOVE SUMMER

# FOXGLOVE SUMMER

## BEN AARONOVITCH

GOLLANCZ

LONDON

Text copyright © Ben Aaronovitch 2014
Cover illustration copyright © Stephen Walter
Cover image Courtesy of the Artist/TAG Fine Arts
Cover image taken from The Island London Series, published by TAG Fine Arts
Design by Patrick Knowles

The right of Ben Aaronovitch to be identified as the author of this work
has been asserted by him in accordance with the
Copyright, Designs and Patents Act 1988.

First published in Great Britain in 2014 by Gollancz
An imprint of the Orion Publishing Group
Orion House, 5 Upper St Martin's Lane, London WC2H 9EA
An Hachette UK Company

A CIP catalogue record for this book is available
from the British Library

ISBN 978 0 575 13250 4 (Cased)
ISBN 978 0 575 13251 1 (Export Trade Paperback)

1 3 5 7 9 10 8 6 4 2

Typeset by Input Data Services Ltd, Bridgwater, Somerset

Printed in Great Britain by Clays Ltd, St Ives plc

The Orion Publishing Group's policy is to use papers that are
natural, renewable and recyclable products and made from wood
grown in sustainable forests. The logging and manufacturing
processes are expected to conform to the environmental
regulations of the country of origin.

*This book is dedicated to Sir Terry Pratchett OBE*
*who has stood like a wossname upon the*
*rocky shores of our imaginations – the better*
*to guide us safely into harbour.*

# Part One

## The Borderlands

*In th'olde days of the Kyng Arthour.*
*Of which that Britons speken greet honour,*
*Al was this land fulfild of fayerye.*
*The elf-queene, with hir joly compaignye,*
*Daunced ful ofte in many a grene mede.*
'The Wife of Bath's Tale', Geoffrey Chaucer

# 1

# Due Diligence

I was just passing the Hoover Centre when I heard Mr Punch scream his rage behind me. Or it might have been someone's brakes or a distant siren or an Airbus on final approach to Heathrow.

I'd been hearing him off and on since stepping from the top of a tower block in Elephant and Castle. Not a real sound, you understand – an impression, an expression through the city itself – what we might call a super-*vestigia* if Nightingale wasn't so dead set against me making up my own terminology.

Sometimes he's in a threatening mood, sometimes I hear him as a thin wail of despair in amongst the wind moaning around a tube train. Or else he's pleading and wheedling in the growl of late-night traffic beyond my bedroom window. He's a mercurial figure, our Mr Punch. As changeable and as dangerous as an away crowd on a Saturday night.

This time it was rage and petulance and resentment. I couldn't understand why, though – it wasn't him who was driving out of London.

As an institution, the BBC is just over ninety years old. Which means that Nightingale feels comfortable enough around the wireless to have a digital radio in his bathroom. On this he listens to Radio Four while he's shaving. Presumably he assumes that the presenters are still safely attired in evening dress while they tear strips off whatever politician has been offered up as early morning sacrifice on the *Today* programme. Which is why he heard about the kids going missing before I did – this surprised him.

'I was under the impression you quite enjoyed the wireless first thing in the morning,' he said over breakfast after I'd told him it was news to me.

'I was doing my practice,' I said. In the weeks following the demolition of Skygarden Tower – with me on top of it – I'd been a key witness in three separate investigations, in addition to one by the Department of Professional Standards. I'd spent a great deal of each working day in interview rooms in various nicks around London including the notorious twenty-third floor of the Empress State Building where the serious investigations branch of the DPS keeps its racks and thumbscrews.

This meant that I'd gotten into the habit of getting up early to do my practice and get in some time in the gym before heading off to answer the same bloody question five different ways. It was just as well, since I hadn't exactly been sleeping well since Lesley had tasered me in the back. By the start of August the interviews had dried up, but the habit – and the insomnia – had stuck.

'Has there been a request for assistance?' I asked.

'With regard to the formal investigation, no,' said

Nightingale. 'But where children are concerned we have certain responsibilities.'

There were two of them, both girls, both aged eleven, both missing from two separate family homes in the same village in North Herefordshire. The first 999 call had been at just after nine o'clock the previous morning and it first hit media attention in the evening when the girls' mobile phones were found at a local war memorial over a thousand metres from their homes. Overnight it went from local to national and, according to the *Today* programme, large-scale searches were due to commence that morning.

I knew the Folly had national responsibilities in a sort of *de facto* under-the-table way that nobody liked to talk about. But I couldn't see how that related to missing kids.

'Regrettably, in the past,' said Nightingale, 'children were occasionally used in the practice of . . .' he groped around for the right term, 'unethical types of magic. It's always been our policy to keep an eye on missing child cases and, where necessary, check to make sure that certain individuals in the proximity are not involved.'

'Certain individuals?' I asked.

'Hedge wizards and the like,' he said.

In Folly parlance a 'hedge wizard' was any magical practitioner who had either picked up their skills *ad hoc* from outside the Folly or who had retired to seclusion in the countryside – what Nightingale called 'rusticated'. We both looked over to where Varvara Sidorovna Tamonina, formerly of the 365th Special Regiment of the Red Army, was sitting at her table on the other side of the breakfast room, drinking black coffee and reading *Cosmopolitan*. Varvara Sidorovna, trained by the Red Army, definitely fell into the 'and the like' category. But since she'd been lodging with us while awaiting trial for the last two months she, at least, was unlikely to be involved.

Amazingly, Varvara had appeared for breakfast before me, looking bright eyed for a woman I'd seen put away the best part of two bottles of Stoli the night before. Me and Nightingale had been trying to get her drunk in the hope of prising more information on the Faceless Man out of her, but we got nothing except some really disgusting jokes – many of which didn't translate very well. Still, the vodka had knocked me out handily and I'd got most of a night's sleep.

'So, like ViSOR,' I said.

'Is that the list of sex offenders?' asked Nightingale, who wisely never bothered to memorise an acronym until it had lasted at least ten years. I told him that it was, and he considered the question while pouring another cup of tea.

'Better to think of ours as a register of vulnerable people,' he said. 'Our task in this instance is to ensure they haven't become entangled in something they may later regret.'

'Do you think it's likely in this case?' I asked.

'Not terribly likely, no,' said Nightingale. 'But it's always better to err on the side of caution in these matters. And besides,' he smiled, 'it will do you good to get out of the city for a couple of days.'

'Because nothing cheers me up like a good child abduction,' I said.

'Quite,' said Nightingale.

So, after breakfast I spent an hour in the tech cave pulling background off the network and making sure my laptop was properly charged up. I'd just re-qualified for my level 1 public order certificate and I threw my PSU bag into the back of the Asbo Mark 2 along with an overnight bag. I didn't think my flame-retardant overall would be necessary, but my chunky PSU boots were a better bet than my street shoes. I've been to the countryside before, and I learn from my mistakes.

I popped back to the Folly proper and met Nightingale in the main library where he handed me a manila folder tied up with faded red ribbons. Inside were about thirty pages of tissue-thin paper covered in densely typed text and what was obviously a photostat of an identity document of some sort.

'Hugh Oswald,' said Nightingale. 'Fought at Antwerp and Ettersberg.'

'He survived Ettersberg?'

Nightingale looked away. 'He made it back to England,' he said. 'But he suffered from what I'm told is now called post-traumatic stress disorder. Still lives on a medical pension – took up beekeeping.'

'How strong is he?'

'Well, you wouldn't want to test him,' said Nightingale. 'But I suspect he's out of practice.'

'And if I suspect something?'

'Keep it to yourself, make a discreet withdrawal and telephone me at the first opportunity,' he said.

Before I could make it out the back door Molly came gliding out of her kitchen domain and intercepted me. She gave me a thin smile and tilted her head to one side in inquiry.

'I thought I'd stop on the way up,' I said.

The pale skin between her thin black eyebrows furrowed.

'I didn't want to put you to any trouble,' I said.

Molly held up an orange Sainsbury's bag in one long-fingered hand. I took it. It was surprisingly heavy.

'What's in it?' I asked but Molly merely smiled, showing too many teeth, turned and drifted away.

I hefted the bag gingerly – there'd been less offal of late, but Molly could still be pretty eccentric in her culinary combinations. I made a point of stowing the bag in the shaded footwell of the back seat. Whatever was in the sandwiches, you didn't want them getting too warm and going off, or starting to smell, or spontaneously mutating into a new life form.

It was a brilliant London day as I set out – the sky was blue, the tourists were blocking the pavements along the Euston Road, and the commuters panted out of their open windows and stared longingly as the fit young people strolled past in shorts and summer dresses. Pausing to tank up at a garage I know near Warwick Avenue, I tangled with the temporary one-way system around Paddington, climbed aboard the A40, bid farewell to the Art Deco magnificence of the Hoover Building and set course for what Londoners like to think of as 'everywhere else'.

Once Mr Punch and the M25 were behind me, I

tuned the car radio to Five Live, which was doing its best to build a twenty-four-hour news cycle out of about half an hour of news. The children were still missing, the parents had made an 'emotional' appeal and police and volunteers were searching the area.

We were barely into day two and already the radio presenters were beginning to get the desperate tone of people who were running out of questions to ask the reporters on the spot. They hadn't reached the *What do you think is going through their minds right now?* stage yet, but it was only a matter of time.

They were making comparisons with Soham, although nobody had been tactless enough to point out that both girls in that case had been dead even before the parents had dialled 999. Time was said to be running out, and the police and volunteers were conducting intensive search operations in the surrounding countryside. There was speculation as to whether the families would make a media appeal that evening or whether they would wait until the next day. Because this was the one area they knew anything about, they got a whole ten minutes out of discussing the family's media strategy before being interrupted with the news that their journalist on the spot had actually managed to interview a local. This proved to be a woman with an old-fashioned BBC accent who said naturally everyone was very shocked and that you don't expect that sort of thing to happen in a place like Rushpool.

The news cycle reset at the top of the hour and I learnt that the tiny village of Rushpool in sleepy rural Herefordshire was the centre of a massive police search operation for two eleven-year-old girls, best friends, Nicole Lacey and Hannah Marstowe, who had been missing for over forty-eight hours. Neighbours were said to be shocked and time was running out.

I turned the radio off.

Nightingale had suggested getting off at Oxford Services and going via Chipping Norton and Worcester, but I had the satnav switched to fastest route and that meant hooking round via Bromsgrove on the M42 and M5 and only bailing at Droitwich. Suddenly I was driving on a series of narrow A-roads that twisted through valleys and over grey-stone humpbacked bridges before expiring west of the River Teme. From then on it was even twistier B-roads through a country so photogenically rural that I half expected to meet Bilbo Baggins around the next corner – providing he'd taken to driving a Nissan Micra.

A lot of the roads had hedgerows taller than I was and thick enough to occasionally brush the side of the car. You could probably pass within half a metre of a missing child and never know she was there – especially if she were lying still and quiet.

My satnav led me gently as a lamb through a switchback turn up onto a wooded ridge and then up a steep climb called Kill Horse Lane. At the top of the hill it guided me off the tarmac and onto an unpaved lane that took me further up while taking dainty little bites out of the underside of my car. I turned around a bend to find that the lane ran past a cottage and, beyond that, a round tower – three storeys high with an oval dome roof that gave it a weirdly baroque profile. The satnav informed me that I'd arrived at my destination, so I stopped the car and got out for a look.

The air was warm and still and smelt of chalk. The late morning sun was hot enough to create heat ripples along the dusty white track. I could hear birds squawking away in the nearby trees and a steady, rhythmic thwacking sound from just over the fence. I rolled up my sleeves and went to see what it was.

Beyond the fence the ground sloped away into a hollow where a two-storey brick cottage sat amongst a garden laid out in an untidy patchwork of vegetable plots, miniature polytunnels, and what I took to be chicken coops, roofed over with wire mesh to keep out predators. Despite being quite a recent build there was something wonky about the line of the cottage's roof and the way the windows were aligned. A side door was open, revealing a hallway cluttered with muddy black Wellington boots, coats and other bits of outdoor stuff. It was messy, but it wasn't neglected.

In front of the cottage was open space where two white guys were watching a third split logs into firewood. All three were dressed in khaki shorts and naked from the waist up. One of them, an older man than the others and wearing an army green bush hat, spotted me and said something. The others turned to look, shading their eyes. The older one waved and set off up the slope of the garden towards me.

'Good morning,' he said. He had an Australian accent and was much older than I'd first thought, in his sixties or possibly even older, with a lean body that appeared to be covered with wrinkled leather. I wondered if this was my guy.

'I'm looking for Hugh Oswald,' I said.

'You've got the wrong house,' said the man and nodded at the strange tower. 'He lives in that bloody thing.'

One of the younger men strolled up to join us. Tattoos boiled from under his shorts and ran up over his shoulders and down his arms. I'd never seen a design like it before, interlaced vines, plants and flowers but drawn with an absolute precision – like the nineteenth-century botanical texts I'd seen in the Folly's library. They were recent enough for the red, blues and greens to still be vivid and sharp. He nodded when he reached us.

'All right?' he asked – not an Aussie. His accent was English, regional, but not one I recognised.

Down by the cottage the third man hefted his axe and started whacking away again.

'He's here to see Oswald,' said the older man.

'Oh,' said the younger. 'Right.'

They both had the same eyes, a pale washed-out blue like faded denim, and there were similarities in the line of the jaw and the cheekbones. Close relatives for certain – father and son at a guess.

'You look hot,' said the older man. 'Do you want a glass of water or something?'

I thanked them politely but refused.

'Do you know if he's in?' I asked.

The older and younger men exchanged a look. Downslope the third man brought down his axe and – crack – split another log.

'I expect so,' said the older man. 'This time of the year.'

'I'd better get on then,' I said.

'Feel free to pop in on your way back,' he said. 'We don't get that many people up here.'

I smiled and nodded and moved on. There was even a viewing platform enclosed by railings on top of the dome. It was the house of an eccentric professor from an Edwardian children's book – C.S. Lewis would have loved it.

A copper awning over what I took to be the front door provided a nice bit of shade and I was just about to ring the disappointingly mundane electric doorbell, complete with unfilled-in nametag, when I heard the swarm. I looked back across the track and saw it, a cloud of yellow bees under the branches of one of the trees that lined the track. Their buzzing was insistent, but I noticed that they kept to a very particular volume of space – as if marking it out.

'Can I help you?' asked a voice from behind me.

I turned to find that a white woman in her early thirties had opened the door – she must have seen me through the window. She was short, wearing black cycling shorts and a matching yellow and black Lycra tank top. Her hair was a peroxide yellow fuzz, her eyes were dark, almost black, and her mouth extraordinarily small and shaped like a rosebud. She smiled to reveal tiny white teeth.

I identified myself and flashed my warrant card.

'I'm looking for Hugh Oswald,' I said.

'You're not the local police,' she said. 'You're up from London.'

I was impressed. Most people don't even register whether the photo on your warrant card matches your face – let alone notice the difference in the crest.

'And who are you?' I asked.

'I'm his granddaughter,' she said, and squared her stance in the doorway.

'What's your name?' I asked.

If you're a professional criminal this is where you lie smoothly and give a false name. If you're just an amateur then you either hesitate before lying or tell me that I have no right to ask. If you're just a bog-standard member of the public then you'll probably tell me your name unless you're feeling guilty, stroppy or terminally posh. I saw her thinking seriously about telling me to piss off, but in the end common sense prevailed.

'Mellissa,' she said. 'Mellissa Oswald.'

'Is Mr Oswald here?' I asked

'He's resting,' she said, and made no move to let me in.

'I'd still better come in and see him,' I said.

'Have you got a warrant?' she asked.

'I don't need one,' I said. 'Your granddad swore an oath.'

She stared at me in amazement and then her tiny mouth spread into a wide smile.

'Oh my god,' she said. 'You're one of them – aren't you?'

'May I come in?' I asked.

'Yeah, yeah,' she said. 'Fuck me – the Folly.'

She was still shaking her head as she ushered me into a stone-paved entrance hall – dim and cool after the summer sun – then into a half-oval sitting room smelling of potpourri and warm dust and back out via the middle of three French windows.

The window opened onto a series of landscaped terraces that descended down towards more woods. The garden was informal to the point of being chaotic, with no organised beds. Instead, clumps of flowers and flowering bushes were scattered in random patches of purple and yellow across the terraces.

Mellissa led me down a flight of steps to a lower terrace where a white enamelled wrought-iron garden table supported a bedraggled mint-green parasol shading matching white chairs, one of which was occupied by a thin grey-haired man. He sat with his hands folded in his lap, staring out over the garden.

Anyone can do magic, just like anyone can play the violin. All it takes is patience, hard graft and somebody to teach you. The reason more people don't practise the forms and wisdoms, as Nightingale calls them, these days is because there are damn few teachers left in the country. The reason you need a teacher, beyond helping you identify *vestigium* – which is a whole different thing – is because if you're not taught well you can easily give yourself a stroke or a fatal aneurism. Dr Walid, our crypto-pathologist and unofficial chief medical officer has a couple of brains in a jar he can whip out and show you if you're sceptical.

So, like the violin, it is possible to learn magic by trial and error. Only unlike potential fiddlers, who merely risk alienating their neighbours, potential wizards tend to drop dead before they get very far. Knowing your limits is not an aspiration in magic – it's a survival strategy.

As Mellissa called her granddad's name I realised that this was the first officially sanctioned wizard, apart from Nightingale, I'd ever met.

'The police are here to see you,' Mellissa told him.

'The police?' asked Hugh Oswald without taking his eyes off the view. 'Whatever for?'

'He's up from London,' she said. 'Especially to see you.' Stressing the *especially*.

'London?' said Hugh, twisting in his chair to look at us. 'From the Folly?'

'Yes, sir,' I said.

He climbed to his feet. He'd never been a big man, I guessed, but age had pared him down so that even his modern check shirt and slacks couldn't disguise how thin his arms and legs were. His face was narrow, pinched around the mouth, and his eyes were sunken and a dark blue.

'Hugh Oswald,' he said holding out his hand.

'PC Peter Grant.' I shook his hand but although his grip was firm, his hand trembled. When I sat down he sank gratefully into his own chair, his breathing short. Mellissa hovered nearby, obviously concerned.

'Nightingale's starling,' he said. 'Flown all the way up from London.'

'Starling?' I asked.

'You are his new apprentice?' he asked. 'The first in . . .' He glanced around the garden as if looking for clues. 'Forty, fifty years.'

'Over seventy years,' I said, and I was the first *official*

16

apprentice since World War Two. There had been other unofficial apprentices since then – one of whom had tried to kill me quite recently.

'Well, god help you then,' he said and turned to his granddaughter. 'Let's have tea and some of those . . .' he paused, frowning, 'bread things with the spongy tops, you know what I mean.' He waved her off.

I watched her heading back towards the tower – her waist was disturbingly narrow and the flare of her hips almost cartoonishly erotic.

'Pikelets,' said Hugh suddenly. 'That's what they're called. Or are they crumpets? Never mind. I'm sure Mellissa will be able to enlighten us.'

I nodded sagely and waited.

'How is Thomas?' asked Hugh. 'I heard he managed to get himself shot again.'

I wasn't sure how much Nightingale wanted Hugh to know about what we police call 'operational matters', a.k.a. stuff we don't want people to know, but I was curious about how Hugh had found out. Nothing concerning that particular incident had made it into the media – of that I was certain.

'How did you hear about that?' I asked. That's the beauty of being police – you're not getting paid for tact. Hugh gave me a thin smile.

'Oh, there's enough of us left to still form a workable grapevine,' he said. 'Even if the fruit is beginning to wither. And since Thomas is the only one of us who actually does anything of note, he's become our principal source of gossip.'

I made a mental note to wheedle the list of old codgers

17

out of Nightingale and get it properly sorted into a database. Hugh's 'grapevine' might be a useful source of information. If I'd been about four ranks higher up the hierarchy I'd have regarded it as an opportunity to realise additional intelligence assets through enhanced stakeholder engagement. But I'm just a constable so I didn't.

Mellissa returned with tea and things that I would certainly call crumpets. She poured from a squat round teapot that was hidden underneath a red and green crocheted tea cosy in the shape of a rooster. Her father and I got the delicate willow pattern china cups while she used an 'I'm Proud of the BBC' mug.

'Help yourself to sugar,' she said, then perched herself on one of the chairs and started spreading honey on the crumpets. The honey came from a round little pot with 'Hunny' written on the side.

'Do have some,' she said as she placed a crumpet in front of her granddad. 'It's from our own bees.'

I hesitated with my cup of tea halfway to my lips. I lowered the cup back into its saucer and glanced at Hugh, who looked puzzled for a moment and then smiled.

'Of course,' he said. 'Where are my manners? Please eat and drink freely with no obligation etcetera etcetera.'

'Thank you,' I said and picked up my teacup again.

'You guys really do that?' Mellissa asked her granddad. 'I thought you made all that stuff up.' She turned to me. 'What exactly are you worried would happen?'

'I don't know,' I said. 'But I'm not in a hurry to find out.'

I sipped the tea. It was proper builder's tea, thank god. I'm all for delicate flavour, but after a stint on the motorway you want something with a bit more bite then Earl Grey.

'So, tell me, Peter,' said Hugh. 'What brings the starling so far from the Smoke?'

I wondered just when I'd become 'the starling' and why everyone who was anyone in the supernatural community had such a problem with proper nouns.

'Do you listen to the news?' I asked.

'Ah,' said Hugh and nodded. 'The missing children.'

'What's that got to do with us?' asked Mellissa.

I sighed – policing would be so much easier if people didn't have concerned relatives. The murder rate would be much lower, for one thing.

'It's just a routine check,' I said.

'On granddad?' asked Mellissa. I could see her beginning to get angry. 'What are you saying?'

Hugh smiled at her. 'It's quite flattering really – they obviously regard me as strong enough to be a public menace.'

'But children?' said Mellissa, and glared at me.

I shrugged. 'It really is just routine,' I said. Just the same way we routinely put a victim's nearest and dearest on the suspects list or grow suspicious of relatives who get all defensive when we make our legitimate inquiries. Is it fair? No. Is it warranted? Who knows. Is it policing? Ask a stupid question.

Lesley always said that I wasn't suspicious enough to do the job properly, and tasered me in the back to drive the point home. So, yeah, I stay suspicious these days

– even when I'm having tea with likable old buffers.

I did have a crumpet, though, because you can take professional paranoia too far.

'You didn't notice anything unusual in the last week or so?' I asked.

'I can't say I have, but I'm not as perceptive as I once was,' said Hugh. 'Or rather, I should say, I am not as *reliably* perceptive as I was in my prime.' He looked at his granddaughter. 'How about you, my dear?'

'It's been unusually hot,' she said. 'But that could just be global warming.'

Hugh smiled weakly.

'There you have it, I'm afraid,' he said, and asked Melissa if he might be permitted to have a second crumpet.

'Of course,' she said and placed one in front of him. Hugh reached out with a trembling hand and, after a few false starts, seized the crumpet with a triumphant wheeze. Mellissa watched with concern as he lifted it to his mouth, took a large bite and chewed with obvious satisfaction.

I realised I was staring, so I drank my tea – concentrating on the cup.

'Ha,' said Hugh once he'd finished chewing. 'That wasn't so difficult.'

And then he fell asleep – his eyes closing and his chin dropping onto his chest. It was so fast I started out of my chair, but Mellissa waved me back down.

'Now you've worn him out,' she said and despite the heat she retrieved a tartan blanket from the back of her granddad's chair and covered him up to his chin.

'I think it must be obvious even to you that he didn't

have anything to do with those kids going missing,' she said.

I stood up.

'Do *you* have something to do with it?' I asked.

She gave me a poisonous look and I got a flash of it then, sharp and incontrovertible, the click-click of legs and mandibles, the flicker of wings and the hot communal breath of the hive.

'What would I want with children?' she asked.

'How should I know?' I said. 'Maybe you're planning to sacrifice them at the next full moon.'

Mellissa cocked her head to one side.

'Are you trying to be funny?' she asked.

*Anyone can do magic,* I thought, *but not everyone is magical.* There are people who have been touched by, let's call it for the sake of argument, magic to the point where they're no longer entirely people even under human rights legislation. Nightingale calls them the fae but that's a catch-all term like the way the Greeks used the word 'barbarian' or the *Daily Mail* uses 'Europe'. I'd found at least three different classification systems in the Folly's library, all with elaborate Latin tags and, I figured, all the scientific rigour of phrenology. You've got to be careful when applying concepts like speciation to human beings, or before you know what's happening you end up with forced sterilisations, Belsen and the Middle Passage.

'Nah,' I said. 'I've given up funny.'

'Why don't you search our house, just to be on the safe side?' she said.

'Thank you very much – I will,' I said, proving once

21

again that a little sarcasm is a dangerous thing.

'What?' Mellissa took a step backwards and stared at me. 'I was joking.'

But I wasn't. The first rule of policing is that you never take anyone's word for anything – you always check for yourself. Missing children have been found hiding under beds or in garden sheds on properties where the parents have sworn they've searched everywhere and why are you wasting time when you should be out there looking? For god's sake it's a disgrace the way ordinary decent people are treated as criminals, we're the victims here and, no, there's nothing in there. Just the freezer, there's no point looking in there, why would they be in the freezer, you have no right . . . oh god look I'm sorry, she just slipped, I didn't mean to hurt her, she just slipped and I panicked.

'Always best to be thorough,' I said.

'I'm fairly certain you're violating our human rights here,' she said.

'No,' I said with the absolute certainty of a man who'd taken a moment to look up the relevant legislation before leaving home. 'Your granddad took an oath and signed a contract that allows accredited individuals, i.e. me, access on demand.'

'But I thought he was retired?'

'Not from this contract,' I said. It had actually said *until death release you from this oath*. The Folly – putting the old-fashioned back into good policing.

'Why don't you show me round?' I said. And then I'll know you're not off somewhere stuffing body parts into the wood-chipper.

Number one Moomin House may have looked like a Victorian folly, but was in fact that rarest of all architectural beasts – a modern building in the classical style. Designed by the famous Raymond Erith, who didn't so much invoke the spirit of the enlightenment as nick its floor plans. Apparently he'd built it in 1968 as a favour to Hugh Oswald who was a family friend, and it was beautiful and sad at the same time.

We started with the two little wings, one of which had been extended to house an additional bedroom and a properly-sized kitchen. As an architect Erith might have been a progressive classicist, but he shared with his contemporaries the same failure to understand that you need to be able to open the oven door without having to leave the kitchen first. An additional bedroom had been added, the no-nonsense brass bedstead augmented with a handrail, the floor covered in a thick soft carpet and any sharp corners on the antique oak dresser and wardrobe fitted with rounded plastic guards. It smelt of clean linen, potpourri and Dettol.

'Granddad moved down to this room a couple of years ago,' said Mellissa and showed me the brand new en suite bathroom with an adapted hip bath, lever taps and hand rails. She snorted when I popped back into the bedroom to check under the bed, but her humour evaporated when she realised I really was going to check the broom cupboards and the wood store.

A circular staircase with bare timber treads twisted up to the first floor, leading me to what had obviously been Hugh's study before he shifted to downstairs. I'd expected oak bookshelves but instead half the circumference of the room was filled with pine shelves mounted on bare metal brackets. I recognised many of the books from the Folly's own non-magical library, including an incredibly tatty volume of *Histoire Insolite et Secrète des Ponts de Paris* by Barbey d'Aurevilly. There were too many books to be contained by the shelves and they had spilled out into piles on the gate-leg table that had obviously served as a desk, on the worn stuffed leather sofa, and any spare space on the floor. Many of these looked like local history, beekeeping guides and modern fiction. There were no magic books. In fact, nothing in Latin but the very old hardback editions of Virgil, Tacitus and Pliny. I recognised the Tacitus. It was the same edition Nightingale had given me.

It was all a bit short on missing children, so I had Mellissa show me up the stairs to her bedroom, which took up the whole of the top floor. There was a Victorian vanity and a Habitat bed and wardrobes and chests of drawers that were made from compressed and laminated chipboard. It was quite amazingly messy; every single drawer was open and from every single open drawer hung at least two items of clothing. Just the loose knickers would have caused my mum to do her nut, although she would have had some sympathy for the drifts of shoes piling up at the end of the bed.

'If I'd known the police were coming,' said Mellissa, 'I'd have had a bit of a tidy.'

Even with all the windows open it was warm enough to pop beads of sweat on my back and forehead. There was also a sickly sweet smell, not horrible, not decay, but all-pervading. I saw that there was a ladder built into the wall and a hatch above it. Mellissa saw me looking and smiled.

'Want to have a poke in the attic?' she asked.

I was just about to say 'of course' when I became aware that the deep thrumming sound that hovered on the edge of audibility throughout the rest of the house was louder here and, predictably, coming from the attic.

I told her that, yes, I would like a quick look if it was all the same to her, and she handed me a wide-brimmed hat with a veil – a beekeeper's hat.

'You're kidding me,' I said, but she shook her head so I put it on and let her secure the ribbons under my chin. After a bit of rummaging in the drawers of the vanity Mellissa found a heavy torch with a vulcanised rubber sheath – she tested it, although in the sunlight it was hard to tell whether the old fashioned incandescent bulb came on or not.

When I climbed up, a wave of sticky heat rolled out. I waited a moment, listening to the now much louder thrumming noise, but there was no threatening roar or sinister increase in pitch – it stayed as steady as before. I asked Mellissa what was causing it.

'Drones,' she said. 'They basically have two jobs – banging the queen and keeping the hive at a constant temperature. Just move slowly and you'll be fine.'

I climbed up into the warm gloom. The occasional bee flashed through the beam of my torch, but not the swarms that I'd feared. I turned my torch on the far end of the attic and saw the hive for the first time. It was huge, a mass of fluted columns and sculpted ridges that filled half the space. It was a wonder of nature – and as creepy as shit. And I personally stuck around just long enough to ensure there weren't any colonists cemented into the walls – or children – and ducked out of there.

Mellissa trailed after me down the spiral stairs with a smug look on her face and followed me outside, more to make sure I was going than out of politeness. When I reached my car I realised that the cloud of bees had contracted down to a solid mass under one of the main branches. To my surprise, it was an ovoid shape that appeared to hang from the tree by a single narrow thread – just like the cartoon beehives that regularly got dropped on characters' heads.

I asked Mellissa if it would stay on the tree.

'It's the queen,' said Mellissa, and sniffed. 'She's just showing off. She'll be back – if she knows what's good for her.'

'Do you know anything about these girls?' I asked.

I thought I heard a pulse of noise from the house behind her – a deep thrumming sound that swelled and then faded into the background.

'Not unless they bought some honey,' she said.

'You don't keep the honey for yourself?' I asked.

The afternoon sunlight caught the downy blond hair on her arms and shoulders.

'Don't be silly,' she said. 'What would I do with that much honey?'

I didn't leave immediately. Instead I leant against the back of the Asbo, where there was some shade, and wrote up my notes. It's always a good idea to do this immediately after an interview because your memory is fresh and also because panicked suspects have been known to assume that the police have long gone and exit their front door carrying all sorts of incriminating stuff. Including, in one famous case, parts of a body. Before I started, though, I looked up the West Mercia channels and switched my Airwave handset over so I could listen in to the operation while I finished up.

A lot of journalists have access to an Airwave, or access to someone who has one, so in a high profile case the cop-speak and jargon can get very dense. Nobody wants to see their 'inappropriate' humour decorating the front page on a slow news day – that sort of thing can be a career killer. I could hear the operation going critical even as I finished up my notes. ACPO don't chat over the Airwave, but it was clear that requests for assistance were now being routed through the Police National Information Coordination Centre (PNICC), commonly pronounced 'panic' – particularly if you've reached the stage of having to call it.

It wasn't my operation, and if I was to travel any further off my manor they'd be speaking a different language, probably Welsh. And if West Mercia Police wanted my help then it would be co-ordinated through the PNICC and I wasn't even sure what kind of mutual aid I'd be providing.

But you can't walk away, can you? Not when it's kids.

I called Nightingale and explained what I wanted to do. He thought it was a 'capital idea' and agreed to make the necessary arrangements.

Then I climbed into my boiling hot car and set my satnav to Leominster Police Station.

For a moment I thought I heard an angry cry come floating over the hills towards me, but it was probably something rural – a bird of some kind.

Yeah, definitely a bird, I told myself.

# 2

# Mutual Aid

Big cities thin out at the edges. Detached houses give way to semis, then to terraces which then grow a couple of storeys before you either reach the historic old town or, more usually, what's left of it after the one-two blow of aerial bombardment and post-war planning. In the countryside the towns start so suddenly that one second you're amongst open fields, the next you're looking at a collection of renovated early-modern townhouses. And then, before you even get a chance to discover whether that was really a genuine Tudor half-timbered building or a bit of late Victorian whimsy, you're out the other side with an ugly red brick hypermarket filling your rear-view mirror.

Leominster, pronounced 'Lemster' in case you wondered, was a bit more interesting than that. And I probably would have taken a moment to enjoy its market square if the satnav hadn't plonked me straight onto the bypass which did exactly what it said on the tin. The town was already behind me when I crossed a bridge back over the railway and spun off a roundabout into the sleepy-looking industrial park where the local nick was kept.

You put your green-field police stations on the

outskirts of town for the same reason you built your supermarkets there – floor space and parking. My first proper nick was Charing Cross, smack in the heart of one of the busiest BOCUs in the Met – there we could just about cram all the IRVs, vans, Clubs and Vice covert units and sundry other pool cars into the garage and nobody under the rank of superintendent got a parking space.

But Leominster nick had two car parks, one for the public and one for police. And, I learnt later, its own helicopter landing pad. The building itself was a three-storey red-brick affair with an exuberant curve that made the far end look like a prow, so that from one side it looked like a jolly storybook boat that had grounded itself kilometres from the sea. The visitors' car park was rammed solid with mid-range hatchbacks, satellite vans and a crowd of white people milling around aimlessly – the famous press pack, I realised. I took one look at them and drove around the block to the entrance to the police car park. To my eye this had a ludicrously low fence around it, easily scalable by any miscreant intent on committing mischief on constabulary property – I was not impressed, helicopter pad or not.

I turned into the automatic gate, leaned out of my window and pressed the button on the intercom mounted on a pole. I told the scratchy voice at the other end who I was, and waved my warrant card at the beady eye of the camera. There was an affirmative squawk and the gate rattled open. For a police car park it was suspiciously devoid of police vehicles, leaving just a couple of unmarked Vauxhalls and a slightly worse for wear

Rover 800. It must have been all hands on deck for the search.

I parked up in a space away from the entrance where I reckoned I wasn't going to get sideswiped by a returning carrier or prisoner transfer vehicle. Never underestimate the ability of a police driver to misjudge a corner when finally coming home from a twelve-hour shift.

A young white man was waiting for me by the back door. He was blond, with a broad open face and blue eyes. His suit, I noticed, looked tailored. But it was hard to tell since he'd obviously been wearing it for the last twenty-four hours straight. He was swigging from an Evian bottle which he lowered when he saw me, stuck out a friendly hand and introduced himself as DC Dominic Croft.

'They're expecting you,' he said, but he didn't say what for.

It was the cleanest nick I'd ever been in – it didn't even have the distinctive smell of a lot of bodies working long shifts in heavy clothing that you expected in a working station. *Eau de stab-vest*, Lesley had used to call it. The place was painted exactly the same colour scheme as Belgravia and half-a-dozen other London nicks I'd been in – whoever was selling that particular shade of light blue must have been coining it.

'This place is usually pretty empty,' he said. 'Normally it's just the neighbourhood policing team.'

Dominic led me upstairs to the main offices where the air conditioning, such as it was, was failing to deal with the sheer mass of police. A couple of detectives looked up as we walked into the incident room, nodding at Dominic then pausing to give me a suspicious once-over before turning back to their work. They were all white and, between them and the press pack out the front, I suspected that on this case my diversity training had been wholly in vain.

Incident rooms during a major inquiry are rarely a barrel of laughs, but the atmosphere that day was grim, the faces of the detectives sweaty and intent. Missing kids are tough cases. I mean, murder is bad but at least the worst has already happened to the victim – they're not going to get any deader. Missing kids come with a literal deadline, made worse by the fact that you don't get to learn the timing until it's too late.

Dominic knocked on a door with a rectangular metal plate marked LEARNING ZONE, opened it without waiting for a response, and went inside. I followed him into the sort of long, narrow room that exists primarily because the architect had a couple of metres left over when dividing up the floor space and didn't know what else to do with it. A small window was open to its meagre health and safety-mandated maximum extent and a desk fan was pushing the warm air around. A desk ran along one wall and an athletic white man in an inspector's uniform leant against it with his arms folded across his chest. Dominic introduced him as Inspector Charles, definitely not Charlie, Edmondson, who was geographic commander for northern Herefordshire, which meant that this was his patch and he didn't seem that delighted to have me on it. Occupying the better of the two seats available was a short squared-off white man with an incongruously long face and pointed chin that looked as if he'd borrowed his features from someone taller and thinner and then refused to give them back. This was DCI David Windrow, senior investigating officer of Operation Manticore – the search for Hannah Marstowe and Nicole Lacey. He waved me to the other seat and I sat and adopted the appropriately earnest but slightly vacant look that is expected of lowly constables in these circumstances.

'Apparently,' said Windrow, 'you've been up here on official business.'

'Due diligence, sir.'

'Yes,' he said. 'I spoke to your Inspector. He said it was just a routine check.'

'Yes, sir.'

'And that you were volunteering to stay up here and lend a hand.'

'Yes, sir.'

'But you're certain that there's no . . .' Windrow hesitated. 'No Falcon aspect to this case.'

The police have a habit of taking a call sign and using it indiscriminately as a noun, a verb and, on special occasions, a burst of profanity. Trojan is firearms, Ranger is Diplomatic and Protection, and Falcon is what a certain DCI of my acquaintance likes to call 'weird bollocks'. The call sign has been in use since the seventies, but it's been getting more of an airing in the last year or two. This portends, depending on the canteen you sit down in, the dawning of the age of Aquarius, the End of Days or, just possibly, that the Folly now has at least one officer that knows how to use his Airwave properly.

Inspector Edmondson unfolded his arms and sighed.

'So you're not planning to continue a Falcon inquiry?' he asked.

'No, sir,' I said. 'I just want to help in any way I can.'

'Apart from the obvious,' said Windrow, 'you got any experience in anything else?'

'Just general policing, PSU, a bit of interrogation, and I'm qualified to use a taser.'

'What about Family Liaison?' asked Windrow.

'I've seen it done,' I said.

'Do you think you could support an experienced FLO?'

I said I thought I could and Windrow and Edmondson exchanged looks. Edmondson didn't look pleased, but then he nodded and they both looked back at me.

'Okay, Peter,' said Windrow. 'If you want to help then we'd like you take over as second FLO to one of the families – the Marstowes. That way we can reassign Richard, the officer taking that role now, to the search.'

'He's POLSA,' said Edmondson by way of explanation. A search specialist.

'If it'll help,' I said.

'We tend to double up roles out here,' said Windrow. 'We're spread a bit thin.'

It's a good thing that the sheep are all so law abiding, I thought but did not say, proving that my diversity training hadn't been wasted after all.

'We probably don't need to tell you this,' said Edmondson. 'But keep clear of the media. Everything is being routed through the press officer.'

'Any of those bastards asks you a question,' said Windrow, 'you direct them there – got it?'

I nodded keenly to show that my egg sucking was indeed proficient and up to date. We tied up a couple of bureaucratic loose ends and then I was dismissed into the care of DS Dominic Croft who was now charged with getting me to Rushpool.

Dominic, being a human being not a satnav, guided me through the town proper – the centre of which boasted one of those completely unnecessary one-way systems that were so beloved of a certain generation of town planners. Most of it was Victorian or Regency terraces crowded close onto narrow pavements with the occasional half-timbered chunk of the seventeenth century plonked down amongst them.

Dominic managed to restrain himself from asking the obvious question until we were safely back in the countryside.

'So ghosts and magic are real?' he said.

I'd had that question enough times to have an answer ready. 'There are things that fall outside the parameters of normal policing,' I said. I find you get two types of police, those that don't want to know and those that do. Unfortunately, dealing with things you don't want to know about is practically a definition of policing.

'So "yes",' said Dominic.

'There's weird shit,' I said. 'And we deal with the weird shit, but normally it turns out that there's a perfectly rational explanation.' Which is often that a wizard did it.

'What about aliens?' asked Dominic.

Thank god for aliens, I thought, muddying the water since 1947. I'd once asked Nightingale the same question and he'd answered 'Not yet'. So I suppose if they were to suddenly turn up they'd be part of our remit. But I hoped they didn't turn up anytime soon. It's not like we don't have enough work to do already.

'Not that I know about,' I said.

'So you don't rule them out?' he said.

We both had the windows down as far as they would go to try and pick up whatever breeze we could.

'Do *you* believe in aliens?' I asked.

'Why not?' he said. 'Don't you?'

'It's a big universe,' I said. 'It's not going to be totally empty, is it?'

'So you do believe in aliens,' he said.

'Yeah,' I said. 'But not that they're visiting us.'

'Why not?'

'Why would they want to travel all that way?' I asked.

We passed through an elongated village that Dominic identified as Luston. Beyond that, the road narrowed and the dense green hedgerows blocked out the view on either side.

'Do you think someone snatched them?' I said, before Dominic could ask any more awkward questions.

'From two separate households?' he said. 'Unlikely. Lured them out, maybe.'

'Internet grooming?'

'Nothing on their computers. At least nothing I've been told about.'

'Someone they knew? Or met locally?'

'Let's hope it's a local,' said Dominic.

Because if it was a local then there'd be a connection. And if there was a connection then sooner or later it could be dug out by the investigation. In the case of Soham the police had their eye on Ian Huntley, the main suspect, from the moment he opened his gob and admitted to being the last person to see the victims alive. Without a connection it came down to hoping they were spotted by the public or came home of their own accord. Or they might be found by the ever-widening search programme – but we didn't want to think of that.

Dominic asked where I was staying and I asked him what was available.

'Today?' he asked. 'Bugger all. It's all full of media.'

'Shit,' I said. 'Do you know anywhere?'

'You can stay in my mum's cowshed,' he said.

'Her cowshed?'

'Don't worry. There's no cows in it.'

I'd have looked for a bit more clarification, but I turned a corner and had to brake suddenly to avoid a white TV satellite van which was trying to park in a gap between a Range Rover and a sleazy-looking maroon Polo. I edged past into the Y-junction that formed the heart of the village, but there were so many media vehicles it was hard to see the houses.

'Lock up your sheep,' muttered Dominic. 'The circus is in town.'

He directed me left again, up a lane that ran up a slope.

'Church is that side,' said Dominic. 'Rectory on your left, pub is back down the way we came.'

37

What I could see of the village was free of rubbish but untidy, long yellow grass obscuring the fences, bushes thrusting out into the lane, and green banks overgrown with white flowers. Trees overhung the road by the church and the air beneath them was hot and still and smelled of overheated car. We threaded our way between another satellite van and a faded blue Transit with a vehicle hire logo on the side. I asked where the actual press might be.

'Going by past form, the senior reporters are in the pub, the photographers are outside the houses and the junior reporters are running around trying to get the locals to talk to them.'

'Is there anywhere for us to park?'

'We'll tuck into my mum's and walk from there,' he said.

Dominic's mum lived in the last of a row of red brick council houses, none of which were still owned by the council, at the north edge of the village. Hers was the only bungalow, set back from the lane with a gravel drive and a front lawn that needed mowing. I followed Dominic's directions and parked in a space by the kitchen door. He told me to grab my stuff.

'We'll dump it in the cowshed and head over to the hall,' he said.

The cowshed was a sturdy one-storey, flat-roofed rectangle built from sandy coloured brick. It stood at the far end of large and unkempt back garden that ended in a barbed-wire fence beyond which stretched a strangely lumpy pasture bounded by an old stone wall. It looked more like a garage extension then a cowshed but when we walked around the back I saw that it had a wide patio window giving a view over the field. Dominic slid open the door to reveal a furnished room with a bed, desk, a flatscreen TV and a walled-off corner that probably held a shower and toilet.

'You guys must really love your cows,' I said.

'Famous for it,' said Dominic.

The inside was as hot as a locked car, so I quickly dumped my stuff by the bed and closed the door. Dominic locked up and handed me the key but, instead of going back out by way of the drive, we headed for the fence where a couple of grey plastic crates and a tractor tire formed a makeshift stile.

'My mum got it into her head that you didn't need planning permission for agricultural buildings,' said Dominic, climbing over the stile with practised ease. 'She wanted to rent it out as a B&B.'

I went over carefully. I didn't want to turn up to my first briefing with a hole in my jeans.

'Is it true about the planning permission?' I asked.

'I think you're supposed to be a farmer as well,' said Dominic. 'You'll be the first guest.'

I followed Dominic along the verge of the field which, as far as I could tell, ran the other side of the thick hedgerow that lined the lane leading out of the village. You could hear vehicles passing on the other side but you couldn't see them at all. I'd been right. Searching for missing kids in this landscape must be a nightmare. Judging from the compacted soil this was a popular back route for the villagers. On those rare times I'd ventured out into the British countryside as a kid

I'm pretty sure I was told not to walk across people's fields.

'This isn't a public right of way, is it?' I asked.

'Nah,' said Dominic, 'but this is an old orchard.'

Which explained the stone perimeter wall, I thought.

'The council bought it up to build houses,' he said, of which his mum's had been the last. They had also allocated a section to a new parish hall stroke community centre and financed that by selling off the rest to a developer.

'He land-banked it in the hope he could change the terms of the planning permission,' said Dominic. Apparently the new plan was to build luxury houses aimed at incomers – it all sounded depressingly familiar – but the villagers had managed to block his application.

'They found a loophole,' he said.

I asked what the loophole was, but Dominic said he made a point of not asking.

'I get enough environmental distress from the boyfriend without wanting to get it from my mum as well,' he said.

The parish hall was about a hundred metres up from the cowshed. It was an odd building with wooden shingle walls and a gambrel roof that looked like it had been shipped over from the Midwest of America and then, presumably, assembled by the Amish synchronised barn-building team. There was an asphalt parking space out the front which was empty except for a shiny new Vauxhall Vivaro in West Mercia Battenberg livery. A lone female PSCO stood guard by the road to make sure nobody else parked there and kept an eye on the scattering of press clustered outside the front entrance.

Them being out front was the reason that Dominic had taken us in the back way.

The hall was just that, a big room that was open to the rafters with a stage at one end and doors off to a kitchen area and toilets. According to Dominic it was where you had birthday parties, amateur dramatics and the dreaded young farmers' disco. 'Feared for miles around,' he told me. It was currently being used as a staging area for the search for Nicole and Hannah, which was why the media was outside. And since every available body was out searching it meant it was deserted. Sausage bags and rucksacks were piled in the corners, shrink-wrapped pallets of bottled water were piled under trestle tables on which Styrofoam cups and jars of instant coffee were stacked. Two Ordnance Survey maps had been pinned to a cork notice board, overlapping so that the areas matched up, and covered in plastic. Arrows, loops and whorls had been drawn on in marker pen – the search so far. The air was warm and still and smelt of creosote.

'Hello,' called Dominic. 'Anyone here?'

'Just a second,' called a woman from behind the door to the toilets.

I had a look at the map while we waited. A modern search isn't just a matter of marking off a grid and working through it one by one. These days you section it off by probability – where your subject could have got to under their own power in the time available. So the search area grows like frost on a spider web, shooting down roads and tracks, spreading out in sheets over fields and gardens.

The door to the toilets opened and a fat woman in a beige cardigan stepped out. She had a round face with a milky complexion and dark brown hair pulled into a no-nonsense pony tail. To go with the cardigan she had a pair of glasses dangling around her neck on a pink strap, knee-length brown skirt and sensible court shoes. She was aiming for dependable parish busybody but it was undermined by sharp blue eyes which were constantly darting back and forth – taking everything in. Proper copper eyes, those.

Still, she did a good professional bustle when she saw me and shook my hand and introduced herself as DS Allison Cole.

'You must be Peter Grant,' she said. 'Thank you for volunteering. Although god knows what the family are going to make of you.'

We sat down by one of the trestle tables. DS Cole yanked a bottle of Evian out of a pallet and offered it to me – I shook my head. She opened it and drank gratefully.

'We're lucky with the weather,' she said. 'If they're out there in the open they're not going to die of exposure.'

'Hottest summer in living memory,' said Dominic. 'You should be right at home.'

I didn't even bother to give him the look – it's not like he'd have understood what it meant anyway.

'Where are you staying?' asked Cole.

'I'm putting him in me mum's cowshed,' said Dominic.

'I thought the council wanted that knocked down?' said Cole.

'They haven't got round to it yet,' he said.

'At least it will be a short commute,' said Cole. 'And it'll be good to have somebody near at hand overnight. Means I can get back to my kids.'

'You think this is going to drag out?' I asked.

'Who can tell?' she said, which meant yes.

'Do you think we're going to get them back?'

'I hope so,' she said, which meant no.

She took another swig of water and wiped her forehead with the back of her arm.

'We'd better get you briefed and introduced,' she said.

The Marstowes lived in one half of a semi built in the watered-down neo-Georgian style that was de rigueur for post-war rural housing developments. Situated at the end of a cul-de-sac, it was, Dominic told me, the last actual council-owned council house in the village. All the rest having been bought up by their tenants in the 1980s and 1990s and then sold on to wealthy incomers.

'Except for your mum,' I said.

'She didn't want to sell,' he said. 'Now of course she looks like a bloody genius – prices being what they are.'

Judging from the decomposing grey VW Rabbit and the empty Calor Gas bottles amongst the long unmown grass of the front garden, the Marstowes were either hoping for a spot on the next Channel 4 deprivation documentary or a two-page spread in the *Daily Mail*. Although to clinch the *Mail* story they'd probably have to adopt a Romanian asylum seeker or something. On the other side of a box hedge the front garden of the other half of the semi was a neat lawn without flower beds.

The windows on that side were closed up and doors were shut tight, and it had a blank empty aspect. The owner-occupier, a senior lecturer at Birmingham University had been amongst the first locals to be TIEed after the girls went missing. That's Traced, Identified and Eliminated, in case you were wondering.

'At his holiday villa in Tuscany,' Dominic had told me. He'd been there since the end of the July.

'A Tuscan villa and a weekend house in the country?' I'd asked. 'How much does he get paid?'

Apparently he'd planned to move his family out to Rushpool, but his wife had divorced him when she found him with an undergraduate discussing Borges' pivotal role in the development of post-colonial literature with the aid of a feather duster, a latex vest and a tub of Ben & Jerry's Chocolate Brownie-flavoured ice cream.

I asked whether the wife or the undergraduate had joined him in Tuscany.

'Wife and kids,' Dominic said. '*And* the undergraduate.'

The semi stood at the far end of a cul-de-sac which branched off the village lane. The media, I noticed, observed a sort of unofficial line of control – never pushing their way beyond the junction. Dominic said that they'd been good about respecting the family's privacy – so far. I wondered how long that would last.

The front door on the Marstowes' side was propped open with a brick and from inside I heard children screaming. Dominic knocked a couple of times on the door, tried the bell which didn't work, and knocked again. He looked at me and shrugged. The screaming got louder. At least one toddler, I thought, and a couple of older kids. One was definitely seriously aggravated about not being allowed out of the house.

Dominic gave up and was about to step inside when a white boy of about nine came charging up the hall and skidded to a halt at the sight of us. He was dressed in a green T-shirt with a cartoon picture of Psy on the front and clutching a pink plastic cricket bat. He stared at Dominic, then at me, bit his lip in consternation and then ran back the way he'd come.

'Ryan,' said Dominic. 'The eldest boy.'

We followed Ryan into the house.

Given the hillbilly front garden, the inside of the house was surprisingly tidy, or at least as tidy as a house with four kids under the age of twelve is likely to get without a full-time professional cleaning staff. I followed Dominic down the short hall and into the kitchen at the back and was introduced to Joanne Marstowe.

She was a small woman with a narrow upturned nose, blue eyes and Midwich Cuckoo-coloured hair. She was slender for someone with four kids. The youngest, Ethan, aged one, was balanced in the crook of one arm. He had the same white-blond hair as his mother and appeared at some point in the recent past to have submerged his face in a bowl of Heinz mashed apple and pork casserole. I could see the open pot on the kitchen table and the high chair with an upturned blue and pink flowered bowl on the eating tray. Ryan had taken up a position behind his mum and now peered cautiously around her body to check we weren't after him. A third child, who by a process of elimination had to be Mathew, aged seven, whose sandy hair was stuck to his forehead with sweat, sat quietly at the table with the air of a child who had been subjected to more than reasonable punishment as specified by section 58 of the Children's Act 2004.

'Hello, Joanne,' said Dominic.

Joanne glared at him, noticed me and turned back to Dominic.

'Who the fuck is this?' she asked.

'This is Peter,' said Dominic. 'He's going to be working with Allison Cole and you.'

'Where're you from?' she asked me.

'London,' I said, which seemed to please her.

'Good,' she said. 'It's about time they took this seriously. Have a seat.'

Mathew watched me sit down with wide suspicious eyes. Joanne asked Dominic if he was staying but he made his excuses and left, though not before giving me a surreptitious thumbs up from the door.

'Would you like a cup of tea?' asked Joanne.

'Thank you,' I said. 'I'll make it, if you like?'

'God, no,' she said and thrust Ethan into my arms. 'But if you can deal with the monster I'd appreciate it.'

I may be an only child, but I've got a lot of cousins. And their parents shared my mum's conviction that once you're big enough to pick up a toddler unaided, you're big enough to babysit while the adults drink tea and discuss the important issues of the day. Ethan gave a startled yelp as I plonked him on my lap, his overheated pink face unclenching as curiosity got the better of his upset. There was kitchen roll on the table. I grabbed

46

a couple of sheets and wiped most of the food off his face. He was a sturdy little boy and a bit heavy to be hanging off his mum's hip. I wondered if he was catching the vibe from the adults around him.

'Have you got anyone who can help out?' I asked. 'Family?'

Joanne looked up from the sink where she was triaging the washing up.

'Lots of family,' she said. 'If you'd been here earlier you'd have been tripping over them. They were very keen to help, so keen that I had to get rid of them – at least for a bit.'

I watched as she paused in front of the kitchen cupboard and nervously tapped her finger on the counter.

'Mummy,' said Ryan, tugging at her leg.

'Shut up,' she told him. 'I'm trying to remember what the fuck I'm supposed to be doing. Tea, right?'

'Or coffee, if that's easier.'

'Which one?' asked Joanne testily.

'Coffee,' I said.

'Can I have coffee too?' asked Mathew.

Which meant that Ryan wanted coffee as well, but in the end they both settled for a can of Coke each and a couple of mini Swiss rolls – the nation's parental bribe of choice. I did my part by bouncing Ethan up and down and making weird noises until he was too confused to be upset. By the time my cup of own-brand instant was plonked down in front of me, Ryan and Mathew had wandered off into the adjacent living room to watch cartoons. Joanne slumped down in the chair across the table from me and put her face in her hands.

47

'Jesus,' she said.

Ethan burped ominously and I stopped jiggling him, just in case. There are limits to the sacrifices I'm willing to make in the name of community policing.

'When's your husband getting back?' I asked.

Joanne raised her head and sighed.

'He won't be back until it's dark,' she said. 'They'll probably have to drag him back – he can't sit around waiting, he'd go mad.'

'What about you?'

'I don't have any choice there, do I?' she said. 'Vicky asked if I wanted to wait it out at her house. I mean it wasn't like she was going to come down and "wait it out" here, was it? Have you seen her house? Can you imagine this lot . . .' She made a gesture that encompassed her children and the state of her kitchen. 'No, if she wants company . . . It's not like she's short of friends.' She gave me an odd look. 'Are you lot trained to keep your mouth shut? Because I seem to be doing most of the entertaining here.'

'We're supposed to unobtrusive,' I said.

'Oh, yeah? All the better to let us incriminate ourselves?'

As it happened, exactly that – amongst all the other roles an FLO is supposed to perform.

'Trained that way,' I said. 'The idea is not to make your life any more difficult than it has to be.'

She laughed at that, a short mirthless bark. Then she made eye contact and held it.

'Do you think I'm going to get my daughter back?' she asked.

'Yes,' I said.

'Why?'

Because you've got to have hope and no news is good news. And because the best you can do is sound like you're being forthright and sincere. If they get their kids back they won't even remember what you said and if they don't – then nothing else will be important.

I was trying to come up with a convincing lie when I was saved by a voice from the hallway.

'Jo? Are you in?' Male, adult, public school.

'In the kitchen,' called Joanne.

We heard him pause at the living room door and ask the boys if they were bearing up.

'Chin up,' he told them, and then he came into the kitchen.

He was taller than me, mid-forties, dressed in cargo pants and green wellies, and a blue and gold rugby shirt that wasn't loose enough to disguise a little pot belly. He had broad shoulders that were going to fat, brown eyes, a narrow nose and a big forehead. He was about to say something to Joanne when he copped sight of me.

'Hello,' he said. 'Who are you?'

Joanne introduced us. He was Derek Lacey – father of the other missing child. He'd been out with the searchers, but they were losing the light.

'I just wanted to be sure you were okay,' he said.

'I'm about what you'd expect,' she said.

Derek pulled a seat out and placed it at the end of the table before sitting down. About as close as he could to interposing himself between me and Joanne without actually sitting cross-legged on the table. I wondered if he was even aware he'd done it. Joanne asked if he wanted a coffee – he asked for something stronger.

'Vicky doesn't approve,' he told me as Joanne snagged a half-bottle of Bell's off a suitably child-inaccessible shelf at the top of the cupboard. 'But by god I need a drink right now.'

He got it in an orange drinking glass with a picture of a happy octopus on it. The Bell's went firmly and decisively back on the shelf. Derek finished his in two gulps. Inspired, Ethan screwed up his face and started to cry until he was pacified with orange squash.

'Where's Andy?' asked Joanne.

'He was with a different party,' said Derek. 'I think they were down towards Bircher.' His eyes flicked up to the cupboard where the Bell's was tucked safely away, towards Joanne, and then back to me.

'I don't wish to sound rude,' he said. 'But I'd like a word in private with Joanne.'

I glanced at Joanne for confirmation – she gave a slight nod.

'Of course,' I said and offered him Ethan just to see what the reaction would be. Derek scooped up the toddler with practised ease and Ethan didn't seem to have any objections – although he could have been distracted by the orange squash.

I could feel them waiting for me to be gone all the way down the hall and out the front door. I considered doubling back and seeing if I could listen in, but I figured that would have been a little bit too Enid Blyton – even for me.

Rushpool was situated in a side valley that ran roughly

north-west to south-east following, I learnt later from an impeccable source, the line of the Rushy Brook – one of the many streams that converged further down the valley with the Ridgemoor Brook before meeting the Lugg at Leominster. Hydraulically speaking, it's actually more complicated than that. But since I fell asleep during that part of the explanation I can't inflict it on you. Although it was still early evening the sun had already fallen below the ridge behind the Marstowes' house in a glare of smoky orange and the village was thrown into cooling shadow. I could hear the pub crowd murmur of the media scrum – still waiting at the entrance to the cul-de-sac – and see the glowing tips of their e-cigarettes and occasional camera flashes. I doubted Nightingale was that keen on me getting my face on the news, so I ducked sideways to guarantee that I was hidden by another box hedge. Then I called DS Cole to let her know I was out of the house.

She told me to stay close in case they called me back in. 'Or a major domestic kicks off.' I didn't get a chance to ask her whether she thought that was likely. The search teams were going to be out until nightfall, but DCI Windrow would be holding a briefing for the investigation team for the next hour or so. Until then I was the man on the spot.

'I'll be back after the briefing to talk to the family,' Cole said. 'There's likely to be a press conference tomorrow morning. If there is, I'll deal with the family. Windrow wants you available in case some actions come up – Dominic will let you know.'

After she hung up I checked through the hedge to

see if the media had eased off yet. As I watched, a shudder seemed to run through the pack, then those on the left hand edge broke away and headed up the lane – they were quickly followed by more and more of their peers until the whole herd had thundered after them. A few stragglers armed with telephoto lenses were left to guard the cul-de-sac. I slouched over in my best nothing-but-us-cockney, or at least in their case probably mockney, geezers-together manner and asked where everyone had gone.

'Leominster,' said a photographer with ginger dreadlocks and freckles. 'In case the local plod make an announcement afterwards.'

They see me and they know I'm police, I thought. But it just doesn't register with them – not really. Which I admit can be handy at times.

'What's the local like?' I asked.

'The Swan?' he said and bobbed his head from side to side. 'A bit foodie but a good range of beers.'

The Swan in the Rushes was not what I expected from a country pub, although it has to be said that my expectations were largely drawn from my mum's prolonged addiction to *Emmerdale* in the 1990s. Situated at the bottom of the village, beside the pond that presumably gave the place its name – not that I could see any rushes – it was a squat late-Victorian building that had originally been built to replace the old water mill just in time for electrification to render it obsolete. It had quickly been converted to a pub misleadingly named the Old Mill before being bought and renamed by the current owner. He introduced himself to me as Marcus Bonneville and told me that he was originally from Shropshire but had made his pile doing something unspecified in London before deciding to return to the country.

People shouldn't be non-specific about where they made their money, not in front of police. The only reason I didn't make a note of his name to do an IIP check later was because I was fairly certain that Windrow's mob had done that on day one – probably before breakfast. When dealing with the law, having a mysterious past is contra-indicated.

He had taste, though, and instead of decking the pub out with the usual olde worlde accoutrements he'd gone for a rather classy Art Deco styling with blond walnut dining tables with matching chairs and circular Perspex light fittings hanging from the ceiling. The mahogany bar had rounded corners and brass detailing and there were framed vintage travel posters on the walls advertising impossibly sun-kissed destinations – Llandudno, Bridlington and Bexhill-on-Sea. All it needed was a murdered heiress and Hercule Poirot would have felt right at home. The cooking was a bit fancy, and while I'm all for transparency in the food chain I'm really not that bothered about precisely which breed of cattle from what particular herd had given its life to make a six-ounce fillet steak served with peppercorn sauce, grilled field mushroom, tomato and chunky chips plus a half a cider for a twenty and change.

I was contemplating an Italian style bread and butter pudding with mocha ice cream when the press pack started rolling in the front door, so I ducked out the back with my glass of Bulmer's in hand. This led me out into a scruffy gravel parking area with a charming view of the wheelie bins and the kitchen doors, which had been left open to let the cool air in. As I finished my cider I watched the staff, in full chef's whites, gearing up for the post-briefing rush. Marcus would be doing well out of the crisis – it's an ill wind, and all that.

The sun was behind the ridge by then and it was almost full dark. Over the top of the kitchen clatter and the voices in the bar I made out the thump of a helicopter travelling low and fast to the south. The search was winding up for the night.

I called Nightingale and told him where I'd be staying – he asked how long I thought I'd be there.

'I don't know,' I said. 'But West Mercia is digging in for the long haul – I don't think they think this is going to end well.'

'I see,' said Nightingale. 'I'll arrange to have some essentials sent up.'

'There's a couple of bags in my room,' I said. 'One under the bed. The other should be in the wardrobe.'

'I'll get Molly to see to it tonight,' said Nightingale, which should have set off alarm bells then and there.

We were interrupted by a call from DS Cole who said that I could consider myself off duty but on-call until dawn the next morning, when search operations would resume. Once I'd signed off with Cole I asked Nightingale if he had any advice.

'Keep your eyes open,' said Nightingale. 'And do your best.'

The village had no street lamps but enough light spilt out from the houses to light my way up the hill. I slipped past the photographers still on guard at the entrance to the cul-de-sac and up to Dominic's mum's bungalow. The lights were on behind net curtains and I could hear the TV inside. I stumbled over something painfully solid left on the path around the side of the building and sensed rather than saw the cowshed as a block of lighter shadow in the darkness. I carefully worked my way to the front. I was fumbling for the key when I looked up and saw the sky for the first time.

When I was very young my mum headed back to Sierra Leone with suitcases full of presents and trunks filled with enough 'as new' clothing to keep a branch of Oxfam in stock for a year and a half. As an afterthought, and probably to secure the additional baggage allowance, she took me with her. I don't remember much of that trip but Mum has several albums filled exclusively with pictures of me looking in turn solemn and terrified as I am manhandled by a succession of relatives. One thing I do remember is looking up at the night sky and seeing that it was crossed by a river of stars.

I saw the same thing that night, a braided stream of light arching over my head while a quarter moon cruised the horizon. For a moment I thought I smelt a sweet slightly fermented scent and the moonlight tricked me into thinking that the empty field behind Dominic's mum's garden was filled with trees. But as soon as I got the lights on in the cowshed they were gone.

# 3

# Operational Flexibility

The sun came up before six the next morning. I lay on top of the duvet and watched blades of light pierce the gaps where the curtains met the walls. I'd left my Airwave on the pillow beside me all night and had heard the search teams up and chattering along with the dawn chorus. It was day three and the girls were still missing. I wondered what the fuck I was doing.

In the absence of coffee, I had a shower, and, by the time I was dressed, Dominic had texted me to say that he was on his way. The air was still fresh but the sun was already sucking up the moisture from the fields and you didn't need to be chewing on a straw to know it was going to be another hot day.

Dominic tooled up five minutes later in a ten-year-old Nissan pickup truck that had been painted a non-standard khaki, dipped in dried mud up to the wheel arches and then randomly smacked with a sledgehammer to give it that Somali Technical look. I found myself checking to see if there was a mount for a fifty-calibre machine gun in the back.

'It's the boyfriend's,' said Dominic. 'He got it second-hand.'

'Who from?' I asked. 'Al Shabaab?'

Dominic gave me a blank look and then asked if I understood about 'mates'.

I nodded. I knew about mates, people from before your attestation as a constable was even a thought in the mind of your career adviser. Some of them are going to break the law and some of those are going to expect you to look the other way. Unless you're a total hard-hearted bastard there'll be at least one who you think you've got an obligation to. Someone you're willing to let slide, or at the very least stand them a pint when they finish a stretch inside. Every copper I know has a mate like that. They're an embarrassment, a pain – and, if you're really unlucky, a sackable offence.

Inside the cab the seats were patched and smelt of overheated dog.

'Well, you see, I've got this mate who's found something that might be relevant to the search,' said Dominic as he deftly steered the massive four by four up past the village hall and onto what laughingly passes as a main road in Herefordshire. 'Only I can't go through the normal channels because she's a bit of an addict.'

And a mate.

'So if we find something?' I said.

'You can say it was your idea.'

'My idea?'

'Something suitably weird.'

'That's a bit presumptuous, isn't it?' I said.

'Presumptuous is my middle name,' said Dominic.

A kilometre further along we reached a crossroad where a crowd of people were assembled. Most of them were dressed in shorts or army trousers, had knapsacks slung over their shoulders and were wearing hats. I noticed that a few of them had Airwave sets clipped to their belts. Dominic slowed down and exchanged greetings with a couple before heading off again. I spotted Derek Lacey on the fringes of the group – looking grim.

'Volunteers,' said Dominic.

Volunteers are good news and bad news in a search. Good because they allow you to cover more ground and have local knowledge. Bad because no copper likes to take a civilian's word that somewhere has been searched properly – we're superstitious that way.

Another couple of kilometres further down the road we came to another crossroad, this one marked with a tall Celtic cross in grey stone – a war memorial, at a guess – where Dominic turned right into a narrow tree-lined lane that climbed towards the top of the ridge. I wondered if this was the same ridge as the Bee House had sat on, but the cell coverage was too intermittent for me to check the location on my phone.

'School Wood,' Dominic said when I asked where we were going. The school in question being a posh independent school we'd actually passed on the drive over. Not that they owned it anymore – it was National Trust property now, part of the Croft Castle Estate.

In places the lane was so narrow that leaves and twigs brushed the sides of the Nissan and Dominic was careful to slow down whenever we approached a blind corner.

'Tractors?' I asked.

'Tractors,' he said. 'Minicabs, horses, Tesco vans,

cows – you never know what you're going to meet around a corner here.'

The entrance to the woods was marked by a wooden five-bar gate with a green National Trust sign on it. Dominic stayed in the Nissan while I got out to open it and let him through. I closed the gate behind him and, because I remembered my Country Code lessons from school trips, I made sure the latch was secure. Once I'd climbed back inside Dominic set off again up a rough track that curved into a forest of dark conifers. The Nissan made easy work of the flinty track bed, which explained why Dominic had chosen it for today's trip. My new Asbo would have been scraping its axles – some of the ruts were that deep.

The track forked and Dominic took the right-hand turn for another hundred metres or so until we reached a place where the greyish brown trunks of felled trees had been stacked in a pyramid by the track. A pale face peered suspiciously around the end of the stack as we drew up.

'That's Stan,' said Dominic as his friend emerged from hiding.

'Stan?' I asked.

'Short for Samantha.'

Stan was about average height, but an habitual stoop made her look shorter. She had brown hair, deep-set eyes, a snub nose, thin lips and a receding chin. As well as the stoop there was a noticeable slackness to the right side of her face. Result of an accident when she was a teenager, Dominic told me later. 'Jumped off the back of a quad bike when she was seventeen,' he said. When I asked why she'd jumped, Dominic just said that they'd all been very drunk at the time.

'Who's this?' asked Stan. She was dressed in a blue boiler suit with the top half undone and tied around her waist by the arms, and a grubby purple T-shirt with the OCP logo on it. If I'd met her while on patrol in London I'd have tagged her on general principles, but she wouldn't have stood out. I realised that out here in the sticks I didn't know what was normal. Maybe everybody dressed like that.

'This is Peter,' said Dominic. 'He's up from London.'

'Oh, yeah?' The words came out slowly, as if Stan was pissed and having to concentrate to speak clearly. I wondered just how badly she'd come off that bike.

'Are you going to show us what you found, or what?' asked Dominic.

Stan stared at me for a moment – her eyes were a pale grey and her right eyelid had a noticeable droop.

'What about him?' asked Stan.

'Peter's from the Met,' said Dominic. 'When he's finished up here he's going straight home. He's not interested in any of your little crimes and misdemeanours.'

Stan's head flopped forward as if it had suddenly got too heavy for her neck.

'Okay,' she said.

After about ten seconds of us all standing there like Muppets I looked at Dominic, who shrugged and indicated that we should wait. Half a minute later Stan's head came up and, as if someone had wound her key a couple of times, she told us to follow her into the woods.

We trooped off behind her into waist-high brack-
en, down something that was not so much a path as a
statistical variation in the density of the undergrowth.
Despite the shade from the trees the air was warm and
humid, and I was just thinking about taking my jacket
off when Stan halted in front of a great wall of rhododendron bushes.

'It's in here,' she said, before crouching down and
crawling into a narrow gap. Reluctantly, I followed her
into a short leafy tunnel that smelt like cheap air fresh-
ener, which opened up into a small clearing surrounded
on three sides by more rhododendron bushes and on
the fourth by a stumpy deciduous tree with shaggy
leaves and branches that were so bent and twisted that
its canopy brushed the ground. The clearing itself was
an unusually regular rectangular shape as a result of
being, I recognised, the foundation of a small building.
At one end was a blackened fireplace defined by a circle
of half bricks and large stones, and at the other a raised
concrete plinth – a coal bunker or cesspit or something
utilitarian like that. The cement floor had been exposed
long enough for a couple of centimetres of powdery
grey soil to build up on top.

'Nobody can find this place,' said Stan proudly.

Only someone obviously had, because Stan showed
us the cast-iron metal door mounted in the side of the
plinth – it looked like the rubbish chute at my parents'
flats. Streamers of plastic, green, white and transparent, drooped from the edges of the door – the remains
of carrier bags. Stan pulled on the door, which opened
with a creak to reveal more strips of plastic and an evil

smell – old meat and rotting paper. There looked to be quite a large void behind the door, but I wasn't that keen to investigate.

'What did you keep in there?' I asked.

'My stash,' said Stan.

'Yeah, but what was in your stash?' I asked.

'Bennies, some blues, some billy whizz, a bit of deer, a couple of coneys and some red.'

Bennies, blues and billy whizz I knew – Benzedrine, diazepam and amphetamines. I asked Dominic what the rest was.

'You know,' said Dominic. 'Deer as in Bambi, coneys is rabbits and red is agricultural diesel. Stan's been siphoning it out of her dad's tractor, haven't you, Stan?'

She bobbed her head. I wondered what agricultural diesel was, but didn't want to look stupid so I didn't ask.

'When do you think the stuff was nicked?' I asked.

'I found it like this on Thursday,' said Stan. 'Afternoon.' She twirled a curl of hair around her finger. 'About five.'

The morning the kids were discovered missing – Day One.

'And when was the last time you came up here before that?' asked Dominic, who'd obviously been thinking the same thing as me.

'Wednesday,' said Stan and stopped when she saw I'd taken out my notebook and was writing things down. For the police, if it isn't written down it didn't happen. And, if the inquiry went pear shaped, questions would be asked. I wasn't going to risk any confusion about who said what to whom – mate or no mate.

'Morning or afternoon?' I asked.

Dominic made encouraging noises and Stan admitted that she'd checked the stash at around seven that evening. A really horrible thought occurred to me then.

'Have you checked to see if,' I hesitated, 'anybody is in there?'

Stan shook her head.

I looked at Dominic and nodded at the yawning hatch. He groaned.

'She's your mate,' I said.

Dominic sighed, pulled a neat little pencil torch from his jacket pocket and dutifully stuck his head inside. I heard a muffled 'Fuck!' followed by coughing and then he whipped his head back out again.

'No,' he said. 'Thank god. And, Stan, do not be storing food down there in future. It's disgusting and probably really unhealthy.'

'We're going to have to report this,' I said and Dominic nodded.

Stan stuck out her lower lip.

'Why?' she asked.

'So the search teams don't waste their time on it when they get here,' said Dominic.

'You think they'll come up here, then?' asked Stan.

'The teams will be here by tomorrow' said Dominic.

'Oh,' said Stan. 'You're still going to help. Right?'

'Help with what?' I asked.

Stan made a little helpless gesture at the gaping hatch.

'They stole my stash,' she said.

'What?' I said. 'All the illegal stuff you had hidden away so that the law didn't catch you?'

'Rabbits isn't illegal,' mumbled Stan.

'Who do you think took your stuff?' asked Dominic.

'Thought it might have been a pony,' said Stan.

'Why would a pony get into your stash?' I asked.

'They're a bugger for food,' she said.

I asked Dominic if there were any ponies nearby.

'There are some a couple of fields over,' he said. 'More down the hill towards Aymestrey. But I've never heard of them drinking diesel before.'

'What about the drugs?' I said. 'What would diazepam even do to a horse?'

We both looked at Stan, who shrugged.

'I don't know,' she said. 'I've never given it to a horse.'

'Maybe we should notify local vets,' I said.

'It wasn't a horse,' said Stan. 'I had the door wired shut.'

She showed us the black iron loops on the door and the frame – remnants of a deadbolt, I thought. Stan said that she always pushed a double loop of heavy gauge steel wire through the loops and then twisted it to keep it shut. I asked where the wire was and she showed me where the unwound strands had been dumped. I picked them up and had a look – they hadn't been cut or melted through or, as far as I could tell, been exposed to magic. In fact there was bugger all in the way of *vestigia* around the stash at all. *Vestigia* being the trace that gets left behind when magic happens.

Flora, your actual growing things, retain *vestigia* really badly and this makes the countryside, leaving aside poetry, not a very magical place. This caused a great deal of consternation to the more Romantic practitioners of the late eighteenth century and early nineteenth century. Particularly Polidori, who spent a great deal of time trying to prove that natural things in their wild and untamed state were inherently magical. He went bonkers in the end, although that could have been a result of spending too much time with Byron and the Shelleys. His big claim to fame, beyond writing the first ever vampire novel, is his work attempting to classify where whatever it is that powers magic comes from. He called it *potentia* because there's nothing quite like Latin for disguising the fact that you're making it up as you go along.

He was amongst the first to postulate that things other than animals must generate *potentia*. Forests, for example, would produce *potentia silvestris* and rivers *potentia fluvialis*. And it is from these sources that the gods and goddesses and spirits of a locality gain their strength.

I've stood in the presence of Father Thames and felt his influence wash over me like an incoming tide. I've seen a lesser river goddess send a wall of water from one end of Covent Garden market to the other. That's sixty tonnes of water over a distance of thirty metres – that's a lot of power, at least 70 megawatts – about what you get from a jet engine at full throttle. And I nearly kissed her just after she'd done it too – makes you think, doesn't it?

We know that power has to come from somewhere, and Polidori's theories were as good as anyone else's. But sticking a Latin tag on a theory doesn't make it true. Not true in a way that matters.

If there had been some kind of supernatural activity,

I would at least have expected to get something off the door, or the concrete of the foundations, both of which stayed stubbornly neutral. Absence of evidence, as any good archaeologist will tell you, is not the same as evidence of absence – I made a note to ask Nightingale about how things went in the countryside.

'What're you looking for?' asked Stan.

'I was looking to see if there are any tracks,' I said.

'There aren't any tracks,' said Stan. 'If there'd been any tracks I'd have seen them.'

'Stan's good with tracks,' said Dominic.

The sun had got high enough to shine directly onto the back of my neck.

'So, no tracks?'

'Nothing,' said Stan.

'So why did you think a pony did it?'

'Don't know,' said Stan. 'That was just the first thing that came into my head when I found it open.'

We were all silent for a moment – something high-pitched yodelled out amongst the trees. The heat seemed to grow around us. I realised that my bottle of water was still in the Nissan.

'To recap,' I said. 'Your stash is gone but the kids are not stuck down there. It must have been people not animals. But they didn't leave any tracks.'

'I thought it might be aliens,' said Stan. 'Because there's no tracks.' She made a motion with her arm – like a claw dangling down.

'Let's hope their saucer runs on diesel, then,' said Dominic. 'Otherwise I think they're going to be a bit disappointed.'

I used an app on my phone to get a GPS fix on our location and then I suggested that we head back to the Nissan before calling it in.

'How are we going to explain what we were doing here?' asked Dominic as he crawled back out of the rhododendrons. I said he could blame it on me doing my due diligence. 'I thought that was the plan.'

Dominic admitted that this was true, but still wanted to know what I was going to say.

'Tell them that I wanted to check on a World War Two military installation,' I said. It wasn't that much of a stretch. The foundations had been the right dimensions for a standard hut and had been made from the poor quality 'economy concrete' used for throwing up pillboxes and air raid shelters in a hurry. In the scramble that followed the fall of France in 1940 a lot of sites had just fallen off the bureaucratic radar.

'Is that part of your brief, then?' asked Dominic.

'Why not?' I said. 'There are all sorts of secrets from back then.'

We pushed our way out of the bracken and back onto the path. It was getting hotter and I could smell the warm resin scent of the trees around me. *Potentia silvestris*, Polidori called the power derived from a forest, the power from whence sprang the antlered gods of Celtic myth, Lemus, Cernunnos and Herne the Hunted – although probably not the last one.

'Who uses this path?' I asked.

'Dog walkers,' said Dominic.

'Ramblers,' said Stan.

'Tourists,' said Dominic, and explained that it was part of the Mortimer Trail, which stretched from Ludlow in the North East, along the ridge that overlooked Rushpool, down into Aymestrey where it crossed the River Lugg and then up to Wigmore, famed in song and story as the ancestral seat of the Mortimer Family. Dominic was a bit hazy about who the Mortimers were, beyond them being powerful Marcher Lords during the middle ages and getting seriously involved in the War of the Roses.

'We did do them in school,' he said. 'But I've forgotten most of it.'

The trail was popular with casual ramblers because of its relative ease and the number of excellent pubs along the route.

'And ufologists,' said Stan.

'Bit of a hotspot,' said Dominic.

'Window area,' said Stan.

There having been a spate of sightings ten years previously, including lights in the sky, cars mysteriously breaking down and a cattle molestation, although Dominic admitted that there might have been an alternative explanation for the last.

'We used to have UFO parties,' said Dominic, in which apparently there was the traditional drinking of the cheap cider, bouts of vomiting and occasional snogging – hopefully not in that order.

'Ever had a close encounter?' I asked Stan before I could stop myself.

'Yeah,' said Stan. 'But I don't like to talk about it.'

We reached where we'd parked the Nissan Technical.

Dominic offered Stan a lift but she said she was fine walking home. She lived with her family on the other side of the ridge near somewhere called Yatton. I watched as she lurched off down the track, making the occasional zigzag and halting every so often to get her bearings.

'She went headfirst into a tree,' said Dominic. 'Spent six months in hospital. The doctors were amazed she walked out on her own feet – everything after that is a bonus.'

Yeah, I thought, that's a mate you're going to go to the wall for.

Despite Dominic having parked it partially in the shade, a gust of hot foetid air struck us in the face when we opened the Nissan's doors. Underneath the aroma of dried shit I could smell rotting vegetables and half-melted plastic.

'Christ, Dominic, what does your boyfriend do for a living?'

'He's a farmer,' said Dominic, as if that explained everything.

We decided to leave the Nissan with the doors open to air out while Dominic called in with his Airwave which got, much to my surprise, better reception than either of our phones. I was that thirsty that I'd just started psych-ing myself up to brave a rummage in the Nissan when Dominic lowered his handset and beckoned me over.

'Were you expecting a delivery?' he asked.

Dominic's mum was a round woman who barely came up to my chest. Her chestnut hair was streaked with grey and tied up into a rough bun at the back of her head. She'd obviously caught the sun that summer, because her skin was brown and she wore streaks of sunblock across her cheekbones. She came hurrying out of the bungalow as soon as Dominic had parked outside and thrust out her hand for me to shake. Her skin was warm and as soft as chamois leather and the bones underneath felt delicate like those of a small bird.

'It's nice to meet you at last.' She was breathing hard as if the short dash from her front door had left her out of breath. 'Is the room all right?'

'Perfect,' I said.

She nodded and withdrew her hand. I gave her a moment to catch her breath before asking about the delivery. She pointed to the paved area by her front door where two old-fashioned oxblood leather-bound trunks had been left side by side.

I sighed and asked Dominic to give me a hand.

'Bloody hell,' he said when he tried to lift his end. 'How long were you planning to stay?'

'It's the housekeeper,' I said. 'She gets carried away.'

Dominic gave me an odd look.

'Housekeeper?'

'Not *my* housekeeper,' I said as I tried to avoid knocking over a garden gnome. 'Our nick has a housekeeper.' Which I decided sounded even weirder.

'Okay,' said Dominic. 'Well, Leominster nick's got vibrating chairs in the rec room.'

'Vibrating chairs?'

'You know. You sit in them and they vibrate,' he said. 'It's very relaxing.'

The inside of my room, a.k.a. the cowshed, was boiling, so once we'd dumped the trunks we retreated back outside with a jug of homemade lemonade provided by Dominic's mum. When the air had a chance to cool inside, me and Dominic had a rummage in the first of the trunks. The top layer, thank god, consisted of about half the contents of my wardrobe, freshly laundered and the creases ironed to a knife edge – which just looks weird on a sweatshirt. The trunk was equipped with a number of convenient drawers and compartments which yielded a miniature brass camp stove with matching pot and kettle and a leather case which contained a cut-throat razor, a shaving brush and a stick of dehydrated soap that smelt of almonds and rum. I wondered if this was all Nightingale's stuff or whether Molly scavenged it from elsewhere in the Folly. A lot of men must have left their belongings behind in 1944 believing that they were coming back.

I put the shaving kit back where I'd found it.

The second trunk contained a tweed shooting jacket, matching yellow waistcoat, a vintage Burberry trench coat, riding boots, a green canvas camp stool and a shooting stick. It was therefore less of a surprise when at the bottom, disassembled in their own oak and leather case, I found a pair of two-inch self-opening shotguns. Judging from the chasing on the mechanism they were Nightingale's two Purdey guns that he kept in a locked case in the billiard room.

I looked at Dominic, whose eyes were bugging out.

'You didn't see that, okay?'

'Absolutely not,' he said.

'Right.'

'The Glorious Twelfth *was* Monday,' he said. 'So grouse is in season.'

I suddenly wondered if Nightingale's contemporaries had bothered with shotguns, or whether they'd trooped out to the countryside and banged away with fireballs. *I say, good shot there, Thomas! Winged the blighter, by god.* It occurred to me that I was currently less than a half hour's drive from a man who might be able to tell me – if the bees didn't sting me to death on the doorstep.

'What the fuck?' said Dominic and, straightening up, looked back towards the front of the bungalow. I joined him just in time to see a column of vehicles roar past the front drive – I recognised a blue Peugeot from the public car park at Leominster nick, likewise a battered green hatchback. A pair of motorbikes with photographers riding pillion raced past, followed by more cars and a satellite van. It was the pack in motion and it was actually quite impressive – like a posh version of Mad Max.

'Shit,' said Dominic. 'They must have got wind of something.'

We exchanged looks – neither of us liked the implications. Dominic pulled out his phone and called the outside inquiry office. After talking for a minute his face relaxed – not bodies, then. He glanced over at me and then told whoever he was talking to that indeed I was here and ready to spring into action – as soon as instructed as to which direction.

'They want you over at the Marstowes' house right away,' he told me. 'Before the thundering herd come rushing back.'

'Have they found something?' I asked.

'Not really,' said Dominic. 'That's the problem.'

Even with all the windows open, the Marstowes' kitchen was stuffy and smelt of hot laminated chipboard. DS Cole had Joanne and her husband sitting on one side of the table and us on the other. Ethan was asleep upstairs and Ryan and Mathew had been packed off to an aunt in Leominster for the afternoon.

'What's happened?' asked Andy Marstowe as soon as we had our legs under the table. He was a short man, just a bit taller than his wife and built with that kind of solidity you get from doing manual labour all your life. He had a pointed chin and deep-set hazel eyes. His light brown hair was receding sharply and he'd obviously decided to bite the bullet and cut the rest of it short. He looked like the classic sawn-off psychopath I used to dread meeting doing the evening shift in Soho, except there was none of the angry violence in his eyes – only fear.

'First,' said Cole, 'let me assure you that we have not found any indication that either Hannah or Nicole have been harmed in any way.' Andy and Joanne didn't look particularly reassured. 'Normally we wouldn't bring something like this to your attention, but unfortunately the media got hold of it and we wanted you to have all the facts before getting a garbled version from them.'

The pack had swept back into the village less than ten minutes after they'd left, and come boiling up the cul-de-sac like the return of a tide, licking at my heels as I ran up the path and only stopping at the hedge line because it was held by a special constable called Sally Donnahyde who was a primary school teacher in her other job and so wasn't going to take any lip from a bunch of journalists. The kitchen was at the back of the house, but I could still hear them as a restless murmur, like surf on a pebble beach.

I watched the parents shift in their seats and brace themselves.

'We found a child's knapsack just off the B4362, four hundred yards from the assembly point. But it was immediately apparent that the item had been lying there for at least ten years, so we don't think it's connected to the case.'

Andy's fists unclenched and Joanne let go her breath. DS Cole opened the case on her tablet and showed them a picture of the knapsack. It had been laid out on plastic sheeting and had a ruler placed next to it for scale. It was made of see-through plastic and although it was fogged by age and neglect it was obvious that any contents had been removed. Cole asked, she said purely as a matter of routine, whether either of them recognised it.

They said they didn't, but I thought Joanne hesitated just a little bit too long before speaking. Then she sprang up and asked if anyone wanted tea. Cole took the opportunity to fill them both in on the current state of the search. Andy fidgeted throughout, and in the first pause said if that was all he'd like to get back to the search now, thank you very much. Then, either not noticing or ignoring his wife's angry look, he got up and left.

I'd have liked a chance to talk with Cole about

Joanne's hesitation, but Cole obviously didn't want to leave her alone. I wondered if I should press Joanne on the subject myself, but I figured it would be a mistake to pre-empt a senior officer. It was probably nothing . . . but that sounded a little bit too much like famous last words.

'He's not dealing with it,' said Joanne when her husband was safely gone. 'He's just keeping himself busy.'

'I'm not sure there is actually a way to "deal" with it, Jo,' said Cole.

'Peter,' Joanne said suddenly, and turned to me. 'Truthfully – what are the chances?'

Now Cole was staring at me, too – no pressure there.

'I think the chances are good,' I said.

'Why?' Joanne's eyes were wide, desperate.

'Because they went out together,' I said. 'If someone had harmed them locally we'd have a lead by now. And if it was someone from outside we'd have sightings of them coming in.'

Joanne subsided. It was all bollocks, of course. Not even very plausible bollocks at that. But I didn't think Joanne wanted facts – just an excuse to hold it together.

It left a bad taste in my mouth, though.

A phone rang, the fake old-fashioned telephone ring-tone that comes as standard on most phones. It rang three times before I remembered that I'd switched it over from my usual tone – the *Empire Strikes Back* theme, because you didn't want *that* going off in front of a distressed family member – and I had to scramble to answer the call before the voicemail cut in.

When I answered, a cheerful woman asked me

to confirm that I was Peter Grant. When I did, she informed me that she was DCI Windrow's Personal Assistant and could I come in, because the chief inspector would like to have a word.

'When?' I asked.

'Just as soon as you can get here,' she said.

# 4

# The Falcon Assessment

The first thing I noticed was that somebody, contrary to Health and Safety regulations, had jimmied the windows in Leominster nick so that they opened all the way out. Given the inquiry offices were all on the first floor, they got a surprising amount of breeze – I figured that, and a truly stupendous amount of caffeinated beverages, was all that was holding the MIU together. I seriously doubted the vibrating chairs were making much of a contribution.

Edmondson and Windrow were waiting for me in the Learning Zone again. They asked me to sit down and offered me some cold water – which I took gratefully. I resisted the urge to rub the bottle against my forehead.

'How are you finding it?' asked Windrow.

'Sir?' I asked.

'The operation,' he said. 'How do you think it's going?'

Nothing unnerves a junior officer quite as much as having a much senior officer stare over a desk and ask your opinion on something. It's always tempting to fall back on that strangled mixture of cop-speak and management-ese that has proved the modern police officer's friend when he wants to talk a great deal and say nothing. Still, from the look in Windrow's eyes, blurting out that I thought that West Mercia Police were taking *an aggressively proactive approach in line with best practice as laid down in national guidelines* was not the way to go.

'As well as can be expected,' I said, which was almost as bad.

Windrow nodded benignly – a gesture I've seen interviewing officers use on suspects dozens of times.

'What's your impression of the Marstowes?' he asked.

'They're hanging in there,' I said.

'There's no possibility that they might have orchestrated the disappearance?' asked Windrow.

God, I thought. But as a theory it certainly had its attractions.

'Is there some evidence that they might have?' I asked.

Windrow shook his head.

'Oh, congratulations by the way,' said Edmondson. 'You've made the papers.'

He passed me a copy of the *Sun* which had pushed the page three girl all the way back to page eleven in order to devote more space to MISSING GIRLS. Since they didn't know anything we didn't, and we didn't know anything, they had a lot of pictures to cover up the lack of text. In the upper right-hand corner of page five was a good one of me and Dominic standing by the village hall. We were obviously talking and, fortunately, both of us were looking suitably grim and intense. The caption read 'ALL HANDS ON DECK: Police from all over the country are involved in the search for Hannah and Nicole.'

'Sorry about that, sir. They must have used a tele-photo lens.'

'Not a problem,' said Edmondson. 'The ACC thought it reflected well on the force – diversity wise.' He gave me a humourless smile. 'Everyone pulling together and all that.'

That's me, I thought. Poster boy for diversity.

Windrow steepled his fingers.

'You've been with the SAU for over a year,' he said. 'Correct?'

'Since February last year,' I said, wondering where the hell this was going.

'So you've had experience of unusual cases?' he asked. 'Cases involving the—' He stalled. Behind him Edmondson shifted his weight uneasily and spoke.

'The supernatural,' he said.

'Yes, sir,' I said, and there was a pause while we all tried to think of what to say next.

The two men glanced at each other.

'Do you see any of that in this case?' he asked.

'Sir?' I said. Because if I've learnt one thing, it is to let the senior officers make their position clear before you risk opening your gob.

'You came up to interview . . .' Windrow checked a yellow sticky note attached to his policy book. 'A Mr Hugh Oswald over by Wylde?'

'Yes, sir,' I said. 'It was a standard TIE.' A Trace, Im-plicate or Eliminate is the backbone job of any major inquiry, find someone and either make them a suspect or eliminate them from the inquiry.

'And you're satisfied that he's not involved?' asked Windrow.

'Yes, sir,' I said. 'On account of him being ninety-three and pretty much confined to a wheelchair.'

'And there's no possibility of an accomplice?' asked Windrow.

There was his daughter, who I hadn't thought to check. But then I'd assumed that the main purpose of the trip had been get to my moping self out from under Nightingale's feet. I should have at least statemented her – Lesley would have killed me for being that sloppy.

'I did a standard assessment,' I said, and wondered just how desperate West Mercia Police were, to be talking to me about this.

Edmondson folded his arms and then unfolded them again.

'I know you haven't been attending briefings,' said Windrow after a pause. 'But you must be aware that we are not making any progress. All we know is that the most likely scenario is that the girls got up in the middle of the night and left their homes voluntarily. After that they just vanish.' He tapped his finger on his desk a couple of times. 'We believe it would be remiss of us not to consider *all* possible angles. And, since you're here and available, we'd like you to do a Falcon assessment on the whole case.'

They *were* that fucking desperate.

I nearly froze up, staring at the pair of them in disbelief. But fortunately my highly tuned bureaucratic arse-saving instincts kicked in and I managed to say that I'd have to clear it with Nightingale first.

They agreed and even let me make the call outside their earshot.

Nightingale thought it was an eminently sensible idea, notwithstanding the fact that neither of us had ever done a formal Falcon assessment before, me because I was too junior and him because in his day such things as assessments and regular case reviews hadn't been invented. At least, not at the Folly they hadn't.

'I don't even know what I'm supposed to be looking for,' I said.

Nightingale replied that he would immediately repair to the library and see what he could dig up in the way of rural supernatural crime.

'And I shall call Harold,' he said. 'This is just the sort of thing he lives for.'

Professor Harold Postmartin being the Folly's archivist, amateur historian and Oxford don voted least likely to get a four-part documentary series on Channel Four, six years in a row.

'And now that I think of it,' said Nightingale, 'it might be worth reaching out to some of our other friends in the demi-monde. Just on the off-chance.'

So I glumly reported back to Edmondson and Windrow that not only would the SAU be happy to do a full Falcon assessment, but we would be tasking our senior civilian analyst and drawing on our covert human intelligence sources – even if some of them weren't entirely human.

They were so delighted they put me in Edmondson's office down the hall which, quite apart from having its own dedicated HOLMES II socket, was out of sight of the main inquiry office. There was a brief delay while Windrow got my access enabled and rustled up a HOLMES-enabled laptop I could use before they closed the door and let me get on with it.

But get on with what?

Part of the problem with doing a Falcon assessment is that it's hard to apply professional best practice to a field of law enforcement that most police wouldn't touch with a one metre extendable baton. Not to mention that the closest the Folly had come to a formal assessment were the times we'd had to tell a senior officer that having occult graffiti sprayed across the crime scene did not make it a Falcon case. Especially if the symbols had been cribbed from Aleister Crowley, *The Lord of the Rings* or *Adventure Time*. The only case like that we ever hesitated over was the kanji characters sprayed onto the front of a private school in Highgate, but according to one of Postmartin's friends at the School of Oriental and African Studies they were from a JRPG called *Sakura Wars* – very popular in the 1990s.

The problem was that once the government pushed through its major cuts in policing, a lot of officers had got the notion that they might be able to unload anything even vaguely weird onto us.

'Although it is noticeable,' Nightingale had pointed out, 'that this never happens if the officer concerned has worked with us before.'

All your cases, I thought, do not belong to us.

So I did what I always did in these situations, and asked myself what Lesley would do – apart from taser me in the back and betray me to the Faceless Man, that is. And what she would do is say – *Start with the action list – duh!*

A modern major investigation runs off HOLMES II, which is a great big computerised mincing machine into which your investigating officers shovel information and turn the handle in the hope that something edible, or at least admissible in court, will emerge from the other end. In order to keep the machine fed, senior officers assign their junior officers 'actions' – interviewing Hannah's and Nicole's teachers is an 'action', as is checking the family phone records against the numbers of known sex offenders. The police never saw a noun they didn't want to turn into a verb, so it quickly became 'to action', as in you action me to undertake a Falcon assessment, I action a Falcon assessment, a Falcon assessment has been actioned and we all action in a yellow submarine, a yellow submarine, a yellow submarine.

Thus, to review a major inquiry is to review the list of 'actions', and their consequences, in the hope that you'll spot something that thirty-odd highly trained and experienced detectives didn't. I sat down and made a note in my notebook – *Commence Falcon assessment with review of action list* – and dated it.

It was lunchtime on day three, Hannah and Nicole had been missing for over fifty hours.

*Day One – 09:22 – first and only 999 call – caller identified himself as Derek Lacey.*

I didn't listen to the sound file, but even from the transcript you can sense him struggling to maintain control. He'd obviously taken a moment to marshal his arguments in the fear that the police wouldn't take him seriously, because he listed off Nicole's and Hannah's ages, the fact that they had left their bedrooms some time during the night, and that none of their friends or relatives had seen them. And he'd clearly impressed the Force Duty Inspector at the Worcester control centre, because he in turn had sent all of available D-shift directly to Rushpool, headed by PS Robert Collington.

Team D had a TOA (time of arrival) of 09:37 at which point Edmondson, as geographic commander, had been informed and had chosen to take ownership of the operation.

Statistically speaking, in cases involving missing children, abduction by a stranger comes at the bottom of a long list that starts with having simply run off, continues down through staying overnight at a mate's without telling their parents and, often, hiding somewhere in the house. In fact, a child is much more likely to be murdered by their parents than be abducted by a stranger. So the first set of actions after arrival involved searching the parents' houses and gathering names and addresses of friends and family.

But Dominic had been right, and the fact that two girls had gone missing from two separate households on the same night must have caught everyone's eye. Because by quarter past ten, less than an hour after the initial 999 call, the girls had been designated as HIGH RISK MISPERS and the on-call POLSA had been notified. Standby PSU officers were called out in Hereford, Worcester, Kidderminster and Shrewsbury. By lunchtime, a sizable chunk of West Mercia Police's available manpower had found itself deployed into the area around Rushpool.

By that time the girls' computers were on their way to High-Tech to be checked for signs of online grooming, and the requisite applications to track their phones in real time had been made. Had this been London, teams of officers would have been poring through hours of CCTV footage. But out in the wilds the surveillance state was unaccountably thin on the ground.

When you deploy for missing children, if you do so at all, the rule is to deploy fast and in numbers. Even if probability and common sense tells you that they're going to skip back into their front door later that day. Had they been older, fourteen or over, then West Mercia might have waited another twenty-four hours before literally calling out the dogs. Still, up until six o'clock in the evening, Edmondson probably thought it likely that the girls would return under their own steam.

Then they found the phones. Both immediately identified as belonging to Nicole and Hannah, both with dead batteries. Since an eleven-year-old girl is more likely to relinquish a kidney than her mobile phone, the working hypothesis changed from runaway to abduction and that's when the fun really started.

Hereford CID was immediately contacted, and the Major Investigation Unit attached to what was now designated OPERATION MANTICORE. Just when most of the detectives had been heading home – they must have loved that. I discovered during a quick trip to the coffee area that despite its fully equipped custody and interview suite, HOLMES-capable offices, canteen, helicopter pad, and not forgetting the famous vibrating chairs, Leominster nick normally only housed the safer neighbourhood team. It was essentially moth-balled against future need – presumably an upsurge in cross-border raids by the Welsh. DCI Windrow, Dom-inic, and all his mates had decamped there from their base in Hereford – which explained why the place was so clean.

The Press Liaison officer contacted the local media only to find that they'd been pre-empted. Somebody had already been in touch with the *Leominster News* and *Hereford Times*, providing details of the two girls' names and a suitably heart-wrenching photograph of both of them in sun hats. I recognised the background – it was definitely the Marstowes' back garden. I spotted a red swing set I'd seen out the kitchen window. Somebody else had recognised it, too, because the assumption in the report was that Joanne Marstowe had contacted the press directly. It was too late for either of the news-papers to change their headlines, but local radio and BBC regional TV news sent journalists and agreed to run an appeal for information. The local news manag-ers must have taken one look at the photograph of two pretty smiling eleven-year-old white girls in matching sun hats and wept tears of joy. The story went national in about the time it took the editors in London to open the jpeg attached to the email. By the time Inspector Ed-mondson was briefing all the new hands on deck at ten o'clock, the media was already assembling in the foyer.

I tried to remember what I'd been doing that night, but nothing came to mind.

Searches resumed at first light and there was a flurry of actions from the newly installed MIU, two hundred plus of which were TIEs on RSOs. Impressively, the MIU had completed over a hundred Trace Implicate or Eliminate on Registered Sex Offenders in Herefordshire alone and had farmed out a bunch more to adjacent police forces. As of when I was checking the list there were only three RSOs within two hundred kilometres of Rushpool that hadn't been checked, and there was a strong suspicion that two of the remaining might be dead.

You can do a keyword search on HOLMES, the utility of which depends on what words you use. I tried, just for the hell of it, *magic, wizard, witch, invisible,* three different spelling variations of *fairy* and spent fifteen minutes weeding out a surprisingly large number of references to books, TV and a fancy dress party many of the kids had attended a week before the disappearance. One statement taken from a school friend of Nicole and Hannah's caught my eye.

**R175 H TST GABRIELLA DARRELL MISC**
PC TASKER: So Nicole had an invisible friend.
GABRIELLA: Yes.
PC TASKER: Like an imaginary friend?
GABRIELLA: Not really.
MRS DARRELL: Nicole always was a very imaginative child. Not like Gaby here who's very sensible. Aren't you Gaby? No imaginary friends for you.

I added a restatementing to my action request list on

the basis that if you don't know where you're going, try as many directions as possible.

By five I'd finished a fast sweep of the action list and took a break. Someone gave me directions to the nearest supermarket, but I got lost and ended up at a huge Morrisons instead. I took the opportunity to stock up on the sort of essentials that Molly wouldn't think of – bottled water, snacks, fruit and shaving gear that had been manufactured this side of the millennium. Inside the store, the air conditioning was fierce. So I parked myself at the in-store café and called Nightingale to discuss my next move. This had the added advantage of keeping Folly business away from the prying ears of other police officers.

'Nothing jumped out, then?' asked Nightingale.

'Not off the action list,' I said. 'The working hypothesis is that they both decided to sneak out of their houses and meet up. And that either they ran away, which is unlikely, or something bad happened to them.'

Nightingale asked why running away was unlikely.

'They didn't take anything except their phones,' I said. 'Runaway kids nearly always take something.' I had, both times, although the first time it had been limited to a peanut butter and jam sandwich and a copy of *2000AD*.

'For the moment we should leave the more run of the mill nastiness to our country cousins,' said Nightingale. 'You should first establish whether the two girls could have come into contact with something uncanny.'

'Like what?'

'A rogue practitioner,' said Nightingale. 'A hedge

88

wizard or witch we don't know about it, or a fae, or demi-fae, or revenant of some sort. Did either of them change their routine behaviour or exhibit strange cravings?'

'The child abuse unit will be looking for the same things,' I said.

'Then I suggest you might confer with them,' said Nightingale. 'You might also want to have a chat with their teachers and the leaders of the Girl Guides or whatever the equivalent body is these days. Assuming they were Guides. Is there a parish priest?'

'I can find out,' I said, and noticed that a couple of white boys at a nearby table were giving me the side eye.

'A good parish priest often knows the more esoteric aspects of his local history,' said Nightingale. 'Or at least they used to.'

They were both dark haired, pasty faced despite the summer. The shorter one had blue eyes and the taller was wearing sunglasses indoors – which told you everything you needed to know, really. The sleeves of their grey and green check shirts were rolled up to reveal the beefy arms of people who actually work for a living. In London I would have pegged them as builders, but out here in the sticks they could have been lumberjacks or sheep shearers for all I knew.

'You might want to talk to Hugh Oswald again,' said Nightingale. 'See if he's noticed anything odd.'

Apart from his creepy granddaughter, I thought. Although she might be worth talking to, as well.

'It's a pity we can't sniff people out like the rivers can,' I said.

'I for one am quite glad that that particular ability

appears limited to them,' said Nightingale. 'I feel our work has become quite complicated enough as it is. Still, as you say . . .'

The white boys knew they had my attention now, but hesitated – that's the trouble with being a racist in the white heartlands, you don't get a lot of practical experience. I gave them a quizzical look, just to fuck with them a bit.

They broke eye contact first. The tall one in the sunglasses turned to his friend and said something, then they both looked at me and sniggered.

What are we, I thought, twelve? So I laughed. It wasn't a genuine laugh but they weren't to know that. They both stared at me and then turned away when I didn't break eye contact. I wanted to provoke them. I wanted to give them a smacking they wouldn't forget.

'Peter?' asked Nightingale and I realised I hadn't been listening.

At the very least I wanted to show them my warrant card and mess with their preconceptions. But you can't do that sort of thing, because there's always a chance you'll end up in a fight. And then you'll have to arrest them. Which, never mind the ethical issues surrounding the abuse of power, results in a ton of paperwork. Not to mention I was way off my manor, so it would piss off West Mercia Police who probably felt they had better things to waste their time on right now, thank you very much. So I took a deep breath and looked away.

That's me – Peter Grant, a credit to his territorial policing agency.

'Sorry sir,' I said. 'I was distracted.'

'I asked how you were feeling,' said Nightingale.

'Fine, sir,' I said.

'Glad to hear that,' he said.

I tensed, hearing the chairs scrape as the boys got to their feet, but they passed on the other side of the table and headed towards the main entrance.

'I'd better get back,' I said. 'I need to get some actions actioned.'

Outside, the sun was frying the car park and my two friends from the café were attempting to lean nonchalantly against the side of a blue Nissan Micra without burning themselves. I wondered whether they were waiting for me, or just didn't have anywhere else to go – it's possible they didn't know either.

The tall one with the sunglasses lit up a Silk Cut and took an aggressive drag.

Magic has what Dr Walid, who would be the Folly's resident man of science if he wasn't actually resident in a nice Victorian villa in Finchley, would call a deleterious effect on microprocessors. We don't know why doing a spell can reduce the chip set of your laptop to a fine sand, but since everything useful from your phone to your food mixer is controlled by chips these days it means you have to be careful. But just because you don't know why something happens doesn't mean you can't attempt to quantify its effects.

And once you've quantified an effect, it becomes that much easier to weaponize it. All you need to do is modify your werelight a bit with a couple of *formae inflectentes* and, after about three weeks of trial and error, you have a projectable spell that will burn out every microprocessor within a conveniently small radius.

I'd got some stick from Nightingale, who has this strange idea that his apprentice should know what he's doing before sticking his finger in the electric socket of the universe. But even he changed his mind when I pointed out that a) it was really just a beefed up werelight and b) you could use it to disable any car fitted with a microprocessor-controlled engine management system – which was pretty much all of them now.

Standing in the baking car park outside Morrisons I came this close to lobbing one into the white boys' Micra, but even as I rehearsed the *forma* in my head I remembered the girls' phones. According to the results summary from forensics, no data had been recoverable from either the phone memories or the SIM cards. But it hadn't given a cause. There are plenty of things that can ruin your phone, but fewer things that are so thorough that a decent forensics team can't extract anything useful. And one of those fewer things, I knew from bitter experience, was a burst of magic.

I gave the two boys a happy smile which almost caused the tall one to swallow his cigarette. Then I moved swiftly back to the Asbo, but not so swiftly as to give them the wrong idea.

Back at Leominster nick I called up the exhibit list and found the reports related to both the girls' mobile phones. They were found at the foot of yet another war memorial, this one a skinny cross set in a raised grassy dais by the B4362 where the lane that runs up parallel to Rushpool to the east switches over to become the lane that runs up the hill to somewhere called Bircher

Common. Which appeared to be both the name of a hamlet and your actual piece of open land for public use. I printed the sketch map and photographs of the site which recorded the exact position of the phones. Then I checked the POLSA notes which hypothesised that Hannah and Nicole had taken the footpath west across the fields until they reached Pound Lane, and walked north up the lane until it reached the B4362 where they had become separated from their phones. The crossroad quickly became the loci of two types of searches, one based on the assumption that the girls had travelled on by foot and the second on the assumption that they had voluntarily or involuntarily climbed into a vehicle driven by person or persons unknown.

The POLSA and their search teams were covering option one, MIU were covering option two – which was a horrible job. With no CCTV and limited ANPR – that's automatic number plate recognition to you, Winston – MIU had to rely on canvassing local witnesses for information about car movements in and out of the area. And even in the countryside nobody's that nosy at five o'clock in the morning. Still, they had managed to amass a staggering number of car sightings around both Rushpool and the crossroads where the phones were found. These ranged from *Some kind of van that might have been white* to *I saw that Citroën belonging to Will Whitton what lives over the hill in Orelton and was up to no good and no mistake.*

Five officers had been assigned to grind their way through these reports. You could tell who they were by the pitiful groans and low moans of despair that floated up from their corner of the incident room.

I noticed from the action list that they were prioritising the period from four to six in the morning – which puzzled me until I found a cross link to the statement by Nicole's mother that she had first noticed her daughter missing at five in the morning. When asked why she hadn't raised the alarm then, she said that Nicole often got up at first light in the summer.

'She likes to watch the sun come up,' she said.

The evidence entry for the girls' mobiles had contact details for a Kimberly Cidre at the High Tech Crime Unit in Worcester, and I gave her a ring on the basis that if you want something done fast it's better to talk than to email.

'Can I help you?' Kimberley Cidre had a strong Belfast accent. I suspected Cidre was not her maiden name.

I identified myself and asked about the phones.

'They're a total loss,' she said. 'At first we thought the batteries had been completely drained, but when we changed them they still didn't work. That's when we took them apart. We tested all the ICs independently and they were all inoperable.'

'Was there any visible damage?' I asked.

'No,' she said. 'No obvious sign of physical damage at all.'

'Have you looked at them under a microscope?'

There was a pause.

'Not yet,' she said. 'What would I be looking for?'

The trouble with scientists is that you can't blind

94

them with science, unless you know more than they do
– which, by definition, I didn't.

'I don't want to prejudice the results,' I said, which is
always a good standby. 'But if you spot something, I'd
like to send pictures to a specialist in London to have a
look.'

'What kind of specialist?'

Explaining that Dr Walid was a world renowned en-
terologist would probably just raise more questions
than it answered.

'I don't know,' I said. 'I'm just the police, but if we
find what we looking for I'll have him call you and explain. How about that?'

There was quite a long pause.

'Is this something to do with UFOs?' asked Cidre.

'No,' I said with complete honesty, for a change. 'Do
you get a lot of UFOs up here?'

'We get a lot of UFO spotters and a lot of sightings,'
she said. 'These two facts may be related.'

'As far as I know there are no UFOs involved,' I said.
'But if we find one, I'll let you know.'

Cidre agreed to check the microprocessors and email
me images of anything she found.

Looking back, I could have possibly been a little bit
firmer about the non-involvement of extraterrestrial
intelligence.

Even when you're part of the investigation you don't
just turn up on the doorstep of a victim's parents, start
asking questions and poking around their bookshelves.
First I had to clear the action with DCI Windrow, who

told me to clear it with DC Henry Carter who was the lead FLO attached to the Laceys. There was a delay while DC Carter checked with DS Cole as to whether I could be trusted or not – obviously I could, because Windrow gave his blessing. But only if either DS Cole or Carter was with me to hold Victoria Lacey's hand.

It was getting dark as I drove back to Rushpool and I realised I was finally beginning to understand how the landscape worked. Leominster sits on a plain where two valleys converge. Travelling northwest, the valley of the River Lugg snakes off towards Aymestrey. And, to the north, another valley drains the land around Orelton and the wonderfully named Wooferton. Between them they make a Y-shape just like a cartoon character's slingshot, with the ridge of high land occupied by Croft Castle and Bircher Common forming the elastic band. Rushpool was one of a string of villages that occupied the slopes below the ridge, nestling in the small valleys cut by streams draining into the flat lands.

In late evening the ridge became a shadow looming ahead as you reached the village, with just a couple of lights visible from isolated houses on the slopes. I drove carefully up the main street, the better to avoid any stray journalists.

The Laceys lived in what was, at its core, an honest to god sixteenth-century half-timbered building. It was the sort of place that had been so heavily modified by each succeeding generation that grown conservationists are reduced to weeping because the whole ill-fitting hodgepodge of styles and periods are equally historical and worth preserving. Except for maybe the ugly PVC frame door which filled the Restoration-era hooded doorway like a cheap set of plastic dentures. The door was opened by Derek Lacey who didn't seem pleased to see me and, judging from his breath, had acquired a bottle of whisky since we'd last met.

'You'd better come in,' he said.

Victoria Lacey was sitting at the huge oak kitchen table and idly rotating a half-drunk glass of red wine. The remains of a snack – bread, posh cheese and a supermarket salad still half in its plastic container – was spread out between her and the seat that her husband returned to. DC Henry Carter was there to watch over them and reassure the pair that I wasn't about to pop them in a cauldron and have them for supper.

Victoria had a thin pale face and chestnut brown hair cut into a bob. She was wearing a man's sized sweatshirt with the sleeves rolled up to reveal painfully thin wrists and long delicate hands. Her eyes, I saw when she looked up at me, were a very pale blue.

I paid my respects and told them I'd try to be as unobtrusive as possible, but they just nodded vaguely. There was half a bottle of red on the table and they were both reaching for it when I left the kitchen.

Much as I'm a fan of Georgian formalism, I do like a house where you can walk down a flight of three stairs on the ground floor and find yourself in what I supposed I'd have to call a 'den'. It certainly wasn't a library, because it only had a couple of Ikea bookshelves. And if Derek Lacey used it as an office, then he wasn't in the habit of leaving his work out. There was a Wii attached to an average-sized flatscreen TV with two sets of controllers strewn at its base – Hannah and Nicole. I found traces of the girls elsewhere in the room, a stack of board games in dog-eared boxes with sun-bleached covers, a collection of teen magazines plonked on a bookshelf, and a battered copy of *Harry Potter and the Goblet of Fire* wedged into a gap between a pristine edition of *Wolf Hall* and the film tie-in of *Life of Pi*.

One corner of the room had a chill that had nothing to do with a physical draft. I felt a waft of dank air and the rattle of some kind of hand-powered machine – a milk churn, if I had to guess. As *vestigia* went, it was about par for a house of this age and nothing to get excited about.

There had been a half-hearted attempt to impose a uniform design on the ground floor of the house, with matt-finished oatmeal walls in a conscious echo of the original wattle and daub, but it fell apart on the first floor. I could tell from the texture that if you scraped the top layer of white, with a hint of peach, off the walls you'd find the history of the families that lived here written in the layers of wallpaper underneath.

More *vestigia* in the hallway, the click and whirr of a cuckoo clock, the smell of Vicks VapoRub and hot steam – sensations that cut off abruptly inside the master bedroom. A modern king-size bed, sturdy antique wardrobe and a nice mahogany Victorian vanity. The scatter of shoes in the corners told me that Derek and Victoria were still sharing the marital bed.

Further down, there was a musty smelling spare room containing a brass bed with a pink coverlet and a double stack of moving boxes in the corner. Next to that, a bathroom that had been refurbished within the last six months, judging by the absence of scale build-up in the shower and the lack of discoloration on the back of the imitation brass taps.

Nicole's own room was bigger than the master bedroom, but an awkward long shape that hinted of two rooms that had been knocked together. It was pleasingly not-pink, but instead wallpapered with subtle lemon yellow and light blue stripes. The furniture was expensive but modern and had taken some punishment around the legs and corners. Again not much in the way of books, just the rest of the Harry Potter set and what looked like textbooks on the fold-down desk. Much less in the way of furry mascots, but stray bits of Lego had worked their way into gaps between the chest of drawers and the skirting board. An obvious gap where the High-Tech Crime unit had had it away with her laptop. A poster of *Hunger Games* over the bed – Jennifer Lawrence taking aim down the length of an arrow.

I pulled out one of the Harry Potters. It was practically mint, probably unread. I put it back and decided that there wasn't anything useful here.

'I understand why you have to do these things,' said Victoria Lacey from behind me – I turned to find her in the doorway. 'I really wish you didn't have to.'

'So do I, ma'am,' I said. 'Did Nicole have a Kindle or any other kind of eReader?'

'Why?'

'I'm sorry?'

'Why do you want to know?' she asked, crossing her arms over her chest.

'They can get emails and other social media,' I said. 'A lot of people don't realise that. We need to ensure we haven't overlooked any avenues of communication that might have existed between Nicole and other people.'

'When you say "other people" you mean paedophiles, don't you?'

Her lips clamped shut on the end of the sentence. I could see she was trying to say the unthinkable in the hope it wouldn't be true – it's a sort of magic thinking, but unfortunately not the kind that works.

'Not just paedophiles,' I said. 'Undesirable contacts, estranged parents, dealers, gang members, that sort of thing.' Christ, I thought. Talk about scant comfort.

'That's your speciality in London, isn't it?' she said. 'Gang violence, that sort of thing.'

'No,' I said. 'I check for things that other officers overlook.'

'Because there aren't any gangs out here,' she said. 'I mean, apart from the Travellers and I suppose some of the Poles, but then they don't live around here as such.' She stopped and stared at me for a moment. 'This is a good place to bring up kids, you know. Not like London. I mean, anything can happen in London.'

I asked her if she'd grown up in London herself, but she said she came from Guildford.

'But I lived in London for a couple of years. Before I met Derek,' she said. 'He's from here. I'm from *off*. That matters up here. But I suppose in London everyone's from *off*.'

Except those of us who are from Kentish Town, I thought.

'Derek whisked me up here almost as soon as he heard I was pregnant,' she said. 'He already had the house by then, bought it off the church when the village lost its vicar. I'm glad he did, because there's room for kids out here.' She looked around the room. 'Do you think they have missed something?'

I glanced around the room – there were still traces of fingerprint powder around the window frames, the door, and anywhere else an intruder might have touched. I estimated that more forensic time had been spent in that one room than in the last fifty local burglary investigations.

'No,' I said. 'I don't think they have.'

She started to cry then. I'm not even sure she was aware it was happening until she felt the tears trickling down her cheeks. I took a step towards her, but she whirled quickly around and fled.

I went downstairs and let myself out.

The next morning my phone pinged while I was in the shower. It was an email from Kimberly Cidre at the High Tech unit. There was an attached image which even my dinky phone display could expand enough for me to see a familiar pattern of microscopic pits and lesions. I forwarded them on to Dr Walid but I didn't need his confirmation.

I know hyperthaumaturgical degradation when I see it.

The phones had been done in by magic.

# 5

## Customer Facing

'Now you're beginning to freak me out,' said Dominic as I squatted down to get my face close to the old stone of the war memorial. 'I still don't see what you need me for.'

'Local guide,' I said.

It was late enough for the search teams to be out, but early enough for the air to still be cool and fresh. Stone retains *vestigia* longer than anything except certain types of plastic, but I'd wanted to check first thing and not waste any time. Magic powerful enough to damage a phone would have left a trace on the monument had it happened here. I know this because I've done experiments in a controlled setting to determine accurately the persistence of *vestigia* following a magical event. Or at least as accurately as you can using your own perception and that of a short-haired terrier called Toby.

'Whatever happened to the phones,' I said, 'didn't happen here.'

It hadn't happened at the Lacey house either. Or, and I'd double checked that morning, at the Marstowe house. I was facing the possibility that I might just have to knock on every door in the village and have a sniff around. This is where it would have been useful to have another practitioner to split the work with.

'So you think this is a Falcon case?' asked Dominic.

'Maybe,' I said. 'But there's no point me going to your governor until I've got something worth telling him.'

'He's going to want to know either way,' said Dominic.

Just then a helicopter clattered right over our heads, the lowest I'd ever seen an aircraft not coming into land. It was a militarised Eurocopter Dauphin in army camouflage. When it banked to head up the ridge we caught the edge of its rotor wash – it was that low.

'Eight Flight,' said Dominic smugly. 'Special Air Service.' He grinned at the expression on my face. 'Finally,' he said. 'I was wondering if anything out here was going to impress you.'

'Are they joining the search?' I asked.

'They've been in it from the start,' said Dominic. 'One of the perks of operating in Herefordshire – the SAS tend to pitch in on these sort of cases.'

Magic only damages microprocessors when they're powered, which meant that whatever happened to the girls' phones happened when they were switched on. But practically the first thing you do with a high priority MISPER is call their service provider and get the snail trail – the track the phone leaves when it's on. That data is kept for three days, but on the night the girls vanished both phones went off the air within five minutes of each other at around ten o'clock. The girls' bedtime.

That was worrying. Because if person or persons unknown had told the girls to turn off their phones, then it displayed a disturbing level of forensic awareness.

'If you were an eleven-year-old girl, what would you turn your phone on for?' I asked.

'Send a text?'

I thought about it. 'Both at the same time?'

'Tweet maybe,' said Dominic. 'Because OMG you'll never believe what just happened.'

Records showed that there hadn't been a text or a tweet, but perhaps whatever made them turn on their phones destroyed them almost immediately.

Accidentally or deliberately? It just went round and round.

Right, I thought. If you can't be clever, then at least you can be thorough.

So I called DCI Windrow and provided exactly enough information to complicate his investigation and not enough to help in a material way. I told him that I was working on the hypothesis that whatever had happened to their phones happened on their way to the crossroad where they were abandoned. I said I needed to do a survey of the whole village so he lent me Dominic, since he was a local boy who people would talk to, and off we went.

There are one hundred and seven separate dwellings in Rushpool, and we quickly fell into a pattern where Dominic distracted the homeowner/resident/dog while I slipped off to do what Dominic started calling my voodoo shit. At least until I told him to stop calling it that, and he switched to calling it psychic stuff, which wasn't much better.

About a quarter of the houses were empty, with their occupants on holiday abroad. Many of the rest had middle-aged or older couples, some on early retirement, others who commuted into a town for work. One of the things that struck me was the lack of young children. Go house to house in a street or estate block in London and you'd have been neck deep in rug rats. But in the village there were a lot of spare rooms, a lot of trim gardens, and no abandoned Tonka toys or Lego punji sticks hidden in the grass.

We paused for a cup of tea in the shade of big tree with a reddish-brown trunk whose canopy spread out like something from a Chinese illustration. The man who made us the tea was called Alec and worked from home as a software engineer. His wife taught in a private school outside Hereford. Both their kids were grown up and moved to London. Their garden was on a terrace that overlooked the churchyard and, beyond that, the twist of the valley as it dropped down towards Leominster. Big trees in a dozen shades of green and brown created a patchwork of light and shade down the lane. It was as quiet as London only gets at dawn on a summer Sunday or in post-apocalyptic movies.

Me and Dominic drank our tea in silence and got on with the job.

During the whole pointless process not one resident refused to let us in or objected to us looking around, which I found creepy because there's always one. But Dominic said no.

'Not in the countryside,' he said.

'Community spirit?' I asked.

'Yeah,' he said. 'That and everyone would know that they hadn't co-operated, which people would find suspicious. In a village that sort of thing sticks for, like, generations.'

Do something frequently enough and you quickly learn to streamline. I worked out early how to identify good *vestigia*-retaining stone items, and how to snatch a few moments of quiet to get a read. I considered teaching Dominic – anyone can do it as long as you have someone to start you off. But I figured Nightingale would have views about it. Even so, I got it down to about ten minutes a house, with just half an hour for the two farms that lay adjacent to the main village.

There was a ton of *vestigia* at the farms. The smell of new-mown grass in a barn conversion, the snort and snuffle of horses by a stone wall halfway down the main lane. Somebody had been really miserable about two hundred years ago in the kitchen of a bungalow – a neat trick, since I judged the place to have been built in the mid-70s. Nothing striking, nothing recent. It was all background. Less activity than I would get from a street in Haringey.

At midday we stopped off for refs at Dominic's mum's bungalow. She was out serving refreshments of her own to the search teams, so we raided her stupendously large American fridge, which was the size of a cryogenic pod and had an ice maker and everything. It was also ridiculously full for one old lady overseeing a totally theoretical B&B business.

'Half my family stops in here of an evening,' said Dominic when I asked about it. 'I think she sees more of us now than when we were all living in the same house.'

I put together a German salami sandwich with sliced tomatoes and lettuce that had *Produce of Spain* on its packaging. The stoneground wholemeal bread, Dominic said, was from a bakery in Hereford. 'I bought it the day before yesterday.'

While we ate, Dominic pulled up the Ordnance Survey map of the area on his tablet.

'You're pretty sure the . . .' He looked at me for a clue but I was too busy chewing. '. . . the "magical event" didn't happen in the village – right?'

I nodded.

'What if the phones were dumped after the event by somebody other than the kids?'

I swallowed. 'Like a kidnapper?'

'That, or a third party who found the phones and dropped them off at the crossroads to be found.'

'To throw us off?'

'Or because they didn't want anyone to know they were in the area,' said Dominic.

'But this has been on TV for two days,' I said. 'If they weren't the kidnapper, wouldn't they have come forward by now?'

'You know it doesn't work like that,' said Dominic.

He was right. Members of the public were famously crap at volunteering information if they thought it might drop them in the shit – even in a serious case like missing children. They could vacillate for days, and often they tried to pass on the information in some devious roundabout way.

'You're thinking they might have called the hotline already?' I said.

'Yep,' said Dominic.

In a case like this there had to have been a thousand calls by now. But the good news was that some other poor sod would have already done the basic follow-up work.

My phone rang and when I checked it was Beverley's number.

I answered and said, 'Hi, Bev.'

'Would this be Constable Grant?' asked a woman with a Welsh accent.

I said it was.

'My name is Miss Teveyddyadd,' she said. 'I believe we have a friend of yours here that needs to be picked up.'

'Picked up from where?' I asked.

Miss Teveyddyadd told me. And while it wasn't either a hospital or a police station, I wasn't sure it might not be worse. I told her that I'd be right there.

'I have to run an errand,' I told Dominic.

'Do you want me to come?' he asked.

'No,' I said. 'I think I'd better do this one myself. You start going through the call-ins and I'll join you as soon as I get this sorted.'

Little Hereford is a collection of houses and a couple of pubs that lies fifteen minutes' drive east of Rushpool in the valley of the River Teme. My GPS turned me off the main road just before I reached the stone bridge and past an orchard to the Westbury Caravan Park. It was a touring park, which meant that it catered for the kind of caravans that people use to clog up the roads in the summer and not the aluminium house substitutes with the suspiciously vestigial wheels. The nice white lady in the camp office looked up from her paperwork and asked if she could help me.

I told her that I was there to meet a Miss Teveyddyadd.

She gave me a broad grin that was slightly worrying in its fervour.

'Ah,' she said. 'You're here to see the blessed sisters.'

I said that I was rather afraid I was, and she gave me directions.

The plots were laid out on neat rectangles of lawn between shaggy olive-green hedges. As I crunched down the gravel access drive I could see heat haze wavering over the white aluminium tops of the caravans. A huge half-naked white man, his belly an alarming lobster colour, dozed in a black and white striped deckchair under a porch awning. In front of the next caravan an elderly couple in matching yellow sun hats sat side by side, drinking tea and listening to *The Archers* on a digital radio.

A fat bumblebee meandered humming past my ear – I gave it a suspicious look, but it ignored me and headed off towards the fat man. Maybe it thought he was an aubergine.

Ahead I could hear high pitched yells and screams – the sound of children playing. Beyond a five-bar gate was what Nightingale insists on calling a sward, an area of naturally short grass, dotted with trees and picnic tables, edged with a steep bank that led to the river. There was a scatter of adults sat at the picnic tables or in the shade of the trees, but the children were all down in the water. Here the river was over ten metres across but shallow enough that I could see the smooth green stones of its bed. I watched from the bank as the kids thrashed around in the water – a froth of bright tropical blue, purples and yellows and distressingly pale limbs. Although I did notice at least one mixed-race boy amongst the others.

I had a sudden urge to pull off my boots and socks, roll up my trousers and go for a paddle.

'Stop that,' I said out loud.

The water stayed cool and inviting but I took a step back. And, because being police is something that never goes away, I did a quick safety assessment to ensure that sufficient adults were supervising.

Satisfied that nobody was about to get themselves drowned in fifteen centimetres of water, I turned left and walked along the bank until I reached the gate which marked the entrance to the orchard. A pale little boy with bleached-white blond hair was standing on the bottom rail and staring inside. When he heard me coming, he hopped off and turned to give me a suspicious look.

'You can't go in there,' he said.

'Why not?'

'Because there's poo everywhere,' he said. 'It's disgusting.'

He was right, I could smell it. Only it was definitely animal – sheep shit, at a guess.

'I'll watch my step,' I said.

'And there's witches,' he said. He had a Black Country accent, so witches came out with a long e – *weetches*.

'How do you know?' I asked.

The boy hopped from one foot to the other. 'Everybody says so,' he said. 'You can hear them singing at night.'

I moved to open the gate and the boy scurried away to take up position at what I assumed he thought was a safe distance. I gave him a wave and stepped through the gate and straight into some sheep shit. The culprits, or possibly their relatives, came scampering over to see if I'd been stupid enough to leave the gate open. At first I thought they were goats, but then I realised that the pale shorn look was due to them having been recently sheared. They looked like a herd of stereotypical English tourists – all they were missing were the knotted hankies on their heads.

Despite the shade it was hot and still under the branches of the apple trees and the air was thick with the shit odour, green wood and a sweet smell like rotting fruit. On this side of the hedge, the slope of the riverbank was less steep and held in place by clumps of mature trees. Right on the edge, sitting amongst the trees and so grown about with long grass and climbing flowers that I almost didn't spot it, was a campervan.

Sighing, I headed towards it – scattering sheep as I went.

It was a genuine VW Type 2 Camper van with a split windscreen and 'A' registration number plate just visible through the long grass and wild flowers, which dated it back to 1963. It was painted RAF blue with white trim and all the windows I could see, including the windscreen, had paisley pattern curtains drawn across.

When I paused to check the tyres – it's a police thing – I saw that they'd all but rotted away and that the van had been there long enough for the roots of a young tree to tangle itself in the wheel arch. From the other side of the van I could hear a woman humming to herself. And I could smell, appropriately given the vehicle, that someone was smoking a spliff. I smiled. Because it's always a comfort when you're the police to walk into a situation knowing that if all else fails you can still make a legitimate arrest.

The humming stopped.

'We don't drive it around much these days,' said a woman from the other side of the van. 'You can't get the wheels anymore, or so I'm told.' I recognised the voice from the phone call – it was Miss Teveyddyadd. Or more properly, as five seconds on Google had revealed, Miss Tefeidiad. Or even more precisely, since we were on the English side of the border, the goddess of the River Teme. Nightingale calls them Genius Loci, spirits of a locality, and says that the first rule of dealing with them in person is to remember that every single one of them is different.

'They are, after all,' he'd said, and smiled, 'spirits of a specific locality. It's only logical that they will be somewhat variable.'

Miss Tefeidiad was as tall as I was, with a shaggy head of blonde hair with a grey streak over her temple, a long straight nose, thin lips and black eyes. It was the sort of face that had become attractively interesting around puberty and was going to stay that way until the owner was carried out of their nursing home feet first. She appeared to be in her well-preserved mid-sixties, but I'd learnt not to trust appearances.

She stood waiting for me on the far side of the VW, where a heavy red and gold awning was attached above the open side doors and stretched out on a pair of poles. In its shade was an old wooden kitchen table covered in a red and white check vinyl table cloth.

'You must be the famous Peter Grant,' she said, and ushered me into one of four grey metal folding chairs set around the table. Another of the chairs was occupied by a handsome middle-aged white woman with long brown hair, hazel eyes and the same long straight nose as her – sister? mother? Relative, certainly. She wore an orange sun dress and broad-brimmed straw hat.

'This is my daughter Corve,' said Miss Tefeidiad.

Corve reached out and shook my hand. Her grip was firm and the skin rough from hard work.

'Delighted to meet you, Peter.' Her Welsh accent was less pronounced than her mother's. I noticed that there was no visible sign of the spliff.

I nodded and said likewise. The Corve was a tributary of the Teme – I'd looked up the whole watershed before coming over.

'Lilly, love,' called Miss Tefeidiad. 'Why don't you be a dear and put the kettle on.'

Something groaned and stirred inside the VW, which rocked alarmingly. I realised then that the back end of the van was dangling over the edge of the bank, as if the ground had eroded away after it had parked.

Beyond where I was sitting a path dropped down to the river, tree roots entangling to form a disturbingly regular flight of steps. At the bottom, the action of the river had carved a pool, deeper and darker than the shallow water immediately downstream. I wondered if the kids playing less than ten metres downstream ever ventured into it for a swim – or what would happen if they did.

A white face appeared in the shadowed doorway of the VW, stared blearily at us from eyes heavily outlined in black, grunted and then swivelled to address the compact cooker that was Germany's contribution to family holidays in the 1950s.

'My youngest,' said Miss Tefeidiad, and got an answering snarl.

'Don't mind her,' said Corve. 'She's been like that since Ralph de Mortimer married Gladys the Dark.'

'So Scotland Yard is back in business,' said Miss Tefeidiad. 'Gaily rushing in where even the saints fear to tread.'

I wanted to ask where Beverley was, and how the Teme family just happened to have her phone. But if there's one thing Nightingale has taught me, it's to let other people talk themselves out before giving anything away. It's something he has in common with Seawoll and Stephanopoulos, and all the top cops that I know.

'I'm just lending a hand with the search,' I said.

'For the missing girls?' asked Corve.

'Yes.'

'Well, we haven't seen them,' said Miss Tefeidiad. 'I can tell you that for nothing.'

Lilly's pale face emerged from the gloom of the camper van and looked around before fixing on me. 'Do you want sugar?' she asked. Her left eyebrow was practically hidden behind a row of studs, and loops of silver pierced her left ear from lobe to tip.

'No tea for me,' I said. 'Thank you.'

'You could have said,' she snorted, and withdrew.

'Don't you go back to sleep now, Lilly,' said Corve. 'We still want a cup.'

'Let me tell you something, Constable Grant,' said Miss Tefeidiad. 'Where you are now is not London – it's not even England.'

'Yes it is, Ma,' said Corve.

'Only in a political sense,' snapped Miss Tefeidiad over her shoulder, before turning a slightly less than reassuring smile on me. 'We remember your lot when they first started, and a more arrogant collection of . . . gentlemen . . . you will never meet. But we have long memories that go all the way back, you see, back to when your beloved Thames was still scuttling around with his tongue jammed up a Roman backside.'

'We used to get heads,' said Corve. 'The druids used to throw them in along with the other offerings.'

'Oh yes,' said Miss Tefeidiad. 'You got some respect in those days.'

'Not that we're looking for heads these days,' said Corve. 'We'll take cash or goods in kind.'

'So when your lot got themselves all massacred or whatever,' said Miss Tefeidiad, 'we weren't exactly crying into our tea. And I have to say that we've got a little bit used to managing our own business in recent years. So, it's not that we don't like visitors . . .'

'We love visitors, really we do,' said Corve. 'Liven the place up.'

'But I think we're going to have to insist on certain minimum standards of navigational etiquette in future.' Miss Tefeidiad gave me an expectant look.

'Sure,' I said. 'Stakeholder engagement is a vital part of our modernisation plans going forward.'

'Look,' she said, 'do you want your girlfriend back or not?'

I wanted to tell them that she wasn't actually my girlfriend and that they better release her before her mother, goddess of the important bit of the Thames, found out they were detaining her and came over to have words. But my life is complicated enough these days and I try not to make things more difficult for myself.

'Yes, please,' I said.

Miss Tefeidiad nodded and then looked over at Corve who got to her feet and went to the top of the tree-root stairs. I got up and followed to look over her shoulder.

'Bev, love,' called Corve. 'Your ride's here.'

She walked out of the pool stark naked – except for the lavender full-body neoprene wetsuit and a Tesco bag wrapped around her hair to keep it dry. She glared at Corve, and then turned her black eyes on me, her full lips twisting into a half smile.

'You took your time,' she said.

'I've been busy,' I said.

Beverley turned to Miss Tefeidiad. 'Can I have my bag back?'

A purple sausage bag came flying out of the dark

interior of the VW. Beverley grabbed it out of the air and slung it over her shoulder.

'And I believe this is yours,' said Corve and handed Beverley her phone. 'Bit of a revelation, that,' she said. 'We didn't know they made them waterproof – very handy.'

'I can't be doing with those things,' said Miss Tefeidiad and sniffed.

Behind her, Corve made a face.

'Laters, ladies,' said Beverley and, grabbing my arm, urged me away.

'So, you won't be staying for tea then?' asked Miss Tefeidiad.

Beverley urgently squeezed my arm, so I told them we couldn't.

'I have to get back to the investigation,' I said.

'That's a shame then,' said Miss Tefeidiad.

And me and Beverley got while the going was good.

'Not a word,' said Beverley, who was so keen to get away we were halfway back to the car before she realised that she was walking barefoot on gravel. We paused long enough for her to extract a pair of flip flops from her sausage bag and then walked briskly the rest of the way. She didn't relax until we were in the car and the River Teme was a kilometre behind us.

'That was close,' she said.

'What was all that about?' I asked.

She pulled off the Tesco bag and shook out her locks, flicking me with water and filling the Asbo with the smell of clean damp hair.

'I thought it would be quicker to get here by water,'

she said, rummaging in her carryall and bringing out a yellow and blue beach towel. 'Should have used an M&S bag,' said Beverly and started squeezing out her locks in bunches. 'That bitch Sabrina failed to mention the weird sisters were still in residence and I ran right into them at Burford.'

'They didn't like you trespassing?'

'I'm lucky to be alive,' said Beverley. 'You don't mess with someone's river without getting permission first.'

'You should have driven up,' I said.

'I'd still have had to cross the Severn, and if you do that you've got to stop and give some respect to Sabrina or she throws a right strop,' said Beverley. 'I thought that if I was getting my hair wet I might as well take a short cut.'

'What are you doing out here, anyway?' I asked.

'I've been deputised,' she said. 'And sent out to assist in your investigation.'

'Who by?'

'Who do you think?' she said. 'Your boss wanted someone out here who knew one end of a cow from the other.'

'And that's you, is it?'

'One of us spent a year rusticating with their country cousins,' she said. 'And do you remember whose bright idea that was?' She bunched her fist and punched me in the shoulder – hard enough that I almost put us in the hedgerow. 'And did I get one visit?'

'It was a difficult time,' I said.

'It was the Thames Valley,' she said. 'Not the moon.'

My phone rang – it was Dominic.

'Guess who I've found,' he said.

The interview room at Leominster's cell block was as clean and as unused as the rest of the station. It was also missing the table that we in the Met have long come to see as an indispensable prop to bang papers on, push cigarettes across, make coffee rings on and, in extremis, put our head down on for a quick kip while no one was looking. Instead, there were two rows of three chairs bolted so that one row faced the other – just over an easy punching distance apart. There was nowhere to put papers or support one of those yellow legal pads while making notes. The briefs must hate it – which, speaking as police, I definitely saw as a feature not a bug.

Dominic who, unlike me, had done a couple of PIP courses (Professionalising Investigation Process) in interviewing, said that the open set-up allowed you to see the suspect's – sorry, the interview subject's – whole body language. You'd be surprised how many people nervously tap their foot when being questioned and how often the frequency of the tapping depends on how close to the truth you are.

Our 'interview subject' had brown hair, small narrow-set blue eyes and an unfortunate nose – he also had a foot tap that just wouldn't quit. He looked like someone who knew he'd been a naughty boy.

Which was how Dominic had tracked him down, by asking himself what kind of no-good would someone have to be up to not to want to help the police with their inquiries. Given the quiet rural nature of the area, the list was distressingly long, ranging from sheep rustling, poaching, agricultural vehicle theft – a top of the line tractor being more expensive than a Lamborghini and much easier to sell in Eastern Europe – to fly-tipping and public indecency. Even hardened criminals, especially those that consider themselves the salt of the earth trying to get by, will come forward on cases involving missing kids. But none had. And, besides, a quick check revealed that nothing majorly criminal had occurred that night. Dominic figured that if it wasn't fear of prosecution it might be sexual shame. And since Bircher Common, just up the lane from where the phones were found, was the local dogging site he concentrated his initial efforts on cars sighted accessing the common late that night. Fortunately, some of the locals, fed up with having their beauty sleep disrupted by the nocturnal revelries, had taken to noting down number plates. Fifteen minutes on the computer had got him a list of names and addresses and, by the time I was fetching Beverley out of captivity, he was knocking at the front door of the first on the list. One Russell Banks of Green Lane, Leominster.

Mr Banks had taken one look at Dominic's warrant card and blurted out that it was in fact him who had left the phones at the crossroad, but he didn't have anything to do with those missing kids, he'd never do anything to harm a kid for god's sake, and please don't tell the wife where he was that night.

'Obviously,' said Dominic, 'the missus wasn't a participant in our Russ's escapades.'

The interview room was part of the custody suite

downstairs and so had thick walls, making it remarkably cool compared to the rest of the nick. Even so, Russell Banks's grey and blue check button-down shirt showed dark sweat patches under the armpits.

Dominic explained to Russell that he wasn't under arrest but, for his own protection, the interview was being recorded on audio and video. And that any time he could just ask to leave. He said he was fine but could he have some water? I passed him a bottle of Highland Spring that we had in a picnic cooler. His hand was trembling.

'We just want to know about the phones,' said Dominic.

Russell nodded. 'I found them,' he said.

'Where did you find them?' asked Dominic.

'Just short of the Mill,' said Russell, which seemed to mean something to Dominic, if not to me.

'Where were they?' he asked. 'Exactly?'

'By the side of the road,' he said. 'On the verge like, just lying there and I thought it was strange but didn't know it had anything to do with those missing girls, you know. Didn't even know there *were* missing girls, until the next day when I heard it on the radio, like.' His leg was practically a blur.

'Why did you get out of the car?' I asked.

His head snapped round to look at me.

'What?'

'You said you found the phones on the verge – correct?'

'Yes.'

'So you'd have to have got out of your car – yes?'

I personally would have gone with stopping for

121

a slash, but I don't think Russ was really thinking that clearly. We were pretty certain we knew rough-ly where he'd been, but members of the public have an unnerving tendency to switch straight from lying to your face to telling you what they think you want to hear – with no intervening period of veracity at all. That's fine when you're looking for them to put their hand up to some crimes and boost your clear-up sta-tistics. But when the lives of two kids depends on the accuracy of the statement, you tend to be a bit more thorough.

He started to say something, but then closed his mouth suddenly and looked at Dominic in mute appeal.

'So,' said Dominic cheerily. 'Where did you really find them?'

He told us the truth, although it took ages to pry all the sordid details out. Which just goes to show that if you want a confession, use a telephone book – but if you want the truth, you've got to put in the hours.

Our Russell had been out enjoying the pleasures of alfresco voyeurism and public sex on Bircher Common with likeminded individuals. Having satiated his carnal desires, he'd made his way back to where he'd parked his car and spotted, when he turned on his headlights, the phones by a gate into the woods. Thinking that one of his fellow swingers had lost them during the throes of passion, he left them at the war memorial in the hope that their owners would find them there – this being the accepted practice, apparently.

'Does you good to see such neighbourliness at work,' I said.

'I bet you don't get that kind of community spirit in the big city,' said Dominic.

It took us another couple of hours to winkle out the names of the participants he'd recognised, and descriptions of others – 'fabulous blonde', 'short hairy guy' and 'let's just say he was lucky we were all doing it in the dark.' Plus makes and models of their cars. This was all going to generate a ton of actions that would be dumped on a bevy of constables who would set forth to TIE every single one. I suspected the dogging scene in North Herefordshire was about to suffer a serious blow. People would just have to go back to having sex indoors for a change.

Fortunately for me and Dominic, what with me being a specialist officer, we could leave that to others.

'We need you to take us to the exact spot where you found the phones,' I said.

'Okay,' said Russell. 'When do you want to do that?'

'How much daylight do we have left?' I asked Dominic.

'A couple of hours.'

'How about right now?' I said.

I hadn't thought the West Mercia Police were quite ready for Beverley, so just before my little tête-à-tête with Russell Banks I'd dropped her off at the Swan in the Rushes in Rushpool, and suggested that once we'd finished for the day Dominic might be able to help her with accommodation.

'Don't worry about me,' she said. 'I can take care of myself.'

I would have offered to put her up in the cowshed, but that sort of thing can be misconstrued. Or to be honest, accurately construed. And I didn't think I wanted to go there.

Dominic put Russell in his boyfriend's truck and I followed on in the Asbo as we drove back to Rushpool, up through the village, across the main road and up yet another narrow lane which twisted onto the ridge. We passed a rather fine cottage with a neat thatched roof, rattled across a cattle grid and parked in the open space beyond, just long enough for me to transfer into the truck. Then we proceeded up a flinty track that was rough enough to eat the bottom chassis of any family hatchback.

'And you drove up here in your car?' I asked Russell.

He said everyone did, which meant to my mind you could track all these doggers by their frequent trips to the garage. Dominic's boyfriend's Nissan made short work of the rough track, as it probably did of wild animals and anti-personnel mines. We climbed towards the ridge with woods on our left and a wide stretch of short grass to our right. After five hundred metres or so we ran out of car-destroying track and set out directly over the grass.

'And you came all the way up here?' I asked as the Nissan bumped and squeaked on its suspension.

'Yes,' said Russell.

'In the dark?'

'Yes.'

'Boy, you really must have been desperate,' I said.

'You get a better class of people at the top of the

common,' he said. 'There's too many weirdos at the bottom.'

Russell directed us to a point just short of the ridge line where the fence that separated the common from the woodland was pierced by a five-bar gate, a wooden side gate and a wooden sign bearing the National Trust crest and a trail marker.

'This is part of the Mortimer Trail,' said Dominic.

We got out of the truck and Russell showed me where he'd found the phones – just on the bare patch that ramblers' feet had worn in the grass in front of the wooden gate. I wasn't going to get anything off that, but the metal was everything an investigatory wizard might hope for. I placed my palms on the top rail, trying not to make it look too theatrical, and attempted to sort through the random sense impressions, stray thoughts, sounds and fantasies that are definitely not *vestigia*. And for a moment I thought the gate was clean, until I realised what it was I was sensing. Nightingale once described *vestigia* as being like the after-image you get in your eyes after looking at a bright light, but what I felt at the gate was different. It was more like stepping out of a cool house on a bright sunny day – for a moment everything is a confusion of light and warmth, and then your senses adjust. Something powerful had happened around that gate and blotted out any other traces with the magical equivalent of white noise.

I didn't like to commit without corroboration, but I was willing to bet that whatever had happened to the phones had happened right where I was standing.

'This is the place,' I said.

'Are you sure?' asked Dominic.

'Edmondson's going to want a POLSA up here,' I said. 'Before it gets dark.'

Dominic pulled out his phone and called in to the nick while I did a slow turn on the spot to see whether anything jumped out. Up on the ridge there was a cool breeze that lazily stirred the grass and the odd clump of bracken. I could hear bird song and far in the distance the lawn-mower hum of a power tool. The sky was powder blue and cloudless – not even a contrail.

I heard Dominic explaining to Windrow that I was certain that the phones had been abandoned at this particular spot. I noticed he didn't mention the M word or call it Falcon. Nightingale says that conspiracies of silence are the only kind of conspiracies that stand the test of time.

'Is this place important?' I asked Russell.

'It's the Whiteway Head,' said Russell. 'This is where all the ancient track-ways cross.'

If I squinted at the dry yellow grass I could sort of see what he meant. The Mortimer Trail came out of its gate and ran west to east, and there was definitely another track crossing it north to south. I went to where I judged the centre of the crossroads was, got on my hands and knees and lowered my face towards the grass.

I was briefly distracted by Russell asking Dominic whether I was praying to Mecca, but I've done this procedure at Piccadilly Circus so it was only for a moment. The short grass was prickly under my palms and filled my nostrils with its vaguely sick-making smell. I idly chased Beverley across the meadows of my mind before letting that go and for a moment I thought there was nothing to sense.

Then suddenly I felt it. Very quiet but very deep, the crack-crack of chisels in stone and the heavy slap of men carrying weight on their shoulders, grunting and sweating and the thirsty smell of salt. You do get *vestigia* in the countryside, I thought, only it seeps in deep and lies there like water under a dry riverbed.

And there was something else, a greasy tension that I remembered from when the Stadtkrone broke open at the top of Skygarden Tower and filled the air with magic. The Romantics had been right. There was power out here amongst all the green stuff – Polidori's *potentia naturalis*.

I broke out Dominic's map. Stan's raided stash was down the Mortimer Trail to the west, Rushpool was along the track to the south, and across a valley to the north at the top of the next ridge was Hugh Oswald's house – less than fifteen hundred metres as the bee flies.

# 6

## Stakeholder Engagement

The next morning I called Beverley as soon as the sun touched the front of the cowshed – she wasn't best pleased.

'If you're going to stay,' I said, 'you're going to work.'

She was waiting for me in the gravel car park behind the Swan in the Rushes, wearing a pair of high-waisted khaki army trousers and a purple T-shirt with the words I'M FROM HERE STUPID written across the chest. In one hand she had what I learnt later was a genuine army surplus gas mask case, and in the other a mug of coffee.

I opened the passenger door and gestured her in.

'Just a sec,' she said, and drained her mug. Then, holding it straight out towards the inn, she called out a name.

A young blonde photographer in skinny jeans and a red sweatshirt trotted out of the inn, smiled, took the mug and trotted back in. I gave Beverley the stare when she got in the car, but she just ignored me.

'You're not supposed to do that,' I said.

'If you're going to get me up this early in the morning, then you don't get to complain when I smooth off some of the rough edges.'

I started up the Asbo and pulled out of the car park.

'How did you get a room there, anyway?' I asked. 'I heard it was rammed.'

'Oh,' said Beverley, 'the nice lady from Sky News let me have her room.'

'Just like that?'

'Not just like that, actually,' said Beverley. 'I had to ask twice! I hate being this far from the Thames Valley.'

After a moment she said, 'Where are we going?'

'I want your professional opinion about someone.'

'My profession in this instance being what?'

'Goddess of small suburban river in South London.'

She nodded and then reached over to brush the side of my face, which was beginning to swell nicely.

'When did you do this?' she asked.

'Yesterday evening,' I said. 'I walked into a tree.'

After finding the phones we still had a couple of hours of daylight, and it wasn't like the POLSA was going to need us looking over his shoulder. So we'd split up. Dominic went east onto the common with our favourite sexual pervert as guide and I went west into the woods.

'And you thought that was clever,' said Beverley.

'It's a National Trust property,' I said. 'It's not like there were going to be giant spiders. The locals call it Fairy Wood. So I had to check it, didn't I?'

'You think they were abducted by fairies?'

'I don't even know if that's a thing,' I said.

I'd asked Nightingale once I'd got back to the cowshed, and he'd said that while he'd never had a case in his lifetime, there were always rumours that it had happened. He promised to look through books and see what he could find.

'Is it a thing?' I asked Beverley.

'Not that I know about,' she said. 'But it doesn't mean it doesn't happen. Mum doesn't hold with it, so someone would have to be pretty stupid to tell me about it.'

'And fairies?'

Beverley hesitated and then – 'Peter,' she said, 'some things you don't talk about.'

'Not even to me?'

'Especially to the feds,' she said. 'Double so the magic feds.'

I cordially hate the use of the word feds – I'd rather be called the filth, at least that would be English English. It's the lack of imagination that pisses me off.

Just short of a crossroad hamlet called Mortimer's Cross we rumbled over a stone bridge and Beverley jolted in her seat and asked whether the river we'd crossed was the Lugg.

'I think so,' I said, trying to remember the map on the GPS. 'Is that important?'

'Nah,' said Beverley. 'Just professional curiosity.'

I turned right onto the A410 which went north with suspiciously Roman straightness towards Aymestrey, which is less a village than a diorama of the last six hundred years of English vernacular architecture stretched along either side of the road. Then another stone bridge across the Lugg where it curved west towards Wales and then a tricky little turn-off that took us through Yatton and the weirdly named Leinthall Earls, where Stan the strange lived. To our right a steep escarpment reared up, topped by the ancient hill fort of Croft Ambrey and Whiteway Head – although our view would have been better if the hedgerows hadn't been higher than our car.

'I'm not totally comfortable with the tops of hills,' said Beverley as we climbed up a steep wooded incline.

'Why's that?'

'You know water,' she said, 'Tends to flow downhill, tends to accumulate at the bottom.'

'That make sense,' I said. 'How do you feel about bees?'

'Why do you ask?'

I told her about Mellissa Oswald's unusual affinity for anthophila.

'And you think she's a bee?' she asked.

'Let's just say I think there's more going on there than an interest in grow your own honey,' I said.

'And that helps us how?'

'Bees cover a wide area. Maybe they spotted something.'

'And told your bee girl?'

'Possibly.'

Beverley kissed her teeth.

'Not unless the missing girls were covered in sugar they wouldn't,' she said.

'They might have seen something and not known what it is.' It was beginning to sound pretty thin even to me.

'Have you ever dissected a bee?' asked Beverley. 'One look inside its head and you'd know that not knowing what stuff is is practically the definition of how a bee operates.'

'When have you ever dissected a bee?'

'I did biology at A-level,' said Beverley. 'Mum insisted. She's still hoping that one of us will qualify as a doctor.'

'And?'

'I'd rather eat a frog than dissect one,' she said. 'And I'm certainly not going to start putting my hands on any sick people.' She shuddered. 'But since I was stuck in the country,' she raised her fist and I dutifully flinched, 'I did pick up a bit of ecology, if only because that's what all the Thames boys go on about.' She punched me in the arm, but gently this time, leaving hardly any bruising at all.

'And let me tell you that I wouldn't be reading too much into the eusocial behaviour of bees if I was you – they're little honey-making machines, that's all.'

'Why don't you wait until you meet Mellissa?' I said. 'And we'll see what you say then.'

It was breathless, bright and hot on the flint road outside the Bee House. I left the windows on the Asbo wound all the way down, because it would be better for it to get stolen than to have the dashboard melt off its frame.

Beverley paused to look at the tower.

'This is nice, isn't it?' she said. 'Nightingale should live here – it's a proper wizard's tower.'

The front door opened before we could reach it and Mellissa stepped out to greet us. She was dressed in orange Capri pants with a fake tie-dye pattern and a matching sleeveless T-shirt that revealed the soft blond down on her upper arms and shoulders.

'Hello, Ms Oswald,' I said. 'I wonder if I could have another word with you and your granddad.'

Mellissa crossed her arms. 'And what do you want this time?'

'First off,' I said and indicated Beverley, who gave Mellissa her best friendly smile, 'let me introduce my friend Beverley Brook.'

'Hi, Mellissa,' said Beverley and took a step forward.

Mellissa's eyes narrowed and then she relaxed and smiled in a sort of delighted way that I was sure she wasn't aware she was doing.

'Pleased to meet you,' she said, and they shook hands.

Interesting, I thought. There's instant recognition, but only if they look for it – they could slip past each other in a crowd.

Mellissa remembered that she was supposed to be hostile and glared at me.

'What is it you want?' she asked.

'We need your help.'

'And why should we help you?'

'Two eleven-year-old girls are missing,' I said. 'Their names are Hannah—'

'I know their names,' said Mellissa sharply, and then softened. 'What is it you think we can do?'

'Provide local knowledge,' I said. 'Of a particular kind.'

Mellissa nodded.

'You're not to over-tire him,' she said and turned to lead us inside.

As Beverley crossed the threshold, I swear I heard a

deep rumble from upstairs in the tower. Mellissa sighed and rolled her eyes.

'Just a second,' she said to Beverley, and then slammed the bottom of her fist into the wall. 'Stop that,' she said and the rumble cut off. 'Some of us are not used to visitors here.'

'Family?' asked Beverley.

'You might say that,' said Mellissa and gestured for Beverley to follow her in.

'I know all about that,' said Beverley.

I followed them both in and tried not to look too obviously smug.

'He's upstairs in his study,' said Mellissa. 'If you go up, I'll bring some tea.'

I made my way up the cool dimness of the spiral staircase to the first floor where I found Hugh Oswald behind his desk, reclining comfortably in a cracked brown leather chair. He looked better than he had the last time I'd seen him, his face more animated and less drawn.

'Ah, if it isn't the starling,' he said. 'Are you going to introduce me to your friend?'

'I'm sure she'll appear,' I said and, remembering this was a man prone to falling asleep at random intervals, I got on with it. 'I was hoping you could help me,' I said.

'Of course, dear boy,' said Hugh. 'Pull yourself up a pew.'

I cleared half a metre's worth of *Bee Improvement Magazine* off a wooden swivel chair and sat down.

'Nightingale suggested that I talk to the local vicar because they often take an interest in local folklore,' I said.

'I believe that many did,' said Hugh. 'But once upon a time being a pastor was a great deal more leisurely occupation than it is now.'

'But then I thought, why chase down the poor hard-working vicar when I have a fully qualified practitioner living in the area?' I said. 'Taking an interest.'

'That's assuming I took an interest,' said Hugh. 'I have broken my staff, after all – *lignum fregit.*'

I nodded at the nearest bookshelf. 'You kept all your books.'

Hugh smiled.

'Ah, yes,' said Hugh. 'Nightingale's starling. Tough and clever, that's what he always said he was looking for – had he been looking for an apprentice at all.'

I didn't get a chance to ask who Nightingale had said this to, or when, because we were interrupted by Mellissa and Beverley arriving with tea and toast. While Mellissa set down a tray on top of a precarious pile of books I introduced Beverley – by her full name.

Hugh looked a bit wild eyed as the implications sank in, but recovered enough to be passably charming. Beverley was charming back and, after giving me the side-eye for no justifiable reason that I could see, accompanied Mellissa back downstairs again.

'Good Lord,' said Hugh. 'Where did she spring from?'

'Nightingale sent her,' I said, watching as he buttered his toast with painful slowness. I was tempted to do it for him, but I didn't think he'd like that.

'Things must have changed back at the Folly,' he said and, toast finally buttered, he lifted the lid on a little white china pot and scooped out some orange marmalade. 'Still, the Nightingale was always a little bit unorthodox in his friends. There used to be this creature, slip of a thing, worked below stairs – never spoke.' He paused looking for the name.

'Molly?'

'Yes, that was her name,' said Hugh. 'Molly. Used to terrify all us New Bugs, but not the Nightingale.' Hugh smiled. 'There were rumours, of course,' he said. 'It was scandalous.'

He bit decisively into his toast.

'Why does everyone call him *the* Nightingale?' I asked.

Hugh chewed industriously for a moment, swallowed and caught his breath.

'Because he was so singular, so extraordinary – or so the seniors said. Of course most of us didn't believe a word of it, but we used it as a nickname – irony, or so we thought.'

He was looking in my direction, but his gaze was somewhere back in time to his young self. My dad does the same thing when he talks about seeing Freddie Hubbard with Tubby Hayes at the Bull's Head in 1965 or being at Ronnie Scott's and hearing Sonny Rollins solo live for the first time.

There were so many questions I wanted answered, but I began to fear that he was drifting off – or worse.

'You should have seen him at Ettersberg,' he said softly. 'It was like standing before the walls of Troy. *Aías d'amphì Menoitiádei sákos eurù kalúpsas hestékei hós tís te léon perì hoîsi tékessin,* but Ajax covered the son of Menoitios with his broad shield and stood fast, like a lion over its children.'

He grew quiet again, and I saw that I'd worn him out and utterly failed to get the information I'd wanted. Lesley would have been well pissed off with me for that.

*Children are missing,* she would have said, *and you're sitting around talking ancient history.*

'I was going to ask you about local magic and folklore,' I said.

Hugh was obviously relieved to change the subject, because he brightened right up.

'I may have just the thing,' he said.

It turned out to be large shabby hardback book with *Folklore of Herefordshire* picked out in gilt on a burgundy cloth cover. It was Ella Mary Leather's classic 1912 work and I had a copy of it on my tablet – after a recommendation by Nightingale. I was about to politely refuse on the basis that it was obviously a valuable antique, when I opened it up to find that the inside pages were covered in handwritten annotations, some in pencil, many in a spiky cursive hand. There was also a stamp that indicated that the volume had been nicked from Gloucester City Library.

'When I first moved up here my doctor encouraged me to go for long walks,' said Hugh. 'But I've always been a bit of an explorer rather than a traveller.'

I wanted to ask more, but I could tell that I'd worn him out. I gathered up the tea things and took them downstairs leaving Hugh alone to 'rest his eyes for a moment'.

There was no sign of either Beverley or Mellissa in the kitchen or in the garden, so I texted Beverley that it was time for us to go. I let myself out the front door just in case she'd gone back the car, and heard her voice from the other side of the hedge.

I looked over to see Beverley and Mellissa emerge from the cottage next door. The older man with the Australian accent and his sons followed them out to say goodbye. As they did so I got a sense of intimacy between Mellissa and the men – nothing overtly sexual, but a lingering touch on the arm of one of the younger ones, the brush of her shoulder against the older man's chest. Beverley saw me and waved, then she turned back to Mellissa and they had a quick exchange. One of the men was sent back inside for a pen and Beverley wrote a number on the palm of her own hand. Then there was another round of goodbyes and Beverley joined me by the Asbo. We paused for a bit with the doors open to let the inside temperature fall below the boiling point of lead.

'Is she . . .?' I nodded back towards the cottage.

'None of your business,' said Beverley.

'What, all three?'

'Like I said,' said Beverley, 'none of your business.'

'Damn,' I said.

'You should be so lucky,' said Beverley.

I realised that Dr Walid was going to want a full report on Mellissa Oswald when I got home. He'd probably like me to get a tissue sample or lure her down to the UCH in London so he could get one himself. I wondered what possible conversational gambit I could slip that into – Are you certain you're completely human? Would you like to find out for sure? Then come on down to Dr Walid's crypto-pathology lab where we put the 'frank' back into Frankenstein!

'I'm sure she could fit you in,' said Beverley.

'Did she say if her bees had spotted anything unusual?'

'Unlike some people, I'm not tactless,' said Beverley. 'You just don't go asking people about their business like that, making assumptions about what they do and how they do it.' Beverley tapped her finger on her chest. 'I merely inquired as to whether Mellissa may, or may not have, noticed anything out of the ordinary.'

'And had she?'

'She said she couldn't be sure, but she thinks her boys . . .'

'Her boys?' I asked. 'Are we talking them next door or the buzzy ones?'

'Her buzzing boys,' said Beverley. 'They've been avoiding the south-west section of the ridge, from the edge of Bircher Common to where the river is.'

Whatever had killed the mobile phones had been on the edge of that area, and I didn't need to check my map to know that Stan's missing stash had been right in the middle.

'Could she relate it to the missing kids?'

'If she had, she says she would have told you when you first came.'

'I can't go to Windrow or Edmondson with this,' I said. 'Even if I persuaded them to change the search area, I don't think it would be a good idea.'

'I'm sure she'll keep her antenna tuned,' said Beverley. 'Got any other leads?'

'Just something I picked up from one of the statements – I'm waiting for Windrow to okay a fresh interview.'

'In that case, can we—'

My phone rang – it was Dominic.

'Are you still up at Wyldes?' he asked.

I told him we were just finishing.

'One of the search teams found something you might want to look at,' he said. 'Just down the road from where you are now.'

'Is it related to the search?'

'Honestly,' said Dominic, 'I don't know. I thought you might be able to tell me.'

I may be a city boy, but I'm fairly certain that the greasy purple and red squishy bits are supposed to stay inside the sheep and not be sprayed across a surprisingly large area.

'Animal attack?' I asked.

Both Beverley and Dominic gave me pitying looks. Stan, who'd been the one to discover the dead sheep and call in Dominic, actually snorted.

'Not unless that puma's come up from Newtown Cross again,' she said.

We were standing in a large field just off the Roman road near where it crossed the Lugg. The wooded slopes of the ridge rose up to the east and hidden on the reverse side was School Wood and Stan's late lamented stash. It was even hotter down here in the valley and missing the breeze we'd had up around the Bee House. Nothing really to dispel the smell of rotting sheep.

'Mind you,' said Dominic, 'when it comes to finding new ways to get themselves killed, sheep are bloody geniuses.'

The sheep lay on its side. It had been sheared recently, giving it a forlorn naked look and making it all too easy to spot the bloody gash in its stomach through which most of its innards seemed to have been pulled out. I'm not very fond of animals, even when they're on their way to the dinner table. But you don't do policing by holding your nose and looking the other way. I put on my surgical gloves and squatted down to have a look and do my due diligence.

The edges of the wound were ragged, suggesting tearing rather than cutting, and the glistening viscera looked like they'd been dragged out, widening the hole. Had she been caught on a hook of some sort? Agricultural machinery looked pretty fearsome to me. Plenty of dangerously sharp bits of metal attached to ridiculously over-torqued diesel engines – an accident waiting to happen. But I couldn't see any tyre tracks in the short grass around the body. I got my face as close to the wound as I could, closed my eyes and held my breath.

There was a kind of *vestigia* associated with the body. Very faint, nothing that Toby would get out of his basket for.

'Do you see any horse tracks around here?' I asked.

'Do you mean hoof prints?' asked Dominic as I stood up.

I told him that, yes, I did in fact mean hoof prints and we all spent five minutes looking around the scene to see if we could find any – with no luck.

'Why did you think a horse had got into your stash?' I asked Stan. 'Were there tracks? A smell?'

'Don't know,' she said. 'It's just what came into my head when I found it.'

*Vestigia* for certain. Which meant what? Something unnatural was buggering about in the countryside, but I hadn't seen any indication, beyond the dead phones, that it had anything to do with Hannah and Nicole. For all I knew, this was everyday life for country folk. What I needed was some of your actual evidence. Or, failing that, a couple of hours with Hugh's folklore book.

'It's Falcon,' I said. 'But it's not necessarily anything to do with the kids.'

'Should I call Windrow?' asked Dominic.

I considered just how much fast talking it would take to explain exactly why I wanted West Mercia Police to put some of their forensic resources into autopsying a sheep, and then phoned Dr Walid.

He said he'd be delighted, and if I could protect the corpse and maybe pick up some samples, he'd send some people over to collect it.

'What kind of people?' I asked.

'There's a couple of firms that specialise in biohazard removal and forensic preservation,' said Dr Walid. 'I consult for them occasionally, and in return they send me anything I might find interesting.'

I got the GPS co-ordinates and texted them to him and he indicated what he wanted in the way of samples. I relayed this to Dominic, who said we should file a report just to be on the safe side.

Beverley said that, although messing with a mutilated sheep seemed like a pile of fun, she was going to take herself down to the pub by the bridge. 'I'm going to have a quick word with the river,' she said. 'Come pick me up when you're finished.'

'A quick word with the river?' asked Dominic once Beverley was gone.

'I'd tell you, but then you'd have to section me,' I said. 'Have you got anything for samples?'

Dominic had a proper Early Evidence Kit in the back of the Nissan, complete with a fingerprint kit, sketch-pad and clear plastic evidence bags – the proper ones with individual serialised numbers and a tear-off strip to maintain chain of custody. We took photographs using a high-end digital camera that Stan fetched from her parents' house.

'For UFO hunting,' Dominic told me when Stan was out of earshot.

'Do we put the entrails back in the sheep?' I asked. 'Or put them in a separate bag?'

Nobody had a clue, so I phoned Walid again and he told us to wrap the intestines in plastic sheeting and then place them by the corpse. I've done some nasty things in my time, but that was genuinely one of the worst. I never did get the smell of dead sheep out of my clothes.

Once our sheep was bagged and tagged we paid Stan to stay with it until Dr Walid's people turned up. Well, I was the one that had to cough up the cash because, as Dominic pointed out, I'd declared this a Falcon opera-tion. I made a point of noting it down with the rest of my expenses. Dominic said he'd talk to the farmer while I picked up Beverley.

'Won't the farmer mind us taking stuff off his land?'
I asked.

'You're joking,' said Dominic. 'The farmer has to pay
for the safe disposal of animal carcasses – we're doing
him a favour.'

The Riverside Inn was a sprawl of a building that had
accreted around a solid sixteenth-century half-timbered
core. Its restaurant was well known and it was best, I
was informed, to book in advance to avoid disappointment. Fortunately you could get snack type food for
eating in the pub garden, although their idea of cheese
on toast was mature cheddar melted onto a slab of
brioche and topped with mustard seeds and cress. As
well as a garden terrace, the inn kept a strip of lawn
hard on the riverbank just by the stone bridge and it
was there I found Beverley relaxing at a wooden picnic
table with the aforementioned posh cheese on toast and
an open bottle of Bordeaux. She offered me a glass as I
sat down.

'Try it,' she said. 'It's on the house.'

'Can't,' I said. 'I'm on duty.'

'So you are,' she said, and poured herself another
glass.

A smart-looking white girl in a black skirt emerged
and on Beverley's recommendation I had the steak ba-
guette which practically came with a genealogy of the
cow and a half-page essay on fresh bread making in
Northern Herefordshire. After all that, it was probably
just as well that it was delicious if a bit under-seasoned
by my standards. Beverley waited till I had a mouthful

before asking me to keep an eye out, and without another word she lay down on the bank and stuck her face and head in the water. I swear she stayed in that position for over a minute, her locks waving like seaweed in the current.

I was just about to tap her on the shoulder when she straightened suddenly, an arc of water from her hair spraying back into the car park and landing on the bonnet of an overheated Mondeo where it sizzled.

'Social call?' I said.

'Nobody home,' said Beverley, flicking out her locks. Water made a sheen on her neck and shoulders and soaked the top of her T-shirt so that the zip of her sports bra poked through the material.

'Sad really,' she said.

'What is?' I asked, standing clear as Beverley flicked her locks again and tied them back with a waterproof scrunchie.

'The terrible Teme trio told me about it,' she said. 'The spirit of the river was done in by Methodists in Victorian times. That really pissed them off – Miss Tefeidiad said you expect that kind of behaviour from the English, but Welsh boys should have known better.'

My phone pinged and let me know that my restatementing of Nicole and Hannah's friend had been actioned. I told Beverley, and asked if she wanted to be dropped off somewhere.

'Can I come to the interview?' she said.

'How would I introduce you – "Hello, my name's Peter Grant. I'm with the police and this is my colleague Beverley Brook who is a small river in South London?"'

'You used to introduce me like that,' said Beverley.

'Yeah, well,' I said. 'I didn't know what I know now – did I?'

## A2457 H TST GABRIELLA DARRELL RE: INVISIBLE FRIEND MISC

Gabriella – *just call her Gaby, she won't answer to anything else* – Darrell was a stolid little girl who was either preternaturally dull, on Ritalin, or biding her time to wreak an appalling revenge on her mother for being clingy and overbearing. Her mother Clarissa was short and unhealthily thin with a narrow intense face and, as far as I could tell, no sense of humour whatsoever.

The barn conversion where they lived just beyond the village of Orelton was seriously nice, its spacious rooms laid out in an uncluttered linear sequence with big windows framed in hardwood and lots of earth tones. It was a Channel Four sort of house with a Channel Four vibe. Mr Darrell was CEO of a mid-sized building services company based in Birmingham.

I didn't need to inquire into their lives since there was already twenty-plus pages worth of information on him and his family, because Gaby claimed to be BFFs with Nicole Lacey and so they had been thoroughly TIEd, IIPed and statemented. West Mercia Police had even gone so far to as check Gaby's claims about her relationship with the missing girls – and had concluded that they'd been BFs maybe, but BFFs? No way!

'I'd like to ask you about Nicole's invisible friend,' I said.

Gaby opened her mouth, but before she could answer her mum spoke instead.

'Why do you want to know about that?'

Gaby rolled her eyes and sighed – see what I have to put up with? I winked back and pretty much from that point on we were allies.

'We're following up any possible point of contact,' I said. 'We like to make sure we haven't missed anything first time round.'

'I see,' she said.

'Gaby,' I said. 'When you talked to my colleague he asked you to make a list of everyone that Hannah and Nicole might know – do you remember that.'

Gaby nodded.

'And you said that Nicole had an invisible friend – is that right?'

Gaby nodded again. Her mother opened her mouth to speak, but I held up a finger to stop her. She gave me a poisonous look, but she kept her mouth shut.

'But an invisible friend is not the same as an imaginary friend, is it?'

Gaby nodded – she obviously planned to make me work for this.

'Did Nicole's friend have a name?'

Gaby screwed up her face realising, reluctantly, that she was going to have to communicate. 'Princess Luna,' she said.

I looked at her mother to see if this meant anything to her, but she shook her head. I turned back to Gaby, but before I could ask another question she asked me why I was brown.

'Gaby,' said her mother in a shocked voice.

'Because my mum's from Sierra Leone,' I said.

'Where's that?' asked Gaby.

'West Africa,' I said. 'Did you ever meet Princess Luna?'

Gaby nodded.

'When was this?'

'At Hannah's birthday party,' she said. 'Mummy didn't want me to go.'

'I thought it started rather late and they had a bonfire,' said Gaby's mother. 'But Little Miss here put up such a stink . . .' She shrugged.

'When was this?' I asked.

'Mid-March,' said Gaby's mother. 'I could look up the date if you like.'

'Thank you,' I said, and she fished out her iPhone and started flicking through the calendar.

'We had sparklers,' said Gaby.

'April the 26th,' said her mother.

I asked where the party had taken place.

'Rushpool,' said Gaby's mum. 'In that field behind the parish hall.'

'And they roasted a whole sheep on a spit,' said Gaby. 'And I got grease all over my fingers.'

Gaby's mum gave a little humourless chuckle. 'We didn't inquire too closely as to where the sheep had come from.'

'Nice,' I said. I turned to Gaby. 'Did you see Princess Luna?'

'Don't be silly. You can't see Princess Luna – she's invisible.'

'Of course she is.'

'Nicole and Hannah were feeding her sheep,' said Gaby, and for a second I thought I'd misheard her.

'They were feeding Princess Luna some of the cooked sheep?'

'Yep,' said Gaby. 'I would have given her some of mine, but I'd eaten it all. I let her lick my fingers, though.'

I felt her mother practically start out of her chair, and then subside again.

'What did it feel like?' I asked.

'Like a big tongue,' said Gaby.

'And was it low down or high up?'

Gaby jumped off her chair and demonstrated by sticking her arm straight out in front of her with her palm turned up. About a metre twenty above floor level, but the way she held her hand suggested an animal of some kind.

'What kind of animal is Princess Luna?' I asked.

'She's a pony, silly,' said Gaby brightly.

A little klaxon went off in my head.

*Aruga aruga*, I thought. *Set condition one throughout the ship.*

When you're police sometimes you've just got to stop and think about what you're doing – even when you're on Day 5 and fears, as the media always say, are growing. I needed somewhere to work, I needed peace and quiet, and I needed a secure internet connection. So I headed back to Leominster nick, because two out of three ain't bad.

A quick chat with Beverley would have been useful,

only her phone went to voicemail. She'd said she was going to have a quick look up and down the River Lugg, so it was possible that she was either in a dead area or currently underwater. I didn't have any luck with Nightingale, either, and calling the Folly just got me the long ominous silence that indicated Molly was the only one answering the phone. I left a message anyway – Nightingale always gets them. I don't know how. Perhaps she writes them down.

I sneaked past the incident room, hid myself in Edmondson office and fired up HOLMES II. First I wrote up Gabriella Darrell's new statement from my notes and sent it off to be processed and then I checked my emails to see if anyone had bothered to solve any of my problems for me – fat chance. Then I opened the annotated copy of *Folklore of Herefordshire* that Hugh Oswald had given me, skipping to the index and looked for *abductions*, of which there were none. Nor was there anything under *changelings, children* but there was something under *The Fairy Changeling*. Ella Mary Leather reported an account of a baby that never grew up and was strangely hairy, who turned out to be a changeling and was tricked into revealing the location of the true baby by an older brother. Leather suggested that such changeling stories might be the result of hypothyroidism or other conditions to which Hugh had noted in the margin *Likely, but what if no gross phys. changes found? What if grows to adult? Oth, rec. foxglove tea (digitalis) to drive baby away – justified infanticide? No evd. Fae this case.*

I was about to move on to *horses*, supernatural or

otherwise, but Hugh's annotations led over to the next page where the name Aymestrey popped out at me. This was in the section on Hobgoblins, which Ella Mary Leather associated with brownies, which she claimed was the Herefordshire name for Robin Goodfellow, the Puck of *A Midsummer Night's Dream*. A name associated with Pokehouse Wood which was located, according to Google Earth, half a kilometre from where Beverley stuck her head in the river and my unfortunate sheep said goodbye to its entrails. It was also on the Mortimer Trail, the same right of way that ran past Stan's stash, and, I found when I checked Inspector Edmondson's Ordnance Survey map, close to the gate where the girl's phones were damaged.

*There a traveller was once so tormented by Puck in the woods that he left a bequest the remuneration from which paid a local to ring the church bell at a certain time of night – to guide future travellers home.* By this Hugh had written: *No ev. of ac. rcntly. wood now F.C. replanted with cons.*

I took a brain break and googled Princess Luna – who turned out to be a character from *My Little Pony*, and a unicorn, and not noticeably invisible.

My phone pinged and I picked it up expecting it to be Beverley or Dr Walid. Instead I read – **WTF R U doing in sticks? <3 LESLEY**

# 7

# Enhanced Interrogation

I woke in the hour before dawn, stuck in that strange state where the memory of your dreams is still powerful enough to motivate your actions. Believing that I'd heard someone outside the cowshed doors I'd stumbled to my feet and slid them open. In the moonlight I thought I saw serried ranks of what I now recognised as apple trees filling the pasture out to the old wall, an orchard of silver and shadow. Above their topmost branches was a white point of light, too bright to be a star. A planet – probably Jupiter. There were a couple of bright stars and there, just visible through a gap in the trees, an orange spark that even I could identify – Mars. In that half-dreaming state I was certain that there was a path running through the orchard and beyond the walls was a darker and thicker forest full of secret places and hidden people.

Then I blinked and it was just a pasture, an old wall and fields of grain beyond.

Back in the cowshed I dug around in the trunks which Molly had sent from London and extracted the antique brass primus stove. It sloshed heavily when I shook it, so there was plenty of paraffin inside.

As soon as I'd got the text from Lesley I'd called

Inspector Pollock at the Department of Professional Standards, who was my designated point of contact with the team that was investigating Lesley's criminal misconduct. I informed him that Lesley had made contact and gave him the details. He told me not to make any response until he'd had a chance to make an assessment. I told him to assess away.

The primus came in a handsome wooden carrying case complete with a brassbound saucepan and lid and a reservoir of white spirit for getting it started. I've practised lighting one of these using lux to vaporise the paraffin, but I didn't want to turn my phone off in case Lesley texted again. It took less than five minutes to fetch water from the bathroom, pump up the pressure, light the white spirit, watch the main burner catch and give a merry flame under the saucepan. Nightingale said that Amundsen had used one of these on his way to the South Pole and that Hilary and Tensing had hoiked one up the slopes of Everest.

Further down in the trunk I found a battered biscuit tin containing half a packet of digestives, loose teabags, some teacakes wrapped in rice paper and a bottle of Paterson's Camp Coffee that was so old that on the label the Sikh was still on his feet proffering a tray to the seated Highland major-general. I decided not to risk it – not least because Camp Coffee is famous for not having any caffeine in it.

After briefing the DPS, I had called Nightingale and told him about Lesley. He seemed rather impressed with it as a tactic.

'Rather neatly pins us, doesn't it?' he'd said. 'I was

considering following you up to Herefordshire.'

'What about the comrade major?' I'd asked.

'Oh, I think I'd have brought her too. And Toby,' he'd said. 'Might have made quite a jolly outing. But if Lesley knows you're out of town I can't get further than a quick rush from the Folly.' And whatever it was that was hidden behind the door in the basement. Whatever it was that Nightingale, I was beginning to suspect, had stayed in his position at the Folly to protect. He wasn't going to leave that exposed.

So no back-up. Apart from Beverley, who seemed more interested in the River Lugg than in the case. I wanted to ask Nightingale about Ettersberg and what, precisely, was behind the black door in the basement of the Folly – but I bottled out and asked him to check the literature on unicorns and brownies.

He said he'd see what he could find, although he was almost certain that brownies were considered entirely mythical.

Inspector Pollock called back and said that I was to engage Lesley in conversation. 'Stretch it out,' he said. 'And if you can entice her to talk directly on the phone, so much the better.'

He didn't have to say that all communication is the policeman's friend, that even if we can't trace your call the mere fact that you're talking tells us something and every cryptic clue, every denial, every weird utterance tells us something. Even if it's just that you're in a desperate need to talk to someone.

He didn't have to say that they were monitoring my phone.

So I texted back: *I'm working where R U?*

And then I did my paperwork and, after that, to bed to dream of apple trees in the moonlight.

Mercifully I didn't have to do the briefing in Windrow's narrow little office, but instead on the first-floor terrace that stuck out in front of the canteen like the flying bridge on a landlocked boat. It may have been an unconscious desire to avoid conferring too much legitimacy on the Falcon assessment, but it was most likely so that Windrow could have a crafty fag. We stood there in the cool morning shade enjoying the chill air as the eastern horizon turned gold under a powder blue sky.

It was Day 6 and things were getting a little bit desperate. Edmondson handed me a newspaper with the headline, POLICE FAILING HANNAH AND NICOLE SAY VILLAGERS.

'If you don't feed the dogs,' said Windrow, 'you're going to get bitten.'

I checked the by-line, because it always pays to know who not to talk to next time you've got something juicy to trade. But I didn't recognise the name – Sharon Pike.

'Writes columns in a couple of the nationals,' said Edmondson.

'What's she doing on the front page?' I asked.

'She considers herself a local,' said Windrow.

'She has a cottage in Rushpool,' said Edmondson. 'I hear she spends most of her time in London, though.'

I suddenly remembered her from me and Dominic's fruitless search for village *vestigia*. She'd been a slight white woman with black hair, dressed in skinny jeans and a salmon-coloured cardigan. I remembered that she'd asked a lot of questions and I hurriedly reviewed my memory to see how much trouble I might have talked myself into.

Windrow must have seen my expression. 'Hasn't mentioned you yet,' he said.

I didn't like the sound of that 'yet' one bit.

Windrow lit a second cigarette off the first and took a deep drag as if trying to fill every cubic centimetre of his lungs.

'I'm stocking up for when I have to go back inside,' he said.

Edmondson checked his watch and glanced at where the sun was springing up above the distant hills.

'So what's your assessment?' he asked.

'Before I start, sir, I need to ask you how much actual Falcon information you want to hear.'

Edmondson blinked and Windrow scratched his chin.

'How much do you normally give out?' asked Windrow.

'As much as people are comfortable with,' I said. 'Some people don't like to use the M-word. Some don't mind that, but want explanations for things we can't explain.'

'Lad,' said Windrow, 'we're so desperate we'll take whatever we can get.'

I started with what I'd already told them – that the phones had been fried by magic up on Whiteway Head where the Mortimer Trail crosses onto Bircher Common. That there was something supernatural moving around in the woods to the south-east along the trail which might, if it was the same thing as Nicole's invisible My Little Pony, be related to her and Hannah's disappearance.

'If the invisible pony really turned up at the birthday party,' I said, 'then we have a clear path from Rushpool, up to Whiteway Head and then west down the Mortimer Trail to where we found yesterday's dead sheep.'

'We were going to have to go into those woods sooner or later,' Edmondson said to Windrow.

'I do have indications that something weird is localised to that area. And there are historical leads to run down, and I'd like to deploy some specialist help,' I said.

'This would be Beverley Brook, aged twenty, resident of Beverley Avenue, London SW20?' asked Windrow.

Well, of course they'd done an IIP check – they'd probably had Dominic do it.

'Yes, sir.'

'And who is she?' he asked. 'Exactly?'

'Best to think of her as a consultant,' I said.

'Good god,' said Edmondson. 'Are you saying she's a . . .' He hesitated as his mandated diversity training caused him to trip over the word voodoo or possibly witchdoctor – I couldn't tell which. 'A traditional spiritualist?' Which impressed the hell out of me, and I was tempted to agree just to reward such a valiant effort. But it's one thing to withhold information from a senior officer and quite another to feed them false data.

'Not really, sir,' I said. 'It's just that there are some people who'll talk to her who wouldn't talk to us.'

'People?' asked Windrow dryly.

'Special people, sir,' I said. 'Bees are avoiding the area

in question. That's why we think something is going on there.'

I waited for one of them to ask whether the bees were 'special people', but luckily both of them had more important things on their minds.

'What's your next step?' asked Windrow.

'I'd like to re-interview both sets of parents,' I said. 'See what they know about the invisible Princess Luna. And then I'd like to have a look at Pokehouse Wood and a couple of other places that have come up in the literature.'

'You're going to have a hard time getting Derek or Andy to interrupt their search,' said Edmondson. 'So I'd talk to them as soon as possible – before we restart operations.'

'I'll ask Cole to facilitate a second interview with the mothers,' said Windrow.

There was the sound of voices from inside the canteen – members of MIU arriving and looking for coffee.

'It's about time we got in there,' said Edmondson. 'Are you ready?'

'One more cigarette,' said Windrow.

Andy had reached the point where he was going to keep going until someone told him he could stop. Even in the bright morning sunshine he looked grey and tired. The next search was staging at Bircher Common, where there was enough room for police and volunteers to park. I took Andy Marstowe aside behind a Peugeot Van with battenberg visibility strips and a West Midlands Police crest, and asked him whether he knew anything about Nicole Lacey's invisible friend. He just stared at me blankly and said he didn't know what I was talking about. I'd have preferred it if he'd demanded to know why I was wasting his time. Which just shows, you should never wish for things you don't really want to get.

'What the fuck is this bullshit?'

Derek Lacey stared at me after I asked him the same thing. He was red-faced and erratic and, if I was any judge, about a day away from coming apart at the seams. His voice was angry but his eyes were sad, pleading, wanting to know why I was tormenting him with these stupid questions. I got him calmed down using the patented reasonable police voice while making sure I stayed out of reach. Fortunately, it's easier to settle people in plain clothes, the uniform has a tendency to set people off, but either way the important thing is to remain calm but firm. This is where doing your two-year probation in the West End comes in really handy.

I explained that we, and it's always 'we' when dealing with aggravated members of the public, were double checking every possible point of contact between Hannah and Nicole and the outside world.

'When kids talk about imaginary friends,' I said, 'sometimes they're talking about a real person. You see, say you don't want a child's parents to know you're talking to them . . . so you tell the child not to tell anyone, tell them that bad things will happen if they do. But kids like to talk, they especially like to talk about their friends. Especially if they're interesting or naughty. I mean, what is the point of interesting or naughty if you can't talk about it to someone else?'

A strange look came into Derek's eyes and I wondered whether maybe I should have avoided the whole 'stranger danger' aspect of my little speech. Served me right for making this stuff up as I went along. Then he pushed his hand through his thinning hair and took a deep breath.

'Yes,' he said. 'I see now – apologies. What was the question?'

I repeated the question and he shrugged.

'Oh, yeah, I remember Princess Luna,' he said. 'I thought that had sort of stopped. Nicky used to demand extra sweets for Princess Luna and then scoff the lot herself. Vicky got very uptight about it – all those childhood obesity articles in the women's section of the Sundays.'

Apparently, there was one of those mother-daughter power struggles – like those that so enliven the lives of my mum's relatives – which Derek had made a point of staying out of. Finally, Nicole stopped talking about her imaginary friend, and Derek just assumed it had been a phase.

'Unless it was real,' he said. 'And just wandered off one day.'

*And how many invisible friends are not imaginary,* I asked myself as he walked off to join the search team. *What if this stuff is way more common than even the Folly thinks it is?* What if it wasn't just children – what if it was schizophrenics as well?

I carry a notebook with a list of these kinds of questions, and it gets longer every month – especially since

Nightingale made answering them conditional on my advancement through the forms and wisdoms.

According to DS Cole, Victoria Lacey and Joanne Marstowe were spending the morning together at the Marstowe house while kind relatives, of which Joanne had almost as many as my mum, were taking the two older boys out for a day in Hereford. When I arrived in the suddenly – and suspiciously – neat and tidy kitchen I found the two mothers seated on either side of the table while DS Cole sat at the end and acted as de facto referee. You could have fried an egg in the space between the two women, and I almost turned on my heel and walked back out again.

'Peter,' said Joanne. 'Would you like some tea?' She was already up and bustling before I could answer, so I said I would and deliberately took her seat to break up the confrontation.

Victoria stared at me as I sat down, her face a mask. 'Is it true you've been asking about Nicky's silly imaginary friends?'

I gave her the same flannel I'd given her husband and I think she bought it, or at least was willing to convince herself that the police hadn't suddenly gone completely bonkers.

'Who wants tea?' asked Joanne.

I said yes again, Victoria said no and DS Cole gazed longingly at the kitchen door.

'You know what it's like with children,' said Victoria. 'Once they get an idea in their head they won't let go – the more you try to stop them the harder they cling on to it. But you can't just appease them forever – can you?'

Joanne plonked a mug of tea in front of me and I asked her if Hannah had ever claimed to have met Princess Luna.

'Hannah said you could only see her when it was a full moon,' said Joanne as she sat down with her own tea. 'I remember because she insisted we have her bloody birthday party on that particular night.'

'I wondered why you'd done that, and it went on so late,' said Victoria.

'The moon wasn't up until past nine o'clock now, was it?' said Joanne. 'I thought they'd got that nonsense from that Hobbit film.'

'I don't remember a unicorn in *The Hobbit*,' said Victoria.

'No, it was the writing in that,' said Joanne. 'On the map.'

Victoria picked a thread off the shoulder of her blouse.

'I don't think I was paying that much attention,' she said. 'It all seemed rather daft.'

'They made us take them to the film twice,' said Joanne. 'They were looking forward to the next one.'

Joanne sipped her tea and looked out of the window.

I took the opportunity to surreptitiously check the phases of the moon on my phone – April 26th had been a full moon.

'I remember when they first went missing we thought they might have sneaked out to look at the moon,' said Joanne. 'Didn't we, Vicky?'

That hadn't been in their initial statements – I saw DS Cole blink.

Victoria nodded her head reluctantly.

'Following the moon,' said Joanne. 'Just like last time.'

'I think I will have a cup of tea now,' said Victoria. 'If that's all right with you.'

'Of course,' said Joanne and got up.

'They'd run away before?' asked DS Cole about two seconds before I could wrap my head around the implications.

'No,' said Victoria. 'Not Nicky and Hannah, they hadn't, but they used to talk about it. As a game – following the moon.'

'They had a song,' said Joanne, extracting a teabag and flicking it into the sink – '*In a minute soon we'll run away to follow the moon.*'

'It doesn't really scan, does it?' said Victoria.

I asked some follow-up questions, but Victoria had been trying hard to ignore the whole 'imaginary friend situation' as she put it and Joanne had three boys under the age of ten and could rarely hear herself speak, let alone Hannah.

Because the media pack were camped outside the front door, I went out the back and hopped over the garden fence and onto the unofficial – definitely not a right of way – footpath that ran behind the houses. Now that I knew what to look for, I could see that nearly all the late-twentieth-century build in the village had gone up on decommissioned orchards. In some places the old fence line had become the edge of people's back gardens. One remnant of the original orchards remained behind the Old Vicarage and I saw a dip in its back wall where a pair of eleven-year-old girls could have easily climbed over. This must have been their semi-secret path. No wonder they'd been inseparable since they were old enough to express a preference – it must have been like having their own secret garden.

The pair would have had to split in September – Nicole would be going up the road to Lucton School, fee paying, while Hannah would be commuting into Leominster to attend a state school. Fear of this separation was put forward as one of the narratives that might lead to them running away together. I wondered what being split up might be like – I didn't have any friends that had gone to posh schools, unless you counted Nightingale.

The path led me out onto a lane by Spring Farm and after a short cut down the back of the graveyard – Rushpool was an old enough village to have two – and I came out by the car park of the Swan in the Rushes where Beverley was waiting with the Asbo. All without attracting the attention of the media.

Me and Beverley parked the Asbo at the Riverside Inn, crossed the bridge and found the official Mortimer Trail footpath a hundred metres further on. We followed it to another gate and stile and through another field munched down to a green fuzz by sheep and then over a barbed-wire fence into a lumpy field of long grass. The path was barely visible as a slightly trampled diagonal, but luckily we could see the next stile at the far corner. A solitary goat watched us go past – we were probably the most interesting thing that had happened all summer.

I paused mid-field to orientate myself using my

phone. We were less than three hundred metres from where we'd found the dead sheep. I looked for it and I could spot where it had lain in the next field.

Pokehouse Wood was not what I expected. For a start, it was missing a lot of trees. It was easy to see where it had been, a rough rectangle of cleared land on a steep slope that ran down to the footpath by the River Lugg. Freshly planted saplings stood in white protective cylinders like ranks of war graves, and between them the scrub and grass were shot through with purple stands of foxglove. I recognised these because I'd googled the plants after seeing Hugh's notes – a famous source of digitalis, which in small doses can save your life and in larger doses kill you.

The missing trees were explained by a sign on the kissing gate which, on behalf of the National Trust, welcomed us to Pokehouse Wood and told us that the area had been cleared and planted with conifers in 2002, but had now been cleared again and planted with native broadleaved trees *to restore the beauty and nature conservation of this important local woodland*. There was a contact number for Croft Castle which I made a note of.

According to the map on my phone, the footpath ran along the river all the way to a historic mill at Mortimer's Cross. Stairs cut into the slope and reinforced with planking marked where the footpath led up to the ridge. We weren't supposed to be searching exactly, a full POLSA-directed team was an hour behind us. But I'd wanted to have a look before all those size tens stirred up the ground.

At the top of the steps was another track, this one cut

level into the hillside and sloping down towards an intersection with the footpath by the river.

'Logging track,' said Beverley. 'That's why it has to be graded flat. You know, this is a bit weird.'

'Good,' I said. 'Weird is what we're looking for.'

'I don't think it's that kind of weird,' she said. 'You see, this bit of land we're standing on belongs to the National Trust but it's been managed by the Forestry Commission.'

The role of which was to deal with the fact the UK was in danger of losing its forests which were, back then, a strategic national resource on account of the fact you needed it to make stuff. This being before Ikea turned up backed by the limitless expanse of the Swedish forests, fabled home to fascist biker gangs, depressed detectives and werewolves.

'Really?' I asked. 'Werewolves?'

'That's what I heard,' said Beverley.

No wonder the detectives were depressed, I thought. And just about managed to stop myself asking for more information – priorities and all that.

'They would have cut down the ancient woodland and planted western hemlock or Douglas fir, probably,' said Beverley. Because back then you wanted a tree with a nice straight trunk that grew fast and was easy to manage. Then, in the late sixties, it began to occur to people that perhaps there was a bit more to reforestation than just planting a ton of trees. By the early 1980s someone had invented the word biodiversity and rural landowners, who up until then had cheerfully been industrialising the landscape, were told to start putting it back the way they'd found it – in fact, better than the way they'd found it, if you don't mind.

'When the National Trust took this place over they probably designated it a PAWS,' said Beverley. Which meant Plantation on Ancient Woodland Site, which led to the next question – what the fuck is an ancient woodland?

'They call it the wildwood,' said Beverley and, according to the men and women with serious beards and slightly windswept hair who make it their business to know this stuff, it used to cover pretty much most of the island of Great Britain. Then, 6,000 years ago, farmers turned up with their fancy genetically modified crops and started clearing the forest out. And what they didn't clear got eaten away by their artificially mutated cattle, sheep and goats. By the Middle Ages most of it was gone, and Britain entered the Napoleonic War desperate for timber.

'Why do you know all this stuff?' I asked.

'It's all anyone involved in working the countryside ever talks about,' she said. 'That and the vagaries of the EU subsidy regime and how evil the supermarkets are. Anyway, ground cover has a critical impact on water tables and flow rates. so you can bet we all take an interest in that – even Tyburn, who's pretty much a storm drain from one end to the other.'

Beverley pointed out the trees that had been left standing when the area was cleared. A long strip of them went along the river bank and beside the footpaths. 'That's deliberate. Those are remnants of the ancient woodlands,' she said.

'And the weird bit?'

'It's the timing,' she said. 'You don't just charge in and clear ten hectares of commercial forest – which apart from anything else is worth a ton of money.' So normally you wait for the current crop of western hemlock or Douglas fir or whatever to mature and then you cut them down and replant with historically appropriate broadleaf trees. Forest management not being an industry for people with a short attention span.

But according to the dates we'd seen on the sign, the trees had only been halfway to maturity before they were felled. 'That would have been a serious loss of revenue, and I doubt the Forestry Commission would have liked it.'

'And that's what's weird, is it?' I asked.

'I told you it wasn't the kind of weird you wanted,' said Beverley. 'What do you want to do now?'

I looked back the way we'd come. The squared-off tower of Aymestrey's church was visible on the other side of the river, and up the road by the bridge I could see the half-timbered jumble that was the Riverside Inn. It was hot and exposed out amongst the seedlings and the air was still and close. It was tempting just to walk back down, step into the bar and a have a beer or nine. I turned to find Beverley looking at me with concern.

'What?'

'Nothing,' she said.

'Let's go up a bit,' I said.

So we followed the trail as it climbed diagonally across the upper slope of what would be, in another twenty years or so, the ancient Pokehouse Wood. We got a taste of what it might look like when the path turned left into a mature belt of deciduous trees. Near the far edge of the trees the path got steep enough that you ended up using your hands to navigate the last bit, and that meant my eyes were just at the right level to spot the little strip of pink hanging from a strand of the barbed-wire fence, just to the right of the stile.

It was a centimetre wide and about six long. Thick pink cotton, the same shade as that of the Capri pants that Nicole Lacey was thought to have been wearing when she left her house. I froze and told Beverley to stop moving. We'd have to be careful backtracking down the path to avoid contaminating the scene any further.

I leaned forward, put my hand over my mouth, and got as close as I dared. When I was sure there wasn't any detectable *vestigia* I leant back and swore.

'What is it?' asked Beverley.

I nodded at the strip of cloth. Along one side there was a distinctive reddish-brown stain.

We're the police. We're accustomed to disappointment. But I've never been in a room full of so many dispirited coppers as we had at the evening briefing on Day 6.

Windrow and Edmondson were good, but there was no disguising the litany of non-results. There had been sightings everywhere across the UK, Europe and beyond. Police were turning out from Aberdeen to Marseilles, which was heartening while at the same time being totally futile. In a case involving missing children the good news/bad news routine is always, the bad news is – we haven't found them yet, and the good news is – we haven't found them yet . . .

But we *had* found a strip of pink cloth. Less than two minutes after I'd called it in, a helicopter had gone overhead and less than ten minutes after that the lead elements of the search team in Aymestrey had arrived, red-faced, sweating and proving that they were much fitter than I was. They helped secure the site, but as the numbers started to pile up me and Beverley made a tactical retreat.

Windrow and Edmondson invited me down to the nick where we had a two-hour discussion about what led me up that particular path at that particular time. The problem being that a search team had done the whole length of the Mortimer Trail on Day 2 and that strip of pink fabric had not been there when they did it.

When this was reported at the briefing a ripple went through the ranks. I knew what they were thinking – a kidnapping, a plucky but futile escape attempt, recapture by the kidnapper, followed by panic. Followed, with remorseless logic, by death and disposal.

When it was over I slipped out onto the terrace to clear my head.

It was still close enough to sunset for the sky to be dark blue rather than black, but it was already cooler. There was a distinct breeze coming from the west and with it snatches of James Brown and the hum of generators – the drone of a funfair as unmistakable as a bagpipe warming up. Much closer below me I could hear the restless murmur of the media pack as they lapped at the walls of the station.

My phone pinged. The caller ID showed 'withheld' but I knew who it was.

**Y haven't you found girls yet?**

Beverley was waiting for me outside the cowshed – which would have been encouraging on just about any other night. The door was open and the light was on, casting a yellow rectangle across the bottom of the garden and into the empty orchard beyond.

Either I'd left the door open or Beverley had broken in.

'Dominic's mum gave me the spare keys,' she said.

'Did you have a good rummage?'

'Yes, thanks.'

'Fine,' I said. 'I'm going to bed. You can do what you like.'

'You're fucking unnatural, you are,' she said,

'Oh, don't start.'

She stepped over into my line of sight.

'I understand you've got self-control and all that,' she said. 'I get it. But you're just . . . fucking unnatural, Peter.'

'Fine,' I said. 'You can come to bed too, but I'm still going to go to sleep.'

'Is that what you think I'm talking about?' Beverley folded her arms across her chest.

'I don't know what you're talking about,' I said. 'Why don't you just tell me?'

'You had your hands on the Faceless Man,' she said. 'And your best friend stabbed you in the back and you're just like "Oh well, you win some, you lose some – ho ho ho." Which is fucking unnatural.'

'And you think this is helping?'

'I think it would be useful if you got just a little bit angry,' she said. 'I'm not asking you to turn green and go on a rampage but, you know, expressing a little bit of displeasure would not be inappropriate given the circumstances.'

'Like what you'd have done, yeah?' I said, because I'm terminally stupid. 'Throw a strop – flood out a few homes?'

'That's different,' said Beverley matter of factly. 'And, anyway, sometimes it's you getting angry and sometimes it's exceptionally heavy rainfall in your catchment area. To be honest, it can be tricky telling the two apart. But that's me, isn't it? I'm a goddess, Peter, a creature of temperament and whimsy. I'm supposed to be arbitrary and mercurial – it's practically my job description. And this isn't about me.'

'What do you want me to do, Bev? Anything for a quiet life.'

Beverley turned and pointed down at a solitary tree that stood by the garden fence. It was squat and a bit twisty; something deciduous is the best I can do.

'Why don't you blow up the tree?' she said.

'What?'

'Give it a lightning bolt, rip it up by its roots, knock it down – set it on fire?' She trailed off.

'What's it ever done to me?' I asked.

'It's a tree,' said Beverley.

'I can't,' I said.

'They're not short of trees round here,' she said. 'They're not going to miss it. And in case you're worried, nobody's living in it or mystically attached to it. Take some of that anger and let it rip – you'll feel better.'

'I can't.'

'Yeah, you can,' she said.

'I can't.'

'What is wrong with you?'

'I can't,' I said slowly. 'It doesn't fucking work that way, okay? It's not about anger, or love or the power of fricking friendship. It's about concentration, about control.' It's hard enough to make a *forma* when you're hungry, let alone when you're angry. 'So you can see that as a form of cathartic release it's a little bit shit.'

Beverley tipped her head to one side and gave me a long look.

'Okay,' she said and cast around at the base of the tree and came up with a section of branch a shade longer than a baseball bat – she held it out to me. 'Hit it with a stick instead.'

'If I hit the tree,' I said, 'will you get off my back?'

'Maybe.'

She smiled as I took the branch. The full moon hovered over the roof of the bungalow and I remembered half dreaming the empty orchard full of trees. I strode up to the tree, swung one handed and the impact jarred the branch loose from my fingers.

'That's pathetic,' called Beverley.

I scooped up the branch and brandished it at the tree.

'Listen,' I said. 'I know you trees are up to something.'

And then I smacked it hard with the branch, keeping my grip loose so that I wouldn't let go this time – it did make a satisfying thwack.

'Now, I thought I was dreaming last night,' I said. 'But I wasn't, was I?'

Thwack.

'They were ghost trees . . .'

Thwack.

'Weren't they? Because people leave a trace behind them. So why shouldn't trees?'

Smack – a fragment of bark flew off the trunk.

'It doesn't have to be a big trace, because you're there for bloody years – aren't you?'

Smack.

'But you can't talk because you're a fucking tree, so really this whole fucking enhanced interrogation shit is a waste of time.' I lowered my branch. 'As if it wasn't always a waste of time.'

I hit the bloody thing as hard as I could, hard enough to numb the palms of my hands, hard enough that the crack echoed off the old wall. Because it's always a waste of time, all those rushed, angry stupid things you do. They never solve the problems. Because in real life that rush of adrenaline and rage just makes you dumb and seeing red just leads you up the steps to court for something aggravated – assault, battery, stupidity.

I hit the tree again and it hurt my hands even worse.

Because getting angry doesn't help, or weeping or pleading or just fucking trying to be reasonable. Because she lost her face, man. Because that had to be like having your identity ripped away. Because you're looking in the mirror and a hideous stranger is staring back. And what would I do if I was her, if I was given that choice? – like there would even be a decision. And getting angry doesn't bring back her face or unmake the choice that she made. Any more than it made a difference when Dad wouldn't get out of bed or when Mum just flat out told you that your stuff was needed by somebody else. When the people you need stuff from are more interested in something else.

At some point the stick broke.

There were probably manly tears.

Beverley Brook may have put me to bed, or it's possible I might have done it myself, just as I've always done.

I woke up to find the curtains open and my bed bathed in sunshine.

I got into the shower and the hot water stung my palms. There were scrapes and cuts across both my hands.

'You think this is bad,' I told the reflection in the bathroom mirror. 'You should see the other guy.'

When I got out of the shower I rolled my shoulders and stretched my neck. I felt better, but there was still a stone in my chest when I thought of Lesley. Some things aren't fixed by a couple of hours of primal screaming – or whatever that was I'd been doing the night before.

It was Day 7 – Hannah and Nicole were still missing.

Me-time was over. There was work to be done.

# 8

## Proactive Measures

First question to ask yourself is – what are you good for? West Mercia Police didn't need me to beat the bushes because they had everyone from Grampian Search and Rescue to the SAS doing that. They didn't need me holding the hands of the parents, even though I bet DS Cole would have paid me quite a lot of money to do so, and they really didn't need me handling the media. What I was was the only Falcon-qualified officer in the area and, along with my specialist civilian support, i.e. Beverley, I was best deployed concentrating on my area of expertise.

The second question to ask yourself is – what the fuck do I do next? Since weird shit was what I was there for, I decided I should work on the assumption that weird shit was what had happened.

We knew that the girls had got up, dressed themselves, and left their separate homes under their own steam. There was no sign of forced entry, and I hadn't detected *vestigia* in their rooms. Assume they were lured out, or possibly one was lured out and then lured the other one out. Assume the luring was done by something supernatural and in trots suspect number one – Princess Luna. Invisible horse-shaped friend, possibly a unicorn, possibly only visible in moonlight – the physics of which I didn't even want to think about.

Closest Princess Luna sighting to the village was at Hannah's birthday party, so stick a virtual pin in the field behind the village hall. Assume the girls go gambolling after My Invisible Pony – following the moon, which had been in its first quarter that night. They wouldn't have walked on the roads, not least because of the danger of being run over by alfresco sex maniacs and, besides, Dominic said that village kids went across the fields – and their paths were not necessarily the ones that were marked on the OS map.

So, up by paths unseen to Whiteway Head – although it must have been a reasonably direct route if the timings were going to make any sense – where something definitely magical happened, and blew both their phones.

Now, I reckoned that they'd met a third party there, perhaps a friend of Princess Luna or maybe an owner, and that would be the point where the girls' fun-filled frolic went sour.

I called up Leominster nick and they confirmed that while they'd had trouble getting a precise DNA match between the blood stain on the pink cotton with hair samples recovered from Nicole's room, a second round of tests using swabs taken from Victoria and Derek Lacey had confirmed a definite parental match. The high probability, the lab had said, was that the blood had belonged to Nicole Lacey.

Which meant that they had gone west down either the Mortimer Trail or the logging road that ran parallel to it, and had probably stayed in that area for at least three days before Nicole had caught her leg on the barbed-wire fence above Pokehouse Wood. A place famous as the abode of fairies – and a mere hop, skip and a jump from where we'd found the dead sheep.

I called Dr Walid and asked whether he'd finished his autopsy.

'Hello, Peter,' he said. 'How're you bearing up?'

I told him I was fine.

'Wonderful bit of mutton you sent me,' said Dr Walid. 'Finished it up this morning. Thought you might like the results.'

'Anything interesting?'

'The sheep itself is your bog standard North Country Mule, a cross between Swaledale and a Border Leicester – a breed known for its meat and for being even more gleckit than ordinary sheep. I've sent some tissue samples to the lab just to be sure.'

'Any sign of magical contact?'

'Nothing in gross physical terms. I sectioned the brain, such as it was, but there was no sign of hyperthaumaturgical degradation. It was a remarkably healthy sheep – apart from the great big hole in its belly, of course. That was cause of death, by the way. In case you were wondering.'

'Could you reconstruct the injury?'

'Well, it's never easy just going by the crime scene photographs. But at a guess I'd say it was struck in the belly, impaled, then lifted bodily and thrown some distance. That's how its guts got spread over such large area.'

'Are you saying it was gored?' I asked. 'By a bull or a goat?'

'I've met some tough goats, but nothing big enough to fling a full grown sheep three metres or so,' said Dr Walid. 'And there's only one piercing wound, so I doubt it was a bull or even a cow – they can get quite territorial, you know.'

I asked what the weapon had been like.

'At least sixty centimetres long, circular cross section and tapering to a sharp point,' said Dr Walid. 'Possibly a spiral configuration.'

'Like a narwhale's horn?'

'Aye,' said Dr Walid. 'Just like that.'

'So you think it's a unicorn?'

'I wouldn't like to jump to conclusions,' he said. 'Not without more evidence.'

'But?'

'If you achieve nothing else,' he said, 'get me a tissue sample.'

Assuming Princess Luna was real, and not a physical manifestation of something incorporeal. There hadn't been hoof prints at Stan's stash and none around the stabbed sheep. And why would a unicorn stab a sheep, anyway?

The girls had let Princess Luna lick the mutton juice from their fingers.

Carnivorous unicorns, I thought. And if it did raid Stan's stash, a meat-eating unicorn that was blissed out on Benzedrine and diazepam and agricultural diesel oil. There were certain 'things' I knew that navigated the exciting boundary between corporeal and incorporeal existence. Ghosts, revenants like my friend Mr Punch, and certain types of Genius Loci. They all had one thing in common in that whatever work-around for the law of thermodynamics they thought they had, sooner or later they had to get their power from somewhere. *Vestigium* was a source. But even better was a bit of raw magic.

And that's when I came up with a cunning plan – one of my better ones, if I do say so myself.

'Got to go, Abdul,' I said. 'I've just had a bright idea.'

Just before I hung up I think he might have said 'god be merciful', but I couldn't be sure.

I called Windrow and cleared my plan with him and Edmondson, who clearly thought I was bonkers, but by that point were getting used to my little ways. Dominic was once again volunteered as liaison, under the condition I explain the plan to him myself.

'Do you have any confidence this will work?' asked Windrow.

'Honestly, sir,' I said, 'I don't know – but if something supernatural is actively working against us, then I suggest it's about time we took a more aggressively proactive approach.'

Windrow gave that last sentence the mirthless chuckle it deserved and wished me luck.

Then I called Beverley.

'Want to come out tonight?' I asked.

'What are we doing?'

'Unicorn hunting,' I said.

'Aren't they an endangered species?'

'That depends on whether they've been helping abduct kids,' I said. 'Don't it?'

\*

It took about thirty seconds on the internet to find a shop in Leominster that sold what they called 'second user computers', five minutes to specify what I wanted, and at least another fifteen minutes to come up with a plausible explanation for what I wanted it for. Then I drove into town, found a café that steadfastly refused to provide a genealogy for its sausages and had a proper fry-up. While I was doing that, I wrote down the specifications for the next job I wanted to do – that would have taken much longer to detail verbally, and even longer to bullshit away.

'So what kind of science experiment is it?' asked the man in the shop as I inspected the devices. They'd done a good job and had gone so far as to add a tiny red LED on the end of each one to show when the power was on.

'I'm looking to see whether high-tension electrical cables really disrupt microprocessors,' I said. 'What did you use for the casing?'

The man was a bit taller than me, with an elegantly clipped black beard that was at odds with his polyester-mix beige T-shirt that had the shop's logo on the front.

'Plastic cricket bats,' he said. 'Kid's size.'

I tested each one carefully and then paid for them.

'You're really out looking for UFOs, aren't you?' said the man.

'You got me,' I said.

'Those kids,' said the man. 'You don't think they were abducted, do you? By aliens?'

'God, I hope not,' I said. 'My life's complicated enough already.'

I handed him handwritten specifications and waited while he read them so that I could clarify a few points and help with the niceties of cursive script.

'Is this supposed to be a detection grid?' he asked.

I told him it was, and he asked me what I was hoping to detect.

'Things that aren't normally there,' I said, and he nodded as if this made sense.

'I'll have to go to Birmingham to get the gear,' he said. 'I can have them ready in two days.'

I paid the guy, packed my stuff, and drove on to the nick to inform Dominic of his role in the festivities.

Strangely, he was less than enthusiastic about me involving his boyfriend.

'We need his Nissan to get us up the rough bits on Bircher Common,' I said. 'And we need someone to drive it.'

'And that's not me, because . . .'

'Because you and me are going to be proceeding down the Mortimer Trail and seeing if we can't attract something supernatural,' I said.

'Have you cleared this with the bosses?' he asked.

'Oh, yeah,' I said. 'Submitted an operational plan, objectives analysis, risk assessment. The whole thing.'

'And what did they say?' asked Dominic.

'They wanted me to take someone from the MIU to keep an eye on things.'

'And that would be me?'

'Yep.'

'We're going to be walking through the woods at night?'

'Is that a problem?'

'It's just I'm not that fond of the great outdoors,' said Dominic.

'But I thought you were a country boy,' I said. 'You grew up in a small village.'

'Yeah, and as soon as I was old enough I moved to the city.'

'You moved to Hereford,' I said. 'That's not quite the same thing.'

'Yes it is. We've got a cathedral *and* an Anne Summers,' said Dominic. 'That makes us a city.'

'Anne Summers?'

'It's right on the square and everything,' said Dominic.

'Hold on,' I said. 'Doesn't your boyfriend have a farm to live on?'

'Sore point,' said Dominic. 'And, anyway, what makes you think we'll attract anything supernatural?'

'For one thing, tonight it's going to be a full moon,' I said. 'Also because I will be doing magical things.'

'Your name is Baldrick,' said Dominic. 'And I claim my ten pounds.'

One thing old jazzmen and old police officers both agree on is that it's important to get your rest in when and where you can. Which is why I drove back to the cowshed, had another shower to cool off, lay down on the bed in my underwear and tried not to think for a bit.

It was hot, even with the doors open. But a little bit of a breeze touched the curtains and brought in the smell of grass and a sweeter smell that I thought I now recognised as cowslip in bloom, although it could have been silage for all I knew.

There were a couple of strands of dusty spider web hanging from one edge of the ceiling. Dominic's mum needed to invest in a proper extension duster or at least learn how to put a J-cloth on a stick.

I lay on my back and let the ceiling go in and out of focus.

My phone pinged – number withheld.

**Do you think they were abducted by fairies?**

I sat up and took a deep breath to calm my nerves. Then I logged the call, contacted the DPS team on a separate phone to give them a heads up, and then texted back.

*Why do you think fairies?*

**Who else?**

*Y not people?*

**No other leads.**

This made me pause. It was the sort of sloppy thinking that Lesley, had she caught me doing it, would have pointed out – just because you don't know something is there doesn't mean it isn't there.

And how would she know that we didn't have any leads?

I called Inspector Pollock at the DPS.

'She's got a line into the secure net,' I said. 'Or access to someone with access privileges.'

'Is it you?' asked Pollock.

'Nope,' I said.

'Of course not,' said Pollock. 'Because that would make my life easier.'

But not mine, I thought. I so hated being on the wrong side of the interview table.

'If she's following the same pattern as last time,' said Pollock, 'she'll make one more response before changing SIMs – try to make the next question count.'

I thought about it for a bit, and then I thought about the tree outside in the garden and the futility of anger.

**I miss you**, I texted.

I waited, but she didn't respond before it was time to go out that evening.

Dominic's boyfriend was named Victor Lowell and was one of the new breed of farmers who got their market price updates via Twitter and drove their tractors listening to 50 Cent. He had floppy blond hair and the posh accent of someone who was privately educated but never got the memo about having to pretend to be just one of the blokes. He also owned the land he farmed which made him, notionally, the richest person I'd ever met.

'Not that I could sell it,' he shouted over the Nissan Technical's engine as he gunned it up the flinty trail to Whiteway Head. 'It's been in the family for, oh . . . months.'

Dominic groaned – this was obviously an old joke.

'You're not a farming family then?' said Beverley.

'Oh, it's a long sad history of farmers. It's just that I'm the first one to own the land I farm,' he said. 'My uncle was a tenant, but my father ran off to London where he made a pile in property. Then I came back and bought the land.'

'He lied to me when we met,' said Dominic. 'Said he was a stockbroker.'

'People have such extraordinary prejudices,' said Victor airily.

We'd come up the slope before sunset to give Victor a bit of daylight to drive back down in. Whiteway Head, I saw, was a saddle between the high points of the ridge to east and west. It was the logical place to cross if you didn't want to schlepp around either end. There was also a clear route of descent on the escarpment side, although I personally wouldn't want to carry a sack of salt down that slope.

We'd brought sandwiches from Dominic's mum's and bottles of water, so we had an impromptu picnic, picking a site at the top of the ridge that gave us a good view across the valley.

The sky overhead was the same hot blue it had been since I arrived in Herefordshire, but to the west the sun was hidden behind a huge bank of grey and blue clouds that were piling up on the horizon.

'The Brecon Beacons,' said Victor. 'The Met Office are issuing a severe weather warning. Could cause some flooding downstream of the Lugg.'

I looked at Beverley, who shrugged.

'Who knows?' she said. 'It's not my part of the world.'

The last of the sunlight seemed to leak out from under the clouds to wash over the valley below. I could just see the A4110 as it crossed the Lugg – a typical Roman straight line aimed at what Dominic identified as Wigmore. *Imposing themselves on the landscape* – they'd always called it that on *Time Team*. Especially the beardy

Iron and Bronze Age specialists – *The Romans imposed themselves on the landscape.* Or, I thought, they wanted to get from point A to point B as quickly as possible.

Dominic pointed out Leinthall Earls and the white angular scar of the limestone quarry that spread up the hillside behind it. Fields covered the bottom of the valley with silvery stands of conifers on the higher slopes. To the north-east I saw the last red of the sun flash off the copper dome at the top of Hugh Oswald's tower. I wondered if the bees were still out and about, or whether they'd retreated to that vast hive under the dome.

Did Mellissa listen to them, or watch over them? Did she sleep up there? There was a thought. Did she dance in front of them, shaking her honey-maker back and forth to tell them where the best flowers were?

We ate chicken tikka masala sandwiches and drank coffee from the big military flasks I'd found in the trunks. Dominic kissed Victor goodbye and we watched the big Nissan rumble and lurch its way down the hill.

The moon rose in the east, swollen and full, but I made everyone wait until it was dark before we approached the gate into the forest.

'Do you think it will make a difference?' asked Beverley as I held the gate open for her and Dominic.

'I just don't want to have to come back and do this again,' I said.

In the moonlight the logging track was a straight milky line between the dark ranks of conifers on either side. I warned Beverley and Dominic to turn off their phones and pulled out the first of my mini cricket bats and turned it on. The LED glowed red in the darkness.

'What does that do?' asked Dominic.

I considered telling him that it saved my brain by providing a power source external to my precious grey matter, but then I'd have to explain everything else.

'Helps me cast spells,' I said.

'Okay,' said Dominic. 'Wait – magic spells?'

I cast a simple *lux impello* combo which put a yellowish werelight about two metres over my head where, hopefully, it would bob about after me like a balloon, only brightly lit. The LED on the cricket bat started to flicker.

Dominic stared at the werelight.

'What the hell is that?' he asked.

'It's a magic spell,' I said, and Beverley snorted.

'Show off,' she said.

'I said I was going to do magic,' I said.

'But ...' Dominic floundered around for a bit before pointing at me accusingly. 'You said that there's weird shit, but it normally turns out to have a rational explanation.'

'It does,' said Beverley. 'The explanation is a wizard did it.'

'That's my line,' I said, and Beverley shrugged.

'You didn't say anything about spells!' said Dominic.

'It's just a werelight,' I said.

It was like having our own personal streetlight, but beyond that bright circle the woods were a jumble of angular shadows – shifting uneasily as the yellow werelight bobbed and wavered in the breeze.

'Can we at least start moving in the right direction?' I said.

'Jesus Christ,' said Dominic, who was still having trouble. 'Is there anything else I should know?'

'We're looking for an invisible unicorn and Bev here is the goddess of a small river in South London.'

'It's quite a big river, actually,' said Beverley.

'How do people normally react to this?' asked Dominic.

'And most of it's above ground,' said Beverley.

'Usually a bit stunned to start with,' I said. 'Then they either get angry, go into denial or just deal with it.'

'Sounds familiar,' said Dominic.

'Unlike some rivers I could mention,' said Beverley.

'What else can you do?' asked Dominic.

'More importantly,' said Beverley, 'what makes you think this is going to work?'

'Because incorporeal entities need power to interact with the real world. And this,' I pointed at the werelight above me, 'is the all-you-can-eat-buffet sign.'

'You know that sounded completely mad, don't you?' asked Dominic.

'Sorry,' I said. 'Professional hazard.'

'Yeah, yeah,' said Beverley. 'Enough distractions. Let's do it.'

So into the woods we went – it was surprisingly noisy. Especially one loud bird whose chirping sounded far too cheerful for the middle of the night.

'That's just a robin,' said Beverley.

I said I thought they were diurnal.

'All day, all night,' she said. 'They don't shut up.'

Somewhere deeper into the gloom, amongst the straight trunks of the western hemlocks, something else made a sound like a ZX Spectrum loading a game off a cassette – Beverley said it was a nightjar.

Even without the sun, the air was warm and spiced with resin and the smell of dusty bark.

About fifty metres up the track it separated and we took the right-hand path which, according to my map, led us parallel to the top of the ridge. Because we were supposed to be looking out for anything weird we didn't talk and in that strange stumbling silence I felt as if my senses had contracted down to the small flickering circle of the werelight.

After a quarter of an hour or so we reached a T-junction where the Mortimer Trail separated from the logging road.

'I think this might have been a mistake,' I said.

'Definitely is,' said Beverley, pointing to the left which was noticeably darker than the right. 'Because we are not going up that way.'

'No,' I said, blinking to try and get my night vision back. 'I mean the light – I should have used a darker point source.' If only *lux* hadn't been so reliable as a ghost attractor. I checked the cricket bat and saw that the LED had gone out. When I shook it next to my ear I could hear sand sloshing around inside. I swapped it for the next bat – the LED flickering as soon as I turned it on.

'Left or right?' asked Dominic.

I considered it. If the point was to *attract* things to us, then taking the easier road made sense. I'd have liked to take the right-hand trail to Croft Ambrey, but I wasn't sure I wanted to be stumbling around an Iron Age fort, what with ditches and ramparts and other convenient limb-breaking opportunities, until I'd had a chance to suss it out in daylight.

This, by the way, is what we call in the trade a risk assessment.

'*Allons y*,' I said, and led off down the left-hand track.

We'd gone on another couple of hundred metres, around a turn and past a turn-off that Dominic identified as heading down to Croft Castle, when we heard the hoof beats.

Beverley heard them first, but as soon as she'd pointed them out I heard them as well. Hooves hitting the ground in a fast jaunty rhythm. A slow trot, I learnt later – sometimes known as a jog.

It took a couple of rounds of shushing and craning to establish that it was coming from behind us. I put down the cricket bat to anchor the werelight in place and 'jogged' back five metres to see if I could re-establish my night vision. With the light behind me the track became a milky strip, snaking between the vertical shadows of the trees, whose pointed tops marched off like fence spikes. The moon hung full and round and almost perfectly aligned with the track.

If this wasn't your actual moon path, I thought, it would certainly do for the postcard.

I couldn't see a horse, but I could hear the hoof beats getting closer – and picking up the pace.

'Let's get off the road,' I said.

Neither Beverley nor Dominic argued, even when we found ourselves pushing through the chest-high bracken that had lain invisible in the darkness until we blundered straight into it. If anything, we were grateful for the additional cover as we crouched down and waited for the hoof beats to get closer.

I glanced up at the werelight obediently hanging directly over the track where I'd left it. The colour was definitely beginning to edge into the red as whatever approached sucked up the magic and lowered the frequency of the emitted light.

The hoof beats slowed to a walk and then a cautious amble. They sounded large, the hoof beats, great big dinner-plate-sized hooves that thumped down onto the dust of the track with authority.

I watched through the gaps in the bracken as the werelight dimmed down to a sullen red and Princess Luna made her appearance. It was transparent but refractive, a statue of living glass, the dying light from the werelight tingeing its shoulders and haunches with red and outlining the long spiralled horn that rose from between its eyes.

Then the werelight popped out and suddenly it was there, huge and real and sweaty and pale in the moonlight, its horn bobbing left and right as it swung its head and sniffed the air.

I resisted the urge to push further back into the bracken.

Then the head snapped back to point down the track, the big muscles in its haunches bunched, flexed and the beast sprang forward, its vast hooves kicking up dust and splinters of rock.

We scrambled out of our hiding place and stumbled

out to stare after the unicorn as it vanished around a curve in the track.

'Okay,' said Beverley. 'I really hope one of you is a virgin.'

'What now?' asked Dominic.

'We follow it,' I said.

Which we did, but incredibly cautiously, all the way down to what Dominic assured me was School Wood – not far from where Stan had had her stash snaffled. I considered launching another werelight, but after a brief discussion with the others we decided to delay that until we were within a comfortable mad panicked rush of where Victor was parked in the Technical.

In fact, I had Dominic turn his phone back on so he could call to make sure that Victor was indeed waiting. You know  just in case.

The track had curved south so that the tall trees cast their moon shadows across the path, making it much harder to continue without lights. The warmth of the day was leaching out of the air and I shivered at a breeze that blew in from the north and riffled the tree tops.

When I figured we'd reached the point where the track started to descend sharply, I decided to give the big werelight another go.

'And what's your plan if Princess Luna turns up again?' asked Beverley.

'I want you two to hang back,' I said. 'While I go and try to make friends with it.'

'And when it inevitably tries to kill you?' asked Dominic.

'You rush in and rescue me,' I said.

Beverley kissed her teeth.

'We have to at least narrow down where it's coming from,' I said. 'So if it runs, we follow it again. And if it attacks, we see how far it follows us.'

'Just for the record,' asked Dominic, 'what were you expecting to happen when we first met it?'

I told them I had thought our invisible friend would be a bit more insubstantial and a bit less like a carthorse with a lethal spike stuck on its head.

'The girls are still missing,' I said. 'We've got to make another attempt.'

'Fine,' said Beverley. 'Just stay out of the way of the horn, right?'

I promised I would.

Then I turned on the last of the cricket bats and put a werelight over our heads, a slightly bigger one than I meant to, one that I learnt later was visible as far away as Wigmore and Mortimer's Cross.

As soon as it went up I felt Beverley clutch my arm.

There was a chill in the air and a sudden coppery taste in my mouth. A smell like smashed flint and a screech like a blade on a whetstone.

At the far edge of the werelight the shadows amongst the trees began to quiver.

'I have to get off this ridge,' said Beverley.

'Why?'

'There are some things you don't do, some places you don't go, unless you are seriously looking for trouble.'

'Are we talking postcodes here?'

'Fuck postcodes,' said Beverley. 'This is a no-fly zone, UN resolution-breaking, war-starting stuff. You know my mum and the Old Man of the River, remember all that aggravation? That's nothing compared to what'll happen if we don't get off this ridge right now.'

'I get that,' I said. 'But who?'

'I don't know, Peter,' said Beverley. 'And I don't think it's a good idea to stick around to find out.'

I heard hoof beats to the north-east, behind us. The fucker must have circled around or just stood invisible in the wings and watched us walk past.

'Which way?' I asked.

Beverley hesitated and then thrust out an arm in a vaguely south-westerly direction.

'That way,' she said. 'Towards the river.'

Away from the unicorn – it seemed like a sensible idea.

'I thought you were going to make friends,' said Dominic as he headed off at a brisk pace.

I would have explained that operational flexibility is the key to successful policing, but I decided to save my breath. I also left the cricket bat and the werelight behind me in the hope that it might slow down whatever was following us.

'How far is it to the car?' I asked.

'Don't know,' said Dominic. 'Half a mile?'

I stopped and looked back.

A hundred metres behind me the unicorn had stopped beneath my werelight to bask in its glow. As I watched, it reared up on its hind legs, the reddening light gleaming along its horn, and gave a deep rumbling bellow.

Nothing that ate grass, I decided, would make a noise like that and legged it after the others.

Suddenly the forest on our left gave way to a single line of trees reinforced with a barbed-wire fence and, on the other side, open pasture silver in the moonlight. Beverley stopped so fast that I nearly ran into her back.

'That way,' she said, pointing at the pasture.

I was about to ask why we couldn't just keep going when I saw something blocking the track ahead. In the darkness it was an indistinct pattern of shadow, but when it moved my brain had no trouble filling in its outline – another unicorn.

'Oh, great,' said Dominic.

I looked back to where the werelight was flickering and our prancing friend came whumping down on its front hooves, head lowered like a bull. I swung back to the fence looking for a stile or a gate, or even a gap that wouldn't involve ripping myself to bits on the barbed wire.

'Peter,' said Beverley – I heard hoof beats from both directions.

'I know,' I said trying to clear my mind.

'Hurry,' she said.

'I know,' I said, summoning up the *impello forma* in my mind and trying to remember the *formae inflectentes* that would make it do what I want.

'I mean it,' she said, and I let the spell go.

It wasn't pretty but it got the job done, ripping out a section of the barbed-wire fence and shoving it to the side so that me, Beverley and Dominic could run through the gap.

'The farmer's not going to like this,' yelled Dominic as we ran past the twisted remains of the fence.

'He can bill me,' I said.

Even in my PSU boots, running at night over uneven ground was difficult and Beverley soon pulled ahead of me and Dominic. Out in the open pasture I was suddenly aware of the blue-black vastness of the sky and the river of stars arching over my head. At the far side of the field I could see a smudged line of shadow against the midnight blue of the sky – I hoped it was another fence line because if it was a cliff or something we were in deep shit.

I heard the bellow of a unicorn behind me and, without looking back, I put on a spurt of speed, the long grass whipping around my ankles.

'There's a fence,' yelled Beverley from in front of me.

Doing magic on the fly, even something as basic as an *impello* variant, is incredibly difficult. Nightingale said that when he was training only half his peers could perform while under physical stress. Which is why, in the Folly, boxing practice goes, jab, jab, right, duck, roundhouse, uppercut, *lux,* jab, jab, *impello.*

I stripped away the sound of my own breathing and the impact of my feet on the grass so that in my head there was only the pounding of my heart and the right *formae* – and then I twisted that shape in the Yale lock of the universe.

Ahead of me I saw bits of shadow splinter and fly away to either side. It wasn't perfect, but I reckoned that even the Russian Olympic judge was going to give me at least eight points for interpretation.

Then I realised that beyond the fence the land fell away in a sixty degree slope, fortunately a wooded one, and I saved myself by deliberately running into a tree and throwing my arms around it.

Beverley screamed my name suddenly and I heard an angry snort from right behind my head and threw myself to the side. There was a horrible crunching sound and a hole the size of a fifty pence bit appeared in the trunk of the tree I'd been holding. Another snort, frantic this time. Bark spooled off from around the hole in the tree and, with a splintering sound, a crack a metre long appeared above.

I smelt it, horse sweat and rough hair, and felt the weight and power of the muscles underneath its invisible skin. And then as if the moon had come out from behind a cloud I saw it, outlined in silver, as big as a carthorse, as shaggy as a pony and as pissed off as a bull in the household goods section of Marks and Spencer. Its mad black eye was fixed on me as it twisted and pulled, trying to get its narwhale horn free of the tree.

'Peter,' Beverley's voice came from a surprisingly long way down the hill. 'Don't play with it – run!'

I know good advice when I hear it, and half scrambled and half slid on my bum down the slope, using the trees to keep myself from spilling over and breaking my neck. Above and behind me the unicorn snorted its frustration and stamped the ground. I was fairly certain it wasn't going to attempt such a steep slope.

This is where the whole ape-descended thing reveals its worth, I thought madly. Sucks to be you, quadruped. Opposable thumbs – don't leave home without them.

The trees ended suddenly and I joined Beverley and Dominic staring down a steep slope planted with white protective tubes and covered with nodding foxglove. I recognised it at once.

'Pokehouse Wood,' I said.

Had the girls been chased down here? Was that why Nicole had left a bloodied strip of her Capri pants on the barbed-wire fence – no handy fence-clearing magic for her. I wondered if there had been a moment when the unicorn had gone from invisible friend to terrifying predator – the point where the mask came off.

'The river's down there,' said Beverley. 'We need to get across it.'

What with the thigh-high grass, the nettles, the springy hummocks and inconveniently foot-sized hollows, it was harder work getting down through newly planted saplings than it had been amongst the full-grown trees. We were seriously grateful to reach the logging track that cut diagonally across the slope of the hill. At least, we were until my mental map of the area reminded me that further up the valley the logging track merged with the one in School Wood. A round trip of about a kilometre – or less than ten minutes as the pissed-off unicorn canters.

I pointed this out, and it was when we turned to flee down the track that we saw them ahead of us.

Two figures, child sized, white faces pale ovals in the moonlight, one of them in a green T-shirt, the other in a pink top,

'Okay,' said Beverley. 'That's strangely convenient.'

I heard hoof beats from up the track, two sets, in what

I was to learn later was an aggressive canter – at the time it sounded like a gallop.

'Not that convenient,' I said.

Normally, I would have approached a pair of missing kids with tact and care, taking it slow so as not to exacerbate any distress. Then, slowly, I would have established who they were while trying to find out, circumspectly, whether their abductors were still in the vicinity.

However, with a couple of tons of enraged fairy tale on our arses, me and Dominic bore down on the girls and unceremoniously picked them up and threw them over our shoulders – practically without missing a step.

Beverley stayed behind us, a hand on my back in encouragement.

'Faster,' she said.

I'm young and I'm fit, but an eleven-year-old is still a weight and even down the slope the best I could manage was a lumbering trot. Dominic was keeping level but I could tell by his gasping breath that it was costing him.

We were getting close to the bottom of the slope, but there the replanted area ran out and plunged into the darkness, cliff face to the left.

'Go right, go right,' yelled Beverley behind us. 'Across the river.'

I went right and stumbled forward as the ground fell away, managed to drop the girl before I landed on her, and came down hard on my shoulder in five centimetres of freezing water. I heard one of the girls give a shrill little scream at the cold.

A hand grabbed my collar and pulled me upright – one handed – it was Beverley. She had her other arm around the waist of a girl and once I was safely up she bounded across the river with her as if the girl weighed nothing.

I scrambled after them, my feet slipping on the pebbled bottom of the stream bed, and threw myself onto the opposite bank.

'Are you all right?' asked Dominic, but he wasn't talking to me. He was crouched down in front of the two little girls and checking them for injuries. 'Can you make a light?' he asked me as I joined him.

There was a stamping and bellowing from the other side of the river.

'Not a good idea,' I said.

Both unicorns were amongst the long grass of the far riverbank, visible as horse-shaped refractions of light and shadow.

Beverley put her hand on my shoulder and stepped forward to face them across what looked, to me, like quite a narrow stretch of shallow water.

'Yeah,' she shouted. 'You want them – you come get them.'

A sapling crackled and split as a horn the length of my arm smashed into it. Hooves smashed down in frustration. But I noticed neither unicorn advanced into the river.

'Come on then,' yelled Beverley, for whom de-escalation was something that happened to other people. 'Get one hoof wet – I dare you.'

Then, with a final snort, they whirled and vanished.

'Thought so,' said Beverley. 'And stay that side.'

Dominic was swearing at his phone which, given how

much magic I'd flung around that night, wasn't working. I pulled my Airwave set, turned it on and handed it over. He called Leominster nick while I squatted down and tried to determine whether either of the girls were injured.

'You'd better go get him, then,' said Dominic to someone at the other end. 'Because we've found them.'

# PART TWO

## The Other Country

*The universe is full of magical things patiently waiting for our wits to grow sharper.*
Eden Phillpotts 'A Shadow Passes' (1919)

# 9

# Post Incident Management

Rule of policing number one – when something good falls into your lap, pass it up the chain of command as quickly as possible before something else bad can happen. Me and Dominic picked up a girl each and let Beverley lead us to the main road. This involved crossing the Lugg again, or more precisely a second stream of the same river because we'd actually been standing on an island.

'Of course we were on an island,' said Beverley. 'You think I'd have risked being that stroppy if we hadn't?'

We stumbled over another barbed-wire fence in the dark, but once we were over that we found ourselves on the lane that ran past Aymestrey church to the main road. We were level with the blunt comforting rectangle of the church spire when we heard the sirens. A traffic duty BMW reached us first, followed quickly by an ambulance and an unmarked Mercedes containing Inspector Edmondson that must have torn up the Highway Code to get to us that fast.

The girls were prised out of our grip and hustled off by the paramedics. Their parents, Edmondson informed us, were already en route to Hereford where they would be reunited at the hospital.

Then we walked back the route we'd come, only this time gloriously mob handed with a couple of dozen officers, two of them armed. We showed Edmondson both river crossings and where, to the best of our recollection, we'd found the girls.

He asked me whether I suspected that there had been Falcon involvement in the kidnapping and I had to tell him that, while there was definitely some weird shit going on in the general vicinity, I didn't have any evidence that it was related to Hannah and Nicole's disappearance.

'We'll have to wait to see what they have to say for themselves,' said Edmondson.

There was no point having officers thrashing around in the darkness, so the decision was made to start search operations, for evidence this time, at first light. And we were whisked off to Leominster nick to be statemented and debriefed. Well, me and Dominic were whisked off. Beverley said she'd much rather go back to her hotel if they didn't mind. Strangely, they didn't mind and even allocated the snazzy traffic BMW to take her back.

I called Nightingale once we were on our way.

'Good work,' he said. 'Do you think you'll be returning soon?'

I thought about the unicorns and Hugh the bee man and his memories of Ettersberg. I thought about coincidences and moon paths and the fact that at that moment nothing which had happened made any sense whatsoever.

'I think there are some loose ends I want to tie up first,' I said.

'Jolly good,' said Nightingale. 'Try not to take more than a week.'

An investigation like Operation Manticore doesn't end when you find the missing kids – but it does get a lot less fraught. Afterwards, you're looking to discover what happened to the poor little mites and feel the collar of whatever despicable scrote turned out to have been responsible. Then you've got to get enough evidence to send them up the steps to court and, if you're lucky, perhaps arrange to have them fall down a few steps on the way there. In fact, from the point of view of DCI Windrow and the MIU, finding the girls was just the start. So it wasn't unusual that me and Dominic had to give statements immediately. What was unusual was that we had to first meet up and discuss exactly what we were going to leave out of the statement. We had that meeting out on the terrace, because then it could be explained away as a cigarette break.

'We normally do two statements,' Windrow, who looked horrified. 'One with all the difficult bits left out and one that goes into our files so we have a complete record – just in case.'

'Just in case of what?' asked Dominic.

'In case it becomes relevant later,' I said.

Windrow took a drag off his cigarette and nodded.

'So, what the hell do we say you were doing up there in the middle of the night?' he asked.

'Witness trawl,' I said and nodded at Dominic. 'After Dom's success finding Russell Banks we decided it was worth running a quick outreach operation to find any witnesses amongst people who visit the area by night.'

'Such as?' asked Windrow.

'Doggers,' said Dominic. 'Birdwatchers.'

'Amateur astronomers,' I said.

'Fox watchers,' said Dominic.

'Druids,' I said.

'UFO spotters.'

'Satanists,' I said.

DCI Windrow gave me a look.

'Just joking,' I said quickly. 'Sir.'

'It's flimsy,' said Windrow.

'We found Hannah and Nicole,' said Dominic. 'Nobody's going to be interested in why we were up there.'

Windrow put his cigarette out in the flower pot that had become the unofficial senior officer's fag disposal unit and sighed – he obviously would have liked to light up another one.

'If that's the way it's done,' he said, 'that's what we'll do.'

I looked over the parapet – the civilian car park was almost completely empty except for one satellite van and a ten-year-old Ford Mondeo that belonged to one of the reporters from the *Herefordshire News*. The pack had migrated en masse to the hospital. I asked Windrow if there'd been any news.

'They're both sleeping now,' said Windrow. 'And their parents are with them.'

They weren't suffering from exposure, and while they were wearing the same clothes they went missing in, both the girls and their clothes were relatively clean. They had definitely been held somewhere with amenities and had been fed and watered. There were no outward signs of physical or sexual abuse but Nicole, so far, had presented as withdrawn and uncommunicative. Hannah, on the other hand, had talked pretty much continuously from the moment she was reunited with her mother until she fell asleep in her arms three hours later.

'What did she say?' I asked.

'Hold up, Peter,' said Windrow. 'I'm not prejudicing either of you before you've given a statement. And, besides, I haven't seen the transcripts myself yet.'

Then we went inside and got ourselves statemented which, this being a serious investigation, meant that it was first light by the time we'd finished. Victor was waiting for us downstairs – well, waiting for Dominic. But he was nice enough to give me a lift back to Rushpool as well.

I had a mad urge to stop off at the hotel and see if Beverley was awake. But between the hiking, the magic, and the strenuous unicorn avoidance tactics I was so knackered that bed seemed more attractive. And I can tell you that doesn't happen very often.

That morning the press went totally bonkers, but fortunately I managed to sleep through most of it.

I woke to birdsong, something with a call like a very high-pitched pneumatic drill. I wondered if Beverley would know what the name was. I patted the other side of the bed on the off chance Beverley might have mysteriously materialised there while I was asleep, but no such luck.

I checked my watch. It was mid-afternoon. I hadn't actually slept that long, but I felt fully rested . . . just not inclined to get up.

Objectively speaking, my whole operation the night before had been a mess from start to finish. I'd gone out to attract unspecified supernatural entities with no real idea what the hell I was going to do if I succeeded. Worse, I'd put Dominic and Beverley at risk through a basic lack of common sense. Nightingale was going to be quietly critical when I explained the thinking behind my actions. If we hadn't found Hannah and Nicole it would have looked even worse – we'd been lucky.

Or had we?

Had it really been a coincidence that two, count them two, invisible unicorns had chased us straight to their location?

My dad would have told me to take the breaks as you get them and not worry about where they come from. But my mum never saw a gift horse that she wouldn't take down to the vet to have its mouth X-rayed – if only so she could establish its resale value.

I decided that I was going to go with my mum on this one.

Eventually I got up, showered and dressed in the one pair of jeans Molly thought worth packing, and a green cotton shirt with a button-down collar that both my parents would have approved of. Having learnt never to trust the countryside, I bypassed my good shoes and stuck my PSU boots back on.

When I stepped outside I found Beverley waiting for me on the lawn.

She was sitting in a folding canvas chair by a rickety outdoor table with a chipped pink Formica top. She was wearing an orange and red gypsy skirt with matching halter top and enough beady jewellery to keep a Camden Market stall in merchandise for a year. A floppy wide-brimmed straw hat had been jammed on top of her dreads, a pair of round smoked-glass sunglasses were perched on her nose and she was reading a battered paperback book with a distinctive cover of black and white diagonal stripes.

'What're you reading?' I asked.

She waved the book at me, and as she lifted her hand a cascade of enamelled blue and silver bracelets slipped down her forearm.

'Val McDermid,' she said. She kicked a blue and white plastic beer cooler that was sitting in the shade under the table. 'I brought you something to drink.'

I sat down in the second folding chair by the table and watched the curve of her bare back as she bent down to fish a couple of bottles out the cooler. They were squat little things made of thick brown glass and sealed with stoppers. There was no label, but when I opened mine I caught a sharp whiff of fermented apple.

'Cider?' I asked.

'Scrumpy,' said Beverley.

'What's the difference?'

Beverley thought about it for a moment or two.

'It's not made in a factory,' she said.

'So, no quality control then?'

'Are you going to talk about it or drink it?'

I took a swig – it was tart, alcoholic and tasted of apples. About what I look for in a cider, really.

'Like it?'

'Let's talk about last night,' I said.

'Which bit?' Beverley folded over the corner of her page and put the book down on the table.

'The "Oh my god I shouldn't be here, we're in violation of treaty, Captain" etcetera,' I said.

'Violation of treaty?' asked Beverley demonstrating why, when you're asking questions, it pays to be literal. 'What treaty is that?'

'You know what I'm talking about,' I said, and took another swig of the scrumpy.

'Okay,' said Beverley. 'If you really want to know.' She leaned over the table towards me and beckoned me to do the same and we didn't stop until I could feel her breath against my cheek, could smell the clean warmth of her skin and see the verdigris discolouring the frame of her sunglasses.

'You see us now?' she murmured. 'Close enough to whisper, close enough for me to smell the magic clinging to your skin, close enough that – if you had the bottle – you could kiss me?'

So I kissed her – just a brush pass, by way of polite inquiry.

'Let's see if we can keep this all metaphorical just for the moment,' said Beverley, which is the story of my life, really. 'The fact that we're close together means that we're undergoing an immediate and involuntary set of interactions – right?'

'Right,' I said. 'Immediate and involuntary.'

'Now imagine you've got your face this close to a total stranger,' she said. 'What happens next?'

'I pull back,' I said.

'What if you can't? What if they literally won't get out of your face?' she asked.

'Then I'd have to take steps, wouldn't I?'

'Exactly,' said Beverley and kissed me

I kissed her back – an immediate and voluntary action. It didn't last quite as long as I would have liked because Beverley pulled back to stare at me over the rim of her sunglasses, her lips twitching into a smile.

'But if you were stuck on the tube you might have to put up with being that close to a total stranger, right?' she said. 'Because all these things are contingent, aren't they?'

Her dark brown irises, I noticed, were tinged with amber and gold around the pupils.

'So it's like personal space?' I asked.

'Only more sort of geographical,' said Beverley.

Because on any other night she might have skipped merrily along the trail with no cares at all. Running into that kind of hostility had been a bit of a shock since Beverley, according to Beverley, generally gets to go where she likes.

I pointed out that I'd had to rescue her from the goddess of the River Teme and her daughters because she'd unwittingly trespassed on their territory, but Beverley waved that away with another cascade of bracelets.

'That was a minor misunderstanding,' she said. 'And anyway, we came to a mutually beneficial arrangement.'

'Which was?'

She leaned back in her chair and reached out to tap my bottle with her fingernail. 'Drink your scrumpy,' she said. 'We're going to a party.

I did as I was told and drained the bottle. Then I followed Beverley over the fence and along the boundary of the old orchard towards the parish hall. Ahead, I heard what sounded like a big pub crowd. Wood smoke rose lazily in the warm air and I realised I was going to get a close up look at what happens when the good people of Rushpool push the boat out.

Or at least how the Marstowe family half of it did.

As it was explained to me, later, by Dominic's mum, it hadn't been planned exactly. The Marstowe family being as widespread and persistent as fungus it had already turned out to volunteer for the search teams. When they got news that Hannah and Nicole had been found, the volunteers had congregated at the village hall to wait for further developments. Naturally, given the good news, a celebratory drink was in order.

By midday, wives, parents, husbands and partners had started driving up from homes in Leominster, Hereford, Ludlow and Kidderminster. Depriving the county, Dominic estimated, of about a third of its taxi drivers and about half its hairdressers. Many of them brought food, and the trestle tables were taken out of the community hall and into the field at the back so that everyone could share. Since there were a lot of people, including a mass of children, it seemed sensible to have a bit of a whip-round and do a couple of runs to the supermarket. At some point someone decided it would be a good idea to build a bonfire – and if you're going to do that you might as well have a barbecue.

Dominic's dad, being Andy Marstowe's second cousin, qualified as one of the family and so was obliged to persuade one of the available PCSOs to keep the media out.

There were a couple of hundred people in the field by the time we climbed over the makeshift stile. I looked over the crowd, the trestle tables covered in bowls and trays and tinfoil, the ranks of bottles, the kids running around the legs of the grown-ups and, oh yes, the granny corner – Dominic's mum plus half a dozen cronies ensconced on a couple of garden loveseats that had been transported in from who knew where.

'This is strangely familiar,' I said, because you could have dropped my mum smack in the middle and she would have felt right at home – although the blandness of the food would have been a bit of a shock.

'Isn't it just?' said Beverley. 'All it's missing is a decent sound system.'

'There he is,' shouted a woman, 'there's my fucking hero.'

Joanne, pale-blonde hair spiky with sweat and dressed in a loose denim sundress, bore down on me and threw her arms around my neck. The open bottle of cider she'd been carrying thumped into my back and I had to throw my arms around her to stop her from falling over.

'God, you're beautiful,' she said, and gave me a boozy kiss – on the lips thankfully, with no tongue. 'I'd kiss Dominic as well,' she said without slackening her grip. 'But I don't know how he'd take it.'

I felt a shudder run through her back and she buried her face in my shoulder. I held her tight for a minute while she shook and then abruptly she pushed me gently back and held me at arm's length. There were tear tracks down her cheeks, but she was smiling.

'We need to get you properly drunk,' she said.

'Where's Hannah?' I asked.

'Over there somewhere,' she said. 'With her cousins.'

'What about Nicole?'

'Still at the hospital, poor thing – running a fever,' said Joanne, and there was definitely a touch of smugness when she told me that Hannah had come out of the experience much better than her friend. She then dragged me off by the arm in search of some alcohol – a manoeuvre that degenerated into a rough spiral movement which probably would have ended in us tripping over a table if Beverley hadn't interrupted and presented us with a couple of bottles of her bootlegged scrumpy.

Beverley casually put her hand on my shoulder and left it there.

Joanne looked her up and down and gave me a grin.

'Oh, you're a lucky boy,' she said. 'You want to make sure you enjoy it while you can – and whatever you do, don't let anyone, ever, tell you who you can fuck.' And with that she lurched off back into the crowd.

'Hail the conquering hero,' said Beverley and held up her bottle to clink.

'*Sic transit Gloria mundi*,' I said, because it was the first thing that came into my head – we clinked and drank. It could have been worse. I could have said *Valar Morghulis* instead.

Beverley took my hand. 'Let's see what the local food is like,' she said.

It turned out to involve a surprisingly large amount of pasta salad. While we were heaping our paper plates I saw a bunch of kids loitering under a canvas sunscreen by the parish hall and recognised one as Hannah. I did a quick scan and swiftly located Andy Marstowe, who wasn't hovering but was definitely maintaining line of sight.

I would have liked to have a quick word. But interviewing a key witness, never mind a child, without going through the SIO would have been a disciplinary offence – not to mention a serious breach of etiquette.

Beverley decided, once we'd eaten, that we needed something to sit on. So we slipped into the dark resin-scented interior of the hall to see what we could scrounge up. The overlapping OS maps were still pinned to the cork notice board, with the last set of search areas still drawn in with chinagraph pencils on the plastic covering. I traced the route we'd taken from the Whiteway Head down to the River Lugg where Beverley had done her Arwen impression. Pokehouse Wood had been searched, so had School Wood – especially near where Stan's stash had gone missing. And so had the ancient Iron Age fort of Croft Ambrey. The big question was, where had the girls been hidden for seven days? Looking at the map, I reckoned that Edmondson and DCI Windrow would be looking north of the ridge. I tapped the spot where, despite not being marked, I knew the Bee House was – they'd pretty much overlooked the whole area.

Another visit might be in order. And if I could prise a little bit more history out of Hugh, so much the better.

Beverley called my name, and I turned to find her trying to pull a stack of folding chairs out from underneath a shelf. She'd had to bend over to get a grip and I watched the play of muscle under the skin of her bare back until she snarled at me to stop mucking about and give her a hand.

We carried the chairs outside where all but two were cheerfully taken off our hands and distributed amongst the needy, the infirm, and the somewhat sloshed.

Just after five, Dominic and Victor turned up with a freshly dead sheep in the back of the Nissan Technical. I thought for a mad second that this was part of the case, but Andy and a couple of other men grabbed hold of it and manhandled it up the far end of the party field. After twenty minutes of discussion, the knives and skewers came out and I made sure I was about as far from the butchery as I could get. Dominic joined me.

'It's a country thing,' he said. 'They're all desperate to prove that they're not a bunch of soft townies.'

'You're not going to help Victor, then?'

'I worked six months on a pig farm,' said Dominic. 'I have nothing to prove – trust me.'

It can take a surprisingly long time to roast a sheep, especially when you have too many cooks. But, by seven thirty, authentically greasy chunks of mutton were being distributed along with a choice between stone ground wholemeal bread or Morrisons' best buy plastic white. I took the wholemeal and the last dollop of English mustard scraped from its jar.

By that time someone had turned up an amp and a deck from somewhere and we were treated to ten repetitions of Robin Thicke's 'Blurred Lines', because it was Hannah's current fave, before she was bundled off to bed by her father, her mother having gone to sleep in a folding chair with a bottle of beer in one hand and a contented smile on her face.

As it grew darker and the air began to cool, the focus of the party tightened around the bonfire, bottles of spirits made their appearance and I was handed a plastic cup with a quadruple measure of Bacardi which Beverley confiscated and handed on to someone else.

'Oh, no,' she said, and drew me away from the fire. 'I've got other plans for you.'

When she steered me out the front and down the lane towards the cowshed I reckoned my luck was in – which just goes to show that Heisenberg's uncertainty principle affects everything, including my love life. Instead of bed we ended up in the Asbo, Beverley driving, and heading into the evening.

Maybe she doesn't like the cowshed, I thought.

Less than fifteen minutes later we turned into the car park at the Riverside Inn, which would have suited me fine. Only, instead of going inside, Beverley dragged me down to the edge of the river. There she threw her arms around my neck and kissed me – hard. I felt her breasts push against my chest and behind them her heart beating with a frightening urgency.

She let go with one arm long enough to untie her halter and then guide my hand into the waistband of her skirt. I pushed it down slowly, letting my palm slide inside her knickers and down the smooth skin of her thighs. Her fingers fought with the belt and the buttons on my jeans and I nearly lost my balance when she grabbed hold of me and gave me a couple of experimental tugs.

I was acutely aware that we were less than five metres from a busy gastro-pub but unless the patrons came out with searchlights and dogs there was no way I was stopping on their account.

We reached the inevitable stage where at least one of you has to do something undignified to get all the way undressed. Beverley let go of me and stepped out of her skirt – laughing as I scraped off my shoes and hopped around getting my jeans off over my feet. My socks stayed on – they always bloody do. At least I got my shirt off without losing any buttons.

It was while I was bending over to pull my socks off that I realised what was coming next. I looked at the river and noticed then that the water was climbing up the wooden slats that lined the embankment, half drowning the bushes that had been planted along the river's edge.

Beverley slipped her arms around my waist and buried her face in my shoulder, the whole exquisite length of her pressed against me.

'It's going to be freezing,' I said.

'Not while you're with me,' she said.

I thought of the three sisters of the Teme.

'Aren't we sort of trespassing?' I asked.

'Nah. There's nobody home,' she said. 'At least nobody who's got an opinion about it.'

It was about then that I probably should have become really suspicious. But, looking back, had you told me then what I found out later I would have carried on regardless.

Letting go of me, Beverley stepped down into the water without hesitation or even worrying about her footing. The river foamed around her ankles, visibly rising as I watched, to cover her calves and then her knees. When she reached the middle of the river she turned back to face me. She was black and silver in the moonlight, a woman made of shadows and curves. Her eyes were hidden but her smile was a pale crescent.

'Aren't you going to join me?' she asked.

'What are you planning to do?'

She put her hands on her hips.

'What do you think we're going to do?'

Still I hesitated.

'You know you can pose on the beach all you like, Peter,' she said. 'But sooner or later you're going to have to get wet.'

So, because one of us had to be practical, I scooped up our clothes and dumped them in the back of the Asbo. Then hid the keys under the leg of one of the picnic tables. By the time I was ready, the water was roiling around her thighs.

'Get a move on,' she called. 'Or we'll miss the surge.'

Oh, the surge, I thought, the rainstorm over the Brecon Beacons that was nothing to do with her.

*Sometimes it's you . . . Sometimes it's exceptionally heavy rainfall in your catchment area*, she'd said. *It can be tricky telling the two apart.*

I cautiously stepped into the water – it was freezing and the footing was uncertain. I carefully felt my way towards the middle where Beverley waited, one hand outstretched towards me. She was still wearing her bracelets.

By the time I reached her, my legs were so numb with the cold that when she touched me her hands felt hot and feverish against my skin. She kissed me again and this time I kissed her back.

Then she leaned back, drawing me down onto the water that was supporting us in such an unnatural way that Archimedes would have given up natural philosophy and retired to the country to become an olive farmer.

I felt it suddenly – the storm surge at my back – there was nothing of people about it, nothing human, it was the smell of morning rain and the gritty touch and scrape of red sandstone. It was the laughing roar of water as it cuts its way through the bones of the earth.

Beverley locked her legs around mine in the darkness.

'Trust me,' she whispered, and drew me down into the water.

# 10

## Intelligence Led

I ended up floating in the sunlight. Beverley was asleep with her head on my shoulder and one leg cocked possessively over my groin. I yawned and wondered where we were – we'd definitely gone with the flow the night before – but I was careful not to wake Beverley, not least because we were still doing that weird buoyancy thing and I wasn't in a hurry to start sinking.

Straight up was blue sky and the dark leafy ends of overhanging branches. If I twisted my head I could see the arches and piers of a bridge that we must have just passed under. Occasionally a vehicle crossed in a flash of metallic reflection and engine noise.

My memories of the night before were already coming apart in my mind. I definitely remembered grabbing some serious air while going over a weir, Beverley's legs locked around my waist, her hips grinding into mine, whooping as her dreadlocks whipped around our heads and we twisted like a dolphin in the moonlight before crashing back down into the drainage basin and slowly sank beneath the surface.

I was sure that that had really happened, but it faded even as I grabbed at it.

I tightened my grip on Beverley – who was definitely real – and basked in the warm afterglow of someone who's just had their brains banged out by the partner of their choice.

It couldn't last. And soon I felt my shoulders scrape along a gravel bank. We pivoted around in the current and beached where the bank had eroded into an alcove. Beverley sighed and rolled herself on top of me, arching her back to look around.

'Where are we?' she asked.

'Somewhere downstream,' I said, and took the opportunity to cop a feel.

Beverley twisted around until she could see the bridge.

'Oh,' she said in a surprised tone. 'I thought we'd go further.'

'Where are we, then?'

'Just past Leominster,' she said, and twisted back to look down at me, her dreadlocks hanging down and dripping water on my face and chest. 'Eight or nine miles,' she said and kissed me. I was firming up nicely again and I would have been happy to see if we couldn't add a couple of kilometres to the total – or maybe just shag where we were, I was easy – but Beverley broke off with a sigh.

'I think we'd better get our clothes back,' she said, and stood up.

As soon as we lost skin contact the water around me turned cold as ice. I leapt to my feet screaming, and stared at Beverley who stood glistening, naked and unconcerned on the bank.

'Bloody hell,' I said. 'Give me some warning next time.'

'Woke you up, though, didn't it?' she said.

'How are we going to get back to the car?' I asked.

'Don't worry,' said Beverley as she climbed up the bank ahead of me. 'I know where we can get some help.'

For a moment I was too lost in admiration to speak, but by the time I'd joined her at the top I'd recovered enough to ask her how far the help was. All I could see was clumps of trees and the metalled track that led up to the main road.

'That's the A44,' said Beverley, pointing to the road. 'Down there and to the left.'

'Just a quick stroll down the road,' I said.

'Ten minutes tops,' said Beverley.

'Stark bollock naked?' I asked.

'If you like, you can stay here while I fetch our stuff,' said Beverley.

Across the road there was a rather tasty regency cottage with cream walls and a red tiled roof.

'Should we just ask them?'

'Come on, come on,' said Beverley and pointed. 'Civilisation is that way.'

Despite the fact that it couldn't have been much more than six o'clock in the morning, the sun was hot enough to quickly dry the water off our skin. Fortunately, out in the countryside pavements hadn't been invented yet. So at least we were walking on grass.

'After you,' I said.

'No, no,' said Beverley. 'It's only proper that the woman walks two paces behind her man.'

I set out down the verge, gingerly watching where I stepped.

Beverley said something I couldn't make out.

'What was that?'

'Nothing,' said Beverley. Then, 'Have you been doing a bit of training recently?'

I squared my shoulders – I couldn't help myself.

As we walked away from the bridge a middle-aged white man came out of the cottage and was climbing into his car when he stopped and did an actual double-take when he saw us.

'Morning,' called Beverley.

'Morning,' said the man and then, noticing me, nodded. 'Nice day for a walk.'

'Splendid,' said Beverley.

Unlike Beverley, you can see when I'm blushing, although the worst bit for me was when we reached the roundabout and the morning traffic picked up.

I tried to remember which offences you got prosecuted under. I was pretty safe from the Sexual Offences Act (2003), because the test for that is whether your intention is to provoke distress, alarm or outrage. Same with the Public Order Act (1986), because I was not intentionally looking to distress, harm or harass anyone – quite the contrary. Now, if I was a total bastard of a police officer I could probably get me on 'outraging public decency' and, judging by the erratic behaviour of some of the oncoming traffic, causing a breach of the peace.

'There it is,' said Beverley from behind me. 'To your left.'

I looked and saw, through the trees that marked the start of the next field along, a scatter of angular shapes and bright colours. It was Travellers of some kind, and when I spotted the signpost to the Leominster Enterprise Park I finally got myself orientated and realised that this was the fairground I'd seen from the terrace of Leominster nick.

I picked up the pace – I wanted a pair of trousers before some passing motorist put us both on YouTube.

There's no such thing as a single fun fair. The different rides are owned and operated by different families, each of who chooses which pitch they're heading for next. Each of the families decorate their rides and vehicles with a different livery, each has its own reputation and own history – some dating back centuries, some who drifted into the life during the last recession and never left. They say that if you're in the know you can walk into a fair and work out who's there by checking the colours. Unfortunately, I'm not in the know. But Nightingale had told me that a few of the families are part of the great informal mesh of agreements that link horse fair to showground to winter camp to the old ways and byways of medieval Europe.

This looked more like a staging area than an operating fair. I made mental note of the names, Wilson, Carter, Spangoli, Reginald. There were a lot of late Victorian steam rides aimed at the nostalgia market and a couple of genuine steam road locomotives. The nearest was a huge beast of black iron painted crimson and forest green – the name *Faerie Queen* emblazoned on the side of its canopy.

A middle-aged white woman in an Afghan coat jumped down from the *Faerie Queen*'s footplate and looked me up and down.

'Cor,' she said. 'I bet you don't get many of those for a fiver.'

Beverley stepped up to my side and smiled at the woman, who responded with a look of wary recognition.

'Good morning,' said Beverley. 'We're looking for a bit of assistance.'

The woman nodded. 'We were told you might turn up,' she said.

Who by? I wondered.

And assistance we got – in abundance. Beverley was ushered off to one caravan while I was taken off to a modern Sterling Eccles by a guy called Ken, who for all he was wearing his hair in a ponytail might as well have had ex-Para written across his forehead. Inside he found some cast-offs that would fit me and made tea while I put them on. Ken worked the steam yachts in the summer but migrated to Ibiza in the winter where he had a job as a bouncer.

'It's mostly Spaniards off-season,' he said. 'So it's nothing like as rowdy.'

He had a Spanish wife on the island and attributed the success of his marriage to his prolonged absences every year.

'I leave just as she's getting sick of me,' he said, 'and I come back when she's ready for some company.'

A cup of tea later I met up with Beverley outside. I got a pair of khaki shorts and a slightly too small Status Quo T-shirt. She got a leather biker vest and a pair of navy cargo pants. All she was missing was a couple of ka-tanas and we could have gone zombie hunting together.

Although, for the record, in the event of the zombie apocalypse I'll be looking to liberate a Warthog PPV from Regent's Park Barracks just for that little bit of extra confidence while dealing with the walking dead.

Transport for us had been arranged in the form of a Series II Land Rover which, despite the marine blue paintjob and a painfully bodged repair to the right fender, was in amazingly good nick.

Leaning against the Land Rover was Lilly, daughter of the Teme, looking pale, pierced and pouty. She wore skinny black jeans and a matching *Keep Calm and Listen to Siouxsie and the Banshees* T-shirt with the neckline cut open so that it hung loosely off one shoulder.

She held up her hand in greeting as we approached and asked Beverley how it had gone.

'Later,' said Beverley and called shotgun, which meant I ended up in the back, where I'm fairly certain a sheep had ridden not long before. A very unwell sheep at that.

For a car that was older than my mother, it had a pretty decent stereo on which Lilly played *Queen's Greatest Hits* but only, she explained, because her sister had borrowed her iPod and hadn't given it back and *Queen's Greatest Hits* was the only CD in the stereo. Maybe the sheep liked it.

We were just into the questionable first verse of 'Fat Bottomed Girls' when we pulled into the car park at the Riverside Inn. After recovering the keys I was sent in to wangle drinks out of the landlord who, because it was out of hours, let me have the ciders on the house. As

I fetched them out I spotted Beverley and Lilly by the riverbank with their backs to me as they stared down into the water.

Now, I'm not saying I sneaked up on them. But I certainly took care not to draw myself to their attention.

'You guys shouldn't have anything to complain about,' said Beverley.

'It's not me,' said Lilly. 'It's Mum and Corve – they've got a lot invested in this, haven't they?'

'I was a bit too busy to update Twitter at the time,' said Beverley. 'But I can give you the bullet points if you want.'

Lilly sighed.

'You know, actually, that's a bit tempting,' she said.

'I was being facetious,' said Beverley.

'No, seriously,' said Lilly. 'It's been that long that I could do with a reminder.'

'Well, not from me,' said Beverley.

'But you're sure it went all right?'

'Trust me,' said Beverley. 'The earth moved – that's all you need to know.'

'Your word?'

'My word,' said Beverley.

'Your word on what?' I asked.

Lilly started, but Beverley just turned and took her drink.

'That no fish were harmed,' she said, and challenged me with a smile to make something of it.

Not when I'm outnumbered, I thought.

I nodded at the river, which was back down to its pre-flood levels.

'What happened to all the water?' I asked.

'It was just a surge,' said Lilly quickly. 'Unprecedent-ed heavy rainfall in the Brecon Beacons.'

'Was that your mum making it rain then?' I asked.

Beverley kicked me in the shins and gave me exactly the same look my mum once gave me when I asked Uncle Tito why he had two families. I was seven at the time and it did seem a bit unfair, what with my dad essentially not being there even when he was, technically, there.

I made a point of mouthing a big 'ow' and acting like I was in pain. You have to do this – if you don't, they kick you again to make sure you got the point.

So I asked Lilly about the Land Rover instead and she said that it still had its original two-litre petrol engine, which I'd thought was only installed in the Series I. As Lilly explained that some early versions of the Series II had been fitted with the smaller engine rather than the 2.25 litre that became standard for the next couple of decades I grinned at Beverley, who was obviously suffer-ing. Served her right.

After a bit more car talk Lilly, having finished her cider, hopped back in her Land Rover and sped off. No doubt to inform her family that Beverley and her chump boyfriend had satisfactorily done whatever it was they were supposed to have done.

I decided that it was time for the chump boyfriend to find out exactly what that was – especially since we were still at the scene of the crime.

At the far end of the car park was the start of a foot-path that led along the river bank. Overlooked by a wooded hillside, it struck me as a nice shady place to have a chat about shady business. We walked in silence until we'd gone far enough for the Riverside Inn to be hidden behind the curve in the path.

'Okay,' I said. 'Just what were we doing last night?'

'I'm hurt you don't remember.'

'What else were we doing?'

Beverley bobbed her head from side to side.

'We were helping out,' she said. 'As well as the other thing.'

'Helping out who?'

'You don't want to know,' she said.

'I think I have a right to know the truth,' I said.

She sighed.

'You see this lovely river here? Got lots of potential but no one to look after it – to care about it,' she said.

'Apart from the National Rivers Authority,' I said.

'Not that kind of care,' she said. 'And do you want to know or not?'

There was a sensation then of disgruntled suburban driver, of car wax and loud stereo, of someone shouting in what I learnt later was probably Korean. I realised that I hadn't felt any flashes of Beverley's true nature all morning. With it came a rush of excitement and desire that I was almost totally sure originated with me – almost totally sure.

'Do your worst,' I said

'It just needed a little spark, a little passion to, you know, get it going,' she said.

I had to think about that for a bit.

'Are you saying we inseminated a river?' I asked.

'Not exactly,' said Beverley. 'It was a bit more . . . diffuse than that.'

I remembered frog reproduction from school, the female lays a huge pile of eggs and the male turns up later and basically hoses them down. It did seem to me that the species had been hard done by in the sex department.

'Are you saying I did it like a frog?'

It was Beverley's turn to pause and work something out. She wasn't happy when she did.

'Ah, fuck no,' said Beverley. 'What kind of fucked-up mind do you have, Peter? Yuck.'

'So it's not like that then?'

Beverley stuck out her tongue and made a face.

'How could you even go there?' she asked. 'Now I've got that image stuck in my mind. Frogs, please.'

'That's what you made it sound like.'

'Did not.'

'Then what is it like?'

Beverley took my hand and led to me along until she found a place where we could sit down on the edge and dangle our feet, minus shoes obviously, in the water. It was midmorning and the sun had come into its full heat so we stayed in the shade of what Beverley identified as a stand of silver birch but which looked more red-brown to me.

'You see this river,' said Beverley. 'Like I said, lots of potential but nobody's home. What it needs is something to stir it up – sometimes this can be perfectly natural, and sometimes you can give it a helping hand.'

I thought of Mama Thames, who claimed to have

gone into the river as a suicidal nursing student and walked out a goddess. And with a personality like that, was it any wonder that she sparked the process in her tributaries, or that they so took after her?

'We were making a donation?' I asked.

'I know you want to be a father,' said Beverley, 'but there were no genes involved whatsoever, no transfer of information, we were strictly catalytic in the process.'

'You're sure?'

'Tell you what,' she said. 'If we come back in ten years and he's watching *Doctor Who*, you can call me a liar.'

'He?'

'I think this is going to be a boy river,' said Beverley, kicking up spray with her feet. 'But you never know – it might have its own view on the subject.'

'You know, I'm pretty certain I'm not supposed to do shit like this,' I said.

Beverley put an arm around my shoulder and leaned in to talk softly in my ear.

'How about this then, Peter,' she said. 'You've been part of something that no wizard has ever been part of before. You know something that's not in their books.'

I wanted to say that lots of things weren't in the libraries of the wise, including plate tectonics, molecular biology and the complete works of J.K. Rowling, but she'd probably say that I was missing the point. I must have hesitated long enough for Beverley to think she'd won the argument.

'You should feel privileged,' she said. And rested her head on my shoulder.

'I shall write it up as a paper, as soon as I get home,' I said.

'You do that,' she said. 'I dare you.'

'My milkshake brings all the gods to the yard,' I said.

'Damn right, it's better than yours,' said Beverley. 'I could teach you but I'd have to charge.'

The next line that came into my head was *Flat bottomed barges you make the river world go round!* But I decided to keep that one to myself.

Back at the cowshed I had just enough time to change into some respectable clothes before DCI Windrow summoned me back to the nick for 'a discussion'. Beverley, who seemed to be in no hurry to leave the cowshed while I dressed, waved me off and climbed under my duvet for a nap while I drove all the way back to Leominster.

DCI Windrow was worried, but it was a whole order of magnitude less worried than he'd been before we found the girls. He was also chewing gum, something I'd never seen a senior officer do before in my life. Nicotine gum, I suspected.

'Nicole remains withdrawn,' he said.

I asked what that meant – exactly.

'Withdrawn,' he said. 'She's not talking to anyone, she's off her feed – unresponsive is what they call it. Indicative of a severe psychological trauma, they say.'

'Like being kidnapped?' I asked.

'You know what modern doctors are like,' said Windrow. 'They're never definite about anything anymore. It's all "maybe, could be, let's see what happens".'

'I saw Hannah running around last night,' I said. 'She didn't seem particularly traumatised.'

'She could be exhibiting a different set of symptoms,' said Windrow. 'The doctors think she may be repressing the trauma by creating an alternative narrative.'

'What makes them think that?'

'There are some fantastical elements in her statement.'

'Like unicorns?'

He handed me a wodge of hardcopy. 'I think it would be better if you read it yourself and then gave me your assessment.'

So back I went into Edmondson's office – where I wasn't going to contaminate Windrow's nice rational kidnapping inquiry with any of my sorcerous ways. Someone, probably Edmondson himself because you don't ever mess with an Inspector's stuff, had jimmied the office window so that it opened all the way, which at least meant the room was warm but not stuffy. It also meant that the drifts of paperwork had to be held down with makeshift paperweights.

I moved a stack of incident reports that were anchored by a spare Airwave handset and started on – *Statement: Hannah Marstowe at Hereford Hospital, 22nd of June.*

Taking a statement from anyone can be a long process on account of the fact that your average member of the public wouldn't know the truth if it donned a pink tutu and danced in front of them singing the Chicken Song. This means you have to ask a lot of confirmation questions and then do some intensive cross-referencing to wring out the facts.

Taking a statement from kids is even worse, because

not only do they like to make stuff up, but if they get scared, hungry, tired or just fed up with your questions they can, especially if they're badly brought-up kids, tell you to fuck off. With impunity. Now add in the suspicion that in a magic-related case it's just possible that the truth really is wearing a pink tutu, and you can end up with six hours of video and a couple of hundred pages of transcript.

You start with the transcript, a highlighter pen and your notebook.

Why had Hannah got out of bed?

Because she'd arranged with Nicole to go for a night-walk.

What was a night-walk?

When you go and walk around at night – duh!

Had they gone on night-walks before?

Only when it was hot.

How long had they been doing this?

Hannah couldn't remember. 'Ages,' she'd said.

What did they do on night-walks?

Go for a walk, silly. Look at the moon. Sometimes they would do naughty dancing.

And what was naughty dancing?

That was when you took off all your clothes and danced around in the buff.

There then followed at least thirty pages where the child psychologist attempted to establish when and where this naughty dancing took place, who instigated the idea and were there any adults involved?

Hannah was cheerfully open that they danced about in the churchyard, sometimes in the field behind

Hannah's house and, if they felt particularly daring, at the road junction by the Rushpool. Generally speaking they weren't totally naked because they left their sandals or flip-flops on. She was amused by the notion that an adult might be involved and asked why an adult would want to watch them dancing.

'They might want to know what you were doing out at night,' said the child psychologist and gently steered Hannah back to the night, as we like to say, in question. On that particular night, whose idea had it been to go for a night-walk?

Hannah said that Nicky, which is what she liked to call Nicole, had suggested it that night.

Was she sure?

She was sure that she would like to stop for a drink and something to eat and could she watch telly because that's what she really wanted to do, and she'd quite like to do all that back at her own home if that wasn't too much trouble.

There followed what is generally known as a multi-agency conference in which the police, social services, the paediatrics registrar and the child psychologist discussed their options for an hour before agreeing that yes, Hannah should go home.

I logged onto HOLMES and had a quick rummage – and there it was. An action for someone to go through all the witness statements and see if there was a reference to the girls going out at night and dancing – with or without clothing. There wasn't any result.

The child psychologist rode back with Hannah and Joanne to their house and noted that Hannah had

238

explained that they had different kinds of dances for different occasions – when Joanne exploded. The child psychologist actually wrote that in their notes – *at that point the mother exploded!* That would have been a fearsome sight even in the spacious back seat of a traffic BMW. The child psychologist felt that the outburst might have been a good thing, because Hannah knew her mother was upset and would have been tense and inhibited in the expectation of parental disfavour.

But she was shocked by the swearing, some of which she had to look up on the internet.

Hannah, now presumably disinhibited, got her dinner, then some telly and then magnanimously agreed to talk to the child psychologist again. Albeit on the condition that she be allowed to watch the Disney Channel at the same time.

When asked what had happened after she and Nicole had sneaked out of their houses and met up, Hannah explained, in a distracted fashion, that they'd taken secret paths up to the moor where they'd met a beautiful woman riding a unicorn. The child psychologist worried at the last statement – did Hannah mean a woman on a horse?

No she meant a lady riding a unicorn – side saddle!

Was this 'unicorn' perhaps Nicole's invisible friend Princess Luna?

Hannah was not impressed – Princess Luna is a completely different unicorn.

Did this unicorn have a name?

The lady never said.

Did the lady have a name?

Yes, the lady's name was Lady.

The child psychologist then sits through an episode of *Phineas and Ferb* before, quite spontaneously, Hannah explains that they walked for miles and miles and miles, then they went downhill and through a cave by a river and then up a hill where they had a sleep.

In the open?

No, Hannah thought there had been tents, old-fashioned tents made of skins or possibly rainbows. And there had been kebabs but she didn't think they were good kebabs because she'd felt sick afterwards. Then they'd woken up and hadn't had to have a wash or clean their teeth or anything.

I made a note to check the medical report and see whether their teeth had been neglected or not.

The next morning they had walked down a hill for a very long way and she'd been really tired and it was getting dark when they went up a hill and into a castle.

What kind of castle?

A castle castle.

Could she remember what colour it was?

Pink and blue and orange.

Had there been any other houses, or roads or signposts?

It had all been trees.

What kind of trees? I asked myself, and a few lines down the transcript the child psychologist also asked, but it was clear by that point Hannah had lost patience with the whole operation and wanted to go out and play with her cousins.

She didn't ask after Nicole – I wondered if that was significant.

She did remember a sort of road in the forest, it was all overgrown but the lady had made them run across it very quickly. There hadn't been any signposts or houses, apart from the castle of course.

I found Windrow in his office reading statements and approving actions which, along with going to meetings with other senior officers, is what senior officers spend most of their time doing. Rather them than me.

I asked if there were any word on Nicole but Windrow said no – the inter-agency care team would send word as soon as there was any change.

'What did you think of the statement?' he asked.

'Don't know, sir,' I said. 'Any chance I can talk to her?'

'Let's see if she sticks to the same story for the next couple of days,' he said. 'Is there any chance it's true?'

'It would be nice to have some physical evidence,' I said. 'She mentioned a cave – any sign of that?'

'From the description it sounded like it might be along the river bank at Aymestrey. There are old quarry workings down there – so it's possible.'

And close to where we found them, I thought, and the scrap of cloth from Nicole's clothes, too. That every vaguely castle-like structure within thirty kilometres of Rushpool was going to get a thorough going-over went without saying. My guess was that the National Trust was going to be seeing a heavy police presence in the next couple of days.

'Any trouble with the media?' asked Windrow.

'No, sir,' I said. 'Is there likely to be?'

'I don't know,' said Windrow. 'I don't trust them when they go all quiet.'

I promised to keep my head down, my nose wiped and to wear a clean pair of underpants at all times.

'What do you plan to do next?' he asked.

'I'm going to do what I didn't do when I got here,' I said. 'I'm going to hit the books.'

Thankfully, he didn't ask me what books. Perhaps he assumed that back at the Folly we had great big tomes full of esoteric lore within which the true history of the world was illuminated. It's true about the esoteric lore, but the illumination has always been on the scarce side. Fortunately, I knew a bloke with a lot of the books I was looking for. All conveniently located in the same place,

I pulled out my phone, found the number I wanted and pressed call – it rang twice.

'Oswald Honey,' said Mellissa. 'Best honey there is.'

'Hi, Mellissa,' I said using my non-policing voice. 'I wonder if I could come up and use your library.'

'Granddad's asleep,' she said.

'I'll be quiet,' I said. 'You won't even know I'm there.'

'Are you going to bring your friend?'

'Who, Beverley?'

'Of course Bev.'

'If you want,' I said.

'Okay,' said Mellissa. 'Come over whenever you like.'

# 11

## Service Delivery Option

In some households you only have to turn up three times before you're expected to make your own tea, draw up a chair in front of the telly and call the cat a bastard. The Oswalds' wasn't that kind of household, not least because they don't have a telly, but at least Mellissa seemed almost pleased to see me – or more likely Beverley.

'She's a bit short of female company round here,' Beverley had said as we drove up the steep lane to the Bee House. 'There are certain topics she can't discuss with her granddad.'

I'd asked her to see if she could find out who Mellissa's parents were, but she made no promises – not even to tell me if she did find out. 'Some things are private,' she'd said. 'Even from the police.'

Which explained why, when we arrived, I was peremptorily waved up the stairs to the study while Beverley and Mellissa hustled into the kitchen with cries of glee and a vague promise that refreshments might arrive at some point in the future. Up in the study, I carefully cleared space on the gateleg table and removed a stack of old *Bee Craft* magazines from the wood and leather desk chair. The cover of the topmost magazine was dark pink and showed a line drawing of a hive and almost abstract pictures of flowers in the bulbous ink style that I associate with Gerry Mulligan covers of the mid-sixties. I remember staring at the cover of *Feelin' Good* for hours when I was twelve but that was not necessarily down to the Art Nouveau stylings of the design.

The trick, when rifling through the library of a practitioner, is to find the books with the notes written in the margins. I don't know why – perhaps it was something they encouraged at Casterbrook – but I've never met a wizard yet who could resist jotting his thoughts down on somebody else's work. *The History of Ludlow* by Thomas Wright Esq., MA, FRS, Hon. MRSL, 1850 had been extensively scribbled on as well as having obviously, judging by the stamp, been lifted from the Bodleian Library. There was quite a lot about wolves and their rampages in the tenth century alongside which Hugh, I recognised his handwriting, had written *alas no more*. One book caught my eye because it had a distinctive plain burgundy cover that I'd learnt to associate with the limited editions published in Oxford for use by the Folly. I opened it to the frontispiece to find the title – *A Survey of Significant Locations in England and Wales* by Henry Boatright. Published in 1907, it was a *vestigium* survey of Earthworks and Ancient Monuments with, where possible, a compendium of any information gathered by reputable practitioners about said sites. I checked the entry for Northern Herefordshire and found listings for Croft Ambrey, Brandon Hill, Pyon Wood Camp and the battlefield at Mortimer's Cross.

Boatright had diligently noted his impressions of

possible *vestigia* as he examined the locations. But, being from the last century, he had yet to take up the ultramodern Yap scale of magical influence.

Should have got yourself a ghost-hunting dog, I thought. That's the way us go-ahead twenty-first-century practitioners calibrate our science experiments.

Boatright was an unspeakably dull writer but, hopefully, conscientious – he certainly went on at length about his sense impressions in a manner that would have made Henry James proud. I did *The Turn of the Screw* for GCSE English, in case you wondered. And I've got to say, I preferred the metaphysical poets – so there.

But Boatright certainly loved Pyon Wood Camp, which was situated the other side of the road from Croft Ambrey – talking about its numinous quality and air of ancient solemnity. He also rated Croft Ambrey because of its lofty aspect, but was disappointed because he found nothing that would verify his theory that this was where Caratacus made his last stand against the Romans. Brandon Hill gave him a weak feeling in his bowels which he later attributed to some dodgy boiled beef he'd eaten the night before. I skipped Mortimer's Cross because it was on the other side of the Lugg and, judging by Beverley's face-off with the unicorn, whatever was running around on the ridge didn't like to cross the river. Why that might be was something I planned to get Beverley to find out.

Caratacus suffered the double indignity of being taken to Rome in chains and having an opera written about him by Elgar. Apart from the need to deal with stroppy British chieftains, the Romans didn't have much interest in northern Herefordshire except as a route up to Wroxeter and places North. They did this by constructing Watling Street, which runs diagonally across England like the zip on a Mary Quant dress, from Dover to Wroxeter. This is the road that crossed the Lugg by the Riverside Inn and that I had admired from up on the ridge – imposing itself on the landscape for certain. I made a note to check and see whether it was possible that either Pyon Wood or Croft Ambrey might be the castle Hannah had talked about. Perhaps the castle had been as immaterial as the unicorns – a product of magic. Or possibly even more insubstantial – a ghost of a castle like the incorporeal apple trees I'd seen in the moonlight. If that were true I'd have pegged the Roman Road to be the one she'd described crossing. Only she'd said it was partially overgrown. According to the OS map the nearest disused section of the Roman road started over a kilometre north of Aymestrey and continued on to skirt the eastern side of Wigmore.

Hugh's annotations were extensive but cryptic, being mainly memos to himself. Things like *BA disagrees* and *See IB07, BA confirms IB06*. Most promising to me was a note on the Croft Ambrey page which read *Activity stops in 1911 BA has no explan*. It took me another half an hour of systematic searching before I located a row of old battered notebooks with dun-coloured cardboard covers on which was handwritten *Incident Book, County of Hereford* and then a year from 1899 to 1912. If I had any doubts about what kind of incidents they recorded then these were dispelled by the words *ipsa scientia potestas est* – knowledge itself is power – written in a ponderous cursive hand on the inside cover of every single notebook. And under that, a name. Barnaby Atkins Esq., MA (Oxon) CP (Herefordshire). CP stood for County Practitioner, a term that I'd heard Nightingale use. But I'd never taken it very seriously. It made me think of pith helmets and tea on the veranda with the District Commissioner. But there he was – Barnaby Atkins, aka BA – and his incident books, or IB, listed by year 99 to 12.

These were working notebooks full of abbreviations and words that I don't think meant what I thought they did. I was particularly suspicious of the number of women Barnaby had a 'brush' with during the course of his activities. Most of his cases were referred to him by the Chief Constable of the Herefordshire Constabulary, local magistrates or, and this surprised me, the Bishop of Hereford. It all seemed very informal, relaxed and entirely lacking in concern for the rights of anyone on less than £160 a year. I knew there was a section of the mundane library at the Folly which consisted of loose pages bound into ledgers – each one had been embossed with the name of a county. That must be where Barnaby Atkins Esquire's formal reports had gone – Nightingale would have to have a look for me – but I suspected a great deal was fixed on the down low and never got reported. Especially things like, *Wednesday Morning a happy bit with Mary who is maid to Mrs Packnar – most satisfactory.*

Barnaby's sexual exploitation aside, it took a while to skim through the material. I started in 1912 and

worked backwards to see what activity BA had no explanation for, and which stopped in 1911. *TH complains
that there have been no more visitations of the ghostly horses
to Croft Ambrey and that he is £5 out of pocket through
loss of custom. He claims that the visitations were common
enough in the summer months but that he has seen nothing of them since the year before last. I told him that it was
in the nature of spirits to be mercurial and that such matters were only my concern when they caused a breach of the
peace. TH remonstrated that a loss of £5 was very much a
breach of the peace but I repeated that I could not assist him
and bade him farewell.*

Ghost horses, Croft Ambrey, the summer months –
any of this ringing a bell?

Barnaby, to give him his due, did investigate further
and found that a number of other magical phenomena at Aymestrey, Mortimer's Cross and Yatton – two
ghosts and, ironically, an unearthly ringing bell – had
also ceased.

I was wondering why Barnaby hadn't asked any of
the local rivers if they knew anything, when I found this
in IB05 – *Came upon one of the river nymphs in a pool
by the bridge at Little Hereford today and overcome by her
beauty foolishly sought to grapple with her. At which point
she landed me such a blow upon the side of the head that I
had to take myself straightway to a Doctor and thereafter to
my bed for a fortnight.*

I took a photo of that to show Beverley later.

1911, I thought, what happened in 1911?

More to the point, did it have anything to do with
my case? The ghost horses said yes, but back in

those days horses were as common as people so . . . coincidence?

I heard a scraping noise from the staircase and, thinking that maybe tea had arrived, I stuck my head around the corner to see if I could help. To my amazement, Hugh Oswald was making his way up the stairs to see me – one step at a time. When he saw me he raised a shaking hand in greeting, but was obviously too breathless to speak. I moved to help him, but he waved me away, shaking his head. It took him at least ten minutes to reach the study, and at the end he accepted my arm over to a hastily cleared spot on the sofa.

He sat down gratefully and wheezed at me while making apologetic little gestures. It was painful to watch. I offered him a drink from the bottle of water I had in my bag and he took it gratefully, making sips between gasps.

'I don't think you should have come up those stairs,' I said.

The wheezing became suddenly ragged, which worried me until I realised he was laughing.

'I had a chance at a bungalow in the Palladian style,' he said. 'But I wanted the tower.' He paused for breath again. 'You can't even fit a chairlift, either – Mellissa spent almost a year trying to find a way. Perils of living in a listed building.'

I offered to go fetch Mellissa, but he was having none of that.

'She'll come looking for me soon enough,' he said. 'I wanted a bit of time alone with you. And she does fuss.'

'If you're sure,' I said.

His face lost some of its livid mottling and his breathing its rasping edge.

'I've got something for you,' he said and directed me over to a chest that had been hidden under a dusty red floral cushion and two volumes of the *Encyclopaedia Britannica*. I opened it up and smelt camphor and the warm smell of old cloth. Inside was a long cylindrical khaki bag with a rough webbing shoulder strap. I've spent enough time rooting around in the Folly's basement to know army surplus when I see it. Stencilled along the side of the bag was *Oswald, H. 262041* and it was held closed with three buckles. The contents were heavy – at least two or three kilos, I reckoned, when I lifted it out of the chest. Under Hugh's direction I placed it on the floor in front of his feet and crouched down to unbuckle it.

When I got it open a thick booklet with a dull red cover fell out – written on the front was *Soldier's Service and Pay Book*. When I picked it up a photograph fluttered out from between the pages – sepia toned and faded, of a young man. Younger than me, I realised with a shock, stiffly posing in his uniform – unmistakably Hugh Oswald. I retrieved the photograph and handed it and the booklet to Hugh, who took them without looking at them. He nodded down at the bag.

'What do you think?' he asked.

Inside the bag were two staves the size and shape of pickaxe handles. At one end they sported grips made of wrapped canvas and leather and at the other an iron cap. Branded neatly into one side was the same number sequence as on the bag, at a guess Hugh's service number, and the hammer and anvil sigil of the Sons of Weyland – British wizardry's legendary smiths.

Makers of staffs.

'Don't be shy,' said Hugh. 'They won't bite you.'

A couple of bad experiences has taught me a certain amount of caution when handling unfamiliar arcane objects, so at first I just let my fingertips brush the surface of the wood. I felt it at once, the rasping, dancing, wriggling honey-soaked warm intimacy of the hive.

'Have you been keeping this in your attic?' I asked.

'As a matter of fact, yes. Well spotted,' said Hugh. 'Take a good grip. It won't hurt you.'

I closed my hand around one staff and lifted it like a club. It was heavy and comfortable and could, if I was any judge, serve usefully as a hand-to-hand weapon in a pinch. Had it ever come to that pinch? Had this frail old man, who had to muster up his strength to eat toast, smacked some poor unsuspecting German with it? *Take that Fritz! Eat English Oak.* I felt the heart of it then, the beating of the hammers and the hot breath of the forge and behind that the rivers of steel and oceans of coal and the clang clang clang of Empire.

I don't know about the enemy, but it scared the hell out of me.

'I want you to have them,' said Hugh

'I'm not sure I should take these,' I said. 'Doesn't Mellissa want them?'

'Now you listen to me, lad,' said Hugh. 'In 1939 we had no inkling of what was to come – the end of the world can arrive with no warning at all and a wise man makes sure he has a big stick tucked away, just in case.'

I nodded.

'Thank you,' I said. I replaced the staff in its bag and buckled it up.

A more practical weapon, I thought, from a less civilised age.

'What did happen at Ettersberg?' I said. The question I'd been aching to ask.

'Operation Spatchcock,' said Hugh.

'What went wrong?' I said.

'What went right? We got greedy, we thought the war was all but over and started thinking about after, what would be our role, what would be the Folly's, the order's, England's, the Empire's.'

He looked at the bottle of water he held, as if trying to remember what it was for. 'Hubris is what it was.' He took another sip and when he spoke again his voice was stronger.

'Nightingale was against it from the start, said we should send in the RAF and bomb the camp from altitude. He said it was the only way to be sure.' He gave me a puzzled look. 'Did I say something funny?'

'No, sir,' I said. 'You mentioned being greedy. Greedy for what?'

'There were some bright young sparks before the war,' said Hugh. 'On both sides. People like David Mellenby, who said they thought it might be possible to formulate a theory that would unite magic with relativity.' Hugh paused again, eyes unfocused. 'Or was it quantum theory? Which one is the one with the cat?'

'Schrödinger's cat?'

'That's the bugger,' said Hugh.

'Quantum theory,' I said.

'Closing the gap, he called it,' said Hugh. 'Had lots of foreign friends, particularly in Germany – all practitioners or boffins – which was damned unusual, you understand. He took the start of the war very badly, saw it as a personal betrayal. You see, the Nazis took his work and . . . I'm not sure what the word is.'

'Perverted it?'

'No,' said Hugh. 'We thought they might have closed the gap, but the methods they used . . .' Hugh was trembling and I considered calling his daughter, but then I saw the look in his eyes and realised it was anger. Not just anger, but rage – even seventy years later. 'They did terrible things to live prisoners, to men and women and the fae and . . .'

He stopped, his chest heaving, and looked around his study, blinking his eyes.

'And, being German,' he said finally, 'they wrote it all down, typed it up in triplicate, cross-referenced it and filed it neatly in a hundred filing cabinets in a central bunker in a camp near a town called Ettersberg.'

'Oh shit,' I said. I realised the implications. Hugh gave me a reproachful look. 'They wanted the research data,' I said. 'That's what the operation was all about.'

'We couldn't let the Russians have it, or the Americans, or the French for that matter,' he said. 'It was obvious to everyone by '45 that this was the Empire's last hurrah. The Russians were gearing up to win the Great Game and the Yanks couldn't wait to get us out of the Far East. I think some believed, including David, that this could put us back in the game.'

'What game?'

'Precisely,' said Hugh and looked so pleased with me that I didn't explain that I meant the question literally. 'And we secured the library, the Black Library we called it after that, for all the good that it did us. Nightingale's job was to cover the extraction, and by god that's just what he did. But even he couldn't save the men who were cut off at the camp.'

And so Operation Spatchcock had fallen apart and the raiding force, over eight hundred men in all, was broken up and destroyed in detail while the remnants fled west in squads or as individuals – werewolves on their tail.

'Were they real werewolves?' I asked. 'Or just special forces?'

'Nobody knows for sure,' said Hugh.

Nightingale being among the last of the few stragglers that made it across the Allied front line.

'He made sure the wounded were on the gliders with the Library, me amongst them, and he gave up his own place so that David could escape,' said Hugh.

'David Mellenby got out?' I said. 'I thought he was killed in action.'

'No,' said Hugh. 'Took his own life, sadly. Locked himself in his lab and shot himself in the head. Wasn't the only one, certainly not the only one, come to think of it.

'You have to understand, Peter,' said Hugh. His voice was shaking and I saw there were tears in his eyes. 'I regret nothing, and if I could go back in time to my young self I would tell him to stop being a weak sister and get the job done. Sometimes you have to make a choice and sometimes you have to act on blind faith and trust that your mates won't let you down.'

I heard his granddaughter call his name from below.

'But when you do that, Peter,' he said, 'make sure you know who your mates are.'

Mellissa bounced into the room and made her displeasure known to both of us. I let myself be chivvied downstairs. Hugh looked done in and I didn't want him to hurt himself. I grabbed the staves along with my other stuff, the heavy wood clonking against my hip as I swung the strap over my shoulder.

In the kitchen I found Beverley seated behind a stack of cardboard pallets containing squat green glass jars with home-printed labels on them.

'I hope you made her pay for those,' I said to Mellissa.

'Got my money's worth,' she said and winked at Beverley, who laughed.

'You can help get them into the car,' she said.

If I couldn't speak to Hannah, I figured I could talk to the next best thing. Her mum. So I called up DS Cole and asked if I could interview Joanne. She said in fact Joanne had been asking after me, so I could visit straight away? Providing I agreed to keep it informal. Which is police speak for waiting until the subject can't see you before taking down your notes. I was getting good enough at navigating the lanes around Rushpool that I could swing around to drop Beverley off at the Swan and then go on to the Marstowe's without having to do any reversing or tricky three-point turns. I did notice that some of the press pack were back in the Swan's car park and, when I turned into the Marstowe's cul-de-sac, I spotted a photographer staking it out. He fired off a couple of shots as I passed, but it was an automatic gesture. Routine.

I also noticed that Andy Marstowe's Toyota wasn't parked outside the house, so imagine my state of unsurprise when I found Derek Lacey with his feet firmly ensconced under the kitchen table. I followed Joanne inside and he jumped up when he saw me and shook my hand.

'Thank you,' he said. 'Thank you, thank you, thank you.'

And then, surprised to find he was still holding my hand, he let go and offered me a seat opposite him and Joanne.

'Thanks,' he said again. 'It seems such an inadequate word.'

There were two open bottles of wine on the kitchen table and two glasses. As I sat down, Derek, obviously familiar with the kitchen, located another wine glass and plonked it down in front of me.

'Red or white?' he asked.

I went with white. After all, I was under instructions to keep it informal. The beauty about the whole 'coppers don't drink on duty' rule is that people think that if you're drinking you're not on duty. They're wrong, of course. We're always on duty. It's just that sometimes we're a little bit unsteady as well. Although, strictly speaking, I should have sought pre-authorisation by a senior officer of Superintendent rank or above before I emptied my glass.

I tasted the wine. A year sitting at Nightingale's table meant I could at least tell good from bad – and this was not bad.

'It's good, isn't it?' said Derek. 'South African.'

'So how's Nicole?' I asked.

'Don't they keep you informed?' asked Joanne.

'I'm just a constable,' I said. 'I'm pretty much the last person that anybody tells anything to.'

'She's coming home tomorrow morning,' said Derek. 'That's why I've been sent ahead to make sure everything is shipshape and Bristol fashion.'

'So she's over the shock?' I said.

'Not entirely,' said Derek and drained his glass. 'But the doctors think that familiar surroundings might help.'

Help what? I wondered, but sometimes it's better just to look interested and hope for the best.

'She's having trouble talking,' said Derek. 'She keeps forgetting words – aphasia, the doctors call it. She was completely *non compos mentis* when we first saw her, but much better now.' He paused to fetch another bottle – a Sauvignon blanc this time. 'I'm just relieved to have them back.'

'Peter,' said Joanne, and then stopped and looked at Derek, who took a breath.

'If something had happened to the girls . . .' he said. 'The police wouldn't keep it from us – to spare our feelings?'

'No,' I said.

Not unless you were suspects, I thought, and even then . . .

'Definitely not,' I said.

'You're sure?' asked Joanne.

'Do you think something happened?' I asked.

Derek filled his glass and topped up mine.

'I don't know,' he said. 'They've always been such happy girls – ask anyone. It's worrying to see Nicky so withdrawn and uncommunicative.'

'And we were worried the last time,' said Joanne.

'The last time?' I asked.

Derek sighed.

'It's not the first time one of mine has run away,' said Derek.

This was not in any case summary I'd read and, believe me, in missing kid cases 'has run away before' tends to be pretty prominent in the initial assessment.

'Nicole ran away before?' I asked. 'When?'

'God, no,' said Joanne. Her glass was empty so I topped it up – it was only polite.

'This was a long time ago,' said Derek. 'And it wasn't Nicole. It was my eldest – Zoe.'

'I didn't know you had an eldest,' I said and thought – if it's in the files Lesley would be so pissed off with me for missing that.

'By Susan, my first wife. She's all grown up now,' he said. 'Lives over in Bromyard.'

I filled my glass and took a sip – the second bottle wasn't as good. Not that Derek seemed to notice. I filled his glass as well.

Given the amount of wine we'd necked, I decided to just come out and ask them what happened.

'Zoe was always a difficult child,' said Derek.

'She was a perfectly good girl,' said Joanne.

'Well, she loved you, didn't she?' said Derek to Joanne.

Joanne turned to me and said in mock confidence, 'I used to babysit her when she was small.'

'And spoil her,' said Derek. 'And listen to her stories.'

'She had a wonderful imagination. Loved Harry Potter and all those fairy books,' said Joanne.

'Did she say why she ran away?' I asked.

'No,' said Derek. But he said it way too quickly, and his eyes shifted unconsciously to look at Joanne, who was pretending to be taking a long sip of her wine while she thought of something convincing to say. I gave her as long as she needed.

'It was just a silly argument,' she said, and then uttered the phrase you should never utter in front of the police. 'It wasn't anything important.'

'And we found her quickly enough,' said Derek.

'Just in time,' said Joanne. 'We were just about to call you lot.'

'Where was she when you found her?' I asked.

'By the lay-by on the main road,' said Derek. 'The one you reach if you go left towards Lucton when you come out of the village.'

I pulled out my phone and got them to pinpoint the location on Google Maps. I think they wanted to avoid the subject, but they couldn't do that without drawing attention to the fact that that was what they wanted to do.

The location was east of Rushpool, the opposite direction from where Hannah and Nicole were reckoned to

259

have crossed the same road while heading up to Bircher Common.

'Why do you want to know?' asked Joanne.

'Habit,' I said and took a gulp of wine. 'It's the way I'm trained – ask questions first, worry about what the information is for later.'

I didn't stay much longer after that, and I left the pair of them polishing off a third bottle. I wondered what was going to happen the moment I stepped out the front door and was tempted to double back and peer in through the windows. I decided not to – even the police have to have some standards. And anyway, they might see me and that would end their use as sources of information.

I arrived home at the cowshed to find Beverley rifling through my stuff.

'What are you doing?' I asked.

She was kneeling by my trunks, dressed only in a pair of blue silk knickers and a matching camisole, and systematically laying out the contents on the floor around her.

'I was languorously awaiting your return,' she said, 'but after ten minutes I got bored.'

'That explains the underwear,' I said. 'Which is very nice by the way.'

'Yes, it is,' said Beverley.

'But what are you doing in my stuff?'

'We need a present to give to Hugh,' she said. 'In return for what he gave you.'

'I don't think he wants anything in return,' I said.

'Don't be stupid,' said Beverley. 'He's given you the

most important thing he owns – that's an imbalance – you can't have that. He's an old man – what if he dies?'

She pulled out the Purdey lightweight two-inch self-opening sidelock shotguns, cracked the breeches and gave them a disturbingly professional once-over.

'Do you think he'd like these?' she asked.

I sat down on the bed and started taking off my clothes.

'I think he's done with weapons,' I said. 'Don't you?'

I decided to leave my boxers on – a man should maintain a certain amount of mystery after all.

'Yeah,' she said. 'And Mellissa would only give them to her harem.'

Beverley closed the trunk and looked at me.

'What are you doing?' she asked.

'I'm waiting languorously,' I said. 'For you to get into the bed.'

'What make you think I'm still in the mood?'

'Unlike some people,' I said, 'I'm committed to this state of languor. I've been putting in the hours. If necessary I can maintain it for an extended period.'

'I could go back to my room at the Swan,' she said.

I slowly put my hand behind my head and cocked my left leg provocatively.

'But then,' I said, 'you'd be all alone and I'd still be here being irresistibly languid.'

She made me wait at least a minute, and then she climbed onto the bed with me. There followed some kissing and some grabbing of parts – the details I will not bother to bore you with, except to say that just as we were getting down to business I paused long enough to ask – 'We're not going to be, like, fertilising this garden or something are we?'

'Peter!' snarled Beverley. 'Focus!'

Afterwards we lay sweating on top of the duvet, spread-eagled to catch the faint breeze coming in through the door, not touching except where her hand rested on my thigh and my hand covered hers.

'When you were eleven,' I said, 'did you ever sneak out of your house?'

'All the time,' said Beverley.

'Where did you go?'

'Into the river of course,' she said. 'Where else?'

'You didn't dance about?'

'On dry land?'

'Yeah?'

'Might have done – don't know.'

'Naked?'

'When I was eleven?'

'I just wondered if it was a fae thing,' I said. 'I've seen you swimming around without your kit on.'

'I know,' she said and rolled over to face me, propping her head up with her hand. 'I've seen you watching me.'

'Couldn't take my eyes off you,' I said.

She reached out and twirled her finger tips around my belly, making me laugh and gasp at the same time.

'Children do strange things,' she said. 'They don't have to be different to want to dance around as free as a chimpanzee.'

She swept her hand up to my chest, pushing ahead a little wave of water, my sweat I realised, coalescing in a way that could not be explained by momentum and surface tension.

'I was naked the first time I saw you – do you remember?' she asked. Her palm swept across my shoulders like a child gathering material for a sand castle.

'That was you in the river at Richmond,' I said. 'What happened to your wetsuit?'

'I was at mum's house and my wetsuit was at my place – when we got the alarm I had to go as I was. We went up the river like crazies – me, Fleet, Chelsea and Effra – if you'd seen us then you'd have freaked big time.'

With a twist of her wrist she held out her hand out palm up, and above it floated a globe of water.

'We'd chased Father Thames's little boys back to their boat, and we're just giving them some lip when down swoops the Jag and the Nightingale comes storming out. I was totally stealthy because, you know, Nightingale ... Mum's got views about us getting into too much trouble. The next thing I know I'm seeing this gormless looking boy standing on the shore.'

The globe started to rotate and flatten out slightly.

'You swore at me,' I said.

'I cut myself on a wire cage,' she said. 'Some stupid environmental anti-erosion measure or something.'

I extended my hand and concentrated, which wasn't easy with one of Beverley's breasts brushing against the side of my chest. *Aqua* was a *forma* I'd only learnt quite recently, but I managed to get a respectable globe of water hovering over my own hand.

'Why, thank you,' said Beverley and without any fuss

my globe jumped over and merged with hers. She saw my startled look and grinned.

'How did you do that?' I asked.

'Wouldn't you like to know?' said Beverley, and with an elegant flick of her hand the globe shot up towards the ceiling and exploded in a puff of vapour. A cool mist floated down around us, beading her shoulders and hip and making me shiver.

I could tell she knew I was going to ask again, because she leaned over and kissed me until I'd forgotten what I was going to say. After that one thing led to another, but fortunately Beverley paused long enough to do the vapour thing again so we didn't collapse from heat exhaustion.

Alas all good things must end – even if only to avoid back strain.

'And what's your plan for tomorrow?' she asked.

'Tomorrow,' I said, 'I'm going high tech.'

# 12

# Passive Data Strategy

'I knew it was something to do with aliens,' said the man from the electronics shop whose name turned out to be Albert but apparently I could call him Al.

'No comment,' I said, which of course merely confirmed Call Me Al's most cherished suspicions. He'd done a good job quickly lashing up a batch of Peter Grant's patented wide-area magic detectors. These consisted of a disposable pay-as-you-go phone, modified to my specifications and mounted inside a brightly coloured plastic box with rounded corners. One third were yellow, another third blue and the rest letter-box red.

I flicked one with my finger – it was heavy duty PVC.

'Where did you get these?' I asked.

'Sports warehouse,' said Al. 'They're children's floats for swimming pools.'

He'd picked them up on his way back from Birmingham where he'd bought the phones. Reputable shops won't sell you more than three disposables at a go, but fortunately everyone else will – especially for cash. One of the advantages of being the police is that when you want to buy something slightly dodgy, you generally know where to shop.

There were thirty of the buggers, and they filled up

the back of the Asbo. I also kept four phones still in their plastic packaging for use later.

'Did you see it?' asked Al, as he helped me carry the magic detectors to the car.

'See what?'

'There was a sighting two nights ago up near Croft Ambrey,' said Al.

We went back into the shop and opened up my laptop and loaded up the tracking software.

'Multiple witnesses, classic Type V, light source, no visible body,' said Al as we waited for the diagnostic test to run. He was surprised that it hadn't made the national papers. 'But your lot did find those kids that day,' he said, and implied that he thought the two were related – which of course they were.

The laptop ran through each of the detectors in turn before putting them into passive mode. Being cheap disposables they didn't have GPS, so I'd have to log each location as I planted them.

'Aymestrey's always been a hotspot for close encounters,' said Al. 'Some of them very difficult to explain away.'

I asked him if he had a list, and he directed me to a website called UKUFOindex.com where all UFO sightings were indexed and cross-referenced for any member of the UFO community to access. I made a point of noting down the address in my notebook.

We ran one last test to ensure that the detectors were registering on my laptop.

'Any abductions?' I asked.

'Loads,' he said. 'But none verified.'

Al, while being a firm believer that extra-terrestrial life had visited Herefordshire, was a firm agnostic on the whole abduction and cattle mutilation thing. Although he lived in hope.

'Just think what would happen if we had irrefutable proof that we weren't alone,' he said. 'Think what a difference that would make.'

It was about then that I got the idea for the investigation technique that I call, for reasons too geeky to mention, the reverse Nigel Kneale. I paid Al in cash, got his personal mobile number in case I needed a technical consult in the middle of the night, and headed for Leominster nick.

The crowd there had thinned out a bit now that the search was no longer being staged from it. MIU was still stuffed into their overheated office space. Luckily somebody had sprung for an industrial-sized cooling fan with a face the same diameter as a dustbin lid and an unfortunate tendency to blow any unsecured paperwork out the nearest window. If we'd had a green screen we could have shot the live elements to a low budget disaster movie. Edmondson had quite adamantly reasserted control of his own office, but the MIU office manager found me some desk space next door in the territorial policing office.

I was just logging into UKUFOindex.com when Lesley texted me. **Have U gone native yet?**

I hadn't been expecting a call until at least that evening, which meant I spent the next ten minutes trying to open the tough plastic clamshell packaging around one of the spare burner mobiles until finally a PCSO on her lunch break took pity on me and lent me a pair of scissors. Fortunately, disposable phones nearly always come with some charge – enough at least to make my initial response.

**No**, I texted back, using the disposable. **But I have been eating sheep.**

I had no doubt Lesley would notice that I was using a different phone but the question was, would she figure out why?

While I waited for a response, I dug into UKUFO-index.com and found that in some quarters UFOs were now known as UAPs – Unidentified Aerial Phenomena – although adoption of this term had proved contentious. The index was just that, a long catalogue of incidents listed by date without any search function, going back as far the 1940s. A guy believed he'd been abducted in Northumbria and Winston Churchill suppressed reports of UFOs sighted by RAF reconnaissance flights. Herefordshire had its own sighting in the summer of 1942 when there was a report of an aircraft crash near Aymestrey, only once the authorities arrived there was no sign of any wreckage.

The disposable phone pinged.

**Does this mean we can talk?**

'We need to push her,' Inspector Pollock had said when we discussed the last text exchange. 'She may be reaching out to you because she's uncomfortable with her current situation. We need to make it easier for her to engage but at the same time you need to push her emotionally. I'm sorry, but that's just what needs to be done.'

What needs to be done, I thought, and texted **How's your face?**

The 1950s saw UFOs popping up from Southend-on-Sea to the USAF base at Lakenheath, but nothing that I could find in Herefordshire or the surrounds. The 1960s proved to be a time of cosmic significance, at least in the number of UFO sightings all over the country. But it was not until August 1970 that I had my first close encounter. A couple travelling towards Wigmore on the A4110 experienced their car mysteriously stopping and then refusing to restart. Although there were no lights available, the couple claim that a tall humanoid, with big eyes, dressed in long dark robes, held up its hand – *just like a lollipop lady, you know, holding up traffic while the kids cross the road.* They were just about to leave their car to have a closer look when the figure vanished and, miraculously, when they tried the ignition the car restarted.

Herefordshire remained blessedly free of alien intrusion until 1977, when there was a sighting in Hereford itself and then nothing until 2002 when a young girl claimed to have met aliens near Mortimer's Cross, just south of Aymestrey. I clicked on the hyperlink and was taken to the relevant page and read the account. Unfortunately, the report was obviously a summary, not an original statement. It described a young girl running away from her home in a nearby village and being 'drawn' up the *footpath north of Mortimer's Mill.*

I checked the OS map – there was no footpath marked from the water mill, but if you did walk north from there you'd find yourself following the east bank of the River Lugg right into Pokehouse Wood.

The anonymous girl is reported to have encountered a tall alien with big eyes and scaly silver skin/clothes like a fish who talked to her for a while and gave her something to drink. The girl believes that what she drank may have been drugged because she went to sleep and woke up later that night on a road near her village.

Three guesses as to who the little girl might be.

Now, what with DCI Windrow and his team being more than just competent, one of the first things they would have done would have been to TIE any spare relatives. So it took just a five second word search to find a nominal devoted to ZOE THOMAS, daughter of Derek Lacey's estranged first wife Susan Thomas and Nicole Lacey's half-sister. They'd done a complete Integrated Intelligence Platform check so I had her, somewhat pathetic, criminal record, as well as a current address, employment and the sad fact that apart from work she used her mobile to talk to precisely three other people. One of whom was her mother.

The disposable mobile pinged. **Still better than yours.**

I called Inspector Pollock and informed him that Lesley had taken the bait.

'Assuming this is Lesley,' said Pollock, 'and not a fake to lead us away.'

'Lead us away from what?' I asked. 'This is definitely her.'

'We'll see. Anyway, I'll brief Nightingale,' he said.

'Do you want me to come back in?'

'Absolutely not,' said Pollock quickly. 'We all like you

where you are right now – a long, long way away. We'll let you know how the operation pans out.'

After I'd hung up, I went and splashed cold water on my face in the bathroom before seeing what could be safely scarfed up in the coffee area. One whole shelf of the fridge was rammed with Morrisons' filled dough-nuts that were apparently free for the taking. Dominic told me later that Inspector Edmondson believed that a squad stuffed with saturated fat and sugar was a happy squad. I ate a custard doughnut while I finished up my UFO research, but I think I should have let it defrost a bit because it tasted funny.

Al the electronics geezer had been right about Ay-mestrey becoming a hotspot for sightings – lots of night-time lights, suspicious movement in the trees, an encounter with an invisible 'entity' and an *inhuman screaming like a pig being tortured*. I made a note to ask Dominic whether pig torturing was a common noctur-nal pastime in these parts.

All of this activity had taken place after the summer of 2002 when Zoe Thomas had met her tall alien in fish scales – it was time to have a chat. I let the MIU office manager know what action I was taking so it could be properly actioned, jumped into the Asbo and headed east along the A44 for the mighty metropolis of Bromyard.

With towns like Bromyard you can tell when you reach the historic section because suddenly the houses are all crowding onto narrow pavements and they assume the squeezed frontage that is typical of a planned me-dieval town. Apart from that, and some startlingly well

preserved sixteenth- and seventeenth-century buildings, it looked like a large suburb with all the exciting
connotations that implies.

Zoe Thomas lived in a bedsit above a Chinese take-
away on the Old Road near the town centre. It smelt
faintly of sweet and sour pork and had that precarious
scruffiness that you get when someone is fighting to
maintain basic standards, but losing. There were no fast
food containers serving a second career as combination
ashtray and biological experiment, but the washing up
in the sink was at least two days old and I could see dust
and cobwebs building up in the corners.

'I've already talked to the police,' said Zoe. She was
sitting on the bed because as the guest I got use of the
only chair, a wooden upright kitchen chair that had obviously come from an expensive set about fifty years
previously and then been repainted in gloss white by
someone with no taste.

I smiled reassuringly and posed with my pen over my
notebook.

'This is just a follow-up,' I said.

'They found them, didn't they?' she asked. 'It was on
the news.'

She had a ruddy white complexion, a square forehead and a beaky nose that must have come from her
dad, and a big toothy mouth that must have come from
somewhere completely different. When she smiled,
which was rarely, she had dimples.

She was wearing slacks and a navy blue uniform shirt
with *Countrywide* embroidered on the breast. Countrywide were a chain store I'd never heard of that provided

all the things country folk needed: wellies – I presumed – organic pig feed, bear traps. The IIP check had revealed that Zoe worked full time as a sales assistant down the road at the local branch.

'This is a related matter,' I said, and she immediately tensed.

She hadn't offered me a tea when she let me inside, which is always a bad sign. According to the PNC, she'd been sectioned under the Mental Health Act two years ago but released after the twenty-eight day psychiatric assessment. There were also a string of arrests and cautions for shoplifting and minor public order offences. Generally, people who've had to deal with the criminal justice system more than three times stop offering random police officers tea. But you can but hope.

'Oh, yeah,' said Zoe.

Sweat was starting to plaster her hair to her forehead, but she made no move to open the windows and let a breeze in. My neck began to prickle in sympathy. There was a smell like microwaved rice.

'I'd like to talk about 2002,' I said. 'When you were eleven and ran away from home.'

'Which time are you talking about?' she asked.

'The time in August,' I said. 'Did you run away a lot when you were a kid?'

'Not before Mum ran off first,' she said. 'That was when I was nine.'

'Were you trying to follow her?' I asked.

She started and looked straight at me for the first time – her eyes were a beautiful hazel colour. Not only was I sure she didn't get that from her dad, I was also pretty certain I'd seen them listed as blue in one of the reports.

'Did *you* used to run away?' she asked.

'Everyone runs away at least once in their lives,' I said.

'Why did you?' she asked intently, and as she did I felt a strange little flutter like the batting of moth's wings on a window. A faint echo of the sensation I felt when somebody supernatural tried to influence me – and trust me, every single one I've met so far has tried it on at least once.

'Why did I what?' I asked, to buy time.

'Run away,' she said, and the flutter came again.

A practitioner can emulate the effect, but it's a ridiculously high-order spell so I was guessing that this was an unconscious phenomenon. *The fae are often lavish in their glamour and I surmise that they deploy it in the same unthinking manner as do young ladies their charms* – so sayeth Victor Bartholomew who despite being a dullard and a wanker has yet to steer me wrong.

'My father was a heroin addict,' I said. 'Sometimes it was like living with the walking dead – so I had to get out.'

'Would you like a cup of tea?' asked Zoe.

'I tell you what,' I said. 'You make the tea and I'll wash up.'

I'd got there just in time – another twenty-four hours and the Environment Agency would have declared the sink a Site of Special Scientific Interest and refused us access. I did briefly consider taking a broom to the spider webs in the corners, but you don't get the full Studio Ghibli from me without a sizable cash advance.

The disposable phone pinged while I was drying up. **Food is terrible here.**

That had to be a hospital reference. Was she trying to tell me where she was? Why was she texting me? Was she reaching out or trying to misdirect?

'Girlfriend?' asked Zoe when she saw me staring at the phone.

'Colleague,' I said without thinking, and texted back. **U only have yourself to blame.**

Zoe Thomas did have a photograph of herself from before the incident, a head and shoulders portrait in school uniform. In it she's smiling lopsided at the camera with her head tilted ever so slightly to one side, as if questioning the whole purpose of the exercise. The picture was big enough for me to see that her eyes were blue. I looked up from the photograph to find Zoe staring at me.

'Your eyes . . .' I said. 'When did that happen?'

'The night I ran away,' she said. 'And do you know something – my parents never even noticed.'

'I think you'd better tell me what happened,' I said, and she did. Over tea and biscuits.

Even when she was small she liked to go out at night – especially when the moon was up.

'That's the best bit about living in the country, isn't it?' she said. 'All the stars.'

I asked her if she used to dance around in the nude and she gave me a funny look.

'No,' she said. 'Why do you ask?'

'I'll tell you afterwards,' I said.

After Mummy had left, she'd started going further away from home.

'And this is going to sound weird,' she said. 'But I felt like I was being called.'

I asked if she'd ever actually heard any voices, but she said no – it was much more like a feeling. 'I wish I'd heard voices,' she said. 'It would have made the whole thing easier to explain. Of course now I realise it was a telepathic compulsion.'

I was afraid to ask from who – but I had to know.

'From aliens,' she told me.

'Aliens?'

'I'm not mad, you know,' she said. 'I've been sectioned. They kept me in for four weeks' "evaluation" and at the end the top shrink calls me into her office and looks me in the eye and says, "You're saner than I am – go away".'

'Did you tell them about the aliens?' I asked.

'I may have glossed over some of the details,' she said, and dunked a biscuit.

Definitely sane, I thought.

'So would it be fair to say that you were summoned out that night?'

I didn't ask whether the summoner had been an invisible unicorn – that would have been leading the witness. You learn about this stuff when you do your PEACE (Planning, Engage and explain, Account & clarify, Closure, Evaluate) training – the not leading the witness bit, not the unicorn. They're one of the things you have to pick up on the job.

'Not exactly,' she said and gave me a rueful smile. 'I walked in on my dad shagging my babysitter.'

'No shit,' I said, and then realised who that must have been. 'Joanne Marstowe?'

'The very bitch,' said Zoe. 'They didn't see me, of course – too busy – so I went upstairs, packed my things and went out the front door. I slammed it hard, too, but they must have been too busy to even hear that.'

'Wait,' I said, doing the maths in my head. 'She must have had Hannah by then – where was she?'

Zoe shrugged.

'I don't know,' she said. 'Not at our house.'

And I'd seen enough of the Derek and Joanne Show to know that they were probably still at it eleven years later. It was outrageous, but I wasn't sure it was relevant – I was certainly not going to write it up this time. To change the subject, I pulled up a picture on my phone of the knapsack they'd found near the B4362 during the search and showed it to Zoe.

'Was this yours?'

'Oh my god,' Zoe grabbed my phone and brought it right up to her face. 'That's my bag. I got it free with a magazine – I loved that bag.'

I explained where and when it had been found.

'I'm amazed it lasted that long.'

'So you had it with you when you left the house?'

'Definitely,' she said. But she didn't know when, precisely, she'd lost it. She certainly didn't have it when she reached Mortimer's Mill. I asked her what had brought her there and she said that it had been a light, only like a light in her brain.

'More telepathy?' I asked.

'I guess so,' said Zoe. 'I think of it being like the guide

beam like they use at airports to bring in aircraft in poor visibility.'

I bet Call Me Al would have liked that explanation.

There was a path from the Mill that followed the bank of the Lugg all the way up to Pokehouse Wood, which wasn't much of a wood back in the summer of 2002, being a bit deficient in the tree department.

'It had just been cleared,' said Zoe. 'There were stacks of trunks by the logging track – it looked really strange in the moonlight – like it was all made of ghosts.'

She'd walked up the logging track, the same one which me, Beverley and Dominic had run down pursued by unicorns, and it was there that she encountered her alien. Pretty much where we'd found Hannah and Nicole.

There was a bright light, like really intense moonlight.

'Only now I think about it,' said Zoe, 'I think that was in my mind as well.'

She was certain that the alien was real, though.

'It was like when you meet someone famous,' said Zoe. 'And I don't mean like *Big Brother* famous. I mean Marilyn Manson famous, proper famous, and it's like a shock when you see them and you think, "Oh my god". And no matter how cool you want to play it, you just talk rubbish. You know?'

I said I did, even though the only time I'd met a celebrity of any stature I'd almost arrested him, and Lesley had to pin his minder to the pavement. It's amazing how fast the famous become just another customer when there's constabulary duty to be done. The joke amongst police being, Do you know who I am? Yes, sir – you're nicked.

Zoe described her alien as tall, human-looking, only with eyes that slanted downwards and had purple irises. She wore a cloak and carried a long staff almost as tall as she was.

'How did you know it was a she?' I asked.

'She had tits all right,' said Zoe. 'Or at least she stuck out in the chest department. And there was the way she moved . . . but you're right – why should aliens even have the same sexes as us? They could have a hundred different sexes, couldn't they?'

'What was she wearing?' I asked.

'A sort of spacesuit,' said Zoe.

'Describe it to me?'

'Like a spacesuit,' she said. 'You know.'

'What colour was it?' I asked.

Zoe had to think about that. 'Silver,' she said. 'Definitely silver.'

It took a lot of questions, but by the end I thought I'd managed to filter out any of Zoe's embellishments. Dressed in silver definitely. There was also almost certainly two other individuals present, but they 'weren't in the light', so Zoe didn't get a good look at them. Zoe said that they had communicated telepathically, for which I could find no evidence either way, and in any case she couldn't remember what they'd talked about.

Nor could she be sure how long they'd talked for, but she did distinctly remember being given a drink which, disappointingly, tasted a lot like water. The next thing she remembered clearly was walking down the road near the top of Rush Lane and meeting her dad coming the other way in his car.

'They went mental,' she said. 'Dad was yelling, and bloody Victoria had to be held back – that's what I heard, anyway. The very next day my mum came and picked me up and took me away. I hadn't seen her for months and suddenly she was there.'

Zoe sighed and shook her head.

'Wasn't like I hadn't run away before,' she said.

'Why do you think the reaction was different that time?'

'See,' said Zoe and gave me a shy smile, 'that time I took the baby with me.'

'You took the baby?'

'Now you sound just like them,' she said. 'It's not like Dad or my "babysitter" were paying any attention.'

'What about your close encounter?' I asked.

'I didn't know there were going to be aliens now, did I?' she said. 'How could I have known that was going to happen?'

As attention-grabbing behaviour it was hard to beat. I had a horrible thought.

'Did anything happen to the baby?' I asked.

'Don't be stupid,' she said. 'I never let go of her.'

I thought about the gaps in Zoe's memory.

'Her eyes didn't change colour, did they?'

'You think lady Victoria muckety-muck would have missed that?' said Zoe. She got up and started piling the tea things in the sink where presumably they would stay until the next Good Samaritan arrived. I'd pretty much got everything I was going to get from that interview, but I thought a follow-up might be in order – perhaps I'd bring Beverley along to see if that would loosen her up.

I thought about Mellissa the bee woman, and how Zoe's eyes had changed. Back in the nineteenth century Charles Kingsley had written of fae and demi-fae and also of people that had been 'touched' by the fae – *so that they themselves seem strange even to themselves.* He seemed to think such people lurked under every hedgerow and I'd wondered whether back then there had been way more activity than in my time. Or it could have just been Kingsley's overactive imagination. Dr Walid often complains that, despite the order being founded by Isaac Newton, for most of the early wizards the Baconian method was something that happened to other people.

'You believe me?' asked Zoe. 'You believe I met aliens?'

'I believe you met something,' I said, and gave her one of Dr Walid's cards. He makes me carry them around for just this purpose.

'I'm going to ask a friend of mine to contact you,' I said, as Zoe gave the card a dubious look. 'He'll be interested in why your eyes changed colour. He'll want you to come down to London for a chat.'

And an MRI, I thought, and blood tests, DNA swabs and anything else he can think of. Although, judging by Zoe's expression, she was thinking a lot worse.

'I can come with you, if you'll feel more comfortable,' I said.

'Why me?' she asked.

Does she want to be a special snowflake or an ordinary person? I wondered. And compromised.

'You've come across some weird shit,' I said. 'I'm not going to lie to you and say it's an everyday thing. But it has happened to a few others – we can help.'

'Okay,' she said. And then almost eagerly asked, 'When do you think he'll be in touch?'

'You need to call him,' I said, and tapped the card in her fingers. 'This is about you, not us.'

Pokehouse Wood, I thought as I walked back to the Asbo. It all keeps coming back to Pokehouse Wood. I paused by the car to check my notebook. I'd been right, 2002 was listed as the last time before this year that the wood had been clear-felled. The time before that, 1970, had been the same year as the ghostly lollipop lady on the Roman Road nearby. I knew where the first set of detectors was getting planted early tomorrow morning.

I called Beverley, who answered with her mouth full.

'I'm having supper with Dominic's mum,' she said.

I could hear cutlery clinking in the background and the sound of the TV being ignored.

I told her I was on my way back, but she said that Joanne Marstowe had popped round and asked if I could come see them. I asked why Joanne hadn't rung me directly.

'She said she didn't trust her phone,' said Beverley.

'Did she say why?'

'Just that she needed to talk to you,' said Beverley.

'No,' I said. 'Why she didn't trust her phone?'

'Sorry, I didn't ask,' said Beverley. 'I told them you'd pop in as soon as you got back.'

Bromyard to Rushpool is half an hour by car, and I knew the route well enough to do that automatic thing when you start preparing for turn offs before your conscious mind has registered where you are. Third exit at the roundabout where me and Beverly had paraded past the locals, left at the next roundabout to cut through Leominster past the Dale factory where the half of Dominic's family who didn't work as cab drivers were gainfully employed bashing metal into structural members. My interview with Zoe had taken long enough that, by the time I reached the turn-off into Rushwater Lane just past Lucton, the sun was starting to flirt with the horizon. I drove up past the village pond and the Swan Inn, past the church, and then left into the Marstowes' cul-de-sac.

Andy opened the door – which surprised me.

'Yeah,' he said when he saw it was me. 'You'd better come in.'

He led me back to the kitchen where Joanne was staring out the back window to where Hannah was playing with her brothers. Ethan was sitting primly in his high chair, his little pink fists waving in cheerful anticipation. He gave me a hopeful look, no doubt believing that my presence signalled the imminent arrival of dinner – or at least the start of the floor show.

'If I told you something crazy,' Joanne said without looking round, 'would you believe me?'

'It depends on how crazy,' I said.

Andy stepped up behind her and put his hand on her shoulder, and she put her hand over his.

Does he know? I wondered. That his wife's been

banging Derek Lacey for over a decade and – if I'm any judge of body language – still is? Or maybe he does know, and this is one of those weird unspoken arrangements that nobody ever speaks about.

Joanne turned and let Andy put his arm around her shoulder. Behind her, through the window, I saw Hannah scramble to catch a ball thrown by one of her brothers.

'What if somebody thought that somebody was not the person you thought they were?' she asked.

I glanced back out the window at Hannah.

'Not Hannah,' said Andy.

'Nicole?' I asked, not liking where this was going at all.

Joanne nodded.

Ethan started yelling – the floor show having been a bit of a disappointment.

Career criminals and Old Etonians aside, people generally like their police to take control of whatever situation they find themselves in. You don't call the police unless things have already gone pear-shaped, and it's nice to have a group of people you can shunt all the responsibility onto. As police, how you assert control ranges from hitting people with an extendable baton through making everyone speak slowly and clearly, to asking them to make you a cup of tea in their own kitchen.

The last being what I did that evening and soon Ethan had his dinner, Hannah was fetched in from the garden, I got a cup of tea, and we all sat around the kitchen table in a calm and productive manner.

'Tell Peter what you told me,' said Joanne.

Hannah screwed up her face.

'Do I have to?' she asked.

'Yes, you do,' said her mum.

'But I want to watch TV.' She slumped in her chair and started sliding off it by inches.

'Hannah,' said Andy gently. 'Just you tell Peter here what you know and then you can be off.'

At her dad's words, Hannah reluctantly straightened up and, after a great sigh, looked straight at me.

'Nicky isn't Nicky,' she said. 'She's somebody else.'

The drama of the moment was somewhat undercut by Ethan, who demonstrated a new mastery of the mysteries of angular momentum by banging his hand down hard on the edge of his bowl, causing it to cartwheel off his tray and create a, no doubt interesting to him, Catherine-wheel effect with his dinner.

The resulting scolding, cleaning and fussing at least gave me a chance to try and think of something more sensible to say than, Are you sure? Of course she was sure, I could see that in the set of her face. But what did she mean? I was willing to believe that families ran a bit different in the countryside, but I doubt it went as far as Victoria accepting a strange child as her own. Presumably, the Nicole currently recuperating at the Lacey house looked and sounded like the one who had gone missing ten days before.

'How can you tell?' I asked Hannah while her parents were distracted.

'Just can,' said Hannah.

'But she looks the same?'

'Looks the same, yeah,' she said. 'But she isn't the same.'

I asked about clothes, dress, speech, smell – which made Hannah giggle – but she couldn't give me a single bit of verifiable evidence that Nicole Lacey was anyone other than Nicole Lacey. Not that Hannah knew who the imposter could be.

'Just isn't Nicky,' she said stubbornly.

When the brothers came in from the darkening garden it seemed prudent to release Hannah to watch TV. She shot off, and I found myself sharing a table alone with Andy as Joanne put Ethan to bed.

'Is it a good job, policing?' he asked.

'It's varied,' I said. 'You never know what you're going to be doing when you go on shift.'

'I was thinking of joining the army,' he said. 'But then Hannah came along and I couldn't do that to the girl.'

'I can see that,' I said.

'Plus I wasn't keen on the whole notion of killing people,' he said.

'He's such a softy,' said Joanne as she sat down next to her husband.

'Do you believe Hannah?' asked Andy.

'There's something going on, but I'm buggered if I know what it is,' I said.

'Yeah,' said Joanne. 'But do you believe her?'

'It's not about what I believe,' I said. 'Let's just say that it's going to form part of an ongoing investigation.'

They gave me the look I've seen from Brightlingsea to Bermondsey, in council flats and interview rooms, from people who remember the Blitz and from kids that are below the age of criminal responsibility. *Yeah*, the look says, *we'll believe it when we see it*.

'The important thing is that everyone stays calm while we get to the bottom of this,' I said and, because the universe likes a bit of irony, it was just then that the wheels came off.

'Mummy,' called Hannah from the front room. 'There's people outside.'

There's no other sound on earth like coppers turning up mob-handed outside your door, two to three vehicles drawing up but leaving their engines running, multiple car doors creaking open in quick succession and then not being closed, the sound of heavy people in big boots piling up with muffled efficiency outside your front door.

'Peter,' said Joanne. 'What's going on?'

Through the kitchen windows I saw flickers of light in the back garden as officers with torches quickly made their way up the side passage to block the rear entrance.

'Peter?' asked Joanne again – rising panic in her voice.

The doorbell rang, twice, three times – insistent.

'Stay here,' I told Joanne and Andy and walked up the hallway to answer the door. I opened it to find DCI Windrow and DS Cole on the doorstep. Behind them waited a line of uniforms.

Windrow was surprised to see me.

'What the hell are you doing here?' he asked.

'Joanne said she had information,' I said.

Windrow nodded quickly to himself.

'Who's inside?' he asked.

'Joanne and Andy in the kitchen. Hannah is in the

living room with Ryan and Mathew,' I said. 'Ethan is upstairs in his cot in the master bedroom.'

'Any sign of firearms?'

*What the fuck?*

'No, sir,' I said.

'Are you sure?' asked Windrow.

I thought very carefully about everything I'd seen that evening and made damn sure.

'Yes, sir,' I said.

'Good boy,' said Windrow. 'Go out the front and stay with Dominic until I have a chance to come and see you.'

'Yes, sir,' I said and got out of their way.

DS Cole led the mob in, calling out Joanne and Andy's names in her best reassuring we're-just-here-to-have-tea voice. I headed down the garden path and out of the immediate operational area as fast I could go. I did notice that none of the cars had their light bars on and that the entrance to the cul-de-sac had been closed off with tape.

Someone called my name – Dominic standing by an unmarked pool car. I joined him and when I asked him what was going on he handed me a copy of the *Daily Mail*.

NICOLE & HANNAH KIDNAP AN INSIDE JOB?

# 13

## Operational Compartmentalisation

I think I must have been awake for some time already, because I distinctly heard the ping from the disposable phone, despite it being muffled under the pile of yesterday's clothes. With a bit of careful wriggling I managed to loosen Beverley's embrace enough to get an arm free to grab the phone and get it in front of my face. The text read, **WTF have U done now?**

I thought for a moment and ended up sending back. **WASNT ME**, because the disposable had crappy predictive text and Beverley's spare hand had grabbed my attention at a crucial moment.

I looked at my watch and wondered why Lesley was awake at five thirty in the morning. Thankfully, Beverley let go of my dick and rolled over, dragging the sheet with her until she became a white lump in the middle of the bed. I took this as my cue to get up and, as quietly as possible, have a shower and get dressed.

'Where are you going?' asked the lump in the bed while I was pulling my boots on.

'I'm off to conduct science experiments,' I said. 'Want to come?'

Beverley lifted her head and looked at me suspiciously. 'What kind of science?'

'Thaumatological,' I said.

'You're taking the piss,' she said.

'Straight up,' I said.

Beverley unwound from the bed, stood up and arched her back – palms pressing against the low ceiling of the cowshed. Then she shook out her dreads before looking at me, head tilted to one side.

'Is it important?' she asked.

I was so tempted to say no, but you can't keep putting shit off.

'A bit,' I said.

'Give me ten minutes for a shower,' she said.

While I waited I pulled up the day's headlines. The *Daily Mail* had the scoop but the media had caught the smell of blood in the water and twenty-four-hour news outlets were running the bulletin every half an hour, with a teaser on the quarter in case your attention span was that short.

According to the *Mail*, who seemed to be the only outlet with any actual facts, Nicole Lacey had accused Hannah's parents of luring them out of their homes with the promise of free gifts. Then they and persons unknown were supposed to have kidnapped them, or at least Nicole, and made them walk all the way to Wales where they had to sleep in a tent until they were made to walk all the way back again. Sharon Pike speculated in a separate column that making the children walk was a cunning ploy to avoid CCTV and automatic number plate recognition systems. She wrote of the existence of a network of temporary camps frequented by new age travellers, migrant labourers, gypsies, asylum seekers and Romanians who were, allegedly, responsible for the shocking increase in rural crime, unemployment and, some said, spreading foot and mouth.

'That's just stupid,' Dominic told me later. 'Nobody believes that Romanians spread foot and mouth – everybody knows that was down to Tony Blair in an attempt to destroy the rural way of life.'

The rolling news networks loved the idea of a shadowy network of camps. It gave them hours of talking heads and a chance to stick a body from Migration Watch or UKIP up against a government spokesman or, even better, someone from the Joint Council for the Welfare of Immigrants in the hope they would both kill and eat each other live on air.

Beverley stepped out of the shower and asked whether there were going to be brambles. I said it was likely. She sniffed yesterday's clothes, kept the jeans, produced an emergency pair of knickers from god knows where, and replaced last night's crop top with a buff linen waistcoat she'd retrieved from the trunk. I winced as she tossed her dirty clothes back on the bed. There was a delay while I found an empty carrier bag and made her put them in there. She seemed to find this inordinately funny, but that's because her mum hadn't been making her iron her own shirts from the age of six onwards.

I watched her tie up her dreads into a ponytail, unconsciously biting her lower lip as she concentrated on getting the elastic tie exactly the way she wanted it. She caught me watching, her eyes narrowing as she smiled at me.

'Why are you hanging about?' she asked. 'I thought we were in a hurry.'

So we climbed into the Asbo with its cargo of magic detectors in the back and headed for School Wood. Beverley asked what had happened the night before.

'Nicole has alleged that Joanne and Andy, or rather some of their relatives, abducted her and Hannah,' I said.

'Fuck!' said Beverley.

'Not only that, but Nicole came out with her story in front of Sharon Pike, freelance journalist and newspaper columnist,' I said. 'With predictable results.'

Which were DCI Windrow turning up mob-handed to 'interview' Andy and Joanne while forensics went over their house with a set of tweezers and a UV light source. Which was a waste of time, because searching that house had happened day one of Operation Manticore – even Beverley spotted that.

'It's in the papers now,' I said. 'Windrow's got to dot his I's and cross his T's etcetera etcetera.'

He'd also told me to stay out of sight.

'It's all got complicated enough,' he'd said, 'without dragging any "additional" elements into the case.' He was too professional to say it out loud, but it was clear he expected the Marstowes to be eliminated from inquiries pretty damn fast – at which point he was hoping the media, and with them the politics, would go away. 'I hear you've got something lined up with Dominic tomorrow,' he'd said. 'Good. You two can keep each other out of trouble.'

I thought I heard, as if from somewhere far away,

Lesley giving a hollow laugh. But I'm pretty sure it was my imagination.

'Are you okay coming back up here?' I asked as the Asbo climbed the hill to the top of the ridge. 'You're not going to be stepping on anyone's territorial imperative, are you?'

'You worry about your job,' said Beverley. 'I'll worry about mine.'

Dominic was waiting for us at the top of the lane. He held the gate open so I could drive in and park by the skeleton of an ancient barn preserved by the National Trust. Stan was waiting with him, both of them sweating even in the shade of the western hemlocks – I think it must have been even hotter than that second day when Dominic had brought me up here to see about his 'mate's' slash.

Stan was wearing the same grubby boiler suit I'd seen her in when we first met, still with the arms tied around her waist. But, in deference to the heat, she was wearing a 1950s blue and white striped bikini top that would have suited a saucy seaside postcard. Her skin was the colour of skimmed milk and I was worried she was going to burn.

Stan was with us because she had a quad bike and trailer which promised to take the slog out of transporting the detectors. The plan was that we would split up, me and Beverley going downhill to Pokehouse Wood while Dominic and Stan deployed the detectors further along the ridge, on the logging track we'd met Princess Luna on, and on Croft Ambrey and the footpaths that converged on it.

'That's a big area,' he said as we piled the detectors into the trailer. 'What's the range of these things?'

'I don't know,' I said. 'It's not exactly an exact science. Put them at crossroads and places that look like,' I hate making stuff up as I go along, 'gateways,' I said. 'Transitional points between one place and another.'

'Boundary points,' said Stan. 'Got you.'

Dominic had brought two rolls of blue and white police tape to wrap around the detectors – the better to deter tampering.

'You star,' I said, after he'd explained. 'Do you think it will work?'

'With the walkers and tourists,' he said. 'But the local buggers will have it away with anything.' He glared at Stan, who gave him a bland look.

We divided up the detectors, the bulk going in the trailer, and me and Beverly watched Stan rattle off on the quad with Dominic riding pillion behind her.

'I notice we have to carry ours,' said Beverley. We each had a courier bag for our share of the detectors. With the strap across our shoulders the weight was even but they banged against our hips when we walked.

'Yeah,' I said. 'But it's downhill, isn't it?'

This time, instead of blowing the shit out of various fences, we followed the official right of way, making sure to stay on the path, close gates behind us and prevent our hypothetical dog from chasing the livestock.

We crossed over into a meadow where the long grass was overrun with clusters of yellow flowers.

'Buttercup,' said Beverley. 'It's poisonous, so cows

and sheep won't graze here – they must be keeping this field for hay.'

Further on we reached the wire fence that marked the edge of the woods and the drop down to Pokehouse Wood and the River Lugg. We found the stile that I'd last seen from the other side when I'd spotted the blood-stained strip of cloth the week before. There was still police tape marking the forensic search around where the cloth had hung on the barbed-wire fence.

Beverley clonked her bag pointedly at my feet and so I took the first detector from hers. Then it was a simple matter to wire it to the base of one of the stile's posts and wrap some police tape around it a few times. I un-shipped my tablet and checked that the detector had some bars and, satisfied it could get a signal out, I noted its position using the GPS co-ordinates app on my good phone.

'Done,' I said.

'You just brought me along to help carry these,' said Beverley and shook her bag at me.

'Actually,' I said, 'I was hoping you'd tell me about the landscape – you being a proper expert and everything.'

Beverley looked around. 'What do you want to know?'

'I don't know,' I said. 'Stuff.'

'Stuff,' said Beverley. And then she put her arm around my neck and kissed me. It went on for a while too – there was some tongue in there and everything. Things might possibly have got a bit impromptu, if not alfresco, except she let go of me and laughed.

'What we're standing on is a limestone ridge,' she said. 'Silurian limestone, as a point of fact. Very permeable, the rain goes right through it and down to the river valley where it belongs, leaving up here nice and well drained – hence the buttercups and the harebell along the hedges.' She put her hands on her hips and cocked her head to one side. 'Helpful?'

'Interesting,' I said.

We followed the path down the heavily wooded slope, past trees that Beverley identified as yew, elder and some oak. I set up another detector where the footpath reached the cleared area which marked the start of the Pokehouse Wood. While I did that, Beverley wandered out into the stands of foxglove that stood between the newly planted saplings. When I'd finished inputting the location I turned to find her gone.

I called her name and she rose out of the nodding purple flowers, the hot sunlight making amber highlights on the strong curve of her upper arms and her neck. I felt a mad rush of desire, not just sex but something wilder and stronger and almost like worship. I wanted to carve statues of her and paint her image on the walls of my cave, where the firelight would make them flicker and jump. I wanted to wrap myself in an animal skin and dance around the campfire wearing a necklace of bear teeth. Had she just asked, I'd gladly have gone mammoth hunting in her honour – although I'd only do that armed with a suitably high-powered rifle. There are limits, you know.

There was definitely power in that place, wild and weird and fae.

'Did you feel that?' I asked Beverley.

'Feel what?' she asked.

I took a deep breath. It's observable but not reliably observable. It can have a quantifiable effects, but resists any attempt to apply mathematical principles to it – no wonder Newton kept magic under wraps. It must have driven him mental.

Or maybe not – the guy had spent almost as much time on calculating the mystical dimensions of the Temple of Solomon as he had developing the theory of gravity. Maybe Newton liked his life compartmentalised, too.

Hugh Oswald had claimed that Nightingale's old friend David Mellenby had found a way to close the gap between Newtonian magic and quantum theory. What might have happened if that had been true, what kind of future had died during that terrible rout from Ettersberg?

'You want to know something strange?' asked Beverley.

'I don't think mammoth goes well with palm oil,' I said.

She hesitated, and then took that as a 'yes'.

'These flowers are weird,' she said, looking at the foxglove.

'They're poisonous, you know,' I said.

'They also like an acidic soil,' said Beverley. 'Which this shouldn't be – not when it's built up on limestone like this.'

'Because calcium carbonate is alkaline?' I asked.

'Exactly,' said Beverley. 'Judging by the trees on the slope, it's pretty alkaline until we get to this cleared area.'

'Can you get local patches of acidity?'

'You can get local patches of anything,' said Beverley. 'Heavy rainfall can leach out the calcium and the potassium, but,' she gestured at the slope with its white support tubes poking out amongst a sea of purple foxglove, 'I don't think so. And this is proper land management we're looking at here, so I can't see the National Trust smothering the land in fertiliser. And even if they did, the run off would have gone into the Lugg and I would have noticed it.'

I put talking to the land management team at Croft Castle on my list of things to do.

'And everything goes well with palm oil,' said Beverley. 'Providing you use enough palm oil.'

I secured another detector at the place where the footpath crossed the logging track. Then we walked down the track to where I judged we'd found the two girls and placed a detector there. The bulk of the detectors were laid out at various strategic points around the wood – anywhere that looked like it was, or might have been, a path at some point in the past. I had planned to walk as far as the Roman Road and place at least four detectors at intervals along that, but looking out across the field where we found the dead sheep I realised I was down to just the spares I wanted to keep against contingencies. I'd have to get Stan and Dominic to swing down and place the ones on the road. So we walked back up through the wood to where we'd left the Asbo.

Strangely, it was while crossing the buttercup meadow that I remembered the way foxglove was used to make a tea to drive away babies that were suspected of being changelings – possibly a form of sanctioned infanticide.

*Changelings*, I thought, and remembered Hannah's absolute certainty that the returned Nicole was not the girl she grew up with.

Changelings – the babies that fairies left with human parents when they nicked a human child. In these enlightened times we didn't have to rely on poisoned tea to determine the ancestry of a child. Although it has to be said that while the science was relatively straightforward, it was the legal issues that were going to be complicated.

'A changeling?' said Windrow, and I could I tell from his tone of voice that I'd used the wrong term.

'A substitution of one child for another,' I said. 'Could be classified as an abduction.'

Windrow's mouth worked, and I suspected he was wondering whether it was medically advisable for him to have another piece of nicotine gum.

You may have chosen the wrong moment to quit smoking, I thought, but I didn't say, because you don't – not to chief inspectors.

'I'm assuming,' he said at last, 'that you have a line of inquiry you'd like to follow.'

'We take DNA samples from both girls and their parents and then we test to see if they are who we think they are,' I said.

'And what do we tell them we're doing it for?'

'For elimination purposes,' I said.

'I know the Met has a reputation for being a bit free and easy with the facts,' said Windrow. 'But you do realise that we're talking about the victims and the victims' families here, and that we're operating with the full sodding media pack camped outside our door. They may not know what the story is, but they can smell there's a story. Not to mention that Sharon bloody Pike has an inside line to the Lacey family. Do you really think that, given all this, it would be a good idea to obtain DNA samples under false pretences?'

'Sir . . .' I said as neutrally as possible in the time honoured tradition of interrupting your senior officer when he's being rhetorical.

'If she is a . . . "substitute",' said Windrow, 'what's the worst case scenario?'

'If she's been swapped, then Nicole Lacey is still being held by whoever made the change,' I said. 'In which case, this is still a live kidnapping inquiry.'

And if there's a case review and it turns up that we didn't do our due diligence, then it wasn't going to be me answering the tricky questions, was it?

Windrow nodded.

'I want you to get the necessary authorisation from your governor and run this as an official Falcon line of inquiry,' he said. That covered him from any case review, and it also gave him plausible deniability should it blow up in the press. 'I also want you to be the one to approach the families and get the samples.'

I said I was fully prepared to do that.

'And don't discuss this with anyone but me and your boss – understood?'

I understood. He didn't want any leaks to the press – or at least, in the event of there being a leak, he wanted to make sure it wasn't traced back to the MIU or, bonus, the West Mercia Police. Mind you, this sort of compartmentalisation suited Nightingale down to the ground – someone had once told him in 1939 that loose lips sink ships and he obviously hadn't seen any reason to change just because the war was over.

'Yes, sir,' I said and rushed off to obey.

Nightingale has his own attitude to the modern world. If he deems something necessary or useful – modern police communications, for example – he is perfectly willing to learn how to use it. This he does with frightening speed and efficiency, although anyone who's spent a couple of months mastering a *forma* will find even the deeper mysteries of the Airwave handset a piece of piss. Still, I wasn't looking forward to explaining to him the finer points of DNA fingerprinting, not least because I'd forgotten quite a lot of it myself. I was just about to start looking things up on the internet when I realised that it didn't have to be me that explained it to Nightingale – I just needed to convince Walid, and then let him do all the heavy lifting.

'Changeling, eh,' said Dr Walid.

'A possible substitution,' I said. I was out on the canteen terrace, which was in full sunlight and no breeze at all, but got the best phone bars in the nick.

'But not as a child?'

'As an eleven-year-old,' I said.

'That would be a rare thing indeed,' he said. 'I'll talk to Thomas. Once he says yes, I'll email you instructions as to how I want you to handle the samples.'

Once he says yes, I thought. Walid really wants that changeling DNA.

I heard a mechanical organ playing in the distance and looking over, across the railway tracks and the bypass, I could just see a swirl of movement amongst the trees. I realised it was a Sunday and the Steam Fair was open for business – not just a staging post after all. Very faintly, over the mechanical organ, the traffic noise from the bypass and the thrum of the generators, I could hear the sound of excited children.

How many of those kids would have been kept indoors until now?

Once I was done with Dr Walid it was time to check in with Inspector Pollock, who seemed to think it was time I took the initiative. I pulled out the disposable phone and texted, **Talk to me!**

'She's not going to fall for this, you know,' I'd told Pollock.

'You never know,' he'd said. 'And it costs us nothing.'

I really hoped so.

While I was waiting to see which train would wreck first, I drove into Leominster proper and put in an order for another twenty detectors on the basis that I could always take them back to the Folly if I didn't use them. Call Me Al was delighted. I was probably doubling his turnover that month. I thanked him for pointing out the UKUFOindex site and he asked whether I wanted to meet up with him and his mates at the pub later. I said I'd see if I was free.

I found a café off the main square which was decorated like a tea shop and served as fine a medley of greasy comestibles as any transport café in the country. Although they did share the regional obsession with providing a lineage for not just your pig but your eggs and potatoes as well. Criminally, I couldn't tell you what it tasted like on account of the fact that I was practically drumming the table by that point. I was just about to distract myself by calling Beverley when Nightingale called and gave me the go-ahead to collect samples.

'I know circumstances are fraught,' said Nightingale. 'But do try to be discreet.'

I checked my tablet and found I had an email with Walid's instructions on how he wanted the samples collected, labelled and transported. *I don't need to tell you how important getting a DNA sample from a changeling might be,* he wrote. We'd discussed setting up a database of 'interesting' DNA samples, but apparently there were legal issues. Patient confidentiality and human rights and all that.

Dominic's mum had a fully equipped office.

'From when she thought she was going to run this place as a B&B,' said Dominic, as he helped me print off the consent forms I was required to get the parties to sign. 'Do you want me to help?'

'Your governor doesn't want you involved,' I said. 'Besides, you must have actions piling up back at the nick.'

'They've got me reviewing statements during the initial investigation,' he said. 'Occasionally I punch myself in the face to keep awake.'

'If anything exciting happens, I'll let you know,' I said.

To avoid just that, I started with the Marstowes. And,

to avoid the posse of photographers at the end of their cu-de-sac, I cut through the adjacent woods, hopped over their back fence and knocked on their kitchen door. Andy answered. He gave me a puzzled look as if trying to work out who the hell I was.

'You'd better come in,' he said.

He sat me down in the kitchen and offered me a beer which I declined in favour of a cup of tea. Despite the open window the kitchen was stuffy and there was the starchy overheated smell of baby food. Andy said that Ethan was poorly and that Joanne was upstairs dosing him with Calpol and would be down in a minute.

I asked him for samples and showed him the forms. He asked why and I decided to tell him the truth.

'If Nicole is not really Nicole, then we should be able to tell by comparing her DNA to her parents,' I said.

'I get that,' he said. 'Why do you need ours?'

'In case Hannah was the one that was swapped,' I said. 'This saves us having to make two trips to the lab.'

I watched his face as he parsed that and then he chuckled grimly.

'Belt and braces,' he said and signed the forms.

I took the swab using the collection kit that I'd borrowed from Dominic who, I realised, had left the Boy Scout scale behind and was now verging on Batman levels of crazy preparedness.

When Joanne came down, Andy persuaded her to sign and swab and then she persuaded Hannah – who wouldn't stop giggling. Then I mounted a detector at the front and back doors, or rather I watched as Andy neatly screwed them into position himself.

'Just a precaution,' I said.

'I don't like the idea of being watched,' said Joanne.

'This doesn't detect you,' I said. 'It's not a motion sensor.'

'What does it do?' asked Andy.

'Hopefully,' I said, 'if certain conditions are met, it will stop working.'

I slipped out over the back fence and made my way down the backs of the village gardens to the Old Vicarage and the Laceys. On the basis that what the eyes don't see the mouth can't complain about, I planted a detector in their huge back garden before banging on their back door.

They met me in what estate agents call a reception room, what I would have called a living room and no doubt Nightingale called a parlour – unless it was a drawing room. In a country home this is not a sign of favour.

They didn't offer me tea.

Derek made a big production of checking the consent forms while Victoria sat beside him on the sofa with her lips compressed down to a line and her hands jammed between her knees.

'I really don't see why this is necessary,' he said.

'A big case like this,' I said, 'even forensic evidence can get challenged. You know, as to collection and that sort of thing. Better to have two sets of samples – that's why they've got me collecting it because I'm not from West Mercia Police and I'm going to send my samples to a lab in London. Separate force, separate samples, separate lab, separate chain of custody.'

Derek was nodding his understanding but Victoria was just staring at me, not angry or hostile, just impatient with one more aggravation she didn't need right now – thank you very much. Still, like the Marstowes, they signed the consents and opened their mouths for the cheek swab.

Victoria insisted on accompanying me when I took the sample from Nicole. I didn't tell her that I was pretty much legally required to have an adult present – it's easier to manage people if they maintain a sense of agency. She led me to the den where Nicole sat amongst a pile of discarded sweet wrappers and empty 600ml plastic Pepsi bottles. She had one in her hand when I walked in and was banging it idly against the floor – fascinated by the *boing* noise it made when it hit. The flat screen TV was showing *Hotel Transylvania* with the mute on – I judged it had got about halfway – and one of the Wii controllers nestled in an empty box of Milk Tray chocolates.

'Nicky, love,' said Victoria. 'There's someone here to see you.'

Nicole stopped banging the Pepsi bottle and turned to look at us.

I'd made a point to study pictures of Nicole Lacey taken just prior to her disappearance. In them she'd looked pretty but slightly odd, the combination of the straight blonde hair and the dark brown eyes meant that even with her photograph face on she stared out of the pictures with a peculiar intensity. She looked exactly the same in the flesh and if the eyes were different or changed then I couldn't see it.

For a moment I was sure that my changeling theory had been totally wrong, but then Nicole smiled at me. It was a wonderful *it's my birthday and I've got a pony* smile. As sincere as a cash donation and equally as suspect.

'Who are you?' she asked, springing to her feet.

'My name is Peter Grant,' I said.

'Peter wants to take a—' started Victoria, but Nicole didn't seem to hear.

'Mummy,' she said. 'There's no more chocolate. Can I have some more chocolate?'

I felt the glamour underneath, and it was strangely harsh and commanding. A play-princess type of glamour, pink and sparkly and hard as plastic. Still, it had its effect. Victoria bobbed her head.

'Of course, Princess,' she said. 'Anything for you.'

The little girl kept her eyes on Victoria's back until she was safely out of the room, before turning her smile on me again.

'You've got a funny face,' she said.

'I'm here to take a sample,' I said, mainly just to buy time while I tried to work out what I was dealing with.

Was she a changeling? Nicole and Hannah had only been missing seven days. How would they, whoever *they* were, produce a duplicate in that time? Mind you, there was a spell, *dissimulo*, that could warp flesh and bone to fit a certain image. Could a substitute have been sculptured to look like Nicole? That would be very bad – when *dissimulo* let go the warped tissue fell apart. It was how Lesley had lost her face. I felt a twist of fear in my stomach that must have shown on my face because the little girl, who may or may not have been Nicole, frowned at me.

And the frown was like a slap in the face – or would have been, had I not built up a resistance to this sort of thing. Still, the girl didn't have to know that. I made a point of looking stricken.

'Do you like chocolate?' she said. 'I like chocolate – I don't know why anybody eats anything else.'

'Chocolate's nice,' I said. 'So your name is Nicky, is it?'

There was a smear of chocolate in the corner of her mouth and a sticky sweet wrapper caught in the hair behind her ear.

'I'm Nicole,' she said primly. 'But you can call me Princess.'

'Well, Princess,' I said, and pulled up out my sample kit and showed her the cotton bud. 'I need to swab the inside of your cheek.'

'What if I don't want you to?' she asked.

'That wouldn't be very nice,' I said. 'A proper princess would want to be helpful.'

She gave that comment the consideration it deserved.

'I think no,' she said, and I got the full changeling Princess Barbie effect complete with Ken's house pool and the train-to-trot homicidal unicorn collectible set with realistic neighing. 'But I don't mind if you think that you did.'

You're so busted, I thought.

I was just dithering about what to do next when I was saved by the return of Victoria with another woman in tow.

I recognised her at once.

'Aunty Sharon's here to see you again,' said Victoria.

The journalist cooed hello to the fake Nicole before turning her beady eyes on me.

'What are you doing here?' she asked.

'I'm just on the way out,' I said, and with that I beat a hasty retreat. But not before half-inching a couple of empty Pepsi bottles. The consent forms merely specified collected biological sample – it didn't specify how I had to collect it.

# 14

# Media Compliant

Now, I was pretty sure that the girl currently living with Victoria and Derek Lacey was a changeling, swapped out by a unicorn-employing supernatural person or persons unknown some eleven days previously. But I didn't have any proof. Yes, she was alarmingly weird. But then so were a lot of children – including, it has to be said, some of my relatives. And, yes, she displayed an ability – the glamour – that I'd assumed resided only with practitioners, Genius Loci like Beverley Brook and the fae. On the other hand, her appearance was unchanged and her own parents fully accepted her as their child. Worse, the media in the form of Sharon Pike, weekend cottage owner and newspaper columnist, had decided that the child was truly Nicole Lacey.

After a careful risk assessment, I determined that rushing in mob-handed and seizing the child would be hazardous, if not actually illegal. In the meantime, I suspected that the girl currently known as Nicole wasn't facing a substantial risk of anything other than hyperglycaemia.

We were going to have to wait for the DNA tests which, according to Dr Walid, would be ready by the next afternoon at the earliest. I spoke to Nightingale, who said he would ask DCI Windrow to maintain a close watch on 'Nicole' and make sure she didn't wander off anywhere.

'Any chance of you getting up here?' I'd asked.

'That rather depends on how Lesley responds to your last text,' he'd said. 'Whatever Inspector Pollock thinks, we are ultimately responsible for Constable May. And it would be risky in the extreme if he tried for an arrest without me present.'

I told Nightingale I couldn't see Lesley falling for such an obvious trap, but he disagreed.

'Not consciously,' he'd said. 'But nobody changes their allegiance so absolutely overnight – she may be looking for a way back.'

I thought of the Lesley May I knew, who was more decisive than a bag full of judges. I still thought it was unlikely, but what did I know?

Nightingale did agree that if Lesley hadn't respond ed within another twenty-four hours, he'd move on site and review my risk assessment in situ – he didn't say it exactly like that of course.

'Give it a day,' he'd actually said. 'If we still haven't heard anything, I'll pop up in the Jag and see what's what. Abdul assures me that all the blood tests will be completed by then.'

So, once I'd ensured the samples were couriered off, I met up with Beverley, Dominic and Victor two villages over in the back garden of the Boot Inn where I had lightly battered Scottish cod fillet, hand cut chips and garden peas.

It was late enough for the sunlight to be slanting into the garden from the west and be cut into shadows by the shades over the tables and splash on the potted trees arranged along the fence.

'Are there no just-pub pubs around here?' I asked.

Dominic blamed Ludlow which, having become a major foodie centre, had raised the pretentions of all the eateries within a fifty miles radius.

'Even the places in Wales,' he said.

'Good for business, if you can get plugged into the supply network,' said Victor who, bizarrely, turned out to be a vegetarian. 'I don't mind raising and slaughtering them,' he'd said when I asked him about it. 'I just draw the line at eating them.' He had the roasted shallot tarte Tatin, roasted pepper, goat's cheese, artichoke and roasted pepper salad.

'That's one too many roasteds in the menu,' said Dominic.

I checked my mobiles at regular intervals – both of them – the disposable and my second-best Android which Call Me Al had rigged to alert me if anything tripped a detector.

Neither made a sound for the rest of the evening, until me and Beverley were back at the cowshed putting the flagrant back into *in flagrante* when, in accordance with the iron principles of Sod's Law, my Android rang. Since Beverley was the only one with at least one hand free at the time, she got to the phone first, glared at it, and stopped bouncing long enough to read it.

'It's just three numbers – 659,' she said, over her shoulder.

'It's one of the detectors,' I said, and extricated my right hand from under her bum and held it out. Instead of handing the phone over, she lifted her hips a fraction and pivoted around to face me – a sensation that managed to be both hugely erotic and uncomfortably weird at the same time. When she finally let me have the phone, I confirmed the numbers.

'I've got to check this out,' I said.

Beverley sighed and flopped forward onto my chest.

It took me ten minutes to get out of the cowshed, and it probably would have been longer if Beverley hadn't decided that she wanted to come with, and so obligingly dismounted without an argument.

The detector that had gone off-line was the northernmost, planted on the Roman road where the lane from Yatton crossed and became a public footpath. Dominic had attached it amongst the bushes by the stile, so there was a good chance it might have just been vandalised.

In the darkness I could only make out the surrounding hills by the way they blotted out the stars, but according to the map on my tablet the shadow to the west was Pyon Wood and to the east Croft Ambrey, with a waning moon hung above like a banner. The Roman road was a straight grey strip between the black hedgerows. I parked the Asbo on the grass verge and left the hazard lights on. Beverley held the torch while I detached the detector from its mount and carried it back to the car. I cracked open the PVC case to expose the bare innards of the device.

'That's a mobile phone,' said Beverley, leaning over my shoulder to look.

I explained that it was, and that the detector worked on the simple principle that a powerful enough source of magic would break the phone and cause it to stop pinging the network, which would then alert the custom program on my tablet.

'So basically it only works once,' she said.

I used a jeweller's glass to scan the electronics, but I couldn't see any visible pitting.

'That's the trouble with magic,' I said. 'It's slippery stuff.' I shrugged. 'What are you going to do?'

'You could bundle four or five phones together and automatically rotate through them,' said Beverley, as I bagged and tagged the phone for shipping back to Dr Walid. 'That would extend the life a bit.'

I installed one of my spare detectors by the stile and packed up.

'But the switching mechanism can't be a microprocessor,' I said. 'And I haven't had time to test the effect of magic on transistors yet – you might have to use valves or electromechanical switches.'

'Do you know why it happens?' asked Beverley as we drove back to the cowshed.

I admitted that I did not have the faintest idea how magic did anything – let alone why it reduced microprocessors to sand and brains to Swiss cheese.

'When you do magic . . .' I said.

'I don't do magic,' said Beverley quickly. 'You get me? It's not the same thing.'

'When you do . . . things that other people can't do . . .' I said, 'it doesn't damage your phone.'

'Not unless the waterproofing fails,' she said.

'I wonder why that is?'

'That's easy,' said Beverley. 'I am a natural phenomenon. So I do less damage than you.'

'Have you visited Covent Garden recently?' I asked. 'They've almost finished the rebuilding.'

'That was collateral,' she said. 'And entirely your fault.'

The next morning I decided to check out Pyon Wood Camp – I took Miss Natural Phenomenon along with me, so she could tell me what all the plants meant.

'They mean,' said Beverley when she saw them, 'that in lowland Britain if you don't chop the trees down you get a forest.'

Pyon Wood Camp is a scheduled monument described in the catalogue as a small multivallate Iron Age hill fort. What it looked like was a round hill covered in trees. When I looked up the meaning of the word *multivallate* I found it meant a hill fort with three or more rings of concentric defences. Since the easiest way to start an argument amongst archaeologists is to ask them what purpose hill forts actually served – as defended villages, refuges of last resorts, ritual centres, palaces of tribal chiefs, cattle herding stations – none of that information was particularly useful.

Neither was Beverley Brook.

'More Silurian limestone,' she said. 'Topped by the usual suspects – oak and ash, some beech, a couple of birch.'

It was particularly hot that morning. Victor had complained that the recent hot weather was buggering up his harvesting schedule, but he hoped that some of the rain they'd had in Wales would shift over his way.

'Not that I want a thunderstorm,' he'd said. 'But a shower or two to take the edge off would be nice.'

It was too hot to walk up the shimmering track from the Roman road, so I risked the low slung underside of the Asbo and drove uphill until we reached the spot, plus or minus twenty metres or so, where the Antiquarian map said that the trail into the monument should start. It wasn't exactly well signposted, and if there was a stile or other public access, me and Beverley must have missed it. In the end we climbed over a fence and slogged through some dense bracken until we reached a close approximation of a path that wound around the hill.

It was close under the shade of the trees and not notably cooler. The air was heavy with a sickly sweet smell that Beverley said was probably the rhododendrons, and the scent of scorched bark and resin that I'd started to think of as overheated forest. Something hooted further up the hill.

'Wood pigeon,' said Beverley.

'I've heard that in London,' I said.

'Yes,' said Beverley slowly, 'we have birds in London. Many of them of the same species.'

Amongst the trees and undergrowth, the ditches and ramparts were hard to distinguish from the steep slope of the hill. It was only when the trail rounded the northeast corner and we found the entrance that I realised the ramparts, despite obvious damage, were twice my height. We laboured up onto what I supposed must have been the central enclosure, although I couldn't see it for the trees. And, despite the heat, we decided to follow the path to its bitter end. Drifts of foxglove started to appear amongst the bracken and bramble, growing more frequent until we stepped out into a glade awash with purple. The clearing was almost too circular to be natural, and certainly large enough that it ought to have shown up on Google Earth.

Beverley kicked at something down amongst the foxglove stems. It cracked and splintered – rotten wood.

'Stump,' she said. 'Somebody cleared this area.'

'The latest imagery on Google Earth was four years ago,' I said. 'It must have happened since then. Is it possible that it might be natural?'

'I don't know,' said Beverley. 'Probably not.'

We worked our way to the centre of the clearing, pushing through the stands of foxglove which seemed taller here than elsewhere, the bells of the flowers larger and more mouth-like as they shivered in the hot, still air. When we stopped I realised that the glade was very quiet. Even the wood pigeon we'd heard earlier seemed muffled and far away.

'There's no bees,' said Beverley. 'And bees love foxglove.'

Mellissa's bees had been *avoiding the south-west section of the ridge, from the edge of Bircher Common to where the river is.* They weren't coming here or to Pokehouse Wood.

'Feel anything?' I asked.

'No,' she said. 'How about you?'

I smelt green stuff, hot and dusty, and sneezed.

'There's no castle,' I said. 'Hannah was very sure about the castle.' The child psychologist had continued her gentle interrogation of Hannah. Heroically enduring countless episodes of *Jessie* and more *Yonder Over Yonder* than was probably medically advisable, the psychologist chipped gently away at Hannah's story, particularly the pink and blue and orange castle which she probably figured for a defence mechanism or a mental block or whatever the psychological term is. Hannah, while growing increasingly fuzzy on every other detail, had stayed firm on the castle.

I thought there had to be a castle somewhere, or at least something vaguely castle-like. But if there was, it certainly wasn't at Pyon Wood Camp.

I had one spare detector left, so I placed it in the centre of the glade and activated it.

'Just on the off chance,' I said.

'Is your work always this vague?' asked Beverley.

'Nah,' I said. 'Sometimes we really don't know what we're doing.'

Beverley had to make what she called a 'pastoral visit' to the Steam Fair, so I dropped her off there before heading back towards the industrial park and the red-brick ship shape of Leominster nick. The media were thick around the public side and there was even a knot of photographers at the entrance to the police car park. I made sure I was wearing a suitably solemn face to avoid 'Police Laugh At Kidnapped Children' headlines from the *Independent*.

'There's going to be a press conference later,' said Dominic when I asked him about the scrum outside.

The broadsheets led with the war in Syria, but the tab-loids were having way too much fun with the idea of child-stealing gypsies to let the mere lack of facts get in the way.

'Copper pipe I'd believe,' said Dominic. 'Children, no.'

I asked him what the MIU had come up with, but he told me to watch the press conference like everybody else.

I settled into my assigned space in the territorial po-licing office and picked up the phone. I called up Croft Castle and asked to talk to whoever it was who managed the forest. They told me his name was Patrick Black-moor and they gave me his mobile number.

'The western hemlock was doing really badly,' Blackmoor said when I asked why they'd clear-felled Pokehouse Wood out of schedule. 'So we decided to fell early.'

When I asked what the problem had been, Black-moor told me that it was a variety of factors. 'The soil remained very poor and acidic, but not enough to ex plain the losses amongst the plantation,' he said. 'It's a vigorous tree, your western hemlock. That's why it gets planted.' It took more than some abnormal soil chemis-try to stunt their growth, but there had been damage to the young trees as well.

'What kind of damage?' I asked.

'In the initial planting phase some of the saplings were dug out during the night. Others had bark damage,' said Blackmoor. But he didn't have an explanation as to what was doing it.

'We called in your lot at one point,' he said. 'In case it was vandals.' Although nobody could think of a reason why, with over 200,000 hectares of Forestry Commission woodlands in England to play with, they'd want to pick on the Pokehouse Wood. I asked whether they might have been protesting the planting of foreign conifers on an ancient woodland site.

Blackmoor found that idea hilarious.

'This was going to be the last commercial crop,' he said. 'Once it was harvested we would have replanted with broadleaf – basically what we're doing now.'

'Maybe someone didn't want to wait?' I asked, which was the bit Blackmoor found most funny.

'Forests are a long-term thing,' he said. 'And the people who care enough about the management of ancient woodlands to vandalise a tree think in the same time frames as us. Besides, there are plenty of ancient woodlands under threat from motorways and infrastructure projects – that's what gets protestors excited.'

'Then who?' I asked, but he didn't have the faintest idea. And the damage had continued. Once the trees began to mature they started to suffer from what looked like an unknown disease, or possibly poisoning.

'At first we were sure it was poisoning,' said Blackmoor. Because most of the affected trees were found to have been drilled. 'Up to a depth of thirty centimetres – in some cases all the way through the trunk.'

I tried to remember my night out with Princess Luna, and to estimate at what height that horn would have been when deployed in skewer-the-policeman mode.

'How high up the trunk did the drilling take place?'
I asked.

Blackmoor couldn't say for certain without looking at
his notes, but he remembered the holes being mostly
chest high. 'Five to six feet off the ground,' he said.

I remembered that night, the glass unicorn refract-
ing the werelight, the crunch as something invisible
and sharp skewered a tree at the same height my head
would have been – had I not been sensible enough to
get out of the way.

'We didn't find any evidence of poisoning, though,'
said Blackmoor.

Some trees just mysteriously fell over. Many others
showed suboptimal growth or other deformities. So
they set up a hide in the woods above and trained a
time-lapse camera on the area.

'It stopped working after the second night,' he said.

I'll bet it did, I thought.

They'd got so desperate that they granted permission
for a pair 'of those UFO nutters' to camp out in the
woods for a fortnight. But they never spotted anything
strange and they were *really* looking.

I asked if there were temporal patterns to the damage.

'It happened mostly during the summer,' said Blackmoor. 'That's all I can give you off the top of my head.'

'Did you keep records?' I asked. And they did, as it
happens – vandalism being an important issue to the
National Trust. Blackmoor said he'd send them to me as
long as I promised, should I figure out what the cause
was, to feed that information back to him.

And if it turns out to be a sacred grove, I thought, or

a faerie place of power or some such mystical bollocks, would he still want to know? Probably yes. And he'd just add it to the long list of issues that makes modern heritage land management such a complex and challenging career.

Inspector Edmondson found the tree vandalism case for me, and when the records from Croft Castle arrived in the form of a great big spreadsheet I started correlating both with my UFO sightings and the timeline of Zoe Lacey's encounter. I was still doing that when the press conference started. Me and Dominic got cold drinks and joined pretty much the rest of the nick to watch it on the internal monitor. These days, sensible police officers make sure they have an independent record of any encounter with a journalist. This meant that we got to see the whole thing – something that very few members of the public did.

For the hard-working lower ranks of the police force there is no entertainment quite as thrilling as watching your senior officer conducting a press conference. Not only is there the possibility that it might be humorously embarrassing, but also if it goes very badly it's useful to have advance warning so one can make oneself scarce. Officers of Inspector rank and above are a power in the land, and they don't like to be mildly contradicted let alone thwarted or shown up in public. I'm sure I wasn't the only officer in the incident room watching the TV and coming up with a convenient list of actions which would keep me far away from Leominster nick – just in case.

It started out normally enough, with Inspector

Edmondson and DCI Windrow sitting at a table elevated on a podium and doing their best gruff, matter of fact, nothing to see here, just doing our job with understated professionalism, manner. We are the police and we have brought order out of chaos – believe it, bruv!

It took them about ten minutes to run down the list of allegations, and why they were bollocks. No evidence that any member of the Marstowe family was involved in the kidnap, no evidence that any member of the local traveller community had been involved, and no evidence of an informal network of child-smuggling camps. Once Windrow had finished, a couple of journalists asked him whether he was one hundred per cent sure that the Marstowe family was not involved and that there weren't gypsies roaming the land stealing children and illegally living off incapacity benefit cross his heart and hope to die.

Windrow repeated himself in the manner of a man who was perfectly happy to sit there and repeat himself until everybody got bored and went home. Unaccountably, he failed to raise the working theory that the children had been abducted by faeries.

It's just that sort of deception, I thought, that breeds distrust of the police.

Sharon Pike certainly distrusted the police, because she stood up and demanded to know what about Harry Plimpton.

'Who Nicole identified by name as one of the men that held her,' she said.

I looked at Dominic to see if the name meant anything to him – his face screwed up in concentration.

'Andy's aunt's daughter's son,' he said after a moment. 'Second cousin. You met him at the sheep roast.'

I was impressed. In my family once you got past niece or uncle it was all cousins, and even that tended to include any random former stranger who'd managed to get his feet under the table.

I heard a flurry of activity from the incident room as someone looked up the relevant nominal on HOLMES. Meanwhile, Windrow stalled by asking where and when the identification had taken place.

'Surely that's not the point,' said Sharon Pike. 'Surely the question is why the police have failed to conduct a thorough investigation.'

I saw Windrow glance down at where he must have had a tablet tucked out of sight.

'Harry Plimpton,' he said, 'has been comprehensively eliminated from the inquiry. Not only did he spend most of the period in question helping as a volunteer with the search, but he can also account for his whereabouts for the rest of the time.'

I looked at Dominic, who nodded at the incident room – the MIU had been busy while some of us were out gallivanting in the woods.

'Has he been put in a line-up?' asked Sharon Pike. 'Has any effort been taken at all to try and identify the men that kidnapped Nicole?'

'Because of the gravity of the offences this inquiry has been meticulous,' said Windrow. He was too professional to let any of his irritation show. 'We have followed every line of inquiry as they came to our attention.'

'Then why haven't you made an arrest?' asked Sharon Pike.

The police had a two-camera set-up in the press room and, after a while switching randomly backwards and forwards, whoever was running the mixing board decided that Sharon Pike was more interesting than Windrow and settled on her.

I noticed that the journalists either side of her seemed alarmed by her behaviour, but I couldn't tell whether it was her manner or her questions.

'And whom should we have arrested?' asked Windrow.

Sharon Pike blinked theatrically, as if the question astonished her.

'Well, Andrew and Joanne Marstowe would do for a start,' she said. 'Since it was their plan from the beginning.'

Windrow fell back on police speak and reiterated that there were no plans to arrest Andrew and Joanne Marstowe, nor were they helping the police with their inquiries or considered persons of interest.

'Of course not,' said Sharon Pike. 'Because the whole hideous plot was facilitated by an officer of the West Mercia Police!' She almost shouted this. The journalists around her were beginning to edge away as if wary of sharing the same frame.

'Sharon,' said Windrow. 'If you have any evidence—'

'Detective Constable Dominic Croft,' she said.

'Well, that explains a great deal,' I said. 'You always were suspiciously one step ahead of the rest of us.'

'That's not funny,' said Dominic, his face pale.

He was right to be worried. A public accusation like that was going to hang around his neck.

Windrow's mouth literally dropped open in shock, but fortunately Inspector Edmondson stepped in.

'That's a very serious allegation,' he said. 'If you have any proof . . .'

'Of course I have proof,' said Sharon Pike and, after rummaging in her bag, held up what looked like an oblong of black plastic and marched towards the podium shouting that 'here was her proof' before slapping it down in front of Windrow.

'This is something you can't sweep under the carpet,' said Sharon Pike. and slammed her hand down on what looked to me like – and on further forensic analysis proved to be – the plastic tray from inside a box of Milk Tray chocolates.

Windrow looked down at the plastic tray, back up at Sharon Pike, and then put his hand over the microphone in front of him and said something.

'Of course I'm all right,' said Sharon, loudly enough to be picked up by an adjacent microphone. 'What are you afraid of? Look at it!'

Windrow spoke again, too low to be picked up.

Sharon Pike glared at him and then looked down at the sad crumpled piece of plastic in front of her. Her head snapped back up and she opened her mouth, but didn't speak. The camera angle was all wrong to see her expression clearly, but you could read the confusion in the set of her shoulders as she looked back down at her 'evidence'.

Then, without a word, she turned and walked away.

The police camera swung madly to keep her in frame as she marched up the central aisle between the ranks of silent journalists and camera operators.

I had one of those 'somebody do something' moments when you suddenly have the realisation that the person supposed to be doing something is *you*. I scrambled up from my desk and ran down the front staircase without a care for health and safety or the two uniforms coming up towards me. They sensibly flattened themselves against the railing and I shouted a thank you as I jumped past.

I missed her in the car park, so I ran around to the police zone and hopped into the Asbo. By the time I was on the main road I'd already done a PNC check to find out what she was driving – a BMW X5 Diesel, which seemed like quite a serious car for someone who lived alone in a small village. Perhaps she had a lot of relatives?

I decided that her most likely destination would be her house in Rushpool, second most likely would be her main house in London. Beyond that, it was anyone's guess. I managed to get Dominic on the Airwave and asked him to ask, politely, if they could keep an eye out for the BMW and Sharon Pike.

'She's going to be acting a bit weird,' I said. 'So she may have to be sectioned.'

I heard Dominic spluttering. Sectioning a prominent journalist would be, as they say, problematic. But both Bartholomew and Kingsley had left detailed case notes about people who had been put under the influence, *seducere* as Bartholomew called it, and had become

*maddened to the point where they rent their garments and*
*would be like to injure themselves if not restrained.*

I considered going blues and twos, but I didn't really want to exceed my authority – and I wasn't sure it would be much help if I ran into the back of a trailer full of hay. I had a worst case scenario growing at the back of my mind, so I went straight to the half-timbered pile that was the Laceys' home. And, sure enough, outside was parked a white BMW X5 Diesel with the right index. I drew up alongside and found Sharon Pike banging on the PVC door and screaming at the top of her lungs.

Before I could reach her, the door opened and Sharon Pike recoiled violently as a small pale figure stepped out to face her. Whatever she'd been planning to say choked off. And in the sudden quiet I heard the little girl say:

'Why're you hitting yourself?'

Sharon Pike smacked herself and the girl giggled and told her to do it again.

I reached them just in time to see Sharon Pike punch her own face hard enough to draw blood.

Some policing situations are the same wherever or whatever you're dealing with. I put myself between Sharon Pike and the girl and spoke in my command voice.

'Stop that!'

Probably-not-Nicole sneered at me.

'I don't like you. Go away.'

'Stop it!'

'Go away,' she yelled.

'Look me in the eye,' I said, and waited until she

reluctantly lifted her head to do so. 'That doesn't work on me.'

Not-Nicole squinted at me.

'Why not?' she asked.

'Because I'm police and it's my job to beat small children if they misbehave.'

'You won't,' she said.

'I can and I will if you don't behave yourself,' I said.

'You wouldn't!'

*You think that because you are small I will not beat you. But I am your mother and I know what is best for you. And if I have to beat you, then that is what I will have to do –* it's true, I thought. As you grow up you turn into your parents.

'Go inside and behave,' I said. 'We will talk about this later.'

She gave me a sullen look before turning and walking back into the house. She wanted to slam the door but she didn't dare.

Sharon Pike was standing with the dazed look of someone who's been hit by a bus. I decided to take her to the parish hall, which would be suitably neutral ground. As I took her by the arm, she gave me one of those vaguely thankful looks that you get from members of the public when they realise you're taking them away from whatever mess they've got themselves into.

The place had been cleared out since the celebratory sheep roast, but there were still a couple of Evians in the fridge behind the serving counter. Sharon Pike took hers gratefully and once I had her sat down on a folding chair she took a dainty sip. I unfolded a second chair and sat down to face her, close enough to be intimate but far enough away to be non-threatening.

'What happened?' she asked.

'You've been put under a form of suggestion,' I said. 'A bit like hypnotism.'

Sharon took another sip of water and then shook her head.

'No,' she said. 'That's not possible.'

'Normally, no,' I said. 'This is a special case.'

'By whom? Who did it to me?'

'I can't say,' I said.

'Can't or won't?' she asked, the confusion wearing off. I didn't think I had to worry about her rending her clothes, but my window for getting useful information was shrinking as she segued from victim to journalist.

'It's part of an ongoing case,' I said. 'But you just stood up and accused the West Mercia Police of conspiring to cover up the kidnap of two children and you did it in front of the whole press corp.'

Sharon held up a hand to make me stop. 'Yeah, yeah, yeah,' she said. 'I was there. Oh god – it's all on tape.'

'Ms Pike,' I said. 'This is important. Can you remember where the ideas come from?'

'You're PC Peter Grant,' she said. 'I looked into you, you work for the Special Assessment Unit – the Met's very own X-Files. I heard you investigate ghosts and aliens and psychics . . .' She trailed off. 'Psychics,' she pinched her forehead. 'Jesus Christ.' She looked at me, eyes narrowed.

'Psychics?' she asked.

'It's an ongoing investigation,' I said.

'You know I'd love to say that little monster made me do it. But I think she just pushed me in the right direction, and I went off and did it to myself.' She sighed. 'It would have been such a good story, too – pretty little girl, chav family, police incompetence – you've got to admit it had everything.'

'You're sure it was the girl?' I said. 'Not Victoria or Derek?'

'Oh it was little Nicky all right,' said Sharon. 'Victoria, I'm sure you may have noticed, has no backbone. And Derek is no better than he should be.'

'Derek?' I asked, wondering what that meant.

'Anything with a pulse,' she said. 'Even me once or twice.' She sighed again and drank more of the water. The good thing about the glamour is that it's all in the mind – she was going to be okay. 'Best lay I ever had.'

'All the names and details you listed in the press conference—'

'You're determined to keep bringing that up,' said Sharon.

'Did you provide the details?' I asked. 'Or did Nicole?' I thought it better not to raise the possibility that the girl was a changeling. Not when Sharon was so obligingly thinking herself down a cul-de-sac.

'No,' she said. 'I provided all the details – so much for professionalism.' She straightened her shoulders. 'Is Nicole psychic?'

'We don't use that term,' I said.

'Really? What term do you use?'

'We just refer to them as people who are unusually good at getting other people to do what they want,' I said. 'It's disconcerting, but luckily it's a bit on the rare side.' As was my ability to talk bollocks, I thought.

'And Nicole is one of these unusual people?'

'Inquiries are ongoing,' I said.

Except they weren't. Because I was stuck waiting for the DNA tests to come back.

First step was to get some bodies out in the field behind the Old Rectory to ensure fake Nicole didn't do a runner out the back. Fortunately, I was in Windrow's good books for so promptly dealing with Sharon Pike.

'Who is where?' he asked when I called him up.

'In her cottage having a lie down,' I said.

'Any sign of the media?' he asked.

'Not yet,' I said. 'What was the reaction after Ms Pike left?'

'Confused,' he said. 'I think they may just pretend it didn't happen.'

'Seriously?'

'We'll find out soon enough,' he said.

So I got some bodies in the fields and on the main lane with instructions to watch out for any comings and goings, but not to intervene unless asked to. I was just trying to figure out what to do next when Dr Walid called.

'In the first instance,' he said, 'Hannah and Nicole are half-sisters, they both share Derek Lacey as their father.'

'Jesus,' I said. 'Sharon Pike wasn't kidding about Derek.' And then the implications hit me. 'Wait. If you could tell that, then the sample I gave you must have come from Nicole Lacey.'

'Correct,' said Dr Walid. 'The samples taken from the

drink bottles were definitely of the child of Derek and Victoria Lacey – assuming you didn't get the samples mixed up.'

I didn't bother asking him if he was sure. When Dr Walid gives a DNA result you can take it into court – literally.

He obviously correctly interpreted my silence as proof that I was floundering, because he went on to tell me that he'd contacted the labs which had processed the DNA samples for the investigation.

'The bottle samples match the blood sample from the strip of cloth you found, but not the baseline samples that were taken from the Lacey house at the start of the investigation,' said Walid. 'Hair follicles, I believe they were. Although they have a parent in common.'

'Derek Lacey?'

'Very good,' said Dr Walid.

Boy, I thought, he really does get about.

Eleven years ago Zoe Lacey ran away with her baby half-sister, met the fae and came back with a different half-sister. And the Laceys had spent eleven years raising a changeling, until a week ago. When the fae, for whatever reason, had swapped them back.

What was I going to tell DCI Windrow? I'd only just managed to sell him on the idea of a changeling. And what was I going to tell Victoria Lacey – actually, genetically, the monster in your den is your biological daughter.

And why were they physically identical?

'What do you plan to do next?' asked Dr Walid.

'I don't know,' I said. 'I'll have to think of something.'

# 15

# Window of Opportunity

I f you ask any copper why they stick at a job which exposes them to abuse from everyone from petty criminals all the way down to government ministers, they'll say it's the variety. It's the not knowing when you go on shift what the rest of the day is going to be like. Accordingly, your training and experience emphasise a loose set of principles which can be applied to a wide variety of situations.

They are: make sure it doesn't spread, make sure no one's dead, make sure no one's going to be dead soon – and make sure you call for back-up before you need it.

I had the Lacey place surrounded, now the next step was to ensure Victoria and Derek weren't dead or injured. So I went back in, but not before I got Dominic to round up some beefy uniforms and wait outside with instructions to come get me if I wasn't out within ten minutes.

I found Derek and Victoria in the kitchen, apparently unharmed except for the valiant attempt both were making to incur alcohol poisoning. They sat facing each other at either end of the vast oak kitchen table. Derek had two half bottles of Bell's in front of him – one empty, the other mostly gone – while Victoria had two bottles of red wine and a dodgy-looking bottle of Bailey's that I suspected dated back several Christmases.

'How are you two doing?' I asked.

'Fine,' said Victoria flatly. 'Thank you for asking.'

Derek rolled his eyes and gave me a look-at-what-us-boys-have-to-put-up-with look which I ignored.

'Where's Nicole?' I said, keeping my voice as bright and businesslike as I could.

'In the den,' said Victoria.

Before I went to look, I paused at the entrance to the kitchen and asked if either of them would like to leave the house.

'Now would be a good time to do that,' I said.

Victoria kept her back to me.

'Why would we want to leave?' she said. 'Everything we want is here.'

They know something, I thought, as I cautiously made my way to the den. But what is it they know? It was hard to imagine that Derek had a tryst with the fae and hadn't noticed anything odd – or maybe the mother of his child had just looked like a tourist or, possibly, a particularly attractive sheep. I really wanted to ask, but I doubted he was going to tell me right that instant. I mentally stuck it on the follow-up to-do list.

I heard her before I reached the door, a very pig-like snoring, and indeed I found her lying on her back asleep surrounded by sweet wrappers. She looked exactly like every annoying eleven-year-old I'd ever been forced to babysit for.

Again I considered just scooping her up there and then and making a run for it. But a run for it where?

And to what purpose? I didn't think that Hereford-shire Social Services would be best pleased about me dumping a poorly socialised pre-teen with mind control powers on them. And, assuming we recovered the *real* fake Nicole, the one that had actually grown up in Rush-pool, we'd end up one child surplus to requirements. In which case, we'd need to find someone to take care of her.

I let sleeping changelings lie and retreated out of the house before Dominic and the brute squad came charging in.

Dominic was outside leaning against the tailgate of the Nissan, which he'd obviously backed into the Lac-ey's drive to serve as a formidable road block. The brute squad, in actuality a couple of PSCOs from the safer neighbourhood team, sloped off as soon as they saw I was okay.

It was getting into late afternoon, but there was no let-up in the heat and no sign of a breeze. I joined Dom-inic at the tailgate, which at least was in the shade of the trees that screened the rectory from the lane. He handed me an Evian that was, if not cold, noticeably cooler than I was. I turned my phone back on and checked for messages. Then I turned the disposable back on and checked that – the same.

I told Dominic I didn't think anyone was going to go anywhere – at least not until it was dark.

'You seem very sure something's going to kick off to-night,' he said. Which translated as *You know something and you'd better tell me what it is.*

'It's the phases of the moon,' I said. 'Hannah and

336

Nicole went missing a fortnight ago when the moon was in the first quarter.'

'That's half and half, right?'

'And when I trawled through all the databases it was clear that all the confirmed events, and most of the suspect events, happened between the first and third quarter. In other words the moon has to be at least half full for any of this shit to happen. And tonight . . .?'

'Is the last night?'

'Yeah,' I said. 'Maybe.'

'Maybe?'

'Why would the moon have any effect on any of this?' I said. 'What possible mechanism is in place?'

'Well . . .' started Dominic.

'You're going to ask about the tides, aren't you?'

'Um, no,' he said. 'I was going to say that the mechanism is irrelevant at the moment.'

'Tonight's the night,' I said.

'So what about the tides, then?' asked Dominic.

'Gravity,' I said. 'That's the mechanism with tides.'

'All living things have water in them,' said Dominic.

'Gravity affects the oceans because they slosh about,' I said. 'Not because they're made of water.'

'That's me told, then,' he said.

'Damn right,' I said.

'So the moon affects magic, why?'

'I'm working on several theories,' I said. 'But I'm currently favouring the hypothesis that the moon has a seemingly arbitrary effect on magic because it likes to piss me off.'

'That's a theory with a high degree of applicability to other spheres of life,' he said.

'Yes it is,' I said, and we spontaneously fist bumped.

The thing about back-up is that when you want it, you want it now, not two to three hours away in London. So, as I schlepped back to the cowshed for a shower and a change of gear, I was rehearsing what I was going to say. I was just trying to find a form of words that would imply that none of what had happened was my fault when the disposable phone rang.

Has to be a wrong number, I thought as I answered. But it wasn't. It was Lesley.

'Hello, Peter,' she said.

'Where are you?' I asked.

'Like I'm going to tell you,' said Lesley, her tone the same as if we were still proceeding down Charing Cross Road with our thumbs hooked in our Metvests. I stopped walking and sat down on a low garden wall. It took me a moment to catch my breath.

'You've got to come in, Lesley,' I said. 'This is not going to end well.'

'Listen,' she said. 'Listen, I called to make sure you were all right.'

'Whether I'm all right?' My voice actually went up an octave. It was embarrassing. 'You're the one who's up to their neck in shit.'

'Yeah, but at least I know what I'm doing,' she said.

'What *are* you doing?'

'I'm not wasting the little time we've got talking bollocks,' she said. 'Are you banging Beverley yet?'

'Why do you care?'

'Because I want you to be happy, you pillock,' she said. 'Because you spend too much time worrying about shit that's not important. And you never know . . .' She hesitated, and this time I heard a catch in her voice. 'You never know when it's all going to get taken away.'

'I tell you what,' I said. 'You come in and I'll let you run my love life.'

I heard something that might have been a laugh, might have been a cough.

'Yeah, that's tempting,' she said.

'You want to make me happy, Lesley?' I said. 'Meet me somewhere – so at least I know you're safe.'

A real laugh for sure – a bitter one.

'I crossed a line, Peter,' she said. 'I'm never going to be safe again.'

'No,' I said.

'And I did it with my eyes open,' she said. 'You always said that people need to accept the consequences for their actions – this is me doing that.'

'You know I was talking bollocks. And anyway, coming in would be a way of accepting the consequences.' I said.

'You've got about a year, Peter,' said Lesley. 'Then it's going to kick off for certain – if you keep your head down I might just be able to keep you out of it.'

'Keep me out of what?' I asked.

'Time's up,' said Lesley. 'Take care.'

The phone cut off.

The evening sunlight sliced across the tops of the trees, a car slowed as it passed me and then accelerated up towards the parish hall. Something tweeted insanely in a bush a couple of metres from my head.

What the hell was that supposed to be – a friendly warning? Something to assuage her guilt? Or second thoughts? Was it part of a plan, and if it was – whose plan was it? A year? Fuck, fuck, fuck. Why a year?

Too late I reached for my own phone to call Nightingale, but there already was a text from Inspector Pollock. **No contact until auth**. Meaning I wasn't to contact Nightingale, or anyone related to Operation Carthorse – the operation to apprehend Lesley May. I'd like to think that Pollock was worried that I was being monitored. But it was more likely that he still hadn't yet ruled out to his satisfaction that me and Lesley had been working together.

So, no back-up until further notice.

I got up and jogged up the lane to the cowshed. I needed a shower to calm down, a change of clothes and a plan.

Containment, then. Stop the little monster currently residing at the rectory from happening to other members of the public. Prevent any further breaches of the peace by Princess Luna and friends. Which left Nicole, our reverse changeling, stuck with the faeries until Nightingale could get up here and lend a hand.

Stuck where? Hannah's pink and orange and blue castle.

I kept the shower cool in the hope it would kick-start my brain.

Get through the night and then ask permission to interview Hannah. Maybe do a little bit of magic to show her I was on her side. Longer term, extend the detector grid out to possible faerie sites. Restatement Zoe Lacey re: aliens and interview Derek Lacey re: his random sexual encounters with the supernatural.

I got out of the shower to find my tablet bleeping at me. The detectors at Pyon Wood Camp and at the crossroads on the Roman road had stopped broadcasting. Coincidence? Don't make me laugh.

I had a pair of khaki combat trousers which were strictly for cleaning jobs and definitely not street wear, unstylish but reinforced at the knees and with lots of pockets. I pulled them on plus my PSU boots.

We could also drag in folklorists and vicars and start working up lists of likely castle sites, plus Professor Postmartin could dig out the County Practitioner records for Herefordshire and the surrounding counties – somebody was bound to have noticed a faerie castle.

East of the Roman Road the detector at Yatton went out.

Next, I put on my utility belt with extendable baton, pepper spray, handcuffs and then my Metvest over what I realised had to be one of Beverley's T-shirts because it was tight on me and had STOP STARING AND GET OUT OF MY WAY written across the chest. As I pulled it on I smelt Beverley, not her *vestigia* but a human smell of sweat and clean skin.

I considered the shotguns – but I'd probably only shoot my foot off. The same probably applied to Hugh Oswald's staffs, but when I pulled one out of their bag it felt solid and comforting in my grip.

The night may be dark and full of terrors, I thought, but I've got a big stick.

'Is there something I should know?' asked Dominic when I re-joined him outside the Old Rectory. I showed him the detector track on my tablet and told him that back-up was on hold. He sighed.

'You were right,' he said. 'Tonight's the night.'

'Looks like it,' I said.

'Have I got time to get changed?' he asked.

'Yeah – I don't think anything's going to happen until the moon gets up.' I checked my notebook. 'Which isn't until about half past ten.'

So, while Dominic was off girding his loins, I called Beverley who seemed to be attending a party in a steam organ.

'I'm negotiating,' she shouted over a background of hurdy-gurdy and screaming children.

'Negotiating what?' I shouted back.

'River stuff,' she shouted. 'I'll tell you all about it when I get back – don't wait up.'

Dominic returned half an hour later wearing cargo pants and real authentic farmer's Wellington boots. Apparently you can tell they're authentic when the muck has permanently discoloured the rubber up to the ankle level. He'd brought his own extendable baton and his stab vest in the beige 'undercover' sleeve.

He'd also brought a folding table, a pair of folding chairs and a picnic hamper. We set them up at the back of the Nissan, sat down and had a drink.

'Outstanding,' I said. 'Now all we need is a deck of cards.'

As the sun set, the detector at Croft Ambrey went offline and we called Stan, who lived close by in Yatton Marsh, to see whether she'd noticed anything. Dominic shouted into the phone for Stan to turn the music off but to no obvious success. He grimaced and turned the phone in my direction so that I could hear a burst of a raw sounding cover of *Children of the Revolution* before Dominic cut the line in disgust.

'She's been sniffing aggro diesel and listening to 9XDead again,' he said. 'There won't be nothing coherent from her until Wednesday.' He put the phone away. 'Do we actually have an operational plan for dealing with the unicorns?' he asked, and then laughed. 'I can't believe I just said that.'

'Priority one, protect members of the public,' I said. 'Priority two, if we can, follow them back to wherever it is they come from in the hope that we can recover the real Nicole.'

Dominic decided to risk a dash for some drinks. While he was away I amused myself by piggybacking onto the Laceys' wifi and looking at the online newspaper front pages. The *Express* went with a new Diana conspiracy theory, the broadsheets went with Syria and a side order of fracking, the tabloids with cricket and the Royals. Windrow had been right. Sharon Pike's little meltdown was being quietly forgotten. It made sense. No profession likes to wash its dirty laundry in public.

Nightingale called at last.

They'd triangulated the signal from Lesley's phone to

a flat in the Dog Kennel Hill estate in Dulwich, and after the requisite amount of time charging about shouting 'police' and 'clear' Nightingale had walked into the kitchen to find an envelope on the table with his name on it.

'It was one of those white envelopes you get with greeting cards and inside was one such, with a cat on the front licking its paw and the inscription *With Sympathy* in pink letters. Inside were written the words NICE TRY.'

'I told you,' I said.

'She could have left us a demon trap,' said Nightingale. 'Or something mundane and equally unpleasant. It's quite maddening, really. I'm certain she's trying to communicate something to us, but I'm damned if I know what. Did she say anything significant to you on the phone?'

'I'd rather tell you about that call in person,' I said.

'Quite,' said Nightingale. 'How are things your end?'

I gave him a quick briefing.

'I think things may be kicking off soon,' I said. 'I could use some help.'

'I'll set off as soon as I'm sure that Lesley has really left the area,' he said. 'That should put me in your vicinity in four to five hours. Can you last until then?'

'Yes, sir,' I said.

'Remember, Peter, the fae are like peacocks. They strut and they boast and they will expect you to do the same,' he said. 'Put on a good show and you may be able to avoid an actual physical confrontation.'

'And if I can't avoid a physical confrontation?'

'I'd really rather that you did,' said Nightingale.

'And if I can't?'

'Fight like a policeman,' he said. 'That should take them by surprise.'

But what kind of policeman? I wondered.

Nightingale said he had to go, and hung up. I sat staring into the growing dark while a robin made a valiant attempt to trill its guts out. But at least the bloody wood pigeon had shut up by then.

Dominic came back with a flask of coffee and we sat in silence for a while, as something in the distance imitated the music from the shower scene in *Psycho*.

'Song thrush,' said Dominic.

The tablet chimed and all the detectors in Pokehouse Wood dropped out – all of them.

'It always comes back to Pokehouse Wood,' I said. 'It's like that's the hinge around which everyone travels.'

'The hinge?'

'I don't know,' I said. 'Axis, roundabout, *entrepôt*, gateway?'

'Do you think we should check it out?' asked Dominic.

'No need,' I said. 'I think they're coming here.'

We drank our coffee and listened to the birds and waited.

'Victor wants to get married,' said Dominic.

'Congratulations,' I said.

'I'm not that keen,' said Dominic.

'Really?'

'Christ, no,' said Dominic. 'I don't want to spoil what we've got.'

'Why would it spoil it?'

'For one thing, I'd have to go live on his bloody farm,'

he said. 'It's not like he's going to move into my flat. This is David Cameron's fault, you know – he had to have his trendy bloody Same Sex Couples Act.'

'Tell him you want a long engagement,' I said.

Dominic sighed.

'Would you marry him?' he asked.

'Who, Victor?'

'Of course Victor.'

I gave it some thought.

'Nah,' I said. 'Not with the hours he works – it's bad enough on the Job when you're doing shifts. But farming, dawn to dusk – no thanks.'

'That's my point,' said Dominic.

'I bet he's going to stay fit, though,' I said. 'All that hard work.'

'There is that,' said Dominic. 'Even if he does smell of cow shit. What about Beverley?'

'What, marriage?'

'Why not?'

I remembered Isis, wife of the River Oxley, telling me that I shouldn't be in a hurry to go into the water. 'It's not a decision you want to rush into,' she'd said. But I had, that night on the banks of the Lugg. Rushed in like the fool I am.

'I'll cross that bridge when I come to it,' I said.

'Peter,' said Dominic.

'Yeah?'

'All the birds have stopped singing,' he said.

We both slowly got to our feet and listened.

I could just hear the sound of a TV coming from a house up the road and a low rumble of voices that was probably the crowd outside the Swan in the Rushes. Far away a car with a diesel engine was labouring up a steep slope.

Dominic used his Airwave to call the spotters we'd stationed in the field to the west of the village, sitting in a Toyota that had a good view of the off-road approaches to both the Old Rectory and the Marstowes' house. They were under instructions to report any movement, strange lights and/or other general weirdness, and to not get out of the Toyota unless told to. So far they hadn't seen anything. Dominic advised them to stay sharp.

'You don't actually have to do this with me,' I said, as I tested the grip on Hugh Oswald's staff and hefted it about a bit.

Dominic laughed.

'My patch, my village,' he said. 'Probably my folklore. So, yeah – actually I think I do.'

'Fair enough,' I said. 'If something weird gets behind me, watch my back and smack anything that's not a small child. As hard as you can – you want to put them down as fast as possible.'

'Put what down?'

'I wish I knew.'

'So, to summarise,' said Dominic, 'we guard the Laceys, prevent anything supernatural happening, follow any . . . thing back to where it came from.'

'Which will probably be Pokehouse Wood.'

'And rescue any missing children we might find lying around. Is that about it?'

'That's the plan,' I said.

Which, right that moment, fell completely apart.

347

My tablet played the red alert sound from *Star Trek*, which indicated that one of the detectors in the village had dropped offline. I turned, naturally, to look at the Old Rectory – walking to the side a bit to see if I could get a look around the back – but there was nothing. Same deal from our spotters in the Toyota – nothing.

I checked the tablet and saw that the other village detector had dropped off – the one at the Marstowe house.

It was at least four hundred metres from the Old Rectory to the cul-de-sac and me and Dominic did it in less than a minute and a half, which is pretty impressive considering all the kit we were carrying and the fact that it was fricking uphill.

There were crashing sounds from inside the house and high-pitched screams, which meant we may even have picked up the pace before a flash lit up the ground floor windows. Followed by the distinctive boom of a shotgun, which caused us to clatter to a halt at the front door.

We stood clear either side of the doorway and I nudged the door open with my foot. It was unlocked and swung inwards.

These country people, I thought, don't half neglect the basics of home security.

We heard Andy cursing, saw another flash and heard another boom.

'Andy, mate,' called Dominic, 'is that you with the shotgun?'

'Yeah,' called Andy from inside. 'The bastards are trying to get in the back.'

Double flash, two blasts close together, the sound of plate window glass shattering.

'We're coming in the front,' yelled Dominic. 'Don't you dare fucking shoot us.'

'Right-oh,' called Andy, almost casually.

Dominic went in first. It was his idea, after all.

We found Andy flattened against the wall by his kitchen door, shotgun at the ready.

'I tried to call you lot,' he said when we joined him. 'But all the phones were buggered.'

'Where're the kids?' asked Dominic.

'Upstairs with Joanne,' said Andy.

I peered around the doorframe. The kitchen light was off and half the windows blown out. The upstairs lights spilled down into the garden, illuminating the swing set, the rotary clothes dryer and a gleaming shape – like a horse spun out of glass. It snorted and its great head swung back and forth – looking for an opening.

Andy meekly handed over the shotgun when Dominic asked for it.

'Out of shells anyway,' he said. Nonetheless Dominic cracked it open and checked. I wondered if Andy had a shotgun licence, but decided now was not the time to ask. Dominic laid it carefully down and kicked it into the living room.

'Andy,' I said. 'I want you to go upstairs, pick the most secure room and barricade yourself, Joanne and the kids inside.'

I expected him to argue, but he seemed to have a touching faith in the police and did as he was told.

'What do we do now?' asked Dominic once Andy was safely upstairs.

'We go forth,' I said. 'And we de-escalate the situation.'

Dominic nodded. 'De-escalation,' he said. 'One of my favourites.'

Peacocks, Nightingale had said.

I squared my shoulders, hefted Hugh's staff and walked into the kitchen, fixed the beast outside with my eyes and said, 'Oi, sunshine! Cut it out.'

The unicorn turned in my direction, the moon-light flashing on the ridges of its spiral horn, and for a moment we stared at each other through the smashed window of the kitchen door. Then, faster than I would have believed possible, it lowered its head and surged towards me.

Its head fit through the broken window, but its shoul-ders smashed into the frame, ripping it out of the brick work with a noise like a JCB ram-raiding a DIY store. Between the kitchen units and the table I had no room to dodge, and turning my back on half a metre of spike did not strike me as a good idea.

But I wasn't some terrified peasant, I was an appren-tice and I had been trained by the man who led the rearguard at Ettersberg. And we were about to find out how good that training was.

*Anticipate*, Nightingale had drilled into me, *formulate, release* . . . and for god's sake, Peter, you have to have the follow-up ready the moment you release the first spell.

I had anticipated the charge and I was speaking the spell even as splinters of wood clattered off the ceiling. It was my shield, famously capable of stopping seven out of ten pistol calibre rounds – on a good day. Had the beast hit it face-on, that horn would have gone right through it. But I didn't have it held face-on – I had it deflected at an angle so that the point slid off to my right, because the surface of the shield is well slippery.

And I knew that not from some ancient text but because I'd logged hours on the range, conjuring the thing at different angles while Molly poked at me with a stick.

The thing bellowed with rage as its horn slid uncontrollably to its left. And where the horn went, head, neck and shoulders were sure to follow. It hit the kitchen table at just over knee height and went down on its side amidst splinters of laminated chipboard. Its great hooves scrabbled on the lino as it tried to get them back under itself. But I had my follow-up ready – I twisted and swung Hugh's staff as hard as I could. I would have liked to have landed one on its head, but my reach wasn't good enough and instead the staff's iron cap scored its way down the unicorn's shoulder.

It bellowed with pain and frustration.

Cold iron, I thought. The stories are true.

I hit it again and it screamed.

I kept the shield aimed downwards to keep it pinned and raised my staff once more.

The unicorn stopped struggling to rise and lay there quivering, staring at me with a mad brown eye – in the darkness it seemed real and solid and all there.

'Are you going to be a good boy?' I asked.

The mad eye rolled in its socket, but the head slumped down amongst the splintered wood of a kitchen unit, stainless steel cutlery and the remains of Joanne's best china.

'Dominic,' I said. 'Are you still there?'

'Yeah,' he said. 'That was interesting.'

'We're going to be stepping back into the hallway,' I said. 'Give Princess Luna here a chance to get up.'

Dominic put his hand on my shoulder and guided me backwards – as I went, I lifted the shield away from the unicorn, although I made a point of keeping it between me and the beast.

It hesitated at first, but then in a crackle of broken glass it got to its feet. I thought it might have another go, but it started turning immediately, incidentally smashing the sink off the wall and bringing down the last intact wall unit. Water hit the ceiling as the cold tap sailed through the air and out one of the broken windows. Even as it sauntered out through the ruins of the kitchen door it had begun to fade, until it was nothing but the sound of hooves vanishing into the night.

'Aren't we going to follow it?' asked Dominic.

'I know where it's going,' I said.

'You know,' said Dominic, 'I think I'm going to marry Victor after all. An experience like this puts your life in perspective.'

'Really?' I said. 'Mine is still passing in front of my eyes.'

'Okay,' said Dominic as we retreated to avoid the widening pool caused by the water fountaining out of the broken sink. 'But are you sure what you're seeing is not just the rest of your life?'

The next step was to get the Marstowes safely out of

the house. We played rock, paper, scissors to determine which one of us would explain to Joanne why she was going to need to wrangle a new kitchen out of Herefordshire County Council – I won. We were waiting downstairs for them to grab some overnight clothes and Dominic had just unshipped his Airwave to get some support in when we heard the siren.

It had the slower tone change that marked it as an ambulance. We heard it come up the slope and then stop further down – about where the Old Rectory was.

'Oh shit,' said Dominic.

By the time we got there Derek was being wheeled out of the house on a trolley. He was wearing a neck brace and an oxygen mask – there was a pressure bandage covering the side of his head. Inspector Edmondson had taken over the scene. We gave him the sanitised version of what had happened to us, and he explained that his people had searched the house and that Victoria and not-really-Nicole were missing.

# 16

# Going Forward

The house of Puck, the Pokehouse, where will-o-wisps were wont to lead travellers astray – and cause police officers to break traffic regulations with extreme prejudice. I'd told Dominic to floor it, and that's just what he'd done.

Whoever had smacked Derek Lacey on the side of the head, and my money was on Victoria Lacey in the kitchen with the bottle of Baileys, had a good twenty minute head-start. But, since they hadn't taken a car, we might have a chance to cut them off – literally at the pass, as it happened.

The big Nissan roared as we did a ton down the B4632 towards Mortimer's Cross. And, trust me, that is not something you want to do without an ejector seat. Behind us I saw lights and sirens as assets started piling in from Leominster – fuck knew what DCI Windrow was going to make of this.

'I think we're going to be asked some questions,' I said.

'What's with the "we", *kemosabe*?' said Dominic. 'I'm planning to blame you for everything.'

He made a sudden right into a turn I couldn't even see, and we went bouncing up a slope. I caught a quick flash of an English Heritage sign and then we slipped about on a rough track until Dominic told me to get ready to open a five-bar gate. So I leaned out the window and knocked it off its hinges with an *impello*. The Nissan bounced noticeably as we ran over the flattened gate.

'That,' said Dominic, 'was not compliant with the countryside code.'

As far as I could tell, we were bouncing across an open field – ahead of us something dull and metallic reflected in the headlights.

'Another gate,' yelled Dominic, and I leaned out and knocked that one down as well. The staff seemed to ripple under my hand as I used it, purring as the metal five-bar gate fell down flat with no fuss whatsoever.

Then we were jolting down a tunnel of trees, with flashes of light grey to our left. I realised we were on the same path that Zoe had followed with baby Nicole over a decade ago. One that really wasn't designed to be driven down at speed.

I saw pale faces suddenly caught in the headlights – so did Dominic, and he hit the brakes. The Nissan skidded, fishtailed sideways towards the riverbank before recovering, and slowed to a halt a couple of metres short of the figures.

It was substitute-Nicole and Victoria. The woman had bound the girl's hands with what looked like duct tape and wound a piece around her lower face to gag her.

We climbed out of the Nissan and approached carefully.

'You can't stop me,' she screamed and started dragging the girl up the path.

When faced with a low-level hostage situation your first task is to calm the hostage taker down long enough to find out what they want. Then you can lie to them convincingly until you negotiate the hostage back, or are in a position to dog pile the perpetrator. Dominic got his torch out and kept it on Victoria's legs to avoid intimidating her – that could come later.

'What can't we stop you doing?' I asked.

Victoria gave me a puzzled look.

'You can't stop me getting Nicole back,' she said.

I looked at the girl who was not-Nicole but probably her half-sister. She glared back over the duct tape as if it was my fault. Which technically, I suppose, it probably was.

So it was a hostage swap – which meant if we were clever we might be able to get Nicole back and keep not-Nicole as well.

'Who are you making the swap with?' I asked.

We were emerging from the tunnel of trees. To our right the treeless slope of Pokehouse Wood swept up the ridge. The white poles that protected the new saplings thrust up amongst brambles and the stands of foxglove stood grey and trembling in the moonlight. I smelt horse sweat and malevolence – I didn't think we were alone.

'The lady who owns Princess Luna . . .' she said. 'She came to see me last night. I thought it was a dream. But it couldn't have been a dream, could it? Because you never remember your dreams, do you?'

Victoria started to drag the girl up the diagonal

forestry track – it was slow going, not least because not-Nicole had gone limp in an effort to stop her.

'This one is your biological daughter,' I said.

Victoria stopped dead.

'No,' she said.

'Remember when Zoe ran off with the baby?' I asked. 'This is where she came.'

'For god's sake, why?'

'For the attention I suppose—'

Victoria cut me off with a disgusted sound.

'Of course for the attention,' she snapped. 'I mean, why did she think it was a good idea to swap Nicky?'

'That was an accident,' I said. 'She didn't even notice it go down.'

'Oh, well,' she said. 'That makes everything okay.' She shook not-Nicole roughly by the arm. 'This isn't mine,' she said. 'Blood isn't everything -- I want my daughter back.'

'So do I,' I said. 'And when the other half of this swap-meet turns up, maybe we can do some bargaining.'

'Um,' said Dominic urgently. 'That would be about now.'

I can't say they materialised out of thin air, but it was as if when I turned my head they arrived in my blind spot, so that when I looked back in that direction they were there. It was creepy, and it was definitely showing off.

And they were real, there in Pokehouse Wood, on the last of the quarter moon. They were flesh and blood. Human shaped but tall and thin, with long delicate faces and hands and black eyes. A woman stood ahead

357

of us dressed in armour made not of metal, but of over-lapping stone scales, slate possibly, polished to a bright blue-grey sheen.

Like the scales of a fish, Zoe had said.

Victoria might have called her a lady but I know a Queen when I'm within genuflection distance.

She wore a silver circlet upon her head with a single large sapphire at her brow. In her hand she held a straight spear of white wood tipped with a leaf-shaped flint blade. I've seen enough *Time Team* to know how sharp a blade like that could be. From her shoulders hung a cloak of white wool, and sheltered under one hem I could see a small figure with a pale worried face. The real Nicole, I presumed.

For a mad moment I considered just stepping up and arresting the lot of them – as a plan it at least had the virtue of simplicity. Its principal drawback being that the Queen was flanked on either side by her beasts, real and stinking. I could see the sheen of sweat on their dappled flanks, and the one on the left had a nasty cut on its shoulder – a streak of dark blood down its side. That one had a particularly mad look in its eye, just for me.

'There's a pair of good looking IC7 boys behind us,' said Dominic softly. 'Carrying bows and arrows. And another two upslope.'

'Good fields of fire,' I said.

'That's what I thought.'

'We're okay as long as we don't do anything stupid.'

'You're giving me this advice now?' said Dominic.

Victoria grabbed not-Nicole by the shoulders and held her out at arm's length towards the Queen.

'I've brought this one,' she said. 'Now give me back my daughter.'

The Queen narrowed her eyes and suddenly I knew I'd seen that expression on someone else's face. She twitched back her cloak and gently laid a long-fingered hand on Nicole's shoulder.

Victoria shoved not-Nicole, who was having none of it and refused to budge.

'Move,' hissed Victoria, and the Queen's lips twisted into a thin smile. She shook her spear and not-Nicole's shoulders slumped and her head drooped – she took a step forward.

What does it profit a copper, I thought, if he should gaineth one hostage but loseth another?

I put a werelight into the air above our heads, the biggest I'd ever attempted. The staff hummed like a beehive and the light came out the size of a weather balloon and bright enough to get three paragraphs in UKUFOindex.com and a special feature in the *Fortean Times*.

I'd been going for sunlight, and it rolled over us like a sudden summer, painting the unicorns in pinks and whites, rippling like an oil slick across the scales of the Queen's armour and flashing off the sapphire at her brow.

'This is the police,' I said. 'Everybody needs to keep calm and stay where they are.'

'You moron,' shouted Victoria.

The Queen turned her eyes on me and I felt the power of her regard push and pull and shove at me as if it were a festival crowd.

'You wouldn't believe the number of people who've tried that on me,' I said. 'I'm afraid you're just going to have to talk instead.'

The pale flawless skin of her brow ruffled, and fuck me if I didn't recognise that expression – every single time I failed to finish what was put in front of me for supper at the Folly. So far the Queen had kept her gob shut, but I was willing to bet she had a mouth full of sharp teeth and, behind them, a long and prehensile tongue.

I laughed for sheer delight at having *that* question answered.

Now I knew what to look for, the similarities to Molly were obvious. Not so much the physical, but the way they held themselves, the way they moved as if they were standing still and the world was obligingly rearranging itself around them.

So Molly was fae or, even better, this particular kind of fae – whatever this kind of fae was. And so we progress in our knowledge of the universe step by step, pebble by pebble.

'Give me my child,' shouted Victoria. The Queen glanced at her, and Victoria fell suddenly silent and slumped to her knees.

'Stop that,' I said.

The Queen looked back at me and inclined her head.

'I can't let you have either of the children,' I said. And, because I was raised to be polite, 'Sorry.'

The Queen's expression went from annoyance to contempt, and on either side her beasts stirred, stamped their hooves and lowered their heads.

I fixed my eyes on my unicorn, the one with the bleeding wound on its shoulder, and feinted with my staff. It flinched and then backed away a couple of steps before rearing up on its hind legs with a frightened whinny.

The Queen shot it a poisonous look and I thought, Just wait till she gets you alone. You're in so much trouble. The unicorn came down at her unvoiced command, but it stayed noticeably nervous.

Then the Queen turned back to me and smiled – this time showing her teeth.

And suddenly there were at least a dozen more armoured fae standing amongst the foxgloves and between the trees that grew down by the riverbank. They wore the same armour of blue-grey slate and in their hands they held half-drawn metre-long bows.

I took a deep breath.

'Peter,' said Dominic. 'Can you even spell de-escalate?'

And I exhaled slowly.

'Let's not do anything hasty,' I said, and lowered my staff.

I heard Dominic mutter something weird about a throne of blood. I looked at the girl half-wrapped in the Queen's cloak, at her half-sister bound and fuming, and her mother on her knees and weeping silently. My mind was suddenly clear and free of doubt and, given what I was about to do, possibly devoid of thought.

'My name is Peter Grant, I am a sworn constable of the crown and an heir to the forms and wisdoms of Sir Isaac Newton,' I said. 'I offer myself in exchange for the children, the mother and my friend. Take me – let everyone else go.'

She made me wait, didn't she? Of course she did.

Then her smile grew wider and she inclined her head in gracious acceptance.

'Dominic,' I said.

'You idiot,' said Dominic.

'Take the girls and Mrs Lacey and get out of here as fast as you can and go to the nearest place indoors where there's lots of people – a pub will do,' I said.

The Queen banged the butt of her spear against the ground.

'I'll be right with you,' I said, and then to Dominic, 'You've got to get a message to my governor, DCI Nightingale. Tell him that wherever they're taking me it will be via Pyon Wood Camp, okay? The castle must be somewhere beyond that, in Wales I think.'

Two sharp raps with the haft of the spear – no more time.

'They don't like the Roman road,' I said quickly, and handed Dominic my staff. 'That would be a good place to intercept.'

Before Dominic could say anything I stepped forward until I was between Victoria and not-Nicole and the Queen. The unicorn I'd injured snorted and pawed the ground – I gave it the eye.

'Now the girl,' I said.

The Queen nodded cheerfully and set Nicole in motion towards her mother. She passed me, a small figure dressed in what looked like a woollen shift. I heard her mum sob with relief.

'Dom?' I called without looking round. 'Have they cleared out of your way?'

'Yes, they have,' said Dominic.

'Then off you go,' I said and stepped forward.


You swear an oath when you become a police officer – you promise to serve the Queen in the office of
constable with fairness, integrity and impartiality, and
that you will cause the peace to be kept and preserved
and prevent all offences against people and property.
The very next day you start making the first of the many
minor and messy compromises required to get the Job
done. But sooner or later the Job walks up to you, pins
you against the wall, looks you in the eye and asks you
how far you're willing to go to prevent all offences. Asks
just what did your oath, your attestation, really mean to
you?

I could have bottled it and not offered the swap. No
disciplinary inquiry would have found me lacking in my
duty had I merely sought to contain the situation and
wait for back-up – in fact that would have been proper
procedure.

And it's not like my colleagues wouldn't have understood. We're not soldiers or fanatics, although I think I
would have heard the whispering behind my back in the
canteen whether it was really there or not.

But sometimes the right thing to do is the right thing
to do, especially when a child is involved. And I reckon
there wasn't a copper I've worked with who wouldn't
have made the choice I did. I'm not saying they would
have been pushing their way to the front of the queue,
and they certainly wouldn't have done it with a glad
song on their lips, but when push comes to shove . . .?

So I did it. Because I'm a sworn constable and it was the right thing to do.

Plus I fully expected Nightingale to come rescue me. Eventually.

I hoped.

They followed the Queen as she turned and walked up the logging track. The unicorns wheeled and cantered ahead. Her heralds, I decided, and the manifestation of her desires. Around me the rest of the party moved in a loose formation, some on the track, some drifting silently amongst the saplings. It was hard to pin down how many there were.

I heard the Nissan start up and, after what sounded like a slightly desperate three-point turn, roar away. The engine sounded weirdly muffled, but at the time I just put that down to distance and the intervening trees.

Either we turned off the logging track or it petered out, because soon we were walking a narrow trail that threaded between mature trees. There was some moonlight to see by, but I found it hard to keep up and the Queen had to stop a number of times to wait for me. Whenever she did, I heard a familiar rhythmic hissing sound from her retainers – I recognised it from Molly. Laughter.

After a long time we emerged onto the bare crown of a hill. One of the unicorns crowded me then, pushing its shoulder against me and guiding me roughly into a hollow between two grassy banks. There the Queen and her retainers made camp, sitting down and wrapping their grey cloaks around themselves. There was a chill in the air, so when one of the retainers offered me a cloak I took it gratefully, although it did smell suspiciously of horse.

The unicorns took station at either end of the hollow and, under their watchful eyes, I slept.

I dreamt that I'd pulled over a flying saucer and was trying to determine whether to charge the occupant with driving while unfit under section 4 of the Road Traffic Act (1988). Which was stupid really because it was a flying saucer and they'd have to be charged as being unfit for duty under part 5 of the Railways and Transport Safety Act 2003. Not to mention breaches of various CAA regulations, and of course Illegal Entry into the UK under the 1971 Act.

I woke to grey skies and damp grass.

Croft Ambrey, that's where I reckoned I was, in one of the ditches that put the 'multi' into multivallate Iron Age hill fort. I smelt wood smoke and, looking over, saw a group of grey-cloaked figures crouched around a campfire.

Never mind Nightingale, I thought, the National Trust are going to have conniptions about that. Quietly, I got up. And angling away from the campfire, I made my way up the side of the lower of the banks. If I was at Croft Ambrey it might be possible to make a dash down the slope towards Yatton. Despite the low cloud it was humid and I was sweating by the time I reached the top.

Stretching away below me was an unbroken sea of trees. Not the ordered ranks of pine and western hemlock, but the spreading multi-coloured tops of oak and ash and elder and all the traditional species of the ancient woodland. I recognised the outline of the hills and valleys from Google Maps and from when I'd stood at the Whiteway Head further up the ridge.

But there was no farmland in sight, no white gouge of quarry works at Leinthall Earls, no village of Yatton – so no Stan sniffing her chemicals and listening to death metal. This was the Wyldewood, spelt with a Y, that once covered the Island of Britain and would again, once the pesky tool-using primates had done the decent thing and exterminated themselves.

I didn't think it was time travel because faintly, like an old scar, I could see the line of the Roman road running north up the valley from Aymestrey towards Wigmore. And, beyond the road, the solitary mound where Pyon Wood Camp had stood – only here was Hannah's castle, blue and orange and, well, I personally would have said salmon rather than pink. A grouping of slender bulbous-topped turrets with rounded roof caps. It looked like a cross between something on the album cover of a progressive rock band and a termite tower.

I realised then that the fae didn't coexist with us within the material world. This was a parallel dimension of some kind. The sort that mathematicians and cosmologists get all excited about and smugly inform you that your tiny maths-deficient brain couldn't get a grip on. But I had a grip on it all right. A terrifying, sick-making grasp of my predicament. Because I didn't think Nightingale was going to be able to get me out of this.

'Fuck me,' I said out loud, 'I'm in fairyland.'

I heard a hissing sound behind me and turned to find the Queen having a good laugh.

They were realer in their own world, particularly the retainers, whose faces showed acne scars and blemishes. Their fingernails were dirty and their armour sported the occasional cracked scale or sign of obvious field maintenance. The unicorns were still beasts the size of carthorses, with the temperament of a Doberman Pinscher and a great big offensive weapon in the middle of their foreheads.

The Queen scared me most of all now that her cloak smelt of damp wool and had a splatter of mud along its hem. As she turned to organise her retainers breaking camp she seemed far too solid for comfort.

It's amazing what irrelevancies you find yourself thinking when it's too late. Because as I looked over the Wyldewood at the disturbingly organic towers of the castle on Pyon Mount, I realised what gift it was that I could give to Hugh Oswald in exchange for his staffs.

We should open up the school, I thought, if only for a day. Bring down Hugh and all his mates and show them the names that Nightingale carved onto the walls. Let them know that they are remembered, now, while some of them are still alive, before it's too late.

And bring their children and their grandchildren – even if, like Mellissa, some of them were definitely a bit odd. In fact, especially the ones that were odd. That way they would know that they were not alone and me, Dr Walid and Nightingale could get a good look at them and take notes for future reference.

And why stop there – let's bring the lot of them. Beverley, the rivers, Zach the goblin, the Quiet People, all the strange and illusive members of the demi-monde and show them the wall and have an alfresco buffet.

Get all of us in the same place so we could all get a good look at each other and come to some kind of proper arrangement. One that we could all live with.

The day was warming up by the time we headed downslope and into the valley where Yatton definitely no longer existed. Being really real hadn't put a crimp in the way the fae moved, though, gliding amongst the trees even as I stumbled down the path and used both hands to steady myself. It got easier once the slope levelled, but the trail stayed narrow and twisty and the canopy of the trees blocked out the sky.

After fifteen minutes of crossing the valley floor, the Queen held up her hand and the band stopped. She made a quick gesture at two of her retainers, one of whom pulled a rope from his pack while the other mimed holding his hands out in front of him, wrists pressed together. I glanced at the Queen who gave me a weary *Just don't get any ideas* look and so I held out my hands as directed. The other retainer wrapped the rope around my wrists, tied it with some care to keep the circulation going but without giving me any leeway, and looped the other end around his own wrist.

I felt a moment of excitement. They hadn't been concerned to restrict my movements before, but the fact that they felt they had to now indicated that they feared I might to try to escape. Which implied that there might be a way to escape nearby.

It was the road. The Roman road. Those imperial fuckers had put their mark on the landscape, all right. Even to the point where it impinged onto fairyland. Had that been their intention, to break up the native fae and ease their conquest of the material world? Or had they just liked straight lines and not cared about the effect?

Maybe the road coexisted in both the mundane and the faerie worlds. Perhaps a bright young man who was quick on his feet might have it away down that road to safety. The Queen must think so, otherwise why bind my wrists? She took the other end of the rope in her own hand – I took that as a mark of respect.

Roman engineers like a nice wide bed, and a cross-country road was often eight metres across with the undergrowth cleared back for another five or six metres either side. I saw it first as a lightening in the wooded gloom and then as a long straight clearing. The Wyldewood had done its best – saplings and under-growth had claimed the road almost to the middle. But none of the mature trees intruded further than a metre.

The band paused in the shadows at the edge. The Queen cocked her head as if listening to something far away. Beside her the unicorns stamped uneasily. Then she whipped around to face me – a question in her eyes.

'I can't hear anything,' I said.

But then I did.

A buzzing sound that dopplered past my ear. A bee and not a fat bumblebee, I saw, but a slender working girl from a hive. She swerved past one of the unicorns which flicked its mane angrily at her, then back to me where she circled once around my head and then buzzed off back down the line of the Roman road.

I thought I heard the sound of tiny trumpets.

I glanced at the Queen who waited, still as a statue,

for at least a minute before raising her hand to gesture us forward. But before we could move there was a crashing in the undergrowth and a huge white deer as tall as me at the shoulder thundered past the spot where we waited. And, as if he had been a pathfinder, a wave of animals followed. I spotted wild pig, more deer, rabbits, red coats and white, brown fur and russet red. Birds whirred overhead, screaming and crying.

By the pricking of my thumbs, I thought, something wicked this way comes.

The Queen let out a low snarl. And then I heard it.

It sounded like a train, like a steam train – huffing and blowing. The flood of animals reduced down to a trickle. I watched a cat the size of a Labrador zigzagging in panic before scuttling around us and vanishing into the undergrowth. I looked down the clear path towards where the noise came from, and saw the forest changing. Trees were falling backwards away from the road, their trunks splintering and fragmenting as they crashed down, so that by the time they hit the ground they had gone to dust. Grey stones the size of my fist were pushing themselves up through the forest floor like stop-motion mushrooms.

The Queen screamed in anguish as her unicorns jittered and skipped back.

I heard marching feet and smelt wet iron and rotting fish as the old Roman road ripped through the forest like a new wound.

The Queen pulled me closer and then, with a savage yank on the rope, drove me to my knees. She shoved her face in mine, lips bared over sharp teeth and her restless tongue snapping like a whip around her lips.

'Make her stop,' she hissed.

'Make who stop?' I asked.

'Make *her* stop,' she hissed and grabbed my head and jerked it round until I could see the engine bearing down on us. I recognised then the black iron painted with crimson and forest green livery and saw the name written on the canopy – *Faerie Queen*. The driver was still hidden behind the pistons, spinning bits and pipes and struts. But I knew, suddenly, who had come to rescue me.

'Oh boy,' I said. 'You's in trouble now!'

I'll say this for the Queen. She was brave – or possibly stupid. It's easy to mistake the two. She stood her ground while all her retainers fled alongside the other animals of the forest. She kept me on my knees by her side as the huge iron machine huffed and hissed and clanked and lurched to an uncertain stop beside us.

We waited for what seemed like a long time as the engine ticked and whirred and let off occasional mysterious bursts of steam. There was a clang from inside the driver's compartment and a familiar voice said, 'Fuck, fuck, fuckity fuck.'

Then silence.

Then Beverley Brook stepped onto the footplate and pointed a shotgun straight at the Queen's head – I recognised the Purdey from my trunk. It was nice to see it getting an airing.

Beverley herself was wearing an oversized leather jerkin and jeans. Her dreads had been tied into a plait down her back and a pair of antique leather and brass goggles were pushed up onto her brow.

'Put your hands on your head,' she said, 'and step away from the boyfriend.'

The Queen hissed and gripped the rope harder.

'I don't care,' said Beverley slowly. 'He is not free to make such a bargain.'

'Nonetheless,' hissed the Queen, 'he made a bargain and he must keep it.'

'Ladies,' I said.

'Peter,' said Beverley, 'you stay the fuck out of this.'

She reshouldered the shotgun.

'I've loaded this particular gun with scrap iron,' she said. 'Now, I don't know if a shot to the head will kill you or not. But just consider how much fun we can have finding out.'

While they were chatting, I created a little shield and, very carefully, sliced off the ropes around my wrist. The Queen felt when they went slack and turned to grab me but Beverley shouted, 'No!' And she thought better of it. She watched sullenly as I picked my way to the traction engine and climbed aboard – managing to burn myself just the once on hot metal.

'The railings,' said Beverley. 'Keep your hands on the railings.'

When I was onboard Beverley ducked back into the cab, pulled what she called the reversing lever, checked the single brassbound gauge and pulled a second lever. The *Faerie Queen* lurched into reverse.

As we backed away, I heard the Queen, the real Queen, shriek with frustration. But even as she did so, the sound began to grow fainter. As it faded, the sun came out and the trees that had crowded the road melted away like dew until we were reversing up the good old A4410 and overlooking the hedgerows to the calm and civilised fields beyond.

The clouds had gone and so had the termite castle.

I sighed with relief.

Beverley stopped the traction engine and spent what seemed to me a very complicated ten minutes, getting it turned round to face in the other direction. Beverley shushed me when I tried to talk.

'This is not easy,' she said. 'In fact, if I wasn't cheating I'm not even sure I could do it.'

I wanted to know how she was cheating, but she glared at me until I shut up.

Once we were safely lurching in the right direction I got her to explain how she came to be the one who rescued me. She'd returned to Rushpool about the same time as Dominic. Beverley had insinuated herself into the conversation – 'I felt it was my duty to offer my expertise,' she said – and, having assessed the situation, made her own plans.

'Your boss approved of it, of course,' she said. 'He's waiting for us at Aymestrey.'

I doubted that Nightingale had been quite that relaxed about Beverley's role and boy was he going to freak when I tried to explain the whole parallel universe thing to him. Not to mention the all-too-human loose ends which were flapping around this case.

I asked whether Nightingale had any idea what to do with not-Nicole.

'Are you saying that you did that whole stupid hostage swap when you didn't even know what you were going to do with the evil little strop afterwards?'

'It was a high-pressure situation,' I said. 'Do you think Molly would like a friend?'

'Not that kind of friend,' said Beverley. 'Besides, Molly has her own friends.'

'Like who?' I asked and thought – like how?

Beverley hesitated. 'That's not for me to say, is it? You'll have to ask her yourself.'

'The girl has to go to social services,' I said.

'Like that won't be a total disaster,' said Beverley.

'I'm open to suggestions.'

'Give her to Fleet,' said Beverley. 'She's already got like a gazillion foster kids, and she's married to a fae. So little Miss Psycho's not going to worry her.'

'Married to a fae?'

'Yeah,' said Beverley. 'Scandalous, isn't it?'

Ahead I could see the bridge across the River Lugg next to which I'd allowed myself to be taken into the water. There were stands of alder on the river's banks and dogwood, hazel and hawthorn in the hedgerows. Robins and thrushes sounded across the fields and a couple of wood pigeon still refused to bloody shut up.

I put my arms around Beverley's waist and buried my face in her hair. Beneath the oil and metal she smelt of peppermint and shea butter.

I was ready to go home to London.

# Acknowledgements

D eep breath – the usual suspects: Andrew Cartmel, James Swallow, Mandy Mills, the Evil Monster Boy. Sabrina and Andreas for rural transportation. John and John at Da Management, Inspector Bob Hunter MPS and Inspector Martin Taylor WMP for everything police. Sonya Taaffe for Latin, Neil Patterson CoE and Clare Greener NFU for country matters. Ben Ando BBC for insight into the media. As always the litany of errors in the book are entirely mine and nobody else's. Finally, I'd like to thank Jon, Simon, Marcus, Gillian, Sophie, Jen and Pandora at Orion, Betsy and Sheila at DAW, Joshua at JABberwocky, Thibaud, Tina and everybody else who have put up with my slow ways – I promise to do better next time.

# Architectural and Historical Notes

Readers with an eye for the esoteric and unusual in architecture will recognise Hugh Oswald's home as *The Folly in Herefordshire* which was built in 1961 by Raymond Erith, whose response to modernism was to pretend it never happened. It sits just as I describe it up on the Wylde and is a sight to see – although please remember that it is a private house and act accordingly.

Hugh Oswald demonstrates the benefit of a classical education by quoting from Book 17 of the *Iliad*:

Αἴας δ᾽ ἀμφὶ Μενοιτιάδῃ σάκος εὐρὺ καλύψας
ἑστήκει ὥς τίς τε λέων περὶ οἷσι τέκεσσιν

Pokehouse Wood is a real place, but I've changed the dates on which it was replanted to suit the necessity of my story. I'm almost totally certain that it doesn't form a gateway to the land of faerie, since if it did I'm sure its owners, the National Trust, would have, at the very least, put up a useful informative sign, if not a visitors' centre with an attached café and small play area for potential changelings.

Since the events of this book, West Mercia Police have entered into a close alliance with several neighbouring police services. As a result Leominster nick is now fully staffed while Ludlow has become as lawless a town as Deadwood ever was – although presumably with better cuisine. This is assuming, of course, that they haven't reorganised again while my back was turned.